GIFTS and BONES

⊱─────────⊰

A BEA AND MILDRED MYSTERY

Barbara Murray

Copyright © Barbara Murray, 2006

Published by Soames Point Press
28 Regency Square, Toronto, Ontario, M1E 1N3, Canada
www.soamespointpress.com

All rights reserved. No part of this publication may be reproduced, stored in a retrieval system, or transmitted in any form by any process—electronic, mechanical, photocopying, recording, or otherwise—without the prior written permission of the copyright owners and Soames Point Press.

Library and Archives Canada Cataloguing in Publication
Murray, Barbara, 1954-
    Gifts and Bones: a Bea and Mildred mystery/Barbara Murray

(Bea and Mildred mystery series; 1)
ISBN 978-1-4303-0117-2

I. Title II.Series: Murray, Barbara, 1954- Bea and Mildred mystery series; 1

PS8626.U773G44 2006   C813'.6   C2006-906399-0

Editor and Production Manager: Emily Dontsos
Consultant and Copy Editor: Emma McKay, www.mudscout.com
Author photo: Jacqueline M. Massey
Cover design: Angi Shearstone, www.angishearstone.com
Layout and Technical Consultant: Danny Wong
Map reprinted courtesy of Bill Burns, http://atlantic-cable.com
Author's Website: www.barbaramurray.ca

Publisher's Note: This is a work of fiction. Names, characters, places, and incidents either are the product of the author's imagination or are used fictitiously, and any resemblance to actual persons, living or dead, events, or locales is entirely coincidental.

This book is set in Garamond

Printed and bound in the U.S.A.

For Allison

Acknowledgements

I would like to thank the many readers of the book throughout its various incarnations. You each generously gave time and courageously offered comment: Edythe Hanen, Erin Jones, Joan MacLeod, Susanne Martin, Allison Murray, Nicola Murray, Jackie Minns, Jacqueline Massey, Barb Kmiec, Stan and Marge Murray, Mary and Bob Younger, Chloe Dayman, Jess Applebaum, Emma McKay, Bruce Murray, Sandra Borthwick, Brian Lord, and Emily Dontsos. I am forever grateful.

Many rich resources provided me with information on ships and the transatlantic cable. I would especially like to thank:

The staff and librarians of the Toronto Reference Library, the Vancouver Public Library, and the University of British Columbia Library, for your patience and expertise.

Dorothy and Eric Lawson, for graciously inviting me to troll your magnificent historical collection for bits of gold.

Dr. Pat Taylor, for an entertaining and informative evening on the art of model shipbuilding.

John Steele Gordon, for your must-read book on the laying of the cable, *A Thread Across the Ocean*.

Bill Burns (http://atlantic-cable.com), for your timely technical proofing of all things cable-related.

And for a wealth of information on body decomposition, skeletons, mummies, and bruising, Dr. D.P. Lyle. Thank you for sharing your extensive knowledge with a complete stranger.

I have had tremendous support over the years. Many thanks to:

Kathie Tolson for inspiring me to write a novel. Your dedication to your own work helped me pursue mine.

Tom, Katie, and Emily Dontsos, and Allison Murray, for your enormous gift one winter of providing this writer with temporary residence, and the food and wine to go with it.

Sheila Moynihan, for your steadfast friendship and for keeping the faith, even when I faltered.

Eli Applebaum, for your constancy and support. Over the years, you never stopped asking about the book's progress. That has been more important to me than you will ever know.

Cam McNaughton, for your gift of patience.

Allice Bernard — your wonderful narration has given the book a whole new life.

My rock, Danny Wong, for your many, kind corrections of my English, for your skill at layout, for your solid loving presence, and for being my companion on this long, literary roller-coaster ride. And to my Wong in-laws, for your generosity.

Emma McKay. Editor extraordinaire. Your gentle, incisive, and strong editorial hand gave the book what it needed: clarity and structure. Thank you, again and again.

Emily Dontsos. For absolutely everything you have accomplished in these last several months to pull the book together: your intelligent, gutsy editing; your attention to every single inch of this production, including the wonderful website; and your energy and enthusiasm. The book would never have happened in the time it did without you. Thank you so very, very much.

My friends and family for your love, support and encouragement.

And, mostly, my sister, Allison. For your unwavering belief, dedication, hard work, support and love. I am so incredibly grateful to have you as a sister.

The accuracies in this book are largely due to the above cast of people. Any errors or omissions are entirely my own.

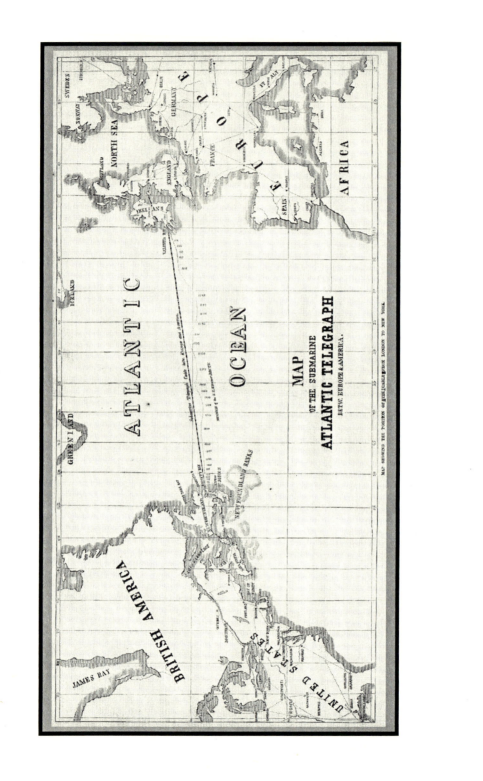

MORSE CODE

Alphabet

A	.-	N	-.
B	-...	O	---
C	-.-.	P	.--.
D	-..	Q	--.-
E	.	R	.-.
F	..-.	S	...
G	--.	T	-
H	....	U	..-
I	..	V	...-
J	.---	W	.--
K	-.-	X	-..-
L	.-..	Y	-.--
M	--	Z	--..

Numbers

1	.----
2	..---
3	...--
4	....-
5	.....
6	-....
7	--...
8	---..
9	----.
0	-----

Punctuation

Full Stop	.-.-.-	Colon	---...
Comma	--..--	Hyphen	-....-
Query	..--..	Error (delete)	....

Contents

St. John's Newfoundland, 1902

Prologue		1
Day One	Tuesday, October 14	6
Day Two	Wednesday, October 15	34
Day Three	Thursday, October 16	61
Day Four	Friday, October 17	94
Day Five	Saturday, October 18	107
Day Six	Sunday, October 19	132
Day Seven	Monday, October 20	150
Day Eight	Tuesday, October 21	160
Day Nine	Wednesday, October 22	176
Day Ten	Thursday, October 23	196
Day Eleven	Friday, October 24	211
Day Twelve	Saturday, October 25	229

North Wales, 1902

Epilogue	281

Prologue
Day Four
Friday, October 17, 1902

"Jean MacDonald. Come along with you," Evelyn called from up ahead, but the message was barely audible by the time it reached Mildred. It could have been the wind; it has a way of dragging the stuff out of words. However, more than the storm pulled at Mildred's concentration, as she and Jean made their long way home. The dark sky had cloaked the last of their afternoon light; trees crowded in on either side of the narrow road; the woods beyond shuddered, as if wary. And the road behind had become sentient, or so it seemed. It's only the wind, Mildred's sensible self would have liked her to believe.

"Hurry, Jean," Mildred whispered to the child, who was walking several paces behind. Bea and Evelyn were already far ahead, almost at the top of the hill. Evelyn lifted her strong right arm, in which she held her unlit lantern, and with the heel of her hand, she brushed a curl off her face. Mildred longed to be walking with pragmatic Evelyn and level-headed Bea. Instead, here she was with dear, fey Jean. They were all a little fey in this family, Jean most of all. She and Jean wouldn't now be lagging behind if it weren't for the girl's premonitions.

As if Mildred's thoughts prompted her into speaking, Jean announced, "I'm not going to talk to Bea ever again. She should have believed me."

Mildred stopped, and turned: "She should have, I'll give you that. But you'll be talking to your cousin soon enough, mark my words. So let's walk a touch faster, shall we, love? A nice, hot cup of tea is calling you. I can hear it from here."

"And Jean, mind your basket now," Evelyn called from near the top of the hill. "I don't go spending the money we don't have for you to be spilling the groceries all over the road. And hold on to your lantern, girl — you're going to need it."

Mildred muttered to Jean, "Not that a lantern'll even stay lit in this kind of a wind."

"I'd think the wind would get to it first," Jean agreed. Then, as if she suddenly realized how far behind they were, her frightened eyes settled on Mildred, then on her mother and Bea, who were getting harder to see. She started to walk faster, struggling with the weight of her basket. She passed Mildred and muttered: "Am I a mule or something? Is that what she thinks I am?"

"I'm sure she doesn't," said Mildred, working to catch up.

"No? Then what's Bea doing, may I ask? She's only got one little basket to carry. Not nearly as heavy as mine." Belatedly, she shouted, if only to let her mother know she was still there: "I'm minding the basket, Mum." But her words were captured by the wind; they never reached her mother and cousin. At the top of the hill the road took a turn, and Evelyn and Bea marched out of sight.

Jean quickened her pace, and Mildred did too, almost catching the back of Jean's coat hem with her foot. The hand-me-down from her much older cousin was too large for the girl. It dragged on the road, picking up a sodden collection of mud, small pebbles, and fir twigs.

"Pick up your hem, Jean," said Mildred. Jean glanced back at her then did as she was told, though it was hard to keep hold of the coat, and the weight of it soon fell away from her small fingers and back to the road.

"At least your coat is warm," said Mildred with envy, fingering the threadbare fabric of her own coat. "Time to light the lamp, dear, don't you think . . . " but her suggestion was interrupted when Jean stopped suddenly and swung around to look downhill. Mildred quickly turned to follow her gaze.

There was nothing down there, only the road at night. Jean watched the path for several more seconds, then peered at the woods to her left, and to her right. Mildred wished even more fervently now that they hadn't lingered, that they'd caught up with Evelyn and Bea. *I'm not as brave as I used to be*, she thought. *Not like Bea. Bea should be here with Jean. I could be up ahead with Evelyn, discussing her customers, or* the children, or Billy — anything instead of being back here with the child. However, she was here to look out for the children in this family, so she couldn't just leave Jean behind to climb the hill alone.

"Come, child, you're making me nervous now. Let's be off, shall we? We've not far to go."

With the near dark, the trees on either side of them had completely lost their shadows. Their spiky shapes blurred into one bumpy mass as each tree melded into the other, and the road became a single elongated tunnel. Ahead of them, it was now too dark to see to the top of the hill. They had gone only a few steps when the wind yanked at their clothing, and a gust whipped Jean's woollen bonnet off her head. The hat would have flown away had it not been anchored to her neck by strong, woven ribbons. It fell to the front of her body and rocked wildly on her chest, but then, seconds later, was dragged backward so powerfully that the ribbons yanked at her thin neck. "Mother!" Jean called.

"She can't hear you, Jean. We're on our own for now. It's not far, though. The lamp, love," Mildred insisted, now for the second time.

"The lamp, you silly," Jean muttered to herself. "Light the lamp."

Jean set her basket and lantern on the road, and hurried to untangle the ribbons of her bonnet from her neck. Mildred tried to help, but the knots were too tight. Sometimes four hands are no better than two, and she let Jean try it herself, though the girl's layers of clothing made freedom of movement difficult. To Mildred, it seemed as if minutes passed while the wind howled around them, but then the ribbons gave way and the bonnet came loose. Jean repositioned it and tied the ribbons tightly. "That's good like that. It'll keep," said Mildred, giving the ribbons a little tug. They stayed taut. Jean reached up and brushed Mildred's hand away.

Jean felt deep into the pocket of her coat and withdrew the box of matches that her mother had given her. She knelt down on the rocky road, lifted the cover of the lamp, struck the match against a rock, and tried to light the wick. But the wind sucked away the meagre flame. "Here, I'll try to block the wind," said Mildred. She stood to the north of Jean, but the wind seemed to go right through her. Jean's third attempt was successful, and as the fire suddenly took a firm hold on the wick, a tight circle of light illuminated the road. But the lantern had also given the black on all sides of them a life it didn't have before. The sides of the road now pressed closer than ever. Sometimes the dark is better, thought Mildred. It's harder to know what's out there.

They set off up the hill once again. At least they had light. Soon they would be home. "Mum! Bea! Wait up!" Jean called.

"Evelyn! Bea! Wait up!" repeated Mildred.

Jean stopped again and glanced nervously around.

"What is it?" Mildred whispered, but she already knew the answer. The sentient road seemed to be watching them once again. Or was it something else? Hiding in the trees further downhill, or along the footpaths that cut north and south through the woods? They started to walk faster. They had gone a mere half-dozen steps when Jean adjusted her heavy basket and the bundle of codfish fell to the ground and started to roll downhill. For a split second, Mildred wondered if Jean was going to keep hurrying away and let the paper bundle roll all the way down to the bottom of the road, or get lost somewhere at the side. After all, this was the fish that Evelyn had got from Billy McLeod when they'd been down on the wharf — "kissing fish," Jean called it. But as the bundle of fish began to roll, Jean automatically stuck out her left foot to break its tumble. "Good girl," said Mildred. Even at ten, Jean seemed to comprehend some of the teetering economics of their small household. Food was food, no matter where it came from. Jean bent down to retrieve the bundle, and as she did so, she glanced downhill, then inhaled sharply and closed her small hand around the damp package.

"Best not put it back in the basket, Jean. Look. It's sprung a leak," said Mildred, pointing to a small rip on the side of the package where cod juice oozed out. Jean turned the package over and examined the tear, then tore a section of paper from the edge and shoved it into the rip. She ignored Mildred's counsel, but kept scanning the dark hill below them, and absent-mindedly crammed the fish deep into a space made vacant by other items in the basket: three cooking onions, two new spools of ivory thread, and a small bolt of fine lace. The best lace — for one of Evelyn's best customers. For a moment, the basket was enough of a distraction for Mildred: Jean was supposed to have put the fabric and notions in one basket, the food in the other, but she had obviously ignored Evelyn's instructions. But, too quickly, the moment was gone.

Jean looked downhill, then grabbed the basket and the lantern and started running up the road. Mildred stayed frozen where she was.

Just now when she had followed Jean's gaze downhill and into the approaching dark just beyond the light of the lamp, she had seen someone standing there. Right in the middle of the road. The red-haired, unsettling boy. Brian. Or was it his twin? He had mentioned a twin. In any case, here he was, not twenty feet away, fading in and out of the dark as if layered with mist. He had been following them. But even more disturbing, he didn't seem to care that she had noticed.

She finally found her feet, and walked quickly uphill away from him. Why would he be following them home? The worry that she had felt for him yesterday disintegrated. Maybe he would leave her alone if she ignored him. As she heard him approaching, she started to run but he kept getting closer. She ran faster but he ran too, and then, just when she realized that she couldn't outrun him, he caught up to her and reached for her arm.

"Mildred," he said, and without even looking at him, with only the touch of his hand, Mildred suddenly knew what an absolute fool she had been.

DAY ONE
Tuesday, October 14, 1902

Brian's toes were blue from the cold, because he still didn't have any shoes and the water was freezing, but it was probably always that way on the beaches of Ireland, even in the summer. Tiny pebbles piled high in the gaps between his toes to tickle his skin with each wash of the tide. Cliffs towered on either side of the harbour and the small beach, where now, standing just off to the left, a full-bearded man in a tailcoat waved his top hat and laughed. He wasn't waving at Brian. He was waving out to sea. Brian lifted his arm and waved too, because that's what everyone was doing. Everyone on board the big vessels and the smaller ones waved to everyone standing around Brian.

All of a sudden, ships and boats had appeared in the harbour, and the beach was now crowded with people. Some, like the man, were dressed in tailcoats and top hats, wearing shoes that shouldn't be standing on a cold beach with salt water lapping at their black patent toes. One particularly fancy gentleman was being addressed as "Your Excellency" by other fancy-looking men. But most of the people smiling and waving to the ships in the harbour were normal people like Brian. Nothing was special about their clothes, and most were barefoot like him, and he knew without asking anyone at all that they were the townsfolk of Cahirciveen and the farming folk of Valentia Island.

Brian glanced at the faces of the people because he wasn't sure why he was waving and smiling. Then, when he recognized the ships in the harbour, excitement rippled through him. The ships out there in the harbour were about to begin laying the transatlantic cable. That was the *Niagara*, the gigantic American steamer far bigger than any English vessel, and over there was the English *Agamemnon*, not as large or as modern, but, still, his favourite. He now knew some of the smaller vessels as well: the *Leopold*, the *Cyclops*, and clearly, the big paddle steamer was the *Susquehanna*. Surrounding the ships were dozens of small vessels and rowboats. Another thrill rushed through him as he realized why some of the large rowboats were heading to shore. They were bringing *Niagara's* cable to land. He ran along the beach with everyone else to help, so that he was there when the men leapt from one of the rowboats as it hit the beach. People all around him cheered and laughed and pitched in: men on shore and off, in topcoats and normal clothes, as well as children, and women, and Brian. They pulled on *Niagara's* cable, which wound off her stern and through the harbour, onto one boat and then onto another and another, until finally the last rowboat brought it ashore. Everyone pulled and pulled on the cable, until they had brought it all the way up the beach and placed it in the tent at the feet of the man they called "Your Excellency." Everyone cheered when it was attached to the battery that would allow a signal on the land's end to speak to the ocean's cable. Brian knew this. He knew everything there was to know about this voyage, and he cheered the loudest of all, and then again he cheered on the beach with the crowd throughout the speech made by a man he felt he should know.

"I have no words to express the feelings which fill my heart tonight," said the thin man with the thin lips and the sharp nose and the warm voice, and the people warmed to him, too, even though many of them couldn't understand English. "It beats with love and affection for every man, woman and child who hears me . . . "

Of course, Brian thought with a shiver: I know his name. This is the famous Cyrus Field, the American who financed the laying of the cable. And once again Brian clapped, but this time the sea swelled and crashed over the beach, and everyone was gone.

Everyone, except Brian. There were no more ships, no townsfolk from Cahirciveen, no Excellency, no Cyrus Field, and they were all gone because by some perverted coincidence another familiar voice had interrupted the proceedings. Brian realized that the voice wasn't coming from the beach or from the harbour; it was coming from Henry's study. The beach and the harbour, the cliffs and the pebbles had suddenly disappeared, and Brian found himself sitting in the hallway outside of Henry's study, listening to the voice that was saying:

"The name Cyrus Newton Norton mean anything to you?"

... --- ...

"I take it that's your full name?" said Henry.

"Damn right. Stevens, this is my daughter, Eliza," said Cyrus, but Henry didn't greet the daughter; he couldn't tear his eyes away from Mr. Norton. The gaunt man with the bad breath had smiled, and now Henry could see why the repellent odour: rotten teeth riddled his mouth, worst of all were those masquerading as front teeth — three blackened, diseased spikes, two on the top, one on the bottom.

"Pleased to meet you, Miss Norton," Henry said finally, turning thankfully to the woman. The antithesis of her father, she was a relief to look at: tall, blond, with delicate facial features and a brilliant smile.

"And you, Mr. Stevens," said Eliza, holding his gaze before releasing the hand he had extended. "What a lovely house you have."

"Thank you, Miss Norton," said Henry. "Please take a seat by the fire, Miss Norton, Mr. Norton."

"Too bloody hot here," Cyrus said.

"Then perhaps this chair, Father," Eliza said, leading him instead to the overstuffed armchair furthest from the fire.

"You sure my name doesn't sound familiar? Think about it. Norton. Cyrus Norton," said Cyrus, shoving her arm aside as he sat down so that he could lock eyes with Henry.

Henry held the back of the other armchair for Eliza.

"Thank you, Mr. Stevens," she said, folding her hands on her lap, twinning one trim ankle over the other.

With his thumbs hooked onto the pockets of his vest, Henry went back to the fireplace. He turned to face the room, and then glanced over their heads toward the door that led to the hallway. He cocked his head slightly and listened.

"Expecting someone, Stevens?" asked Cyrus.

"No," he said. "Just the maid with our tea."

"Really?" asked Cyrus, shifting his gaze in the direction of the door. "Thought I heard someone in the hallway."

"You must be mistaken, sir," Henry said, glancing at the doorway again, and then back at Eliza.

"If you say so," said Cyrus, his head still half turned to the doorway. Henry nodded but no one spoke for several seconds as they all listened. Finally, Henry replied to Cyrus's query.

"I didn't say I didn't know your name, sir. In fact, I recall it very well."

"That so?"

"Yes. My father mentioned you."

"I bet he did. But he didn't tell you everything about me, did he?"

"What should he have told me, Mr. Norton?"

"That I broke the cable."

"What cable, sir?"

"*Niagara's*, of course," Cyrus snapped. "Didn't your father tell you I broke the cable?"

"No, sir, I'm afraid he didn't."

"Well, that's good, because it's a lie. It was never me, and he knew it. It was him. He broke the cable." He stared at Henry for several seconds. "Don't look so dazed, Stevens. 1857. Not 1858, mind you. No. The first try. 1857. The *Agamemnon* and the *Niagara*. Mean anything? Sound familiar?"

"Yes. Of course. The first transatlantic cable ships," said Henry.

From Niagara's *deck, Brian could see the majestic* Agamemnon *off in the distance, her sails stretched tight by the storm.* Niagara's *cable really had no beginning and no end, just like they had always remembered, just like he had always been told. None that you could see, anyhow. In front of him, the cable stretched forever through the paying-out gear that ran almost the entire length of the deck. To his left toward the stern, the brake wheel. No wonder. He stared harder. It wasn't nearly strong enough. Anyone could see that. To his right, more paying-out gear, and way further along the deck toward the bow, the massive hold with its coils of cable. He tried to run toward the hold.*

His feet didn't move and he looked down at them, bare against the wet wooden deck, seawater running over his toes, shining white like snow. White like the dead of winter, like ice, like dreams leached of colour. He watched the gale throw the rest of the crew off balance as it pitched the ship's stern vertically upward and then down again. Not him — he was steady on his feet, and dressed in fresh whites like a sailor. Just like he'd always imagined.

All the men were too busy grabbing hold of something, scrambling to adjust something, trying to fix something. Some of them just stood and watched, but most of them were yelling. Everyone worried about the cable. But nobody worried as much as Brian.

Far beyond the huge waves and the dark and the rain that lashed the Niagara was his Agamemnon, carrying the Atlantic's last half of the cable.

"We were aboard the *Niagara*, Judson and I," Cyrus Norton was saying. "Together on the first voyage."

"No, sir," replied Henry. "My father sailed on the *Agamemnon*. Quite an experience, he said . . ."

"Is that what he told you? The *Agamemnon*?"

"Yes."

"Bloody nonsense. Wasn't the *Agamemnon*. Was the *Niagara*."

"No, sir, you have it wrong, I'm afraid."

"No, sir, I don't. Ever heard the story about the brake failing on the *Niagara*? Snapping the cable? Losing over 300 miles of it 2,000 fathoms down to the bottom of the sea?"

"Of course. Terrible. Heartbreaking for the men involved, I can well imagine. I take it you were one of these from the way you talk. But I can assure you my father was not involved. You must have the wrong man. My father was Judson Henry Stevens, originally from Greenwich. Died there two years ago."

"That's him, the one and the same."

"He wasn't even on board the *Niagara*. I heard the accident was caused by some idiot applying the brakes too quickly on the paying-out cable."

"Wasn't too quick, was too heavy — too much pressure. And was your father in fact. He was the idiot. He and I, we were together on the paying-out gear."

"Look, Henry," Brian said. He pointed to the stern, not at the man who was throwing up over the side, but at the man standing at the brake wheel. Even from here, Brian could tell that he was leaning too heavily on the handle. "Ease up!" he hollered. The man didn't hear him, but it didn't matter because Brian was running in his bare feet down the deck until he was standing beside the man and the brake.

"I can help," he said, but the man wasn't listening. He was turned away, looking at the gauge. "That's 3,500 pounds," called Brian, pointing at the numbers. "Ease up when the ship comes up out of the swells! That's too much pressure on the

cable! *Do you feel it? You have to feel it.*" *Brian tried to show him how to feel what the cable was saying, but he still wasn't listening. Brian tried to grab the brake wheel from his hands, but the man shrugged him off and Brian fell backwards and almost went over the side with the impact. He got up onto his knees and then onto his feet, and he ran back to the man. "Feel the way the ship dips and rises. You've got to follow her lead; apply the weight, release it, apply it, release it."*

"Apply the weight, release it," Cyrus was saying to Henry. "Apply it, release it, I kept saying, but then I heard the sound I had been trying to prevent. I grabbed the wheel from his hand, but it was too late."

The cable snapped! Brian didn't act fast enough. He tried to grab the cable before it went over the side, but he couldn't. The sound it made when it exploded over the ocean ripped them all in half. Everything was screaming: the ship and the ocean and the cable and everyone on deck, and Brian's ears couldn't stand it. He clamped his fists to the sides of his head, but the noises from the ship and the ocean made it past his fists, as did the voices from the study. He could no longer see his Agamemnon *in the distance.*

"We both looked at each other then," said Cyrus. "I could see it in his eyes. The fear. He knew he'd done it. Lost all that cable. Eyes like yours, in fact. Brown, dark brown. They went almost black with the fear. Anyhow, I'm thinking fast and I said, 'We'll say it got stuck, Judson, you don't need to worry, we'll say the gear stuck, that the wheel wouldn't turn.' He just nodded stupidly and then everyone arrived at once: the engineer, Charles Bright; the big men, Samuel Morse himself and Cyrus Field — same first name as me, funny, isn't it? — the foreman; the entire goddamn crew; newspaper reporters; the whole world, and who's holding the brake wheel? Who's still got the brake wheel in his hand? Me, of course. Not Judson.

"And you know, I realized later that while everyone ran down to us at the stern of the ship, Judson had stepped away from me a couple of paces. As if I was diseased. That should have been my first hint of what was to happen. Field was a gentleman, I must say, didn't yell or scream, but the foreman, was he mad. Not that he said anything to me; just glared at me. Judson couldn't even look up; he was just staring down at his feet. Hanging his head in shame, he was. I could hear the foreman thinking as he looked from one of us to the other, why the bloody hell does Norton, goddamn Norton, have the brakes in his hands? Judson didn't speak. I didn't speak. I was too stunned. I wanted to wheel back time, give the damn wheel back to Judson, wished I'd never grabbed it from him. But you can't turn time around, can you? I couldn't even look at all of them, the whole crew, not 'cause I was guilty, 'cause I wasn't, but the disappointment in their eyes; everyone had worked so hard, been so excited, and then people are grabbing the wheel out of my hand, and the whole ship is thinking bloody Norton, goddamn Norton, and that was the end of it. I got blamed, and Judson never said a thing, never confessed. Never owned up."

When he stopped talking, no one spoke until he said, "There it is, Stevens, that bloody sound again. Out in the hallway."

"I don't hear anything, Norton."

But Brian had heard it. It was the sound of the cable crying as it sank to the bottom of the sea. The man continued to stand at the brake wheel, staring down at it as if the cable was still united and whole. Brian tapped the man on the shoulder. "You can't wish it back," said Brian to the man responsible, who now turned to face him. "I know. I've tried."

"Aah, Natty, our tea. How welcome," said Henry, while Natty crossed the room and placed the tea tray on the coffee table in front of the Nortons' two chairs. She gave a small curtsy and as she left the room, Henry stared after her, while Cyrus rapidly knocked the end of his cane up and down on the floor.

Brian had returned his fists to his eyes to stop his mind from thinking, and he hadn't heard her coming down the hallway toward the study. When he did, he scrambled up off the floor, and pressed his back against the hallway wall underneath a portrait of his father. By the time she reached the study carrying the full tea tray, he was standing still, his forefinger to his lip. "Sshh," he said. She nodded and smiled. Natty liked to spy too, and he knew that she would never give him away, just like he would never give her away. Before she went into the study, Natty turned her head and winked and gave him her slightly crooked grin, then she straightened out her face and stepped into the room. When she came out a minute later, she looked at him as if she was confused. She seemed distracted; her gaze barely grazed him, and she didn't smile at him again. He wondered what was bothering her, and why she hardly paid him any attention. He wanted to follow her, but he also wanted to know what else was going on in the study. He would get to Natty later, he decided, as he went back to peeking around the corner of the study door.

"Father," whispered Eliza, and she reached out to steady her father's vibrating cane. She turned to Henry, and said: "Shall I pour, Mr. Stevens?"

"Yes. I'd love a cup, thank you, Miss Norton. A drop of milk would be fine." He took the cup from her hand and then went back to the fireplace. Eliza poured a cup for her father. She helped him settle back in his chair.

"Don't spill it, Father," she whispered as she placed the cup and saucer in his tremulous hands, even more so now since he'd told his story. He gripped the cane with his knees.

Henry smiled down at Eliza, and stepped toward her as she passed him the plate of biscuits. "Thank you, Miss Norton," he said.

"He gets clumsy sometimes," said Eliza quietly, nodding at her father and smiling gently at Henry, then dropping her gaze to her lap.

"Don't need you interfering saying I'm doing this, doing that," Cyrus said to his daughter, spilling tea onto his lap. "You're always on about something, you are."

Brian waited for it to come. The thing that always came. The yell. The fist. The slap. He fell to the floor and crawled back up against the wall and arranged himself into his cross-legged position. He couldn't listen anymore, he just wouldn't, that's all. He closed his ears by closing his eyes, then sealed them off with his fists.

"Oh, Father," she said, leaning over with a linen napkin to wipe the area above his knee.

"Leave it," he said again, swatting at her hand.

"I won't have that in my house, sir," Henry said, stepping toward him, but when Cyrus just glared at him, he took a deep breath, turned away from the pair, and went on, staring into the fireplace: "In any case, the brakes were the problem, not the brakeman. My father remarked on that several times. And the cable itself, it didn't weigh enough, wasn't strong enough. He said it could have happened to anyone."

"Maybe it could have happened to anyone. Didn't. Happened to him. And you know what?"

"What, Mr. Norton? What should I know?"

"No one believed me. I couldn't get work in the cable business after that. Me — Cyrus Newton Norton? I was the best, and I couldn't get a job. All because of your father. Spread rumours about me afterward. They didn't for one minute think that maybe he was lying. The foreman, what was his name? Jack, maybe."

"Jake?" asked Henry. Eliza spilled a few drops of tea onto the floor as she was pouring.

"I *am* sorry," she said.

"Not a problem," Henry replied with a smile.

"Yeah. That's right. Jake," said Cyrus. "Now how'd you know that, heh?"

"Let me top up your tea, Father," Eliza said, reaching for the pot.

"I don't want any more goddamn tea," Cyrus said, whacking her hand with his cane. Henry strode across the room and grabbed the cane, his knuckles white as he gripped the wood.

"That's enough," he said, and then he turned to Eliza. "Miss Norton. Excuse my gruffness."

"Quite alright, Mr. Stevens. No, really, I understand completely. I think it's time we were on our way. Father?"

Cyrus made no move to leave. Eliza continued to stare at the floor, twisting her scarf in her hand. "I'll have a biscuit, though," said Cyrus, his voice suddenly soft and sweet. "Yes, believe I will. Thank you, Eliza. Where was I? Gotta finish what I came for, don't I?" She nodded and handed him the plate, her hand shaking as she did so. He grabbed three biscuits, two of which he thrust in his jacket pocket. He sucked like a half-dead fish on the third biscuit, slurping at it with his cracked lips and rotten teeth, soggy bits slipping down his chin and onto his already-stained shirt. Henry stared, horrified, at the man's mouth and at his pocket, both tarnished with newly-acquired oatmeal debris in addition to the older bits of mysterious dried food matter. He rolled his eyes and swung around to the fireplace.

"And what did you come for, sir? I thought you came to tell me your little story about the brake."

"Well, there's that. Time you knew that. But I wouldn't've tracked you down all the way from England just to tell you my sad story, would I?"

"I have no idea, sir. You confuse me, I must say."

"Well that's unfortunate, isn't it? But, you see, I had other reasons for coming here."

"Is that so? And what might they be?"

"Three of them, Stevens. The first is betrayal, like I just told you. Destroyed my life with that. The second is blackmail. Your father blackmailed me for years, if you can believe it. Did you know that? *He* blackmailed *me*. Should've been the other way around, and now it's going to be, Stevens. I've come for my money back and then some. And you'll pay. There's things I know about your family that you probably wish I didn't."

Henry didn't answer, but just turned to stare into the fireplace.

"And so the third reason, as you've already figured out, is murder. You've known all along who did it, heh, Stevens?"

With his hands, Brian was pushing Cyrus's words away from his brain when he glanced up to see Penelope coming down the hallway. She was almost at the study door, and looked as though she was about to interrupt her husband and his visitors.

"Sshh," said Brian, standing and putting his finger to his lips.

Penelope acknowledged him, and did what he said. She stopped outside the door just as Henry said, "So. You intend to blackmail me for a murder. That is why you are here, sir, I see now. How stupid of me. Now I understand what my father meant when he told me about you."

Penelope looked over at Brian, her eyes wide with apprehension, then she stepped to his side of the door. She leaned up against the wall just like he was doing. "You can hide here with me," he whispered, moving aside to give her more room. They both fell totally silent as they listened intently to the conversation in the study.

"What did he tell you?"

"That I should be wary of you if we were ever to meet."

"You wary of me? Now there's a twist. But he's making it sound like I threatened him, Eliza. Did I threaten him?"

"No, Father, I don't believe you did. Not him."

Henry glanced between the two of them and frowned. "My family, Norton? Are you threatening my family now?"

Penelope's hands flew up to silence her own mouth and she turned to face Brian. He had also sealed his mouth with his hands.

"Heavens, Stevens, don't go off half-cocked," said Cyrus. "Why would I do that? I'm not threatening you or your family. You see — I don't need to. But. Now that you mention it, Stevens, let's just say the word got out around town here, and back home in England, and down in New York, of the murder. Time the whole world knew about it anyhow, I'd say. Let's just say people found out somehow. You with me?"

"This is absolutely insane. I don't believe I'm hearing this. But I'll humour you. Go on."

"And the word got around to your business associates. Your reputation's awful important to you, isn't it?"

"Yes, I'll grant you that. Where are you going with this, sir? I have another engagement."

"Of course you do. Well. Just thought you should think about all this, Stevens. Think about how much your reputation is worth."

"I see. My reputation. However, my dear sir, I still have no goddamn idea — excuse my language, Miss Norton — what you are talking about!"

"No need to yell and no need to apologize to her. She's heard far worse than that. Yes, you do know, I think, Stevens. You know very well."

"It's time you left, sir."

"Father?" Eliza said, rising abruptly from her chair. "It's time we left. Mr. Stevens has been most kind."

"Like hell he has. But, alright," Cyrus said, grabbing hold of her hand and thrusting himself pelvis first off his chair. "You think about what I said, Stevens. You'll be seeing me again."

When Cyrus and Eliza emerged from the study, a young, red-haired man was standing at the end of the hall by the front door. "Brian?" called Cyrus, leaning heavily on Eliza's arm as they hurried toward the young man.

"No, sir, I'm George," he said, turning to greet them with a polite smile.

Cyrus stared at him for several moments before shaking his hand. "Cyrus Norton. My daughter, Eliza," he said, not taking his eyes off George. "Unbelievable. Can't get over the resemblance. Identical." He followed Eliza's gaze to a portrait above George's head on the wall of the foyer. It was of identical twin boys in riding gear. One red-haired boy stood angled toward the left, the other to the right as if they were talking to one another. The boys appeared to be about twelve years old. "The resemblance is striking, quite striking," he said, his gaze going from the portrait, back to George, then to the portrait again.

"Yes, it is, sir," said Henry, striding down the hall behind them. Then he turned to his son and said in a low voice, "George, stop it." At his father's tone of voice when he spoke to Cyrus, George had reached up behind his left ear to start scratching. Now, he let his hand fall and grabbed it with his right.

"Sorry, sir. Habit."

"Runs in the family, heh Stevens?" said Cyrus.

George glanced from the Nortons to his father, and then said, "If you'll excuse me sir, ma'am, Father, I have a class to get to." He bowed slightly to them, then took his coat and hat from the coat stand and started out the door.

"Did you build this *Agamemnon?*" asked Cyrus, and George turned back around. Cyrus was pointing with his cane to a model of a sailing ship that stood upright in the case tucked into a little alcove in the hallway.

"No, sir."

"Well, I have the same model ship at home. Funny that, heh? The *Agamemnon*. Come see her. If you'd like to take a look."

"Not on my life," said Henry, opening the door.

George again glanced anxiously between the two men, and then stepped backward out onto porch. "By all means — come on by," continued Cyrus. "We'd like to see more of George, isn't that right, Eliza?"

"Yes, Father," said Eliza, taking her father's elbow and leading him out the front door. George had nodded to them again, and then had run down the path and out the front gate. "Come, Father. We must be off," said Eliza. "It's time for your medicine."

"Ah. Yes. My medicine."

As Cyrus stepped onto the porch, Henry said, "By the way, Norton. Ever hear from Jake?"

"The foreman?"

"That's right."

"Don't believe I have. No. Think that's the last I saw of him."

"That so?"

"Yes."

"Well, I heard from him. He wrote to me a couple of years ago after my father died."

"That so?"

"Yes. Funny thing was, he was already dead, Jake was. Never thought I'd be getting letters from someone already buried. You wouldn't happen to know anything about that, would you?"

"Me? Don't be ridiculous. What would I know about that?" Cyrus said as Eliza tugged on his arm. He turned his back on Henry, shoved his hand through Eliza's arm and, without another word, headed down the path.

... --- ...

From Penelope's second-floor bedroom, George could be seen in the distance. He hadn't stopped running since he left the house. Eliza and her father, on the other hand, walked slowly toward the front garden gate. Eliza didn't seem to want to leave. She kept looking back over her shoulder, searching the windows of the house, hoping, perhaps, for someone to rescue her. But Cyrus propelled her forward, dragging on her arm. Eliza opened the garden gate and led them out of the yard. "How did you find out, Mr. Norton?" Penelope mused at the window, then turned smartly on her heels. "Enough of this malingering," she said, before heading out of her room and striding down the hall, toward her refuge.

Brian nodded and followed her. He had been hiding with Penelope, she in the curtains on one side of the window, he on the other side. He caught up with her just as she reached the top of the stairs. She turned as he approached. He hesitated, trying to determine whether she was happy or sad. She smiled at him. He wasn't sure if that meant anything or not, but he took the chance and reached out. Hardly touching her soft skin, his fingers wrapped themselves around her hand.

... --- ...

"Don't call me girl, I said to him. I'm not a girl. I'm now a woman. Lady. Call me lady," said Natty, with a grin. "'Oooh,' he said, and bowed. 'Lady, is it? Toronto, m'lady? Why on earth would'ya wanna go to bloody Toronto? You'll never do it, Natty. You're not like your mum. And what would Toronto want you for, by God? Best stay here where you're wanted.' Then, Clara, I says to myself, 'Oh, Natty you're a troubled lady.' You know why, Clara?"

Clara shook her head.

"Because you should have seen my little heart jumping about in my chest, if you can believe it. He wants *me*, I thought. He wants me."

Clara smiled as she nodded. She coughed loudly and started to re-tie her shoes for at least the tenth time that day. "You're nearing twelve years old and you still can't tie your shoes?" her mother had screamed at her again that morning as she headed out before dark. "What do I need to know about shoe tying?" she called back. "I deliver coal is all I do. Coal don't care about my laces." She dropped the laces and hugged her knees to her chest as she gazed up at Natty. Natty looked at her and frowned. She always did when she coughed like this; it was the same look her mother gave her. Natty bent down and quickly tied Clara's one shoe, then the other. When she grew up, she wanted to be just like Natty. Natty was something special.

"But you know, he must have seen my feelings on my face because he says, 'Not me,' he says, just like that. 'It's not me that's wanting you to stay. God in heaven,' he says. 'Sure, you're of some use 'round here, but it's them I'm thinking of. Those people ya work for. The Stevens'.'"

"The Stevens'?"

"That's exactly what I said to him. 'The Stevens'?'"

Both of them glanced out the doorway of Natty's bedroom and into the dark of the cellar. Then they both looked up at the ceiling. "Is that her up there, Natty? In the kitchen?"

Natty nodded, and lowered her voice. "She'll be down any minute if you don't go, Clara."

"I know."

"She said last time, 'You tell that little coal girl to drop her wares and leave. I don't want you two wasting time when you should be working.'"

"What'd you say?"

"What'd'ya think I said?"

"Yes, Mrs. Stevens," they chorused, then giggled and glanced again at the ceiling, then at the door. They suddenly stopped giggling, and stared into the darkness beyond.

"Was it raining when you arrived, Clara?"

"No. Not a drop."

"Always sounds like it's raining down here, doesn't it?"

Clara listened, but must have looked confused because Natty said, "Hear that?"

"Mrs. Stevens?"

"No. Something else."

"Don't hear anything. Just the cellar. Though it feels like someone's watching us, Natty," she said, dropping her voice to a whisper.

"Always does."

"Does?"

"Yes. Oh, don't worry, Clara — it's usually just Brian. He's alright. Not like the rest of them that lives here."

"Is he out there now, watching us?" whispered Clara, peering into the basement. "Did you hear him come down?"

"No, but I don't always. I'll be working away, up in the kitchen, in the laundry room, and then, there he'll be. Awful quiet. Not like most boys. Clara, it's alright. Don't fret. Besides, Brian's nice to me; he's my friend. And it's good he's got me to stand up for him, is all I've got to say. You should see the way they treat him. If ever there was a boy in need of a friend, it's him. I'll introduce you next time. You still haven't met him, have you?"

Clara shook her head.

"Anyhow, Clara, I was telling you the story of talking to my Pa."

Clara nodded, looking slightly more relaxed.

"My Pa says, 'those people you work for,' and I says to my Pa . . . "

"The Stevens'?" they both repeated and giggled again.

"The bloody Stevens', who cares about Penelope and Henry? I says. Anyways. Soon, Clara. I'll have the money saved, and I'm going to Toronto."

"I know. I'm coming with you."

"I know. Now, before you go . . . there's something I've got to show you."

"What is it?" asked Clara, scrambling up off the floor to stand beside Natty.

"I haven't opened it. I was waiting for you." Natty bent down under the bed and pulled out a package. "It's from the catalogue, see? Look at the return address: Sears and Roebuck." Natty pointed to the lettering on the front of the package.

Clara just stared at it and said, "Unh-huh."

"Clara?"

"Unh-huh?"

"You haven't been practising, have you?"

"Don't have time."

"Nonsense. That's an *s,* see? That should be easy to remember."

"I know, I know. And that's a *d,*" she said, pointing to the *b*. "I'm just too excited to be bothered to read. Just open it, Natty, alright?"

"Alright. It's not a *d,* but anyways, we'll work on it later. You've got to practise. If you want to go somewhere, Toronto or anywhere, Clara, you've got to learn to read."

Clara nodded, and Natty ripped open the brown paper and then the layers of soft white paper underneath. Out of the shredded package spilled a bundle of creamy fabric. Natty reached into the bundle and pulled on a section of the material until she held in her hands a long muslin empire gown. She stared at Clara and Clara stared back, and then the two of them pulled the rest of the items from the bundle. In the end they had another five beautiful pieces: a muslin skirt and drawers trimmed with a lovely embroidery, a cambric gown with the same embroidery on the yolk and trimmed with pretty ivory ribbon at the neck and sleeves, and two corset covers, one muslin and one cambric.

"From him again? Your secret admirer?" whispered Clara, nodding at the silk stockings Natty had hung to dry at the end of her bed.

"Yes," Natty said, grabbing up the underwear pieces and hugging them to her chest.

... --- ...

Penelope pulled the swollen, damp mass from the pantry, set it on the counter and stared down at it for several seconds. Then she placed her elegant hands on either side of it, leaned over and sniffed. One long deep inhale. Yes. Fresh meat. Raw beef. The smell of life. Of tomorrow. Of the whole of next week. She could stretch the meat and make it last ten days if she put her mind to it. Just like her mum could do. Pies, stews, soups — even dried is good, her mum had said. Dried is better than nothing.

Penelope liked being in the kitchen. She didn't want to come back to it permanently, nothing like that. But it was good to be here alone, in her very own kitchen; one that belonged to her. She loved the smells, the canisters full of flour and sugar and salt and soda, the pots and pans and cooking implements. The clean surface of the counters. The shiny white sink. The tiny residue of bread dough in the corner of the large wooden block in the middle of the kitchen. She'd asked for the block when they moved here. She had had one in France; it was one of the things she'd loved about that house. She stood up to her full height of five feet, six inches, and straightened the front of her crisp white blouse and green skirt. Emerald, like her eyes. She wore colours to accent her eyes. How unusual, people had said when she had been working in France. Two girls with eyes so much the same. And look at your hair. You two could be the same person.

She walked along the border of the cutting block. She had more sharp knives than she needed, each with a different handle. She had asked for these as well. They've got to have good knives; the servants can't chop with a dull knife. Not that I would know, she'd said, correcting herself, like she knew nothing about kitchens, about cooking, about food, blocks, knives, when she knew everything. As if she hadn't spent half her life in one. She knew more about the kitchen than about the library, or the parlour.

In the end, Henry gave her money for the kitchen. Spend it how you like, he had mumbled after his third scotch. And she had. She had even had the new laundry room built, only a couple of steps down, just off the kitchen.

Each night before she went to bed, she crept down with her light and opened the door to the pantry. Just to look at all that food. Everything you could ever want. Vegetables, fruit. Potatoes. Onions. Salt. Tea. Bread, still fresh from the morning's baking. Rolls, a half a sweet tart. She would open the icebox. Milk. Butter. Eggs. Bacon. Sausage. Everything you could ever want. She had only been caught once, a year ago, when her son came down to the kitchen. He had looked at her strangely when she turned around, but before she faced him, she wiped the guilt from her face and replaced it with a smile. Her confident smile, the one she had made her own. The smile she had perfected over the last eighteen years. Even so, when he looked at her, while the shadow from the hallway played on his features, while he chewed on a piece of string, it was as if he knew. But perhaps that's because he always had that look about him. Half-smile, half-sneer. Her own son. She wanted to follow him back to his bedroom and ask: What were you thinking just then?

She didn't ask, she didn't follow him. What would she have done if he had said, I know who you are. I know what you did.

She picked up the beef and carried it to the far counter that faced the side yard of the house. Beyond was a high hedge, and no neighbours within watching distance. She liked that. She liked to work alone. But when she set the beef down, she noticed that the door to the cellar stairwell was open — just an inch, but that was enough. She walked past the end of the counter, grabbed on to the handle, and was about to close the cellar door when she stopped to listen. She waited a full minute, but she didn't hear it again. An unfamiliar sound from below — probably just Natty, no doubt, with her little friend, Clara. Or, perhaps, it was Brian. The thought of Brian almost made her laugh. "Mentally afflicted, is he ma'am?" Natty had asked her some time ago. Always more chatty than was really appropriate for a person of her status, Natty carried on: "To be honest, hope you don't mind my saying, but he reminds me of some of the patients I cleaned up after at the hospital for the feeble-minded. Especially the way he's always batting the air around his head with the palms of his hands — as if he's trying to push some invisible bother away."

Penelope had been in a light-hearted mood that day, and answered readily: "Oh, yes. A troublesome habit, that is. Most distressing."

"I've tried to get him to stop, ma'am."

"Is that so? It's of no use, I suppose you've realized."

"Yes, ma'am, but there's no harm in trying, is there?"

"None at all, Natty."

"I mean he does look so awfully disturbed when he's doing it. Ma'am?"

"Yes, Natty."

"Is there anything that can be done for him, ma'am?"

"No, Natty, I'm afraid not. Nothing at all. Sad to say, but there you have it."

"Ma'am?"

"Yes, Natty?"

"I was wondering if I could ask you another question about Brian?"

Natty was obviously feeling like she could milk this rare opportunity with Penelope. Still, Penelope was feeling generous, so she said: "Well, Natty, I don't know. However, I won't know until you ask it, will I? So, ask away."

"Well, then . . . was he born that way, ma'am? Has he always been unfit, or did he get afflicted later?"

"Oh, much later, Natty. When Brian was born he was rather perfect — I suppose," she said, and then she'd turned from the sink to the doorway that led to the hall. "Much like our George." Standing in the doorway was her George. He had heard the last part of the conversation, and smiled at his mother — a most charming, engaging smile. She really had the most wonderfully handsome son.

Now, she smiled at the memory, quietly shut the cellar door and went back to work. She took another sniff of the beef before placing it into the large meat grinder. She'd grind a section for meat loaf, and chop some of it for a pie.

She cranked the handle as she pressed down on the muscle of meat, but she should have known what would happen next. Before she could stop it, her mind had raised another memory, but this one she would forever banish if she could. Instead of the muscle of meat before her, she now remembered human muscle. And bone. And legs, twisted horrifically under the body at the bottom of the staircase. And the body, tumbling over and over itself as it fell down the stairs. There was never any hope for that body. None at all. The body was broken well before it reached the bottom.

"George, please pass the butter," Penelope said, and her words shattered Brian's memories into a million pieces. His mind stopped in mid-stab, and he sat immobile, staring helplessly at the dreaded steak and kidney pie. But he was worried about more than the pie, he knew that much. He just didn't know what it was. He knew that he was about to tell Henry about his friend, Morna. He should tell someone about Morna. He remembered coming home with his brother; he remembered his brother falling. And he remembered another thing: he and George had been late for supper.

Though it felt like hours, or centuries, they had arrived only minutes before. Penelope and Henry were already seated, she at one end of the long dining room table, he at the other. Mouth full of pie, Henry grunted when they had rushed into the dining room. Penelope, her meal untouched, hands folded on her lap, sitting erect, glared at them when they took their seats on opposite sides of the table. Being late for supper was equal only to other dining infractions, such as eating with the wrong fork or using your own knife for the butter. Brian forever tried to understand all her rules, but never could get them right. Natty knew it, and she would be there to help him when he needed it. At the sideboard behind him, Natty had filled Brian's and George's plates. As always, she served George first. Penelope would have been upset otherwise. When she put the plate in front of Brian, it held only a two-inch wide sliver of pie, and a dozen or so peas.

"Oh, Natty!" Penelope had uttered.

"Should I give him more, Mrs. Stevens? He won't eat more, I shouldn't think."

"Not more, you fool. Less. For heaven's sake."

"Is this better, Mrs. Stevens?" Natty asked, after she'd brought Brian's plate back to the sideboard, removed an inch of the slice, and returned with the plate. She didn't like to cross Penelope when it came to Brian.

"That's better," Brian implored Natty with his eyes. "Don't worry about it, Natty. You'll just get her upset."

"If he has to have any at all, then, yes, that is much better. Otherwise it's simply a waste, isn't it, Natty?"

"Yes, ma'am."

Brian didn't like it when Penelope got angry, and she was angry now. He didn't know whose fault it was: Natty's, his own, or — and he looked across the table — George's.

"George! The butter!" he hissed in a conspiratorial whisper. But George was elsewhere. He wasn't listening, and this was very upsetting: Penelope would get even more cross. And far more concerning, Brian couldn't figure out why something else about George was bothering him. It wasn't the clean clothes he had on; George always changed for supper. It wasn't that he'd just had a long bath; though not a common occurrence before supper, that in itself wouldn't be distressing. It was his fringe. George had combed it straight down over his forehead so that the hair ends tickled his eyelids. Seeing Brian watching him, he patted his still-damp fringe so that it sat even flatter on his forehead. Oh, stop worrying, Brian told himself, as George returned to his task: boxing his peas with the tines of his fork.

"More peas, Brian?" Natty interrupted as she came over to his side of the table and held the serving dish out to him. He shook his head like the top of a rag doll, his red hair flopping back and forth. She returned the peas to the sideboard, and came back with the pie that she was going to offer to Penelope. "You should eat something, Brian," she whispered, and they caught Penelope casting them a dark look. She didn't like it when Natty tried to assist Brian. Natty and Brian both knew it. And they both knew better than to talk at the dinner table. So they communicated with their eyes.

It's kidney, Natty! What am I going to do? I can't eat the stupid pie. I'll throw up all over the table, over Penelope's fine linen, my knickers, this old shirt, her new rug.

Who cares about the stupid ugly rug, Brian, go ahead, throw up all over it. You can't pick the kidney out —

I know. You can't pick at the table —

Picking's not allowed.

I know, Natty. I know, I know, I know. What am I going to *do*?

"George," Penelope said again, but this time Brian was so absorbed by the horrors of kidney that he hardly heard. Her voice passed him by, almost unnoticed, almost uncared for until Henry bellowed:

"George!" and Brian's head spiked upward, making Natty drop the pie's serving spoon on the floor, sending pastry, loathsome kidney, gravy flying, landing on his plate, the white tablecloth, his crystal water glass, his stained shirt and grey knickers, the new rug. Brian swiped the mess off the ripped shoulder of his shirt and his bruised knee. Penelope glared at Natty. Natty rushed to the sideboard to get a cloth. Penelope rolled her eyes, and, finally, George looked up from his picking — blatant and unabashed food-picking — and said: "Yes, Father?"

"The butter, goddammit."

"Right. Sorry, Mother. I'm surprised Brian didn't get it for you," George said, grinning at Natty. He reached farther than Penelope would have had to and picked up the crystal butter dish. George passed the dish to his mother, careful that the butter knife, balanced just so and cleanly sitting in its slot, did not fall out and drop onto the white linen tablecloth, or worse, the rug. As their fingers touched around the butter dish, Penelope's eyes widened as she stared at George's forehead. Brian followed her gaze, and as he did, whole big pieces of memory tumbled back into his brain.

He remembered the visit today from the Nortons. For some reason, he had totally forgotten about that, and he knew as he stared at Penelope and George and then back at his kidney mess, and then back up at them, all the while trying to find a place for his eyes to settle, that this was tonight's reason for Penelope's distress and Henry's silence. And he knew something else. Something bad had happened to George. Penelope knew it, too — she was still staring at George's fringe, which he had combed brilliantly over his forehead. But the fringe had parted and there, red and sore and undeniable, was a large, unhealed gash. "George?" asked Penelope softly. "Whatever happened to your head?"

Brian stared at the gash as if he was seeing it for the first time. But, of course, that was nonsense. He was with George in the alley when it happened, just over an hour ago.

...---...

He knew the feeling. Wet from the waist down. And the smell. How could he ever forget it? "Oh, God," George moaned without opening his eyes, and Brian thought, yes, that's always the first thing — reality through the nose. Scent before sight. George moaned again, and reached for his forehead.

"What will you tell Penelope?" Brian whispered, leaning forward over George's face, which he could see quite clearly despite the dark. He tried to stifle a giggle. "Perhaps you won't tell. I didn't ever — never ever — but mothers always know. They figure it out, you know. But come. Get up. Up, up. I'll help you." George didn't answer, didn't move. He just kept groaning. Brian could understand. The smell of urine is the absolute worst. "Are you going to wash the sheets yourself? Doesn't work, you know. Just throw them in the fireplace. Light it. Quick. Done. Find a new set. Where's the cupboard? I'll get you fresh sheets."

He looked around for the doorway to the hall, but the room was too black. When did it become nighttime? He wanted the day and the light and then, as if the air was responding to his wish, shapes started to become visible. That's better, and he felt a sudden thrill at knowing what he would find in George's room. He wondered why he had decided to visit George tonight.

Why indeed? Now *that* was a very good question, he thought as he looked around the room. But he would think about that later. He had noticed something familiar coming into focus on the other side of the room. Even in the dimness, he could see her name inscribed on the wooden hull: *Agamemnon*. Oh, my. The 1857 *Agamemnon*. He had had an 1857 as well; it was the favourite of all his model ships. He had loved those three main sails, the tiny portholes, the small, lean wooden masts. He couldn't wait for the dark to go away so he could see the model that George had built. Perhaps when George's bed had been changed and the sheets burned, he could help him with any pieces still under construction. Had George begun the cable, he wondered, starting across the room toward the ship. Brian could still remember his father's words when he had began his own *Agamemnon's* cable and brought it down to his father's study. He could still feel the hard, small copper wires as he showed them to him. At first his father hadn't responded, and had folded his hands in front of his stomach and bowed his head. He did this when he was getting angry, and Brian was about to back away when his father breathed heavily and said simply: *You almost have it right, Brian, but it was made of seven copper wires, not eight.* Brian had relaxed. His father's voice was, as always, deep and kind, but this night it was more sad than usual. Brian remembered wondering why copper wiring should have made him so sad. *And what are you going to use to wrap the wires? We don't have gutta-percha. I suppose rubber would do — there's some in the shed.* But Brian had shaken his head. He couldn't use rubber. Only gutta-percha would work; his father knew that. Why was he saying to use rubber? They wouldn't have used rubber on the real transatlantic cable now, would they? It needed to be gutta-percha to properly insulate the wires. Brian had said all of this and his father replied that he would try to find some gutta-percha the next day. Now, as Brian approached the other side of George's room, the memory just slipped away, as his memories always did. He tried to recall, once again, what had happened next — had his father found some gutta-percha? had he himself finished constructing the cable? wrapping it with gutta-percha? then with tarred hemp? finally, with iron strands? — but as if nothing had ever happened beyond that moment, the memory came back hollow.

Suddenly, he felt a rush of nausea as he gazed at the slowly forming shape of the *Agamemnon*, and realized that this wasn't the *Agamemnon* after all. It wasn't any kind of model ship, just a mess of wood scraps and wire bits. And no words were inscribed on anything. The night had been playing with his eyesight. Brian reached up and started scratching above his right ear. His father always hated it when he scratched like that. *Stop it, Brian.* But he didn't, he couldn't; something was making him nervous, and he didn't know what it was.

He glanced around as if the room would tell him why, but instead a sick ripple washed up into his throat as other questions leapt out at him. Why did George's bedroom have stone walls? And only on two sides? Where were the windows? The drapes? The desk? The bed? What were lobster buoys doing in the bedroom? This room was turning out to be unlike any boy's room he had ever seen.

"Where are we?" he whispered, turning back and walking over to George. "Do you know?" George still wasn't speaking, and this was becoming very irritating. "Just get up. Stop worrying about it. We've got to get out of here."

Wherever *here* was. Now everything was in focus. He scratched the spot above his ear furiously. Yes, indeed, indeed, indeed, this was no bedroom, not at all. *Stop it, Brian, stop it.* How could he? They were in an alley, of all places. No models of ships, no toys of any kind. No, indeed.

They were halfway down an alley, as a matter of fact, in a city it would seem — he could tell by the sounds and smells coming from the street up ahead. A clip-clop and the scratching of a horse-drawn carriage. A second later, two men rushed by. He could tell by their heavy tread, and their harsh laughter. Were they drunk? Was this even St. John's? He hoped so. At least let it be St. John's. Brian didn't know where he was and he wanted to go home. Home? Yes, *home*, alright? Home. Then he looked over at George. He wasn't in his bed in his own house, and he didn't need clean sheets. He was lying on his back beside two lobster buoys in this alley. His shirttails were hanging loose over his urine-soaked trousers. But the worst thing by far was that George's red curly hair was soaked with blood.

Now why on earth does he *have to have* blood on his head, Brian thought, jumping up and down on the spot. George brought his hand away from his head and laid it over his stomach, and the red blood from his hand saturated his urine-soaked shirt. "You've cut yourself, George," Brian whispered, leaning over him again. "Did you fall? What happened?" He didn't fall, don't be silly, Silly. Another sound from down the alley — another horse? another man? — made him glance quickly at the cobblestone walls on either side of them. Someone could jump out at any time. People jump out of the night out of walls out of holes that you don't know are there. Even though you should have known. Because you knew everything. No, you didn't, not everything.

You should have listened.

I know. I should have listened. George groaned again, opened his eyes and saw the blood.

"Oh, God, I must have fallen," he moaned again. At least he was speaking. And then he sniffed and closed his eyes.

"I know. It stinks," Brian said, glad for the distraction of the urine. "There's no getting used to it." He'd never have thought he'd be glad to be talking about piss.

It took George another five minutes to pull himself to standing while Brian strode back and forth and back and forth across the width of the alley. He had tried to help George up, but he didn't seem to want it. "Come. Get up then, let's go," he said now, as George stood uneasily against the damp wall of the building. "Let's go. Let's go." You've got to go, you know, you've got to get out of here. I know.

Just as he knew absolutely too late that he should have listened to himself the half-second before the hole opened in the dark, and life fell out.

He could tell now that George hadn't fallen. He had been hit on the head and his bladder had released all on its own, and at least it was just his bladder and not his bowels and oh, God, I need to hide, Brian thought. *Now.* You can never be safe, ever. *Never, ever.* Ever. He rushed over and crouched behind a collection of old traps and netting that had been tossed further down the alley. A fine drizzle had begun to fall. He looked down at his still-dry arm. And he began to giggle again. The nervous laugh that used to drive his father crazy. "What the hell am I doing here?" George suddenly cried out at him.

"I wish I could tell you, old man. I've been asking myself the very same thing. It doesn't look good for you though. Were you drinking, do you think?" Brian said, trying to sound as calm as could be. As if he was fooling anyone. Still, he tried to keep his voice level. Tried to act grown up. If you act scared, you are scared. He knew that. Not that it mattered. Pretending doesn't stop life from happening. "You've been drinking, haven't you?"

"I haven't been drinking."

"So you say. But you might not remember. Maybe you take after Henry and Judson. Nonetheless, Henry and Penelope will be none too pleased. Look at you." This was better. Keep talking. Scary things go away when you're talking.

"What's this?" asked George, pulling apart his unbuttoned shirt and looking at his still-hairless chest.

"What's what?" asked Brian, not wanting to know, hating to look. "Tuck it in, George. Let's go. Don't worry about it, whatever it is."

"Some fool has put something on my chest."

"So? We don't need to know; we don't care what it is. Let's go."

"What the hell is it?"

Brian didn't want to look but he did anyhow. A note had been written on George's skin. It ran diagonally upside down across his chest. That was smart, Brian thought suddenly. In a flash of admiration for the perpetrator, he realized that if it was written right side up, how could George have read it? He would have had to try to decipher it upside down. Someone had been thinking. But it didn't matter, he realized as he stepped closer, because the note contained only a two-word sentence.

George looked down at his chest and said: "What on earth is this nonsense?"

...---...

"And then I lifted my shirt," George finished as Henry fingered his own forehead, and Penelope and Natty stared at George. They hadn't said a word the entire time he had been talking.

"What was on your stomach, George?" asked Penelope, her voice barely a whisper.

"A message," said Brian.

"Nothing," said George.

"Nothing?" said Brian. "It was more than nothing, George. Didn't you read it? You must have read it. Tell them. For God's sake, tell them, you idiot."

Instead, George lied: "It was just a bunch of squiggles; I couldn't make them out."

Of course you could read them, George, Brian thought. Why are you lying? Then he turned in his seat and saw Natty looking at him. She was staring at him with the most horrified expression.

"It wasn't me," he said, because that's what she seemed to be thinking. She didn't answer but just turned from him, quickly gathered up some dirty dishes from the sideboard and with a nod to Penelope, almost ran out of the dining room and into the kitchen.

Penelope and Brian stood side by side at the kitchen block, trying to decide what knife to use. Each in its respective slot in the wooden holder, there was every type of blade you could ever want: long, short, cleavers, bread, paring — all of them sharpened by Penelope herself with the stone she'd brought from France and kept in the drawer under the cutting block. There was every type of knife, Brian thought, except the one he really wanted her to use — his father's, the one with the stag handle. What had Penelope done with it? It was his favourite. Why wasn't it here? He was about to ask her when he remembered: he was the last to use it. In fact, for some reason, he had stolen the knife from his father, and he had hidden it — in his secret alcove in the cave that belonged to him and his brother.

"Use that one," he quickly suggested, successfully subverting memories of the knife, the alcove, the cave. Penelope didn't argue with his choice, and selected a medium-sized, sturdy tool with a seven-inch blade and a black leather handle. She started to chop professional, efficient slices, and juicy red chunks fell away and onto the board.

"I imagine *you* know what happened to George, don't you, Brian?" Penelope said, lifting a handful of the meat and putting it into a ceramic bowl. She wiped her hand on the towel on the counter and returned to her cutting. Her activity gave the kitchen its only vigour. Natty had cleaned up the supper things, and the kitchen sparkled. Natty had retired for the night, as had the rest of the household. Brian and Penelope were left to their nocturnal selves. He shook his head to her question about George. He didn't know the answer to that. Why was she asking him?

"Another pie tomorrow?" Brian asked, once again outsmarting himself.

"Meat loaf tomorrow. Beef for the whole of next week, just about," she said, and he hoped against hope that kidney wasn't part of her week's meal planning.

Soon the meat was completely sliced and put into the bowl. She covered the bowl with a glass lid and stored it in the cooler. She returned to the block, wiped down the top, and brought the cutting board and knife to the sink. She poured warm water from the stove's kettle into the sink, and began to lather the implements. "One more thing. Perhaps you can help me with this as well, Brian."

He nodded and waited again for her to speak, mesmerized by the bubbles slipping down the flat of the shiny steel of the blade.

"How do you think Cyrus Norton knows, Brian?"

Brian shrugged. Why was she asking him?

"I wonder if he found the body."

What body, Brian wondered. What was she talking about? He scratched behind his ear. He didn't want to be with her anymore. He backed away from her. He was going to go upstairs to visit Henry.

"But that's impossible. I buried it extremely well, didn't I?"

He stopped and stared at her, as if hearing the story for the first time.

"One would never know there was a body buried in that cellar. So, how did he find out, Brian? Do you know?"

Of course he didn't know! He followed her gaze to the cellar door. It was closed, as it always was. Shut tight. The way she always kept it. But it didn't help, he thought, fixating on it; he knew what lay on the other side. Natty was downstairs, sleeping in her room. That, at least, was reassuring. But the staircase was steep, and dark at the top. And at the even darker bottom, Penelope's memories, and some of his own, lay waiting. Well, he wouldn't remember them. That's all. Not tonight. Too many bad things had already happened today, although those memories were already sketchy, and only bits nagged: George, of course, but even worse, even more worrisome, that miserable Cyrus and his talk of murder and blackmail, and now Penelope with talk of a dead body. Brian started to rush away from Penelope, but when he got to the door leading to the hallway, he had a sudden thought that made him stop. He turned to look back into the kitchen: Did she mean *this* cellar?

He didn't know. He didn't want to wait around to find out. He ran along the hall and up the stairs. He would visit Henry. With him, at least, he would be safe.

Day Two
Wednesday, October 15, 1902

"Hand me those boxes, will you, love?" Bea whispered to her young cousin. From the basket in the aisle, Jean picked out two boxes of Italian Cream Candy and handed them up to Bea, who was standing on a short stool in order to reach the back of the shelf.

"These ones?" asked Jean.

"Yes. No. Actually, the larger ones. Sorry."

"That's alright, Bea. These?"

"Yes, love. Thanks. I can fit three more. Hurry, Jean. Let's get this done before you have to go."

Standing at Shulman's front window, Mildred paid little mind to their conversation as they worked in the aisle behind her. Instead, she concentrated on the street outside the window: horse-drawn wagons carrying people, horse-drawn carts carrying dried fish, a streetcar going west, women shopping with their children, fish merchants, three cyclists, and a worried young couple who had just now stopped in front of the store to tend to their infant in its pram. She noticed all of this, but none of it wanted her attention — that had been consumed by Mrs. Stevens and her son. It had gone with them out of Shulman's door and into their carriage, and it had then parked itself on Water Street and waited for them to emerge from a store down the block. As Mildred so often did when she needed to think, she looked to see what her charges were doing.

Jean was handing Bea three thin blue boxes, and Bea took them and placed them in their row. She got down, moved the stool a third of the way down the aisle, and climbed on it again. "Spanish Peanut Sticks this time, love," said Bea. "Four of them." Neither of the girls spoke while they continued to work: a quiet had come over them that had begun when Mrs. Stevens and her son had been in Shulman's, and now Bea stood on the stool, boxes in hand, gazing toward the store window, as if she would find the answer there.

"Miss MacDonald?" Mr. Shulman called from the front of the store.

"Yes, Mr. Shulman?" Bea answered too softly. She began working for Mr. Shulman when she was sixteen, now more than two years ago, and had never grown accustomed to him calling to her from the front counter. She would never answer in kind.

"The delivery for Mr. Snead," he called. He probably hadn't heard her reply but he had grown used to her ways, and rarely asked her to speak more loudly. "Would you be so kind as to retrieve it from the back room? And little Miss MacDonald?"

"Yes, Mr. Shulman," Jean answered in a voice even less audible than her cousin's. It had always been that way, thought Mildred, watching the flush rise to the cheeks of both the girls: they abhorred being the focus of attention.

"Your mother is here to pick you up."

Sure enough, Evelyn had arrived, Mildred saw as she glanced at the front door and smiled. Evelyn returned the smile and went to find Jean. Mildred crossed her arms in front of her chest and turned around to face the window. Down the street, Mrs. Stevens was being assisted into her carriage by her driver. Her son wasn't helping — which was no surprise to Mildred — and he climbed into the carriage after her. Mildred figured the girls were onto something: it was clear by looking that trouble of some kind had befallen the Stevens', and now it was tied to them like an anchor. Its urgency had been evident when they had been in Shulman's a half-hour before.

"Essence of Jamaican Ginger, Mrs. Stevens. For the sinuses," Mr. Shulman had explained to her at the front counter. From where Mildred stood next to Bea as she filled the bin of oats at the far end of the aisle, she could see him touch the right side of his nose with his finger. He smiled at Mrs. Stevens as if she was the only customer to whom he would impart his medicinal knowledge, and with a dramatic gesture, he untwisted the top of one of the newly-arrived bottles to display the pale brown liquid inside. Mrs. Stevens nodded, her camel-coloured hat tilting as she did so, but she averted her head from the odour. Her son seemed to like it, though, and leaned closer to the jar as Mr. Shulman held it out for him to smell.

"What do you think of it, Jean?" Mrs. Stevens then asked, leaning partway over the counter so that she could see Jean, who was seated on a crate on the other side. Mr. Shulman let her sit there while she waited for Evelyn to pick her up, and he always gave her a job to do. Today, she was using another crate as a table to make a sign for the sale on Blackberry Cordial.

Jean hesitated before answering. She seemed distracted and deep in thought. After several seconds she looked up and smiled at Mrs. Stevens and said, "Don't mind it so much, ma'am. It doesn't make my nose hurt like some of the other ones."

"Well, there you have it then, Mr. Shulman," Mrs. Stevens said, smiling over at her son and then down at Jean, before looking over at Mr. Shulman. "An endorsement if I've ever heard one: A product that is not a nose-hurter cannot be all that bad."

"And yet," Mr. Shulman said, reaching down to pat Jean on the head. He lowered his voice and continued, "You did not come here for my Jamaican Ginger, did you, Mrs. Stevens?"

"No," she said in a whisper, touching her tan-gloved fingers to her forehead. Before she continued speaking, Bea had quickly wiped the oat dust off her apron and sauntered over to the counter to get one of the ledgers out of a drawer behind Mr. Shulman. She pretended to peruse the columns while she listened in on the conversation. Mildred went to stand next to Mrs. Stevens, but she tried not to stare at the woman who continued speaking in a hushed tone. Pointing toward her son's forehead, Mrs. Stevens nodded and said, "A deep cut."

"Requiring stitches, perhaps?" asked Mr. Shulman, gazing at the forehead, trying to see past the fringe to the cut beneath it. Mrs. Stevens had brought her son with her so that Mr. Shulman could examine him, but he was clearly one of those taciturn young men who would rather be anywhere than shopping with his mother. He turned his back on them and stepped away from the counter before Mr. Shulman could see more of his forehead.

"I don't think it needs stitches," she said, glancing nervously at her son. But when he didn't voluntarily turn around so that they could get a better look, she spoke for him, "I don't think he'd want them." He shook his head and walked away from them to go and stare out the window. It was obvious that he was embarrassed to have people discuss him, but Mildred was shocked at his rude behaviour. The least he could do is be civil and answer his mother.

"I see," said Mr. Shulman quietly, keeping his attention on Mrs. Stevens. "Well, we will want to keep it clean so that it will not become infected. I am not a physician here, you understand."

"Quite clearly," Mrs. Stevens replied. Mildred had heard him say this many times before: he always prefaced any medical advice with the qualifier about "not being a physician *here*."

"Miss MacDonald?" he said.

"Yes, Mr. Shulman?" Bea answered slowly, as if distracted by the importance of the ledger in her hands.

"The Tincture of Arnica. Take a look for it, if you please. It is on sale this week, as it happens."

"I'll check for you, Mr. Shulman. I won't be a moment, Mrs. Stevens."

Mildred went with her. They excused themselves as they brushed by several customers before arriving at the middle aisle. They worked their way past a boy — he had been looking at the glycerine suppositories but then when he saw them he pretended it was the pomade that interested him — and made their way to the centre of the aisle. Bea reached up to the fourth shelf. Next to the bottles of boil remedies, she came to the arnica. She answered in a voice not loud enough to carry, "Yes, Mr. Shulman. It is on sale."

"Speak up, love, he can hardly hear you," said Mildred. Then she shook her head and returned to the counter where she said to Mr. Shulman and Mrs. Stevens: "It's always like this. So often I ask them to speak up, and they don't. You'd think they were raised in a church, the way they whisper." Mildred noticed that Mrs. Stevens' son had left the store. He'd no doubt had enough of people talking about him, and was waiting somewhere outside for his mother.

Bea rounded the corner of the aisle and got closer to the front counter so she wouldn't have to holler, then she repeated what she had said.

"As I thought," Mr. Shulman said. "And the prices?"

"Nineteen cents on the four ounce bottle, thirty-six on the half-pint, and sixty-three on the pint."

"You will only need a small amount," he said to Mrs. Stevens. "Bring us the four-ounce, Miss MacDonald," he said to Bea as she headed back to the arnica aisle.

Mrs. Stevens hesitated, then said, "That's alright, Bea. I'll take the half-pint."

"The half-pint it is," said Mr. Shulman, and Bea returned once more, bringing both sizes up to the counter. Mr. Shulman wrapped the bottle, then placed it gently in Mrs. Stevens' small basket between the handful of carrots and a large bag of rock candy. He spoke quietly as he did so, giving her instructions on the use of arnica as well as other details on the care of cuts. Then he dipped his pen in the ink well and on the day's ledger he wrote "36 cents" beside Mrs. Stevens' name.

"Thank you, Mr. Shulman. Your advice is always appreciated," Mrs. Stevens said, and he bowed slightly in acknowledgment. "I've a few more things to get," she said.

"Do you need Bea to assist you, Mrs. Stevens?"

"I can manage just fine, thank you."

"Oh, Mrs. Stevens, I meant no offence. I did not think for a moment that you were incapable of managing. It is just that, if you will excuse me, your maid is usually the one to make the daily purchases."

"Natty's not working for us anymore."

"Oh, I see, well . . . "

"Yes. Walked out. Left without a word. Haven't seen her all day," said Mrs. Stevens, heading back into the aisles, just as Dr. McTavish stepped up to the counter. Mildred looked him over, and she had to resist the urge to reach out and touch him, even just a little bit, a small, light fingering of his sleeve for instance: he was such a handsome gentleman and always so smartly dressed. She had always fancied virile men. His business must be going splendidly considering he could afford such fine clothes — such as this dark worsted suit he was wearing — as well as the care of his wife and seven children. Bea added up and wrapped his purchases: a measuring glass, six small paraffin candles, and one dozen post office papers, and then placed them in his bag. He tipped his bowler hat to them. Mildred put up a hand to fix her hair. She smiled and nodded good-bye to him, just as Mrs. Stevens returned to the counter with one dozen eggs and a box of toothache remedy.

"Having a touch of tooth pain, are we, dear?" asked Mildred.

Mrs. Stevens looked at her and frowned and Mildred took that as an affirmative.

After Bea had tallied her order and Mrs. Stevens had adjusted her coat and hat and was preparing to leave, Mr. Shulman asked Bea: "Will you be making a mending delivery to Miss Norton for your aunt this afternoon?" She nodded and he added, "Then if you would be so kind, might you also deliver the pomade to Miss Norton, Miss MacDonald? She came in looking for it the other day but, unfortunately, we were out of stock."

Mrs. Stevens looked over at them, hesitated a moment and then said, "Did I hear you say 'the Nortons' — would that be Mr. Cyrus and Miss Eliza Norton, perchance?"

"Yes, Mrs. Stevens," replied Bea.

"Then I wonder if you could perform a small task for me, Bea?" asked Mrs. Stevens.

From her stool's perch, Bea frowned at the bustling scene outside of Shulman's storefront window. Even though the source of her disturbance, arnica in hand, had departed minutes earlier, Bea's mind kept wandering back to the window. Trying once again to focus, she began to shelve the tins she had been holding.

"Best get this done, enough of this lallygagging. Jean, hand me a few more, will you, love? You'll have to go any minute now," Bea said, straightening the tins she had put on the shelf.

As if she knew they were talking about her, Aunt Evelyn called from the back of the store: "I won't be a minute, Jean. We need to get a few more potatoes. And carrots. Perhaps I should get a couple of those, for a soup . . ."

Jean didn't respond to her mother, nor had she answered Bea seconds earlier. She stood beside Bea's stool — she had followed her gaze outside the window, and there it had stayed.

"Jean. *Jean?*" Bea whispered.

"Sorry, Bea," said Jean, turning to look up at her, her eyes dark with worry.

"Don't fret, love, I don't know what's the matter with us today. Let's finish, shall we?"

Jean nodded, and handed Bea the two tins she had been holding. But as Bea placed those next to the others, Jean remarked, "Do those tins go there, do you think, Bea?"

No, of course not, Bea grimaced. The tobacco tins belonged behind the front counter. Unfortunately, Jean's correction came many tins and boxes too late. Bea scanned the shelves above and below — tobacco wasn't the only thing she had mis-shelved.

"Did you fall, Morna?" Brian asked. When she didn't answer, he bent down and gently poked her on the knee. There was no reaction. "What are you doing at the bottom of the stairs, Morna? How did you get here?" She didn't respond. She was all twisted every which way. "Come. Get up. Up, up. Here, I'll help you." But before he could reach for Morna, he heard a movement from the top of the stairs. The stairs were too steep, and they were too dark at the top. He couldn't see if anyone was up there. He quickly knelt down beside Morna, and whispered in her ear: "Are you dead, Morna? Did someone kill you, Morna?"

...---...

He still didn't know if Morna was dead, or if she had been killed, and he wished he'd stop thinking about it. He would think of Natty instead. From Henry's bedroom window, Brian could see the tree-lined street for a short distance, but Natty wasn't coming. Where had she gone? What was taking her so long to return? She had better hurry. He had to tell her about Morna.

...---...

Morna had just brought a load of clean clothes up from the laundry room when he came into the room. She cried and dropped the laundry onto the kitchen floor, and one of the new white blouses fell against the metal legs of the stove. A tiny speck of coal landed on the lace-trimmed collar and immediately widened into a circle of dark grey. She fell to the floor and Brian got down on his knees beside her.

"I didn't mean to scare you."

"What am I going to do?" she cried, flicking a curl off her forehead, and holding the collar of the blouse close to her eyes. She had grown nearsighted several years back.

"Cold water? Soda?" Brian suggested.

"Soda, perhaps," she said, and she scrambled painfully up from her arthritic knees and rushed over to the sink. Brian went with her, and watched while she dragged the ceramic canister of white powder across the counter and spooned three small scoops onto the black smudge. She poured a tablespoon of water onto the mound from the pitcher on the counter, then more to make a paste. "Please, please, please. She'll be furious," she cried.

"It'll be fine. It will. Don't worry," he said, touching her for the first time ever. He had never ever touched her before. He didn't know why. At first she started, shocked, then she relaxed slightly.

"It'll be fine. Just fine. Not to worry," she said, repeating his words.

"Yes," he said.

"Yes, absolutely fine," she said, fingering the soda paste gently into the smudge so as not to make the stain bigger. After several minutes, she brushed the extra soda onto the counter and held the garment up to her eyes again. "I can't see. Is it gone? I can't see. It doesn't seem to be there." The smudge had faded, but not disappeared.

"It's gone," he lied.

...---...

A sound outside of the window brought Brian's mind back to the present. Two women had just entered the yard through the front gate. He recognized the older one, small-boned and not more than five feet tall, with short black hair and a kindly face, her eyes dark and intelligent. The younger woman he felt he should know. He'd seen her somewhere, but couldn't recall where. She was taller than the other woman by a few inches. He liked her hair, full and wavy, and dark brown. On the lawn outside, the older woman stopped, touched the younger woman's shoulder, and spoke to her as she turned. The older woman must have decided to wait outside, and she walked over to the oak across the street. She looked up to the second-floor windows and Brian waved to her, but she didn't wave back. Was she ignoring him? Brian waited a moment for her to see him, and then turned his attention to the young woman who approached the front porch on her own. When the doorbell rang, he was already at the top of the stairs. He held tight to the banister, but he did not descend. He waited first, listening for Penelope.

There was no welcome here. No comfort. Nothing to call "home." You'd be worried all the time, thought Bea, of smudging, of denting, or, God forbid, of spilling. Of living. Where could you put your feet up? Or read a book? She'd never seen such an immaculate, perfect foyer, and it gave her the jitters.

The dark wooden floor gleamed far too radiantly. The wood had been polished until it sparkled. Even the mahogany banister alongside the winding staircase shone with an excess that was worrisome. Natty cleaned all this? Gawd. Bea tapped her foot and shifted on her chair, wishing Mrs. Stevens would hurry with that delivery for the Nortons. "Since you're going, might you also deliver something from me to Miss Norton?" Mrs. Stevens had asked in Shulman's. Bea couldn't very well say no, could she? She wished now that she had. She struggled with herself to stay seated and tried to take her mind off her nerves, but there was nothing consoling to rest her eyes on. Even their coat rack was orderly. Oh, for a few sweaters strewn about on chairs, an overweight coat rack that listed to the right, the odd dent in the wall, a bit of dirt tracked in on a shoe. A bit of life to let you know someone actually lived here. But it would have to be someone whose hand-me-down clothes didn't sound such a discordant ring in a place like this.

The grandfather clock told her she'd been waiting for ten minutes. She'd restocked the store shelves, and then had made the first two deliveries for her aunt. She was anxious to do this third delivery to the Nortons so she could get home for supper.

Across from her, on the wall next to the staircase, two red-haired boys gazed down. The portrait was of George and his identical twin brother. Strange that they're wearing such old-fashioned clothing, she thought. And neither seemed at all like George. The portrait painter didn't do a very good job. Far too affable, both of them — can't imagine George ever looking like that, even at a younger age.

George often came into the store — to buy tobacco, most often without his mother. Now, Bea wondered if perhaps she had seen both twins, but had thought them both to be George. The boys in the portrait were absolutely identical. Then, as if he had heard his cue, Bea heard a sound on the staircase, and there was George, looking somewhat dishevelled, as if he had just woken from an afternoon nap. He had crept down unheeded by Bea, and now stood against the banister, watching her examine the portrait.

Bea looked quickly away and to her right toward the parlour door. She disliked people staring at her, as George was doing now. She fixed her eyes on the floor in front of her and reached into her coat pocket, and then into the other one. Surely she had something in her pockets that needed doing. She was about to search her basket when he said, "Identical twins."

She looked up at him. Well, that was blatantly obvious, wasn't it? She nodded, and was about to avert her eyes again when curiosity compelled her to ask, "You and your brother?"

At first, George looked confused by the question. He stepped into the hallway to stare up at the portrait, as if to remind himself which one it was, although there was only one such picture in the hallway. When he turned back to face Bea, he had a half-grin on his face: "Yes, of course. My brother and I."

"Have you both been into Shulman's?"

"Most certainly," he said, looking at her. It was his turn to be curious. She'd seen that look before. People thought that because she was shy, she was incapable of coherent speech. In this instance, as had happened before, her inquisitive nature took precedence over her bashful one, and speech flowed freely.

"Well, I'm sorry, I never realized you had a twin."

"Most people don't."

Then Bea had a thought: once again she had presumed that she was talking to George. "And which one are you?"

"George," he said, smiling while reaching up to scratch behind his left ear.

"So I thought," she said as she concentrated her gaze again at his forehead. She had tried to sneak glimpses of it, but now she felt an overwhelming desire to leap off her chair and brush the hair from his forehead, for he had hidden the cut with his fringe. Since Mrs. Stevens had mentioned the cut in Shulman's, Bea had been positive she would know exactly what it looked like. Now, sitting so close to George, she was even more certain. Suddenly, she realized that she had been staring. She glanced away and quickly said, "What's your brother's name?"

"Brian," he said, just as the parlour door opened. Bea was relieved to hear Mrs. Stevens come out, and she glanced at her as she started down the hallway toward them. When Bea looked back, George was no longer there. It was as if he had disappeared into the air, but of course he hadn't: he had returned from whence he came, up the stairs without making a sound.

...---...

Eliza opened the doorway to a waif. The young woman's oversized coat and floppy hat did nothing for her looks. "Miss Norton?" she asked softly, gazing across at Eliza. She did have wonderful eyes. A dark green, almost brown. Stunning, really. And her hair wasn't bad, either, a dark brown.

"Yes? What can I do for you?" Eliza asked, and smiled.

"I'm Bea MacDonald, Miss."

The poor lass could hardly get the words out. She reminded Eliza of herself as a young woman. At least ten years separated them, probably more. "Yes?" Eliza replied softly, not wanting to scare her.

"I have a few deliveries: Your lace collar from my aunt . . ."

"Oh, of course, I didn't recognize you at first — you're Mrs. Mac-Donald's niece, from Shulman's."

"Yes, Miss. And here's the pomade from Mr. Shulman, if you still want it."

Eliza accepted the cloth bag containing the bundle of mending, and the bottle of pomade wrapped in paper. "Yes, lovely. How sweet of him to remember."

"He often does, ma'am," said Bea. Then she hesitated, and Eliza looked down to see that she was also holding a letter in her hand.

"Is this for me, Miss MacDonald? It seems to have my name written on it."

"Oh, yes, sorry, ma'am. It's a note for you, from Mrs. Stevens. She asked that I await your reply so that I can return it to her."

"I see," Eliza said, and Bea handed her the letter. "I won't be long," she added, closing the door almost all the way so the young woman wouldn't be able to see into the apartment. Still, she felt uneasy, as if Bea was trying to look in, and when she reached the kitchen and sat at the table, she was sure she heard her talking to someone.

"Who are you talking to?" Eliza called, still sounding friendly. "Did you bring someone with you?"

"No, Miss. No one, Miss."

A lie, no doubt, thought Eliza. Girls lie more than they tell the truth. She knew; she had been one. She carefully opened the envelope and pulled out the letter. She could hardly believe what she was reading. "France?" she almost shouted. She couldn't have wished for more, and she felt like crying. Now she wouldn't have to initiate a communication with Penelope. She could sense life opening up; its doorway had come, curiously, in the guise of this most interesting first letter from Penelope:

> *Dear Miss Norton,*
>
> *I hope this letter finds you well. My husband told me about the blackmail discussion from earlier and as you no doubt must know, your father's remarks about murder are alarming and of serious concern to my husband, as they are to me, so I was prompted to write. I am also concerned that a recent event concerning my son, George, might be linked to the blackmail that your father mentioned.*
>
> *I realize that you probably know nothing about any of this, but two women often have an easier time of resolving things, as you will no doubt agree. Therefore, I thought it worthwhile to write to you about this situation. Without causing you any distress, I wondered if you would mind answering a question about the matter. I realize you might not have any answers, and that they might all rest with your father, but my question is simply this: Has your father ever been to France?*

Sincerely,

Mrs. Henry Stevens

Eliza looked down the hallway, and noticed that the door was further ajar than she had left it. Bea had pushed it open and was trying to sneak a look. Without saying a word, Eliza walked to the door and closed it shut. She stared down at the letter still in her hands. She hoped that Penelope would understand her answer; that she would be able to read through the lines. She then turned to the table in the hallway, withdrew the pen, and in a quick flourish across the bottom of the same letter, she wrote a single word.

...---...

"*Yes?* Is that all she said? *Yes?*" Mrs. Stevens asked from the backseat of her carriage. Her coachman had driven them down to the Nortons', and then they had waited for Bea to finish the errand.

"Don't know what it says, ma'am," said Bea, unable to take her eyes off Mrs. Stevens' face. She had so many questions, and the more she looked at her, the more she felt as if the answers would come clear. The least of the questions was why Mrs. Stevens had even asked her to do the errand. If she had the time to come and wait outside the building, why hadn't she delivered the letter herself?

"Of course you don't," said Mrs. Stevens, folding the letter and stuffing it back into the envelope and then into her satchel, and handing Bea ten cents. "Well, thank you, Bea," she said, as she started to tap the back of the front seat to indicate she was ready to depart. But just as Bea was about to turn and leave, Mrs. Stevens said, "Bea?"

"Yes, ma'am?"

"Might you do a bit of work for me tomorrow?"

"I have a half-day at Shulman's in the morning, ma'am."

"In the afternoon, then," Mrs. Stevens said, but she seemed to catch the harshness in her voice, and with a softer tone, she added, "Would you?" When Bea hesitated, she added. "I'll pay you, of course. Forty cents for the afternoon."

As if I'd do it for free, Bea thought, but forty cents was rich, and besides, her interest had been piqued: George and the scar; Mrs. Stevens and Miss Norton and the contents of that note she had just ferried back and forth. "Yes, that'll be fine, Mrs. Stevens," she said.

"Splendid. I'll see you when you're finished at Shulman's then. Around noon?"

"Thereabouts. Yes, ma'am."

Mildred watched Bea bolt down the short stretch of Duckworth Street before weaving down Hill O' Chips and turning right on Water Street, her head bent and her hat pulled tight to shield her face against the wind. Then, Mildred turned back to the building where the Nortons lived. The windows of those apartments now occupied were illuminated, leaving the four remaining windows looking all the more vacant. But the Nortons' apartment wasn't one of these; it faced the back, and that's where Mildred went now. When she got there she could see their brightly lit kitchen three floors up, but she was unable to see movement from inside. Not that that would tell her anything; it would simply be Eliza making an early supper or setting the table or making tea. It would not tell her what she needed to know.

She needed to know what drew her to the apartment, what compelled her to want to go up there right this minute, even while Bea walked home alone in the dark. She suspected that what pulled her had little to do with the note that had been passed back and forth between Penelope and Eliza. She had read the note, of course. So had Bea. Both Eliza and Penelope had acted so odd; how could Bea not slip the paper out of its unsealed envelope and read what was on it? Then, as Mildred watched, the Nortons' kitchen window suddenly went black.

She walked around the front of the building, and waited. Several minutes later, Eliza emerged, fixed her collar and adjusted her hat, and headed briskly along Duckworth Street. Mildred resisted following her, partly because what she really wanted was to be inside their apartment, not away from it, and partly because she should really be accompanying Bea home. But mostly, something about this whole affair made her nervous. Soon, her curiosity overcame her, and she set out after Eliza.

Eliza wove along one street and up another until she came to the part of town where the rich people live. The Stevens occupied a large house with a treed and spacious yard, and Eliza stopped outside of it. She stayed a moment and then went and stood behind a tree across the street to look up at the bedroom windows, much as Mildred had been doing some minutes before at Eliza's building.

Now, why would she have come here, Mildred wondered, as she watched the cold work its way into Eliza; it didn't have far to go. No matter how much she tightened her collar or pulled on her gloves or adjusted her hat, she could not keep the damp East Coast air from seeping through every fibre of clothing and into her bone. Eliza had come here for a reason: that was evident from the way she kept taking her watch fob from her pocket, checking the time, and glancing up at the bedroom windows on the second floor. All were lit but the one on the far right.

Before long, George came out the front door. He closed it quietly behind him, and then went down the front path and out the gate and headed toward the city. Eliza checked her watch again and was about to leave her post, when Henry emerged from the house. He had the distinct air of someone being secretive. He checked right and then left and then ran to the front gate, and opened and shut it quietly. He stood on the street for several moments, and seemed to be trying to see behind the tree across the street. For a moment, Mildred thought Eliza was going to step out from behind it and make herself known. But she stayed where she was, hidden and invisible to Henry. Mildred glanced up at the bedroom windows and realized that someone had entered the far right bedroom: the light had been turned on.

Finally, Henry departed in the same direction as George, and after a minute, Eliza departed as well, but not to follow either of them. She headed home, and this time Mildred did not go after her.

Mildred wrapped her shawl tightly about her, and ran after her ward. She was glad to leave the Stevens' house behind, although she wasn't entirely sure it had left her. It seemed to follow far too closely at her heels as she hurried to the outskirts of the city.

"Now what do you suppose it's all about?" Bea muttered when Mildred caught up with her. It was good to have Bea's reassuring, pragmatic company. Bea was always pondering and analyzing, the opposite to Mildred and Jean, who so easily got caught up in flights of fancy — such as the one Mildred had experienced just now. She glanced behind her. There had been no one after her. She really must stop being so easily scared.

Bea must have lingered because she hadn't yet reached the trail going up the south shore. "This blackmail business. The Stevens'?"

"Speak up, love, heavens," Mildred said.

"Why blackmail, do you suppose?" Bea said, still speaking so softly that Mildred could hardly hear her.

Mildred shrugged in answer to Bea's question, but it was a problem to which she was sure she should know the answer. Before she could comment further, Bea said,

"And what's France got to do with it?" They walked another half block before Bea muttered, "I don't like the feel of it."

"Nor do I," Mildred said, trying to keep up. Bea's much longer legs gave her a bigger stride, and Mildred was always lagging behind. By the time they reached the edge of the city and were about to veer onto the path that would take them home, Bea suddenly stopped and said, "I'd like to hear what Natty knows. She might have heard something about this blackmailing business and the rest of it; George, and so on."

"Oh, Bea, not now," said Mildred. The dark had become black. No light was left from the day. And it was beginning to rain. The wind had not abated, and now it pulled and twisted Mildred's long skirt about her legs. "Let's go home to supper."

"Supper can wait," pronounced Bea as she turned and began to march back toward the city centre.

"Where does Natty live?"

"Don't know where she lives. Never been. I'll find someone to ask."

"Bea," Mildred called, stopping dead in her tracks on the path. "I'm going home. You can go on if you like, but I don't like the look of it. I remember where she lives now — and it's a house that's worse than the one I've just come from; it's one that's better seen in the day than by night. Whatever it is you've got to ask her, it can wait until tomorrow. But have it your way. I'll not be stopping you." She turned on her heels and bravely headed for home on her own. But before she had gone twenty feet, Bea ran up beside her, then stopped to wrestle her umbrella out of her basket.

"Tomorrow might be better. In the full light of day," Bea said.

"Isn't that what I just said?" quipped Mildred, striding ahead and leaving Bea with her uncooperative umbrella. She didn't know why she bothered with it. It's not as though it would stay open in this kind of wind.

Eliza hung her coat and hat on the rack, listened for the familiar greeting and then softly called out, "Papa?" She tore one of the silk roses off her hat then walked down the hall toward his bedroom, but stopped outside the room on the left. He was in there muttering and cursing. He was working, she supposed, or that's what he called it — his work. She tapped three times, quietly, to let him know she had returned. He didn't like to be disturbed when he was in there, so she didn't knock again; she just waited silently for him to emerge, but when he didn't, she headed down the hall toward the kitchen. She was surprised he hadn't come out; he had been so angry when she left.

"A walk? Now?" Papa had said when she had left a while earlier.

"Yes, Father," she had replied, and had boldly not given him any more explanation.

She had been reticent about leaving. She didn't like to go out without him, or, especially, to leave the apartment alone. She was never sure what he would do when she was out. She needed to be there, on guard.

She entered the kitchen and smiled at the red rose as she placed it tenderly in the vase: cut glass, a gift from her mother. She gently put the vase dead centre on the white linen tablecloth and picked up the scarlet placemats from the counter behind her. She slowly circled the round table, laying the placemats in their respective places — one, two, and then three. The third setting had been her idea, and tonight she wasn't going to let it upset her. She would just do it and not think about it. She wouldn't think about today at the Stevens', either. If she thought about that — about Penelope watching her from the top window; about the way Henry looked at her and spoke to her so kindly; about blackmail that she had long known about — it was as if someone had taken a carving knife and slit her open from the inside. The ache of loss and longing would pool under her skin until her chest seared. It was almost too much. She closed her eyes, took a deep breath, and gathered herself. She would continue. She would find a way. She had found a way. She just needed to get there. And she would, she decided, exhaling. One minute at a time.

She smiled again at the rose and its cut glass vase. Now. Enough of being maudlin. She must be resilient. She would only think about the good things that had brought her to this small apartment in this dank, godforsaken colony a world away from England. She would remain hopeful and imagine a different future, and that's what she did now as she smiled and hummed to herself, and walked around and around the table. First she laid the two forks on each setting, the entrée fork on the inside, the salad fork on the outside; then the knives, the soup spoon, and the teaspoon. The napkins came last, scarlet, the exact red to match the placemats. This red is safe, she would have told her mother years ago. "It's not a wet red, Mother." She would have felt foolish for saying it; she would have felt that she, too, was going a little mad. But there was no need to say such things to her mother now. Since her accident, Eliza didn't need to tell her mother anything.

"Mother is dead, Papa? Is that what happened?" Eliza had suggested that day in Greenwich a year ago. She had spoken tenderly because she had never seen her father cry. She didn't think he was capable of such emotion. He didn't answer as Eliza walked up to him as he stared down at his wife's limp body.

"Yes," he finally said. Then he turned to face Eliza. "Who will talk to me now, Eliza? Who can I talk to? Do you know?"

"You can talk to me, Papa," she replied quietly, and started to reach out to touch his arm, but she pulled her hand back when she saw his eyes. They had darkened and narrowed, and she didn't know what he would do or say next. He was always threatening her with his cane, or his fists. Then, without another look, he turned and walked away from her and out the front door of the house.

Later that day, Eliza had left to go to the market, for flowers, for her mother. "I'll have two of those," she told the heavyset, red-aproned woman at the flower stall, pointing to the chrysanthemums, "and six of those," pointing to the daisies. She might as well be extravagant, she thought, and she kept picking more and more buds and blossoms until she had an immense, colourful bouquet. On her way back she saw the

Gladstones, the neighbours from two doors down, heading up the stairs into their row house. They turned when they noticed her coming down the street.

"Hello, Eliza," they called in unison, grinning down at her with an appreciative glance. "Beautiful flowers. Stunning," Mrs. Gladstone added.

She smiled up at them. "Good afternoon, ma'am, sir," she said. "Aren't they?" she agreed, turning her smile on the flowers. "They're for my mother."

"Really?" they commented, again in unison, and Eliza could hear the edge in their voices. They had never liked her mother. Many people had never liked her mother.

"She died today," said Eliza.

"Oh, my!" said Mrs. Gladstone. "Really? How horrible. What can I do to help? You poor thing. Would you like me to come over for a while? Help with the funeral arrangements? Something?"

"Thank you, no. Father and I will be fine. Really," and she nodded solemnly to them and took her leave. Mrs. Gladstone had long been trying to get an invitation into their house. They didn't have people over. She should know to stop asking.

"Bye then," they called and waved. "If there's anything . . . "

She nodded and opened the door to her house, again hearing them talk about her as soon as her back was turned. She had heard it plenty of times before: "Poor thing." "How has Eliza managed?" And now they were saying: "I wonder how she died? Well, thank God she's gone. It's a blessing, really. Poor girl, what with that father and mother. Well, at least one of them's gone now. She's the better off for it, I suppose, although I'm not sure how she'll cope."

Now, she admired her table, and its happy scarlet settings, and decided she would only think of good things. With her right hand, she lifted the side of her black skirt, and, as if dancing a waltz, she stepped back one pace and bumped up against kitchen counter. She still smiled, even though the cramped kitchen was a huge source of irritation with this apartment. She kept dancing with her arms. In one movement she deftly released her skirt and dramatically folded her forearms across her white blouse, freshly pressed and starched for supper. But her smile faded when she looked back at the rose.

It's not centred. Move it to the right, she thought.

She smiled again, danced toward the table, and carefully slid the vase one quarter-inch to the right. She danced backward again. *Not like that. Not enough. Another bit.* She frowned, danced forward again, shifting the vase slightly. Another quarter-inch. *Too much.* Back an eighth of an inch. *Not enough.*

Penelope retired early to her room with its sky blue ceiling, walls, and carpet. Her very own. Every morning and every evening she was surprised to find her room as she had last left it. She expected, instead, cold stone walls and ceilings, and steel bars for a door.

She removed and hung her clothes, donned her dressing gown and slippers, and sat down at her vanity. She took the pins from her greying hair so that it fell long down her back. With her silver brush, she worked slow even strokes through her hair while she reflected on Cyrus Norton. How did he know? How did he find out? Only two other people knew: her mother and her mother's friend, Freda Murphy.

"We'll have to tell Freda, won't we dear?" Mum had suggested as she poured weak coffee into Penelope's cup. Penelope had added two large spoonfuls of sugar — the only way to make the coffee palatable.

Penelope would give anything for a pot of her mum's horrible coffee now. That visit eighteen years ago to her mother's tiny cottage in Yorkshire was the last time she'd seen her. She had gone to tell her that she was getting married to Henry Stevens and moving to Newfoundland. But her mother knew there was more, and soon got it out of her. The wedding. Ever practical, her mother soon saw the problem: "Can't very well have a mum like me showing up at the wedding of a rich girl, can we, love?" her mum had said gently. Penelope nodded and cried, while her mother leaned across the table and patted Penelope's elegant hand with her pudgy one. When Penelope had stopped crying, and had dried her eyes with the hankie that her mum handed her, her mother had said: "Tell me the rest, love. How did you become so rich so soon?"

Penelope knew the question would come, of course, and had had a lie all prepared. From France to England by boat, and then up land to Yorkshire by train, she had practised what she would say. Instead, she told her mother the truth. Most of it, at least. When she was done, her mother brewed another pot of coffee, put another slice of apple cake on Penelope's plate, and said they needed to tell Freda.

"Why would we tell Freda, Mum?" Penelope had asked, but as soon as she said it, she knew the answer. With the coffee cup halfway to her mouth, she paused, but didn't look at her mother — she was so ashamed that she could have forgotten. And, yes, as her mother had said, Freda would have to know everything her mother knew.

Penelope stopped brushing her hair, and then tossed the brush on the vanity and rushed over to her desk by the window. From the bottom drawer she extracted a locked box. She took a key from the locket that hung on a silver chain around her neck, and unlocked the box. Off the top of the pile inside the box, she removed the last three letters from her mother, sat down and opened the first, and then the final two. Yes, just as she had recalled, the handwriting of the final two was different from the first. She had noticed something different about these letters when they had arrived, but she had put it down to old age, or illness. But now, she wondered — had something happened to Freda? Was Freda still her mother's scribe?

Ever since Penelope could remember, Freda had been her mother's writer and reader. When Penelope was old enough, she had taken over the job, but then when she left at seventeen to work at the rich girl's house, the job of scribe reverted to Freda. Now, Penelope wondered if the difference in these letters could have something to do with Cyrus Norton's discovery. For the last eighteen years, Penelope regretted telling her mother everything. She trusted her mother, but she had never really trusted Freda Murphy. However, her mother had never learned to read and write. And so, they had had to tell Freda everything.

Brian had been waiting all evening, it seemed, for Natty to come home. He had waited from long before the sun set and painted pink shadows on the house across the street until now, when the streetlamps sent circles of light onto the street below and in through the big leafed trees on either side, and it felt like he had been waiting all day. He didn't know what had happened to Natty, or why she wasn't coming home. Then suddenly, just like that, he remembered — Natty wasn't coming back, and it was his fault.

He got down off the armchair on which he had been kneeling, went over to the unlit fireplace, and sat cross-legged on the wooden floor beside the rug. He missed the heat from a good fire and he missed Henry and he missed Natty. If Henry came back soon they could light the fire together. Did Henry still throw his clothes into the fire? First the paper, then the twigs, then some clothes if you've got them. That's how it went. If not, wood would do, and Henry had plenty of that, Brian realized, seeing the pile in the metal bin to the left of the stone hearth. To the right of the hearth and at the back of the room, Henry's closet door stood open. Fine suits and jackets and pants, pressed and neat, lay on their hangers, and Brian realized with disappointment as he watched their serious greys and navies that Henry probably didn't burn his clothes any more. He probably didn't need to.

With the tip of his forefinger he started to write words on the wooden floor like he used to do when he wanted to talk to Natty, and to Morna. Morna would always answer. She knew what he was saying.

Brian knew why Natty had left. He had scared her again. He hadn't meant to. He had only wanted to talk.

"He's watching you," he had told her from the doorway of her bedroom, and she had let out a little scream and spun around to face him.

"Brian, you scared me. Don't creep up on people like that."

"Sorry."

"What did you say, Brian? Someone's watching me? Who?"

"Him," he said, and he had pointed at her new underwear garments that had fallen on the floor.

Brian was pulled away from remembering Natty by Henry's footsteps coming down the hallway. He could always tell when it was Henry. He scrambled up off the floor, leaving the words half-written on the floor, as Henry opened the door and slammed it behind him and strode over the words to his desk. He sat down at the chair and cupped his forehead in his hands.

Brian walked over to Henry and put his hand on his shoulder, as he often did when Henry was upset. Henry didn't mind being touched, not like some people, and Brian could feel the skin beneath his shirt and sweater start to relax. "Worse today?" Brian remarked, as Henry continued to massage his forehead. "How about we light a fire?" he suggested. Henry sighed and nodded and pushed back his chair. When the fire was built — from paper and wood, as Brian had already predicted — and they were both sitting in front of it, Henry in the rocking chair on the rug and Brian beside him, cross-legged on the floor, Henry finally spoke:

"I didn't think anyone else knew who committed the murder, Brian."

Brian nodded. He must have been thinking the same thing because he remembered what he had written on the floor. He finished it now, quietly, while Henry nursed his scotch and watched the fire's flames, and he wondered to whom he would write now that Natty was gone. When he was finished, he read the words aloud to Henry: *"Morna knows."*

... --- ...

"Was someone murdered?" Brian whispered, looking around nervously because conversations such as this didn't belong in a restaurant at high tea. He and Morna came to this popular Greenwich restaurant when Morna wanted tea, and he wanted to talk. Brian glanced across the aisle, then grinned at the middle-aged woman seated at the table opposite, just in case she overheard. She had taken to sliding her eyes their way. His smile settled her and she turned her face away from him, presenting him with the back of her wide-rimmed hat. She focused once more on her table-mate, a woman almost half her size and twice her age, also dressed entirely in brown. Across his own table, Morna had begun to reply. But before she did, she looked over at him with that expression he got from so many people: confusion, apprehension, finally, pity. He detested the latter.

"Yes, Brian," she said.

Morna had answered as she always did initially, with patience and a smile. In the same fashion that he had spoken, she spoke quietly while, at the same time, the fingers of her right hand strummed the tabletop. Her left hand lay poised on the doily next to the porcelain teapot.

"Who did it?" he asked, the words racing out of his mouth before he had a chance to chase them back in.

"Do you remember this?" Morna said, shifting her gaze away from his face, looking anywhere but at him. No! Brian wanted to scream. No!

No! No! He didn't remember. Why else would he be asking? But he didn't speak or scream. Instead, he tried to keep quiet while he waited anxiously for her to continue. She took a few slow, civilized sips of tea, in between which she dabbed her mouth and tried to furtively wrap a stray thread back around her loose coat button. Finally, just as his patience was running out, Morna gave up on the thread and, resuming her strumming, said:

"You let the body fall. Don't you remember hearing the head hit the ground and absurdly wishing you had brought a pillow? The soft hair still grows from where it slipped away from the palm of your left hand. Do you see it?" She stopped tapping and turned her left hand palm upward, and then glared at him across the table. She scared Brian into looking at his own hand sitting in his lap. She had mentioned this before, he now remembered, and once again he didn't see any hair growing there, but it soon would, he imagined. Morna knew everything. She was prescient. She seemed to know all of the past and all of the future; that's why he talked to her as much as he did. He only remembered anything when he talked to Morna.

She started strumming again, her fingers going faster than before. "And do you remember this? Afterward, holding the knife tenderly between your right thumb and forefinger as if by loving it you could bring back life?"

"I remember that," said Brian. "I remember the knife. What did I do with it afterward?"

"You let it fall to the floor of the cave."

"And then what, Morna? What did I do with the body?"

"Why do I have to keep telling you?" And just like that, her patience was gone. He was never sure how long it would last, or how much time they had to talk — about the past, about the future, about his life, most of all. "Aren't I doing enough to make up for it?"

Brian was trying to find something to say to mollify her when a voice beside them asked: "Are these seats taken?" They had been interrupted by a young woman, fashionably dressed in a grey and white outfit: matching dress and jacket; grey gloves and pocketbook; white folded parasol; and a grey hat trimmed with a wide white ribbon. Morna had deliberately taken this table for four in Annabelle's Tea Shoppe. They didn't come to this crowded restaurant because it was a popular spot for young people such as this lady; they came because they had been here once and were satisfied. This would do. It was private enough for conversations such as theirs. Except for today, apparently. The spare seats at their table were the only free ones remaining.

Morna glanced away from Brian's face and up into that of the pretty woman. The woman's hat was cocked over one eye, and Morna automatically reached up to her own hat — green and years old; Brian had never seen her wear anything else — and stuffed the stray grey curl on her forehead under the worn brim. It immediately strayed out again and she let her right hand fall into her left, where it began a light, rapid pawing of the palm. She did this when she was nervous and that was almost always. Brian reached over to lay his hand on hers, but as her fingers stilled themselves, his own reached up to scratch behind his right ear. "Please have a seat," said Morna to the woman.

"Thank you," said the woman, frowning down at Brian. He smiled at her in a manner he thought becoming, and, in fact, it seemed to help. Her face softened and she said, "I'm Joan, and this is my fiancée, Hubert."

Neither Brian nor Morna had realized that the woman had a companion, who now approached the table. The tall, darkly dressed, black-haired man, sweat or oil shining on his frowning forehead, had been waiting off to the side while his friend got them a table. Brian could tell by the look on Morna's face that the man disturbed her; just as he knew that she wished she had not relinquished their privacy to strangers. This was confirmed a moment later when she tapped out a message with the tips of her fingers, this time using the leg of the table as her implement.

"Let's leave. He looks like my husband."

Brian nodded, though he didn't see the resemblance. They didn't even have the same colour hair, after all. But Morna was always saying things that he didn't agree with, or that didn't make sense.

"Please, no, stay. Don't leave on our account. You haven't finished your tea," said the woman named Joan, as Morna pushed back her chair and stood up. She immediately sat back down, like an obedient child. She didn't meet Joan's eyes or Hubert's as she slouched into her chair and reached for her teacup. She allowed her thumb and forefinger to tenderly touch the china handle before she gripped it tightly and brought the cup to her lips. She then set it too loudly back on its saucer, so they could know she was upset. If there had been a door handy, she would have slammed it, but if they were to have asked, "Is there something wrong?" she would have lied, "No. Nothing. Why do you ask?" However, the couple, who had taken their seats, he next to Brian, she next to Morna, didn't notice Morna's mood. Their server had arrived, and they were busily ordering tea and crumpets.

After Joan had placed her order, and while she waited for Hubert to finish placing his, she leaned over to Morna and whispered: "I hope we haven't intruded. You weren't expecting company, were you?"

Morna looked at her as if she'd just said the silliest thing, then she turned to fix her gaze on Brian. "I have all the company I'll ever need," she replied in a small voice, before taking a quick sip of her tea. After she swallowed, remembering her manners, she gave Joan a small smile and added, "But thank you for asking."

... --- ...

Morna and Brian pushed open the large wooden doors of the main Greenwich post office and walked into the spacious and airy room. They weren't going to be doing this too many more times, which was too bad because Brian loved coming here. Every Tuesday, apparently. Not that he remembered one from the next, but that's what Morna said: "It's Tuesday, Brian, off we go."

The grand but sparsely furnished space was dotted with three high tables in the centre of the floor at this end, and two of its walls were lined with steel boxes. The entire post office was topped by high ceilings, and decorated with ornate woodwork. At the other end the post mistresses, behind their high wooden counters, stamped envelopes and chatted with their customers.

Each one of the steel boxes held a secret, and now Morna took the key out of her coat pocket, inserted it into the lock, and opened her box to reveal theirs: a single envelope at the back. She pulled it out, re-locked the box, and walked over to a high table. With her increasingly arthritic hands, she tore open the envelope, and out fell the pound notes. Brian nodded. It was the same amount every week, never a pound less. "Yes. More than enough, I should think," he said. "He should be happy with that."

She smiled — the whole thing had been her idea — and then she took a blank envelope out of her purse. She carefully put the money from the first envelope into the new envelope, sealed it, turned it over, and addressed it as she always did: *Mr. Henry Stevens.*

Day Three
Thursday, October 16, 1902

"How *could* you?" hissed Mrs. Marsden as Bea stepped around her to get to the front counter. At first Bea thought she had inadvertently done something terribly rude, but she couldn't think what it was. So she quickly sorted through a long list of possible infractions — her dress, clothes, hair, the whole of her life — but whatever her crime, she would not soon be forgiven — that much was obvious from Mrs. Marsden's stiff back as she turned it to Bea and marched away. Having said what was on her mind, she seemed to want to make a quick exit, and the fake flowers and grapes atop her hat bobbed up and down as her short legs took her toward the door. Bea was about to apologize for God knows what, since she couldn't discern the cause of the woman's disfavour, when she caught herself.

"You can't be serious! That was months ago," Bea wanted to call out to her when she realized the source of the woman's wrath. But she didn't say anything. She reacted as she so often did to criticism, with a pithy rejoinder that never made it out of her mouth. But at least this time she had an excuse for not speaking her mind: she couldn't very well bawl out a customer in Mr. Shulman's store. But, honestly. Months had gone by since she'd sent those letters about Marconi to the *Newfoundland Telegram*. That was January; it was now October. She'd had no trouble writing what was on her mind; she just didn't realize the public flogging she'd get once the letters were published. She'd have to think long and hard before doing something like that again. People whispered about her when she was still within earshot, and they'd avoided her gaze even here in the store. It got to the point where Bea would cross the street so she wouldn't have to greet them. She was only recently beginning to feel less a pariah, and now this. Honest to God, she was fed up with the whole Marconi debate, and with people like Mrs. Marsden harbouring ill will toward her. The woman must have been trying for months to get up the courage to say something to her. But Bea now didn't have the courage to reply.

Instead, she watched Mrs. Marsden get to the front door, and then she stepped behind the counter to help Mr. Shulman wrap Dr. McTavish's photographic equipment. But Mrs. Marsden wasn't done. She turned and called harshly, glaring at Bea,

"I don't know why you thought you should interfere. It's got nothing to do with you, does it? I'm sure Anglo-American didn't need you fighting their battles for them." She made no attempt to lower her voice, but her eyes skitted around the room, not meeting Bea's. Bea could feel the heat rise to her cheeks and she wanted to disappear through the floorboards. The entire store was watching. Mr. Shulman had glanced at Mrs. Marsden, and then at Bea, and Bea realized he was waiting for her to answer the woman. He had never liked Mrs. Marsden and her ill-mannered nature, and now he was giving Bea permission to reply. Fantastic, grimaced Bea, bloody fantastic, as she continued to stare at the counter and fold the paper over Dr. McTavish's items.

"Well, missy?" growled Mrs. Marsden.

Bea could feel without looking that the entire store had riveted its attention on her. People had moved so that they could see what was going on and all chatter had stopped; Bea knew that, courage or not, she had to respond. She straightened her shoulders hoping to look stronger than she felt, and then she walked around the counter and over to the front door. She would answer, but she wasn't going to engage in a shouting match with the woman.

"You're correct, Mrs. Marsden: the argument had nothing more to do with me than it had with you. And Anglo-American doesn't need me fighting its battles any more than Marconi needs you. But we all have a right to express our opinions," Bea whispered, forcing herself to look Mrs. Marsden in the eye. It was more than Mrs. Marsden was doing. Then Bea turned and started away. She had said her piece.

"Well, you're an awful woman," hissed Mrs. Marsden. "I've always thought so. Think you're so smart." There now, thought Bea, turning to look at her. Intelligence is a terrible crime, and I should be burned on the stake for it. Mrs. Marsden's loud voice had invited people to move closer and stare: Women with baskets filled with everything from fabric to canned goods; a few children of varying ages; two babes in arms; and three men. Mrs. Marsden looked as if she liked the attention they were receiving. And Bea wasn't surprised they were getting it: the topic had consumed the citizens of St. John's since the previous December, when Guglielmo Marconi had successfully sent his wireless message from their own Signal Hill across the Atlantic. But on the tails of that achievement, the Anglo-American Telegraph Company had insisted on its monopoly rights and was able to prevent him from conducting any more experiments on Newfoundland soil. The citizens of St. John's had been outraged. And some of them still were. Bea was one of a handful who had come down on the side of the Anglo-American company. She had never been sure why, and she certainly had never understood why she felt compelled to write letters about it, for God's sake; Aunt Evelyn had said it was because she just liked to be contrary. "Once it's out there for the world to feast on, you can't pull it back," she had said about the first letter that Bea had written and then submitted in a flash of anger. Bea wished she had listened. Still, she wasn't sure she wouldn't make the same choice again. Marconi's achievement was spectacular, but so were the achievements of the telegraph industry in the previous century. Everybody seemed to have forgotten about them. And they also seemed to have forgotten that the transatlantic cable endeavour had been initiated by a Newfoundlander. She had said as much, and more, in her letters to the newspaper.

"Furthermore," Mrs. Marsden continued in an even louder voice, her gaze darting around the room before settling, mean and dark, on Bea. " . . . Furthermore, the entire city's on my side, isn't it?" A fleeting smile crossed her face as she looked at her audience.

"Do you think so?" whispered Bea. "Shall we do a poll, here in Shulman's? Marconi versus Anglo-American?"

"And furthermore," continued Mrs. Marsden as if Bea hadn't spoken. Now Bea really wished she had never confronted the woman. "I don't need to know what they think, do I? It was your letters against him that got printed in the *Telegram*. It was because of people like you that he was ousted."

"It is quite true that I submitted my letters to the paper, Mrs. Marsden. Still, you can hardly blame Marconi's departure on me." Bea was no longer whispering, but she still refused to raise her voice to meet that of her opponent.

"Well, I do. If you hadn't written those awful letters, Miss MacDonald, if you had kindly kept your thoughts to yourself, he would still be here, wouldn't he?" said Mrs. Marsden, her voice increasing in strength and volume with each word. She was now almost shouting. "He'd still be running his experiments up on the Hill. Still bringing fame to our fair city. It was a fantastic thing he did, Miss MacDonald, and the whole world knew it and he did it from here, didn't he? Here. That made us someplace special. That's something you don't seem to understand. What he did was special. And we were all special because of him."

"There's something you don't understand," Bea replied slowly, her voice deepening as more anger took hold. "Of course he was special. Anybody could see that. My quarrel was never with him." She stopped speaking for a moment and took a breath. She was beginning to sound defensive, and consequently shrill and strident. Mrs. Marsden had noticed the shift in Bea's manner, and she smiled and pressed her point:

"Anglo-American had had its day. You should never have tried to interfere."

"Had its day? Are you certain of that — Mrs. Marsden, is it?" asked a woman from the small group that had gathered near the barrels of sundry items lining the wall near to the cash register. Customers previously lurking in the six narrow aisles now came to the front of the store to see who belonged to this voice. "I really don't know that much about the topic, and excuse me for interfering — but do you really think this young woman had the power to make Mr. Marconi leave St. John's, no matter how many letters to the paper she wrote?" Bea could not have been more relieved: she had an ally in the room. She knew who belonged to the voice, although she would never have thought her a person to take a stand in public — she seemed even more shy than Bea — but Bea was glad that she had. Her defender was Miss Norton, whose gentle beauty was now made greater by the flush that had risen to her cheeks after her small speech: soft and without rancour, a stark contrast to the diatribe of the now-sweating Mrs. Marsden. Miss Norton adjusted her small navy blue felt hat that matched her navy and white pin-striped coat. With her navy-gloved hands, she firmly gripped her basket filled with several items from the store, and took a step toward them. Despite her obvious discomfort, she wasn't going to back down.

Mrs. Marsden seemed surprised by the interruption, and reticent to take on this new opponent. "Well . . . I don't see why not," she equivocated.

"I wonder, Mrs. Marsden, if you are all that correct in blaming Miss MacDonald here. I'm not certain that she influenced the decision all that much. As I understand it, and I am a newcomer here, so please forgive me, Anglo-American continues to have the rights to all communication industry in Newfoundland, and this dates back almost fifty years. Those are the facts, as I understand them. I also understand that Marconi had to respect those rights, is that not the case?"

That was the case, thought Bea, but one that most people would willingly refute. Marconi had departed St. John's, but the argument wasn't settled. This debate appeared to be, however. Miss Norton's gentle tone had had the effect of diffusing the tension that had been building, and neither Mrs. Marsden nor the crowd seemed interested in continuing the dispute. The crowd whispered amongst itself for a moment, and then dispersed throughout the store; Mrs. Marsden harrumphed and high-tailed it out the door; left alone at the front of the store, united in an awkward silence, stood Miss Norton and Bea.

"Up and left, that's what she did. No by-your-leave. No fare-thee-well. Left her things behind for us to deal with. Be sure to throw all her belongings in the rubbish, Bea," Mrs. Stevens called over her shoulder. "Do you hear me? Are you listening? Answer me, Bea. I cannot abide people who don't reply when asked." Mrs. Stevens held tightly to the banister as she descended the steep, narrow staircase into the cellar.

Bea followed behind, her eyes focused on the back of Mrs. Stevens' head, as if she would find the answer there.

"Bea, are you deaf?" Mrs. Stevens asked.

"Sorry, Mrs. Stevens I was just thinking."

"Thinking."

"Yes, ma'am . . . " Bea said, but her thoughts hadn't given her a solution: Why was Mrs. Stevens so jumpy? She'd been like this since yesterday at Shulman's. But now, since they'd begun their descent, she was worse, and her uneasiness was wearing off on Bea.

"No by-your-leave, Bea."

"Yes, ma'am," Bea replied, and she glanced behind her up the staircase to the partially open door of the kitchen. Light from the kitchen streamed through the opening, but it didn't flood the stairwell.

"Not a word, I tell you. Do you hear me, Bea, not a fare-thee-well."

"Yes, Mrs. Stevens," said Bea, shrugging off what felt like a touch on her shoulder. She was already beginning to imagine things.

They were almost to the bottom of the staircase. Bea leaned down and tried to see past the low ceiling and the diffused light of their lanterns, but the only visible part of the cellar was the small portion at the bottom of the staircase caught by the orb of their lights. She followed Mrs. Stevens down the remaining two steps, but just as they got to the bottom, a pipe creaked from the other end of the cellar. Or at least, that's what Bea had heard; Mrs. Stevens' sharp intake of breath indicated otherwise. Bea stepped onto the wooden floor behind Mrs. Stevens, who had come to a dead stop. Bea waited for her to speak or move, but she seemed to be listening for more sounds from the cellar. Bea didn't hear anything. Finally Mrs. Stevens released a long exhale; she had been holding her breath. When she spoke, it was with a rare softness in her voice. "Can't say I like cellars. They're strange things," she said.

"Isn't that the truth," Bea muttered in reply. And then she heard another sound, but one that seemed somewhat out of place. "I guess the rain's started up again," she said.

Mrs. Stevens swung around and glared at her. "Have you been talking to Natty? Have you two been gossiping about us?"

"No, ma'am. Don't know what you mean, ma'am."

"Don't lie. I know a liar when I see one."

"I am not lying, Mrs. Stevens," Bea said definitively. "I haven't seen Natty for days, since before she left here I imagine."

Mrs. Stevens continued to study her face, and then she turned away. "I won't have it. No more of this nonsense about imaginary things, do you understand?"

"Yes, ma'am," answered Bea, although she had no idea what Mrs. Stevens was talking about. She wasn't imagining the rain, but then she had a thought: "You don't hear the rain, Mrs. Stevens?"

"There is no rain! I told that to Natty, and I'm telling it to you. Honestly, Bea, I cannot abide this gibberish. There is no rain. No leak.

No dripping water. I'll ask you never to mention it again so long as you work here."

"Yes, ma'am," Bea said, thoroughly baffled. Gawd. It's just a little rain.

Mrs. Stevens mumbled something, and then her high English voice shifted to its polished tone and slashed at the pregnant space: "Clean it up, Bea," she announced, striding briskly toward the tiny room tucked between the coal bin and a small storage cupboard, her lantern splashing light over the dark in front of her. "Toss everything of Natty's in the rubbish." Bea fingered the fabric of her apron as she followed behind.

"Natty lived down here?" Bea blurted when she saw the room. She would never be able to sleep a night in a place like this. Dark. Windowless. Your imagination would always be playing tricks on you. And besides, it felt more than empty. It felt lived in.

In response to her question, Mrs. Stevens turned and glared at her again. "Get on with it," Mrs. Stevens said, turning to face the room. She folded her arms across her chest.

"You want everything in the rubbish, Mrs. Stevens?" Bea asked, walking past her and into the room.

"You heard me," she said.

Mrs. Stevens stepped forward to stand in the doorway, rubbing her arm where Bea had brushed against her as if she'd just been infected. Bea had seen that look before: as far as Mrs. Stevens was concerned the room had been tainted by the lower classes. Heaven help her if she ventured any closer, she might get servant germs. Bea walked over to the side of the narrow bed. On the floor beside it sat the first of Natty's sparse, rubbish-bound possessions: a pair of brown, sensible shoes. She bent down and picked them up.

She turned the pair of shoes over in her hand; they were polished and shiny with good soles. "Someone could use these, Mrs. Stevens," she said. "My cousin could." She looked at Mrs. Stevens and held her gaze.

"Yes, I suppose she can have them," Mrs. Stevens said after a second. The shoes alone might be just payment for this work. Bea could envision Jean's smile at seeing the shoes. She put the shoes on the bed and turned toward the closet. "I'll leave you to it then, Bea. I'm stepping out to do some shopping. You're on your own."

"Yes, Mrs. Stevens."

"In the rubbish, everything except the shoes. You can have the shoes."

"Thank you, Mrs. Stevens," Bea said while the woman's footsteps retreated through the cellar and up the stairs, her lamp's light weaving with her, diminishing and then disappearing altogether. Bea had thought she'd be relieved to see her gone, taking her fearful, irritable nature with her, but when Mrs. Stevens had left, the cellar still felt occupied. Bea couldn't help but wonder if she was alone and she felt foolish, but nevertheless she called out: "Hello?"

Was that a reply? Don't be daft, she thought. She gave it a second or two, and then called out again. Nothing. Just the cellar playing tricks like they do. Still, when she started to tiptoe to the bedroom door she almost expected an apparition to jump around the corner. She was beginning to feel like her friend, Callum. He was often so jittery he made Bea feel confident in comparison. "Is it haunted, do you suppose, Bea?" Callum had asked her several years back when they'd been reading in her attic. They had been home alone, and he was asking about her house. "S'pose," she'd answered. She'd said it to scare him; he was almost as nervy as Jean, but, honestly, what else was she supposed to say to such a question? "Does our house scare you?" Bea had tested him. "No," he'd said, and she couldn't tell if he was fibbing. "Not really. Odd is all; like we're not alone."

That would be an apt description for this cellar, she thought. She got to the doorway and stayed quiet, listening. She had heard something, she was sure of it. After several seconds, she decided that it must have been a creak from an old pipe again, or from a floorboard overhead. "Be brave, you silly," she muttered, twisting her fingers tightly in her apron and swinging around to face a narrow cupboard on the other side of the small bedroom. She strode over and flung open its doors. "Aah. Anyone would've wanted these, Jean," she gasped. She would often do this: speak out loud to Jean or whomever, whether they were around or not. Jean did it too. Of course, they'd both picked up the habit from Aunt Evelyn. Bea frequently came upon her midway through a one-sided conversation as if someone was right next to her.

Natty's cupboard was laden with treasures: a dress, a sweater and a nightgown. Bea took the dress off its hanger and held it in front of her. It was beautiful: brown, like the shoes, and homemade.

It's a fine hand that made it; has a nice bit of lace, Bea thought. The lace trimmed the high-buttoned neck and the wrists of the long puffy sleeves. Why would she have left something like this behind? Bea glanced up at the shelf high in the cupboard. She ran her hand along the surface, then pulled her fingers away. Nothing there but dust.

Bea removed the tan woollen cardigan from its hanger. It had two small patches on the elbow where Natty had mended it, but otherwise, no holes. "This is your good outfit, then, Natty — the shoes, the dress, the cardigan — I've seen you wear it. Why would you leave it behind? I can't throw these beauties in the rubbish. If you really have left Newfoundland, I'll save them for you. If you never come back, then Jean could use them. Maybe not this year, but soon." Suddenly, her voice sounded overly loud against the naked silence of the cellar. She looked out the open doorway of Natty's room, into the dark space beyond, then turned back and quickly placed the items on top of the bed. The clothes and shoes were going anywhere but into the rubbish.

On the floor behind the doorway was a pair of stockings. Bea picked them up — silk. What's Natty doing with silk stockings, she thought. I'd have to save for a million years to own a pair of silk stockings.

The hat for the outfit — tan, like the cardigan, with two flowers on the brim — perched on a hook on the back of the door. Bea stretched her long arm up and removed the hat. She was placing it next to the clothes when she heard the rain again. Mrs. Stevens was wrong. This was certainly rain. No doubt about it. She fingered the rim of the hat and wondered why such a familiar sound would keep wanting her attention. She wished she could just ignore it and keep working. But soon, she couldn't help but stop and listen closely, and after some time she realized that she was the one who had been grossly mistaken. Mrs. Stevens was correct. This wasn't rain at all.

...---...

"Where are we going, Bea?" asked Mildred, rushing after her down the street.

Bea didn't answer; she just walked quickly as she muttered: "I think I've got it now."

"The sound from the cellar?"

Bea didn't reply, but with her right hand she slowly drummed her fingers against her thigh. Tat-tat-tat. Taat. Taat. Taat. "That's an *s* and an *o*. Yes, I'm almost certain the first word spells 'someone.'"

"Someone?" asked Mildred.

"I think I have the whole sentence. Here we are," said Bea as she burst through the door of the small telegraph office. Mildred came in after her. Besides Bea and herself, there was only one other customer in the small space. A runner, Mildred thought, from one of the businesses. He's come to send a message, or to pick one up, for his employers. They must be working him hard: the child looked exhausted and in need of a good meal. Mildred felt a strong impulse to wrap her arms around him, hold him for awhile on her lap, have him lay his head on her shoulder. He motioned for them to go ahead; he didn't seem to be waiting for Winifred, who now looked up from behind her cubicle.

"Hello, Bea," she said brightly, taking off her spectacles and setting her book aside.

"Hello, Winifred. I wondered if you could help me decipher something?"

"Absolutely. What have you got?"

"I'm certain I know what the first three words mean, and then I get confused."

"Let's hear it."

Using the spare unit that Winifred had pushed across the counter toward them, Bea set her piece of paper beside her on the counter and tapped out the series of dots and dashes that she had heard in the cellar, the sound that she had been fooled into thinking was rain:

... --- -- . --- -. . / .-- .- ... / -.- .. .. -..

"It means 'someone was kissed.' Am I right, Winifred?"

"Yes, if you have it right. Though those last two *s*'s are a bit murky. Are you sure those were dots that you heard?"

"I think. I can't be sure."

"Well, let's see what the rest of it says."

"A bunch of dots, five or more, I think."

"Eight?"

"Let me see," Bea said, and closed her eyes. With her forefinger she tapped the key, and counted: "One two three four, yes, you're right, eight dots. Of course, how silly of me, that means . . ."

"Delete. The sender wanted to delete the last word; they made a mistake or wanted to make a correction. What did they send instead Bea? What was the word that followed?"

"I can't remember, Winifred. I'm going to have to remember. When I do, I'll come back. Thanks, Winifred. Bye for now," Bea said, turning on her heels and rushing out the door. Mildred went out after her. The boy had gone before them, and Mildred hadn't even noticed him leave.

"You're welcome!" Winifred called to the closing door.

Bea put the kettle on to boil and tiptoed through the kitchen to the top of the cellar stairwell, and listened. She had not wanted to come back to the Stevens' after her visit to Winifred; she only wanted to go home, but she had given her word that she would prepare the supper, and she still had the laundry to do. She didn't know why she had not given Winifred that last line of Morse. She'd wait until she got home, she had decided on the spot. She could get it deciphered as easily there.

The family was still out for the afternoon and now, as she listened, no sounds emanated from the cellar. No water dripping this time. No sounds of rain. No Morse code. She *must* have imagined it. *Someone was kissed.* Ridiculous. "Ah, Callum," she said aloud to the open door. "Do you suppose we're imagining things today?" But when she turned toward the kitchen her hand flew to her mouth to stop from screaming. Through the glass window of the outside door, a pale-eyed creature stared at her. Surely this was an apparition that Callum would have imagined: a child, about ten or twelve perhaps, almost albino with long, thin white hair and pale blue eyes and a face so gaunt that the wide jaw and high cheekbones pushed painfully at the skin as fine as silk and as white as her hair. Her shirt was black as were the hands that she cupped to see through the window. When she saw Bea, her mouth broke into the most magnificent grin. Bea muttered to herself, "Don't be daft," as she went to the door to unlock it. It's just a young girl, you idiot, not a bloody ghost. But when she opened the door she could see why she might have thought so. The child was sick, and very near death, it seemed. "Hello," the girl said brightly, then followed it up with a loud, painful cough, and it was the second time for Bea to be shocked. She had a throaty, beautiful voice to go with her exquisite smile.

"I'm Clara, come with your coal delivery."

"I'm Bea. Seen you about," she said because she now realized that she had, but it had been a long time and the girl had lost more weight recently. She came in, wiped her hands on a remarkably clean rag from her pocket, and sat down at the kitchen table as if she was perfectly at home in this kitchen.

"Yeah. Seen you about, too. So where's our Natty, then?"

"You're her friend, also?"

"Yeah. We're pals, me and Natty."

"You don't know?"

"Know what?"

"Well, she's gone. Mrs. Stevens said she just up and left."

"Not my Natty. Not without telling me."

"She's probably at her house."

"No. I went by today. Her pa said she's not there."

"She's not here, either, I'm sorry to say. I'm taking her place for now. I wish I knew what to tell you. I'd like to know myself. It's strange that she'd leave like this."

"Yeah. I'll say."

"No, you don't know what I mean," said Bea. "Tea?"

"Yeah. Love it. Thanks."

Bea wondered what Mrs. Stevens would think — her making tea for this child — but the girl needed some sustenance; that was clear to see. She poured hot water from the stove into the teapot, and brought it over with milk, sugar, cups and a plate of biscuits. Clara immediately wolfed down three biscuits, and shovelled three teaspoons of sugar and a dollop of milk into her tea, took a loud sip, then asked, "Whaddya mean?"

Bea sat across from Clara, who had tucked herself into the window seat. Bea poured her own tea, took a sip, and said, "She left her things behind."

"What things?" the girl asked, and for the first time she seemed to clam up.

"Her clothes."

"No. Natty wouldn't leave her clothes. She just wouldn't. They're special."

"Well, she did."

"Which ones?"

"The hat . . . "

"Brown, nice little flower . . . "

"That's the one. A jacket . . . "

"Brown too."

"Yes. A dress . . . "

"With nice lace. Always liked that dress. Natty said she'd give it to me when I got bigger, whenever that is," she said, looking down at her bony legs, and then coughed several times very loudly. "Where're they now?"

"The clothes?" asked Bea. The girl nodded, and drank some more of her tea and ate another biscuit. Bea got up and grabbed another handful from the jar and put them on the plate, then went to the pantry and shaved off thin slices of leftover pork pie, butter and bread, though not enough that anyone would even notice it was gone. She set these in front of Clara, along with a fork and knife. "I'll take the clothes home for safekeeping," said Bea as Clara spread a wad of butter on her bread and took a bite of pie. Then, seeing the dubious expression on the girl's face, she lowered her voice and said, "Mrs. Stevens wanted me to throw everything in the rubbish. Everything. Can you imagine?"

Clara shook her head. "Penelope? Bet that woman got rid of our Natty. She's evil, she is. She didn't like Natty. Didn't like any of us. Won't like it that I'm here eating this." Clara glanced behind her out the window. Bea followed her gaze. They still had the house to themselves but any minute, one of the Stevens' could come home. "Any blood?"

"Pardon?"

"Yeah," Clara said, and then she leaned across the table and whispered, "If Mrs. Stevens killed Natty, there'd be blood somewhere wouldn't there?"

"No. No blood, but . . . "

"What is it?" asked Clara, still whispering, her big pale eyes widening in her white face.

"Did you spend much time in the cellar with Natty?"

"Lots of it."

"Ever hear strange noises?"

"Not so much. Just regular strange ones like every cellar. You know."

"Yes. I do."

"But Natty heard things. She was always hearing strange things down there. Said she could hear it raining inside when it wasn't, things like that."

"Is that what she said? Rain?"

"Yeah. And she was surprised she didn't hear the sound of breathing."

"Why is that?"

"Because there was someone down there watching her, she said. I felt it too, and she said not to worry. It happens all the time here, she said. There's always someone watching."

"In the cellar?"

"Yeah. But up here too, she said."

Bea sat back against the chair back, and said, "Where do you think Natty went?"

"I don't know, Bea."

"Clara?"

"Hmmm?" she asked while chewing on her bread. Suddenly she looked exhausted. She could fall asleep any second. She glanced at the bench to her right and smiled and nodded, and Bea wondered if she was already drifting off into dreamland.

"You said her clothes were special," Bea said, speaking louder to wake her up. "Any particular reason?"

Clara was slow to respond and when she finally did, she simply said, "No," but Bea could tell that she was lying.

"Clara. She might be in trouble. What if she is? Besides the fact that the clothes are so nice, what else is so special about them?"

"Alright. I guess she wouldn't mind if she's dead, or kidnapped, or something. She told me never to tell and I haven't. I haven't told a soul."

"I believe you. I know she would trust you. I would."

Clara smiled and her eyes lit up, and she lowered her voice and whispered, "She's got a secret admirer."

"Really?"

"Yeah."

"How d'you know?"

"Those clothes?"

"Yes?"

"They're from him, some of them. Did you see the silk stockings?"

"Yes. I wondered about them."

"And the hat. He sent the hat to go with the dress and the jacket. She'd made those herself. She's good."

Bea nodded.

"He knew a lot about her," said Clara.

"Did he?"

"Yeah. Even like what underwear she liked."

"Underwear?"

"Yeah. Didn't you see it down there?"

"No, I only saw the clothes that I mentioned. And I checked everywhere for her things. In the cupboards, under the bed, in the drawers, on the back of the door. No underwear."

"It was new. Just came the other day, the last time I saw her. A new present. She knew it was from him."

"What kind of underwear, Clara?"

"An underwear set with lots of pieces: there were gowns and drawers and corset covers. Five pieces, I think."

"Six?"

"Yeah. You're right. Six. How'd'you know? You saw them down there, didn't you?"

"No," said Bea. "I didn't see them there. But I know the set you mean: they're in the catalogue at Shulman's, Clara. Natty comes in all the time to look at them."

...---...

Bea held the damp pyjama bottoms in her hand, and was suddenly filled with an urgency to get out of this house. It was the Morse code, no doubt; the strange, pale little girl; the talk of Natty going missing. She took a deep breath. She still had this laundry to finish. But the feeling escalated as she worked: Just drop what you're doing. Leave.

She tried to calm herself. She was almost done her day. She just had the last of this laundry to hang; she had made their supper and it was waiting for them in the warming oven. The laundry had taken far longer than it should have. Bea had had to fiddle repeatedly with the new iron, trotting up the few steps into the kitchen for more coal from the bucket, and another match from the match holder, and then back down again to the laundry room, to the ironing board. Why had they set the laundry up like this? She couldn't figure it out. One should iron in the kitchen, with the stove at the ready. But Mrs. Stevens must have wanted this newfangled iron, one that didn't need the heat of the stove. So they must have built this laundry room, away from the easy heat, and purchased the new iron. It was supposed to be "self-heating." But all of Bea's efforts this afternoon couldn't get the iron hot enough — the coal inside the iron wouldn't stay lit or would burn poorly. Bea had finally abandoned the self-heating iron for the old irons buried at the back of the kitchen cupboard. She heated them on top of the stove, running back to get one and then the other off the stove top as need be. A laborious affair. If she was going to continue to work here, she would have to talk to Mrs. Stevens about this arrangement.

She started to pin the grey and green-striped pyjama bottoms next to the tops, when she heard the sound of footsteps. The garment slipped out of her hands. It must be Brian or George coming home, she thought. Silly for her to still be so nervy. With sweaty hands, she bent to pick up the damp pyjama bottoms from the wooden floor. She gave them a quick shake. Brian's. Or George's. Too small to belong to Mr. Stevens. She continued to hurriedly hang the laundry, now and again stopping and listening, but there was no further sound from the kitchen or from the small set of stairs leading up from the laundry room. She was almost through the remaining items in the laundry basket when she heard a creak from the staircase and turned. It was neither of the twins standing there; it was Mr. Stevens, and he had been drinking.

"Bea MacDonald, is it? Heard you'd be here. Those my things you touching there, Bea? You like 'em, heh?" he said, pushing himself off the doorjamb, and taking the two steps down into the laundry room with more balance than Bea would have thought possible. "No," he said, shaking his head, and then trying to smooth his hair back with his hand. His hand failed and his hair remained askew, sticking out at odd angles, as if he'd earlier run his fingers through it. "I can see they're not mine. They're the boy's. Too bad." Bea watched him carefully as he wove his way to the large table along the far wall of the room. The table held the pressed and folded laundry, and some damp sweaters drying on racks. She didn't take her eyes off him.

He picked up her newly pressed linen tablecloth and mangled it. His hands groped her work as if it were mere paper bound for the fire and not a thing that she had worked on carefully for the good part of an hour, each wrinkle examined and re-pressed until the entire cloth was sharp and perfect. The section of the tablecloth that he had scrunched was now thoroughly wrinkled. He dropped it onto the table, a careless reject. He turned and smiled at her, his eyes an alcoholic glaze. "There's things that a man wants . . . " She couldn't believe what she was hearing and his words adhered like skunk to her skin, her throat and the back of her nose, igniting her stomach with a panic that flooded throughout her. She had left it too late to run, she realized as she belatedly began to edge her way along the wall toward the stairs, his eyes on her the entire time. But there was a reason why she hadn't fled: as illogical as it was, she had wanted to see his face again. His was a face that she had seen many times, of course, in the store and on the street, but just now when he'd stepped from the shadowy stairwell she had glimpsed something else unexpected, something she was shocked to see. Despite the threat inherent in his behaviour, she needed to get another look at it. And now when he turned, she saw what she needed to know, saw that she was correct. Yesterday, she had been mistaken. She was sure that she would have recognized the cut on George's forehead, but it was this scar on Mr. Stevens' forehead — square-like, deep and wide, positioned dead-centre and high on the forehead above the wrinkle lines — that was the exact match to the image in her mind. She recognized it straight away, and she also recognized something else — his smile. She had been seeing both the smile and the scar in her dreams. Now, of late, the dream images seemed to be seeking out their real-life counterparts. He smiled again and took a step toward her as she took several more toward the door.

"Do you know what I mean, Bea? Do you know what I mean by needs?" he said, taking another step, his voice throaty and soft, like the purr of a cat. Bea felt her skin grow a thin shield against it, against him, and then another shield and another.

She was about to break into a run, when, without warning, he suddenly stopped coming toward her and started scratching furiously — his head and his neck, his chest and his crotch. She didn't stop to think what had got hold of him. She ran up the stairs and into the kitchen, grabbed her basket and coat, and was running out the door as he screamed: "What have you done to me?"

"Aunt Evelyn?" called Bea as she burst in through the front door, but she slowed when she reached the kitchen. "Hello, Billy," she said.

"'Lo," said Aunt Evelyn's friend, looking up from his *Evening Telegram* and then, unfolding his long torso out of the chair by the fire, he stood to greet her as she came into the room.

"Hello, Bea," said Aunt Evelyn, looking up with a smile. "Just in time. Want a cup? What're you wearing that old smock for, Bea? Didn't you leave the house with your dress on this morning?"

"Had to go back to Shulman's and change into this thing I keep there," said Bea, taking off her coat. "Spilled molasses on myself at the Stevens'."

"That so?" asked Aunt Evelyn, giving her a skeptical look. Bea nodded as she set her basket on the floor and draped her coat over the back of a chair. She had felt compelled to change her clothes after the incident with Mr. Stevens, and now she knew that her aunt could tell by looking that molasses didn't have anything to do with her change of clothes. But Aunt Evelyn would not ask her any more about it with Billy McLeod in the room.

Her aunt finished pouring a cup of tea for Billy, who sat back down on the small bench by the stove, then she returned to the table and poured a cup for herself and one for Bea. Bea plunked down onto one of the chairs. After several seconds she said,

"Do you know a young woman named Natty, Billy?"

"Natty Cooke?" asked Billy.

"Yes," said Bea.

"Angus' daughter. Proud of her, he is. 'Going somewhere, my Natty,' he always says. I seem to remember him saying something about his girl getting a good job at one of the new English houses. Her pa's all she's got — mother's dead, or gone, can't remember."

"Why do you ask, Bea?" questioned Aunt Evelyn.

"Well, she worked at the Stevens' before me and she left without a word, and left some beautiful clothes behind — beautiful, Aunt Evelyn — and Mrs. Stevens just wanted me to throw them in the rubbish, and then . . ."

"What, Bea?"

"Well, I'm wondering where she is, is all."

"Why, Bea? Do you think something's happened to her?"

Bea just shrugged and instead of answering, asked, "Is Jean around?"

"Upstairs."

Bea strode to the bottom of the staircase and called for her cousin. Several seconds later, Jean came bounding down the stairs and into the room.

"Bea! You're home!"

"Jean, how are you, love?" Bea asked, hugging her cousin. Jean sat on Bea's lap — a habit they'd had since Jean could walk.

"Good, I'm good. How're you?" asked Jean, pecking Bea on her cheek and wrapping her arms around her neck.

"Fine, but listen, Jean."

"What is it, Bea?" Jean asked pulling her arms away and peering into her cousin's face. "Something's wrong with you," she said with absolute certainty.

"Not really," said Bea. "It doesn't matter. But can you look at something for me?"

"Yes," said Jean, getting down off her lap, taking a seat beside her at the table, and moving the chair right next to Bea's. While keeping one ear on their conversation, Aunt Evelyn prepared the tea, as Jean asked, "What is it?"

Out of her pocket Bea withdrew the scrap of paper on which she had written the Morse code. "I know what the first line says," Bea said, sliding it across the table to Jean.

Jean nodded, and took the paper from her hand. Bea put her arm around her shoulder and the two cousins bent their heads over the paper. "Morse," said Jean.

"Morse code?" asked Aunt Evelyn and Billy in unison as they both came to stand behind the girls.

"I heard it and wrote it down," explained Bea.

"Unh-huh," said Jean. Then a few seconds later, she said, "Bea? Are you sure you got it right? You've written 'someone was kissed.'"

"Yes, unfortunately. Does it say any more, Jean, like who did the kissing?"

"I don't think so, Bea."

"Somebody sending silly kissing notes to a young woman?" asked

Aunt Evelyn, gently rustling Bea's hair.

"There's nothing silly about it," snapped Bea, shaking her head.

"Well my, aren't we grumpy!" Aunt Evelyn sniped back.

"It's not that anyhow, Mum," interrupted Jean.

"No?" Bea and Evelyn said.

"No. You see, I don't think the sender meant to say 'kissed' at all."

"No?"

"No," said Jean. "I think those must have been *l*'s you heard, Bea. Not *s*'s. Otherwise it hardly makes sense, does it?"

No one spoke while they determined the outcome of the word once the *s*'s were replaced with *l*'s.

"It says 'killed,' Bea, not 'kissed.' Otherwise it doesn't make sense," Jean muttered almost to herself.

"What doesn't make sense, Jean?" asked Bea.

"The last line. After the delete line — the eight dots? — there's the last line that is supposed to replace the first line. Do you know what I mean? The sender wanted to delete that first line — someone was killed — and replace it with another line instead," said Jean, speaking to her elders as though instructing children much younger than herself. Then she began tapping the tips of her own small fingers on the tabletop. "If you got the dots and dashes right . . . " she referred to the paper where Bea had written it down and tapped out the code on the table:

-- ..- .- -.. . .-. . -..

At the sound of the last "dot space dash dot dot," she looked up from her own fingers. "Bea?" she said.

"What does it say, Jean?" asked Bea.

"What is it, Jean?" asked Aunt Evelyn.

"You've figured it out, haven't you?" asked Bea.

"Oh yes. But I don't like it anymore than that first line, Bea."

"Please, Jean. Tell us," said Aunt Evelyn.

"Mum, it says 'murdered,' Mum. It says, 'someone was murdered.'"

Silence came over them all, and then Billy walked over to his chair by the stove, picked up the chair, and brought it to the table. Before he sat, he moved a chair over for Evelyn, who sat heavily down on it and reached for her sewing basket.

"Where did you say you heard this?" asked Aunt Evelyn after many seconds where the only sound was the overriding rhythm of Jean tapping her fingernails on the tabletop.

"At the Stevens'. In their cellar, while I was cleaning up Natty's things."

"It's daft, Bea," said Aunt Evelyn, sending her needle with excessive speed through the hem of a black linen skirt.

No one spoke for several more seconds, until Billy finally said,

"I think someone's having you on, Bea."

Evelyn nodded. "I agree. But it's a mean trick. Stop tapping, Jean. Please."

"One thing I don't understand, Aunt Evelyn," Bea said as Jean stopped her tapping, got up off her chair and sat again on Bea's lap. Bea wrapped her arms around her cousin's waist.

"What's that, love?" asked Evelyn.

"Why would Natty have left her clothes behind?"

"That's right. So you said. Well, you brought them with you, didn't you?" Evelyn said, cocking an eyebrow at Bea and setting her sewing back in the basket. "You could hardly throw them in the rubbish."

"Hardly," said Bea, and she leaned over to pull the garments from her bag. As she brought them out and handed them around, no one spoke. Evelyn examined each piece closely, turning them inside out to look at the seams and the lining. "Billy?" she said, staring at Natty's dress on her lap and fingering the fine lace.

"Yes?" he asked as she looked up at him.

"You'd best get us an introduction to Angus Cooke. I think we'd better find out where his Natty has gone."

Mildred reached for her glass of single-malt scotch. She could use the drink; the evening was not over — more disturbing news was still to come before the night was out. As if today's events thus far had not been enough: there was the Morse code that Bea had discovered and Jean had deciphered; that uncomfortable episode in the laundry room; and then Mildred's own upsetting experience a few hours earlier. She must have dozed off, and had a daydream — of breaking into the Nortons' apartment of all things. As the years went by, she was having these lapses of fatigue more and more frequently. She would suddenly get weary and drift off, often at the most inopportune moments. She was unable to fight the powerful exhaustion that would wash over her, and in the end, the deep sleep was a balm. Her only real fear: that she would never wake up, that she would be gone forever.

Her hand touched the table beside her, and discovered disappointment: she had not poured herself a drink after all. Restless and frustrated, she got up from her chair and joined Jean by the window as the storm's salty seaweed wind bit sharply at the room and into her thoughts of the Nortons' apartment. While Bea lay in bed and stared up at the ceiling, Jean watched the black of the stormy night. She had been doing so for at least twenty minutes. The child was having a premonition but didn't know it, and that was why she couldn't leave the night alone. And, as much as Mildred tried, she could not shake the after-effect of her daydream. It was still with her, as if pondering the night with her and Jean at the attic window:

"Have you come for supper?" the red-haired boy had asked. Mildred had seen him somewhere before, but she couldn't think where. He was seated at the round kitchen table set with pretty scarlet placemats.

"No, thank you," Mildred had answered politely, because she didn't know how else to reply. What could she possibly say? She had tried to keep the surprise off her face. He, on the other hand, didn't seem at all perturbed that she had just barged into his home uninvited. She had no longer been able to resist the pull of the Nortons' apartment. It had grown stronger throughout the day. So as soon as she had known that Bea was home safe, and away from that horrid Mr. Stevens, she had returned to the city. She had no idea what she thought she'd find in the apartment, but when she had come down the hallway to the kitchen doorway, she had stopped, dumbfounded. She was amazed to find this boy addressing her so calmly, as if she was not out of place. He was the child she had seen hours earlier in the telegraph office. She felt as if she had also encountered him elsewhere, but she couldn't place the feeling.

"Why not?" he asked, toying with his salad fork and looking her in the eye. She had never seen a child so forlorn. He seemed to have just been crying, though she couldn't see the tears.

"I've eaten, thank you," she said, which was a lie, of course, but even if she was hungry, now was not the time or place. Besides, you don't stay and eat food from the home you've just broken into. You can take it with you, of course, if you need it. But you certainly don't linger.

There are certain rules to being a burglar, and this must surely be one of them. You don't eat the food, even if it *is* offered to you by a strange little boy who apparently lives there, but shows absolutely no surprise that you've arrived. "I'm quite full," said Mildred, trying to sound calm as she sat down in the chair to the left of him. In fact, she was feeling entirely distracted and wished she had never come. "Otherwise I'd love to join you." Mildred looked behind her down the empty hallway, and then back at him. She wondered if he was the reason why she had come. The Nortons had stepped out, but why would they have left the child behind?

"I like company. *Natty* used to eat with me," he said, staring at his hands.

"Natty? I thought I recognized you from somewhere else. From the Stevens'." She was reminded of the portraits of the two boys on the wall in the Stevens' hallway. She was about to ask him about the pictures when he said,

"My twin lives there."

"And you live here?"

He shrugged, and Mildred said, "So that's how you know Natty — your twin introduced you?"

He looked at her as if wondering what the right answer to the question might be, then he shrugged again and said, "My *father* used to eat supper with me."

"Yes, I would imagine," Mildred said, trying to be encouraging, although now she knew for certain that there was something terribly wrong with this child. He was mentally unsound; there was no question about it. She couldn't understand why the Nortons had left him alone in the apartment. He should not be on his own. It was obvious to anybody that he couldn't cope.

Mildred started to get out of her chair. She was feeling increasingly bewildered, and, more than that, disturbed. She didn't want this conversation to go on. She wished she hadn't come, and she didn't understand what had prompted her.

He didn't seem to notice her discomfort. "Do you know Natty?" he said.

"Well, yes, but only slightly, from the store. Bea has been wondering about her, you see."

"There isn't much to wonder about," he said.

"No. I know," said Mildred.

"Are you looking for her here?" he asked.

"No." For a moment she had felt compelled to say, "I came looking for you," but she didn't, even though she wondered again if perhaps he was her reason for being here.

He looked around the kitchen. "No," he said. "I didn't think you'd come for Natty. Neither have I. But I know why else you're here." He lifted the thin forefinger of his left hand and pointed past Mildred and the kitchen door toward the bedroom hallway.

She stood up to look out the kitchen doorway in the direction he had pointed. She glanced back at him and the small, pristine kitchen and then, to her right, down the hallway. She could see four doors: one partially-opened at the very end of the hall — that was the water closet — and three closed, two on the right hand side of the corridor, and one on the left. Suddenly she tensed. Something was not right down there. She again felt a familiar urgency, as if something was calling her toward it. She was confused. Should she stay here with this child, or explore the hallway? Getting away from the child might be a relief. He disturbed her, but, she decided, as she looked at him sitting there so lonely, she would sit with him awhile longer. Company might be just what he needed. She listened for the sound of life coming from the hallway, then she walked softly back to the kitchen table and sat down.

"It's locked," said the boy, reading her mind.

Mildred nodded. He continued,

"That room. You know the one I mean. It's always locked." He nodded as he spoke, and then looked at his hands. "It doesn't matter."

It didn't matter, Mildred knew. She could get into any locked room she wanted, but she rarely did. People locked rooms for a reason: to keep other people out, even her. Nowadays, she usually only went where she was invited. She had been law-abiding for many, many years now; her days of being a burglar were long over, or so she had thought, looking around at the unfamiliar apartment. The child continued to gaze at her, and, as he did, he conjured up a memory of another child from her past: a boy she had robbed when she herself was just ten.

She resisted the memory and concentrated on the boy sitting across the table. He had put his hand back on his lap and had returned to staring at the scarlet placemat in front of him. His was the only one of the three place settings that was fully set — plate, cup, glass full of water, cutlery, napkin — while the other two had been cleared clean leaving only the mat.

"I really must leave," Mildred said. It was suddenly all too much: this strange boy, her memories, the feeling in the apartment. "Sorry for the short visit," she said, standing up and heading out of the kitchen. He didn't want her to leave, although he never said so. He didn't say goodbye either, but as she got to the front door of the apartment, he looked along the hall toward her and smiled. Then, as if his words would keep her, he said, "He laughed when the blood fell from the palm of my hand, and onto his."

...---...

The wind reached up and blew straight dark strands around their eyes and cheeks. In appearance, Jean had taken after Mildred's side of the family: small, and dark. She could even be her doppelganger, right down to the shape of their ears and the way they walked — imperial and ethereal, as if princesses from another realm.

But it was Bea who took after her in character. Sometimes she found it startling how much they were alike. Except, while Mildred had always considered herself smart, Bea was so much smarter. Brilliant, really.

Mildred had heard that adopted children often grow to resemble their adoptive parents not only in personality, but also in mannerisms and voice. Bea could be that adopted daughter, for no blood ran between the two of them. Mildred's line ran through Evelyn's, not that of Bea's uncle and Evelyn's late husband, Ian. Mildred had immediately taken to Bea the moment she found her on board the vessel thirteen years ago, sitting beside her mother's cot. She knew then that they were related in a special way, and she had often wondered what it was that bound them. Was it the similarity of their pasts, or the ties that she already had forged with Evelyn and their kin; bonds that had begun with Mildred's own daughter, Sarah — bonds that nothing could destroy.

"Aren't you cold?" Mildred asked Jean, but the girl shook her head. She looked freezing, and she should have been: dressed like a vagrant in her thin nightgown that dragged long on the floor, gathering dirt onto its hem. Bea was still lying on her back on the bed, ignoring them, staring up at the ceiling, deep in thought. Mildred resisted the urge to interrupt, to tell her to sit up and pay attention: if you think today was bad, more is to come, and here is some of it now. Jean suddenly gasped and reached out her right hand to touch the window with the tips of her fingers.

"You see it now? At last?" asked Mildred, following her gaze into the infinite black beyond the pane.

Jean nodded. Of course she had; the child got her gift from Mildred.

"The ghost?" Mildred asked, just to be sure.

Jean didn't respond this time; perhaps she couldn't hear her above the storm, but Mildred knew she had seen it. The bad tidings: a ghost ship that had just now appeared above the trees, dipping and bobbing on the wind as if still sailing the seas, its crew calling home to their loved ones, cries that were carried seaward and cast pell-mell onto the waves.

Still, Mildred wanted Jean to confirm her sighting and she was about to again ask her question, when Jean responded with a nod and a whisper:

"Bea, a ship's gone down."

"Oh, Jean, not again. I've had enough of this kind of thing for one day. Quit your imaginings and come to bed."

"Bea. You're becoming dim-witted," said Mildred, spinning and staring at Bea. No wonder. The girl really had had a disturbing day, what with her experience with Mr. Stevens and the Morse code news of someone being murdered, and so on. Still, Bea needed to act smart. "Bea," Mildred said more gently. "I would listen to Jean if I were you, Bea, I really would. There's a ghost ship out there."

But Bea ignored her, just as she dismissed Jean. "It's just a storm, Jean. I'm sure everyone's fine."

"It's far more than a storm, Bea," said Mildred.

"More than a storm, Bea. You don't know," Jean mumbled, as a gust of wind tucked in through the quarter-inch crack between the pane and the wood.

"Close the window," said Bea. "I'm getting cold." Mildred glanced her way. Bea's melancholy had turned irritable.

"The events of your day are not Jean's fault," Mildred scolded her, and as Bea's gaze fell onto Jean, Mildred was relieved to see that she was chagrined.

"Sorry, Jean," she said, sitting up.

"S'alright. Doesn't matter."

Bea nodded and a few seconds later said, "Jean?"

"Unh-huh," said Jean, still facing away from her toward the window.

"Tomorrow?"

"Unh-huh?"

"Tomorrow I have to work late, so does your mum. Want to come meet me at Shulman's, or do you want to go with Aunt Evelyn to do the fittings?"

"Meet you at Shulman's, Bea," Jean said, coming to sit down beside Bea and cuddling up to her. She lay her head on Bea's lap, and Bea tousled her hair and said, "That's fine, Jean."

Jean rolled over and looked up into her cousin's eyes. "I saw it, Bea. A ghost ship. I did."

"It doesn't necessarily mean anything, Jean. It's probably the night playing games with your eyes. It does that. It's probably because of the Morse tonight. That's what's on your mind, Jean. It's on mine too, how can it not be? I'm sorry, Jeannie. I wouldn't have given it to you to decipher if I'd known what it said. Stupid of me."

"No, wasn't," said Jean, slipping off Bea and the bed, and going over to the window, her voice so faint Mildred could hardly hear it. Bea got up and put her weight to the top of the wooden sash. Mildred reached up to help.

"I am sorry about the Morse code, Jean. Really I am."

"Oh, for heaven's sake," said Mildred. There really wasn't time for this type of nonsense.

"I know. It's alright," said Jean.

Mildred could hardly believe her ears. Both girls were becoming maudlin and distracted. It was entirely unacceptable. Mildred had raised them better than this. Granted, little could be done about the ghost ship. A vessel had gone down somewhere near here, that was a fact. Everyone aboard had perished, and even if the townsfolk were to conduct a search this very minute, the chance of crew or passengers being found alive was extremely remote. Mildred looked at the shadow of the ghost ship as it left. More than remote, she realized sadly: hopeless. But the girls needed to keep their wits about them. There was much worrying yet to be done.

"I didn't raise you to be addled, Bea, Jean," she said, turning toward them. "Are you listening to me?"

They certainly weren't. With her bare toe, Bea sought Jean's bare foot under the girl's long nightgown. She left her foot there, her cool skin on Jean's. Bea finally said, although Mildred rolled her eyes when she did because she could tell that Bea was just playing along, "I'll do what I can about the ghost ship." Jean looked up at her, a wisp of hair falling across her cheek, her dark eyes showing complete faith in her cousin. "I'll try and tell Aunt Evelyn."

Oh, Bea, thought Mildred, because she knew she wouldn't.

After Bea tucked Jean into bed, she put on her housecoat and strode to the top of the stairs, mumbling to herself.

"Aunt Evelyn, Jean saw a ghost ship. Someone's gone down," Bea muttered, rehearsing what she would tell her aunt. She paused at the top of the stairs. "You've got to tell somebody, Aunt Evelyn."

"That's right, Bea," said Mildred. "And Evelyn will say: 'Tonight, Bea?'" She held onto her shawl with one hand and stood beside Bea, her other hand on the banister.

"'Tonight, Bea?'" Bea repeated. "'Are you out of your mind? You want me to walk into the city in the pitch black and say what? My daughter has predicted a ship going down again?'"

"'She's been wrong twice, Bea,' Evelyn will say," said Mildred. "But right four times, five if you include tonight, Bea. Tell her that. Don't forget to tell her that, Bea. She needs to know that. You should know it too, for that matter. Jean can see."

Filled with resolve, Bea marched downstairs and Mildred followed, more hopeful now that Bea would tell Evelyn about the ghost ship. Better that people tried to find it than do nothing at all. Better they tried, even though all they'd find was the dead, if they found anything at all.

At the kitchen table, Evelyn sat with her back to them. Without seeing the front of her face, Mildred knew she was squinting at the garment in her hands, her eyesight thwarted by the inadequate light of the lamp. They approached from behind, and as always, Evelyn acknowledged their presence without looking up. Bea came up beside her, and Mildred looked over her shoulder, amazed once again by the tiny, perfect seam that, in the near-dark, Evelyn was stitching in the hem of a white blouse. Bea took a deep breath, but just as she was about to begin her story about Jean's ghost ship, Evelyn said: "Something you want to tell me, Bea?"

Bea glanced back at Mildred. Evelyn hadn't meant the ghost ship, and they both knew it. She had meant something else. Evelyn had always known when Bea was lying or feeling guilty or worried. And this afternoon she had detected something amiss in Bea's manner. She was waiting for Bea to tell her about the incident in the laundry room, but for reasons that Mildred couldn't fathom, Bea had decided against it.

"No," said Bea, talking to the floor.

"No?" asked Evelyn, looking once at her, then back at her sewing. "What brings you down, then? Something."

Mildred watched Jean's ghost-ship news teeter on the edge of Bea's tongue, begging to become a word or a full sentence, but Bea just swallowed it back. She shook her head.

"Nothing."

"You sure?" Evelyn said.

"Yes," she said too quickly, and then after a couple of seconds said, "Absolutely. Of course I'm sure."

Evelyn glanced over at Mildred. Mildred answered by raising her eyebrows, but Evelyn didn't need any confirmation from her. She already knew that Bea was lying. She returned her gaze to Bea, and let it settle there for a few seconds. She went back to her sewing, nodded at the pile of mending to be done and said, "Idle hands." At that command, Bea sat down, picked out a needle, a spool of beige thread, and a beige glove to be mended, and tried her best to help. But after a few minutes of fruitless effort, she put the thread and needle back on the table, and kissed her aunt on the cheek.

"Remembered something I've got to do. See you in a bit, Aunt Evelyn."

"Where are you off to? Look at it out there!"

"I know. But I need to see Callum. Got to ask him something," she said as she strode into the hallway and put on her boots and Uncle Ian's old oil coat.

"Can't it wait until morning, Bea? Surely to God."

"No, it can't. Don't worry. I won't be long," she said as she lit a lantern and walked into the night.

Bea ran first along the trail to the bluff, but of course he wasn't there. No one would be daft enough to be sitting outside on a night like tonight. She left the bluff and headed up the trail that led to his house. She didn't have far to go, but she could hardly see through the torrent of rain that came straight at her, and she had not gone far when her lantern blew out. It took her a few minutes to get it lit again. Finally, up a hill and over a rise, she came to his house. He was still awake: a light shone from a window near the rear of the house. The rest of his family all went to bed early, but Callum was often up well past midnight.

"Cup of tea?" he asked with a smile as he opened the kitchen door to her knock. He'd spoken as if it was the most normal thing in the world for her to appear at his house in the dead of night dripping wet; but then, it wasn't the first time she had done so.

"Something a little stronger, if you've got it," she answered as he let her in and helped her off with her coat, which he hung next to the stove.

"Beer? Rum?" he asked, as he went over to crouch down in front of a small stand-alone cupboard several feet from the stove.

"Rum in a nice hot cup of tea. What do you think?"

"Sounds lovely."

"Your dad won't mind?"

"It's my rum, not his. He's welcome to it, and he helps himself, let me tell you."

She took a seat at his kitchen table while he prepared her drink, and she reached out to touch a wrench sitting on top of the table. She'd sat here innumerable times since she arrived in Newfoundland when she was five, and she still drew the same comfort from the table, through all its changes from Callum's mother's influence to how it looked now: male-dominated, mostly. Callum, his three brothers and their father had littered the table with assorted tools, a pipe and its holder, and a couple of tobacco pouches. But Jean's friend, fiery little Laura, had claimed a corner and marked it with her old rag doll, a present from Aunt Evelyn.

"Hungry?" he asked, setting a steaming cup of tea flavoured with rum before her. She added milk and sugar to it.

"No. Thanks," she said, taking a sip.

He sat down across from her with his own mug, and waited for her to speak. He knew she'd get around to it. She sipped on her tea, and finally she said, "Do you know Henry Stevens?"

"Only slightly. Met him once last year."

"What did you think of him?"

"Dishonest, to be frank. He was brokering for a chap in England. He tried to get us to sell cheap. Kept insisting. Called Dad all kinds of names. Must have been drunk. Never seen anything like it, actually. We wouldn't come down in price so he bought from someone else in the end, though God knows what he got for what he was willing to pay. Wasn't quality fish. Why the questions, Bea?"

"I've been doing work for Mrs. Stevens. Had an encounter with Mr. Stevens today. Got me wondering." Callum looked up from his focus on the table and gazed intently at her with his heavily lashed, hooded eyes. "It wasn't anything to worry about," she said, answering his look. No sense telling him the rest. He would just get worried.

"But something's got you anxious," he said, cocking his head at the kitchen door and the storm that raged outside.

She nodded, and wrapped her shoulders with the blanket that was hanging over the back of her chair.

"Cold?" he asked.

"Little," she said. He got up and checked the stove, then brought the teapot and rum over to the table. After she'd added more tea and rum to her mug, she said, "Do you remember the dreams — about the boy and the box, the man and the knife?"

Callum nodded. He knew what she was talking about. She had had the exact same dream three times, each time frightening enough to wake her out of a deep sleep. Each time, Callum happened to be on the bluff when she'd run up there afterwards, and he'd always been captivated by Bea's recounting of the dream. He'd been listening to her dreams since they were children, and they both knew from experience that some of her dreams contained portents, while the vast majority were simply ordinary dreams, the kind that most people had. He chewed on a twig he'd found in his shirt pocket, and drummed his free fingers on the tabletop. Bea wasn't surprised to hear him ask: "Tell me again, Bea. Remind me." He never tired of hearing her dreams.

"Father has left me and my little brother standing alone on the deck of a ship," she said.

"Well, that part's the truth, isn't it?"

"So I've been told," Bea said, pausing for a moment. The disturbing story of her arrival had long been a subject of conversation in her household. Aunt Evelyn and Uncle Ian, while he was still alive, had never tried to hide the truth from her. "Behind us, sitting on a life preserver box, is a strange boy, and standing next to us is an old man. The man is not wearing a hat, scarf, or gloves. In his thin hands he is clutching a bright red box to his chest. I think the box belongs to me and I wonder what he is doing with it. It is a child's box. It might belong to the boy . . . I'm not sure. I look back, and the boy is standing in front of a mirror. He's reached his right hand up and has laid his palm on the mirror. His hand is bleeding. On one side of the mirror, the boy has blood gushing from a cut on his forehead. I can see the cut quite clearly. On the other side of the mirror, his forehead is clear: no blood, no cut.

"I look back at the man, and he is holding a bloody knife in his hand. Together, we look back at the boy, but he is gone. I'm sure the man has something to do with the boy. I think that the knife is the same one used to hurt the boy.

"The man looks like he just woke up: he has whisker stubble on his chin and cheeks and on the limp folds of skin that hang off his face. I want to point this out to Little Ian. But I don't. He doesn't look like the type of man to make fun of, not unless we have a clear escape, which we don't. The man seems shrunken while his clothes are gigantic, everything almost falling off. He is wearing a long grey coat, tattered and drooping from his shoulders, and its collar flops open, showing his wrinkled, bare neck. He is ugly with boils on his face and a horrible nose and he scares me, but I keep looking over at him, to the box that he is holding. The box lid is written all over in gold. I can almost read the name on the box, but I can't quite see it. He is gripping the box so tightly, I think it will break. His hands look like eagle's talons, but each finger has a nice shiny nail filed to a sharp point. Like a girl's. I wonder if his hands are a woman's hands. He fiddles and fiddles with the new-looking lock. He keeps fiddling and I keep staring. Then, suddenly, I can see inside the box as if the sides have become invisible.

"The box is much bigger inside than it appears from the outside. It is divided into three compartments. On one side is a pile of letters and papers, dirty, as if they had been covered with soil. On the other is a single letter written on a lady's writing paper. Pink, I think, or peach. And in the middle is a pocket knife, and I realize that it is the same knife, but now it is not in the man's hand, but in the box. I wonder if the letters are addressed to me. I want to know what the letters say. It's important I see the letters. I need to read them.

"Suddenly he turns, and glares down at me. I look up at his face and realize he is smiling, only it isn't a real smile, it is a pretend smile, and a horrible one, as if someone has just yanked his dry lips back over his toothless gums. He suddenly tucks the box up under the opening of his coat, where one button hangs loose just below his rib cage. He glares at me again and I am scared from how much he hates me. I look over and see that the sailors have finally got the ramp in place and we are all supposed to disembark off the ship and fall straight into the ocean. We are not docked at all, but nobody seems to notice and nobody seems to care, and everybody is just going to do what they're told. I don't want to go. I look back and the man is gone. Then, all the passengers are suddenly gone too, and it's just me and Little Ian, alone on deck. I realize all of a sudden that we're on one of the cable ships, and I am holding on to Little Ian's hand, and our two trunks are at our feet."

When she finished recounting the dream, she blurted, "Callum, quit it. Please."

"Sorry," he said, and he stopped his drumming that had increased in intensity while Bea was talking. After a few seconds, while he chewed on the twig and she took a sip of her tea, he said, "I take it Henry Stevens fits in here somehow."

"It was the exact same smile, Callum, I swear. Except for the teeth. Mr. Stevens has teeth. And the cut on the forehead: absolutely identical." She wrapped herself in the blanket, and then poured one more shot of rum into her mug and, to Callum's nod, one into his as well. They both had more questions about her dream, but neither seemed to want to ask them. Another important question now nagged at Bea, and it had been doing so since she'd shown Jean the Morse code. The question had kept her occupied throughout Jean's bantering about ghost ships, and it was still with her. Had someone really been murdered, as the Morse code had said, and had Mr. Henry Stevens done it?

Day Four
Friday, October 17, 1902

The door opened to the smell of stale beer and tobacco, and a small, unkempt man propping himself on one shoulder against the doorframe as if his feet were going to give out on him any minute. Mildred just about fell over from the stench. She put one hand on the balcony post to keep her balance.

"'Lo," he mumbled.

"Angus," said Billy, stepping toward him as the rest of them stayed behind him on the porch. Billy had met them at the corner of the road leading to the Cooke house. In the bright light of day, yesterday's Morse code incident seemed silly. That morning over breakfast they had talked about it, and even Jean became convinced that it had just been someone playing tricks on Bea. Still, they had Natty's clothes to worry about, so they decided to go ahead with their plan to meet up with Billy. Bea had run ahead to Shulman's and set up the shop, and when he arrived, she asked for a half hour off, which he willingly allowed. "How've you been, good man?" asked Billy.

"Good 'nuff. Who's asking?" said Angus, peering at the daylight.

"Billy. Billy McLeod."

"Nah. You're not. 'E's dead."

"Not so far as I know. I'm right here, aren't I?" he asked, and turned around to glance at Evelyn, Mildred, and the girls, who nodded. "You're thinking of Bobby, my cousin."

"Right y'are. Well, there y'are," Angus said. "I'll be. Look at ya. Younger than last time, Bobby."

"Billy."

"Yeah. Want a nip o' my spruce beer, Bobby?"

"Billy. Sorry, Angus, we don't have time. Here's the thing, Angus, is your daughter about?"

"Nah. H'ain't seen her in days. Said she'd come around for my birthday. Forty-five, you know. Bake me a cake, she said. H'ain't seen her, never saw her, she still owes me that cake so if you see her tell her to get on over here."

"So she hasn't come back home recently?"

"Not that I know. I would've known, wouldn't I?"

"Yeah. Angus, do you think she might have left the island?"

"Left Newfoundland?"

"Aye."

"Left here and gone where, d'ya suppose?"

"I don't know. Somewhere else. New York. Montreal."

"Toronto."

"She went to Toronto?"

"That's not what I said. I said Toronto, but that don't mean she's gone there. That's just where she'd go if she were going somewhere. Talks about it. Threatens to leave. Tells me she's going to pick up and go." Then, as if he suddenly realized the nature of the conversation, he said: "Why? Why d'ya ask?"

"She's left her job at the Stevens', hasn't returned. How long's it been, Bea?"

"A few days, I think," said Bea.

"Those bastards. If they've done anything to my Natty . . . "

"She must have gone to Toronto. That's what's happened, don't you think, Bea?" asked Billy, turning to her.

"Sounds likely . . . " said Bea.

"Likely," said Angus. "Probably left me, just like her mum." He seemed to sober suddenly. "Say. Ya don't think something bad's happened to my Natty, do ya?"

"Well, you see, Angus," said Billy. "That's what we're wondering. But she's probably fine. Probably gone to a friend's or some such thing."

"She don't got no friends. Not that I know of, anyhow."

"Well, a suitor perhaps. Could've got a suitor."

"Nah. Said she's never going to get married. Said she'd rather be a nun. Got to be a Catholic first, I told her. And you're not going to become no goddamn Catholic, I told her, not over my dead body." He started to close the door on them. "Ye let me know if ye find anything. Can't interest ya in a nip?"

"Not today, another time, Angus."

"Right then. Well, can't say the same for me. All this talk's got it calling me, I tell ye." And at that he slammed the door, leaving them on the front step.

When they turned to leave, Mildred glanced up at the second floor window just as a drape fell into place. She nudged Bea. "Someone's up there, in that room," she said, pointing.

Bea glanced up behind her, but by then the drapes were still.

...---...

Bea lifted the three-foot long rectangular bolt of black Indian linen and stood it between the black chambray and the black sateen, then stepped back to survey the shelf. It was better this way, she decided; Aunt Evelyn had been right. "You should sort all those bolts by colour, Bea, not by the type of fabric," Aunt Evelyn had said when she was in the store last week. "Most people come wanting a navy or a red, before a cotton or a silk. Some of them don't even *know* what they want when it comes to fabric, believe you me. You can still have the black silks together, for instance, but every time I come in here I have to go all over the store just looking for the right colour. I'd rather the same colours were all grouped together."

So Mr. Shulman had given his consent and Bea had rearranged the shelves. Most customers seemed to like the change. She finished with the blacks, and had a bolt of newly-arrived white Gibson cloth in her arms when a voice to her left said:

"This is far preferable."

"Hullo, Mrs. Stevens," said Bea, glancing toward her, then averting her gaze and hoisting the bolt up to the white shelf.

"I need more errands done, Bea. Another bit of correspondence to the Nortons," Mrs. Stevens said.

For a moment, Bea had thought Mrs. Stevens had found out about yesterday's nasty episode with Mr. Stevens. She was so relieved when it wasn't mentioned that, without thinking, she agreed:

"Tomorrow, perhaps, ma'am. In the morning. I don't have to be here until noon."

"Fine, I'll see you then," said Mrs. Stevens as she turned to leave, her emerald satin dress swishing with her.

Before Bea had a chance to respond, Mrs. Stevens stopped, and turned.

"Bea?"

"Yes, ma'am?"

"What in God's name was that concoction you made for us for supper last night?"

"Codfish, ma'am."

"I know that, dear. I'm not that obtuse: I've become familiar with that fish since we first arrived. That other thing — what was it?"

"The pudding, ma'am? That's figgy duff."

"Charming. You don't say."

"Yes, ma'am."

"And what is in it, pray tell?"

"Easy, ma'am. Water and flour and raisins and molasses."

"Really? Then what?"

"Pardon, ma'am?"

"How do you make it?"

"Oh, boil it in the cloth, ma'am. Easy. My aunt's recipe."

"You don't say. Old family recipe, is it?" said Mrs. Stevens as she turned away again and headed down the aisle.

"Mrs. Stevens?" Bea called.

"Yes, Bea," she said, stopping and glancing back at her.

"Did you like it?"

"Well, I can't speak for Henry or George, but, yes, Bea, in fact," she said as she swirled away, talking over her shoulder as she left. "I found it quite delightful."

Bea smiled as she smoothed out the wrinkles on the side of the bolt. But seeing Mrs. Stevens again reminded her of several things she was still curious about: Was the image from her dream correct? Had Henry Stevens actually injured someone with a knife? Or worse? And in the upset since the laundry room, she had forgotten all about the blackmail in the note to Miss Norton from Mrs. Stevens. Bea was curious to know if there was any further development on that front. For some reason that she couldn't explain, she wondered if the correspondence between Miss Norton and Mrs. Stevens was related to the letters in her dream. But the only thing she had to go on was the colour of Mrs. Stevens' writing paper: pink, as in her dream. While she felt that she had settled the dream images of the scar and the smile, she still had others to lay to rest, and until she did she knew they would persist in pestering her: most importantly, the image of the red box and of the letters. She tidied up the ends of the fabric that spilled over the side of the shelf, and suddenly decided that she needed to ingratiate herself to the Nortons. Somehow or other, they were connected to the images in her dream.

She was lifting the next bolt of Gibson cloth onto the shelf when she had an unrelated thought: Why hadn't Mrs. Stevens mentioned Brian? She had spoken of Henry and George and herself, but why had she made no mention of what Brian thought of Bea's figgy duff?

Mildred waited anxiously beside the wharf's shed and waved frantically to Jean and Bea as they quickly approached from the street, weaving through fish merchants and cullers, and horse-carts stacked high with dried cod. She was desperate to get home. She usually enjoyed the wharf at this time of year, with its bustle of industry: fagots of dried cod everywhere; schooners tied up at every available berth and waiting out in the harbour to unload cod or take on winter provisions; people crowding the wharves and the boats; all the sorting, selling, and bargaining. But today, home was where Mildred and the girls and Evelyn needed to be. Home was peace safely contained, where comfort was.

Bea and Jean ran up to her and she said, "Best tuck them under here," indicating the space between the bench seat and the wharf. The wind was picking up, and with one sip it could suck their wares out to sea. The girls shoved their baskets and lantern securely under the bench alongside Evelyn's two baskets, then they all went to stand beside Evelyn, who was at the railing looking down at the mercantile wharf.

"She went down in last night's storm is what I heard," Ralph Whelan was saying to the McNees as he yaffled dried, salted cod off his schooner and handed it to Callum, who tossed it on the culling table.

"Who was aboard?" asked Callum's father, Mike, rapidly grading one fish from another and then flinging them onto the sorted piles lined along the length of his table.

"Stuart's cousin, Douglas, and two of his sons," said Whelan, handing Callum's older brother, Adam, a pile, and then another to Callum.

Mike was culling the fish almost as fast as it took for the next pile to hit the table. "Damn bloody shame," he said.

"I *told* Bea I saw a ghost ship," Jean cried to her mother, but the wind had shifted momentarily and it carried her young voice down to the wharf and to the men.

"You knew a boat had gone down, Jeannie?" called short, dark-haired Callum. Jean didn't answer, but hid behind her mother's skirt. "C'mon lass, it's me." It was true; Jean was fond of Callum. If it had been Callum by himself she might have said something, but she wasn't going to say it to the group of men who now gazed up at Jean and her family.

"She didn't know a thing, Callum, Mike," Evelyn called down.

"Is that so, Evelyn?" answered Mike.

"That's so, Mike. You don't believe those rumours about us, do you? Leave her be."

Evelyn swung around, taking Jean by the hand and propelling her back toward the bench. Bea and Mildred followed as Mike's big voice drifted up to them from below. "That child's got the gift of sight, I swear: that's not the first time. If only she'd use it, we'd all be the better off."

...---...

"Jean MacDonald. Come along with you," Evelyn called from far up ahead, but the message was barely audible by the time it reached Mildred. It could have been the wind; it has a way of dragging the stuff out of words. However, more than the storm pulled at Mildred's concentration as she and Jean made their long way home. The dark sky cloaked the last of their afternoon light; trees crowded in on either side of the narrow road; the woods beyond shuddered, as if wary. And the road behind had become sentient, or so it seemed. It's only the wind, Mildred's sensible self would have liked her to believe.

It's only the wind, Brian reassured himself as he ran quietly after the woman named Mildred and her young companion. Still, wind such as this terrified him. It brought with it thick dark skies and heavy rain, and no comfort. None at all. What was he doing here? He should not have strayed so far from home. Home, Brian? Yes. Home, alright? Home.

What *are* you doing here, Brian?

I don't know.

Are you following Mildred?

Yes, come to think of it.

Why?

He didn't stop to think about it. He kept going up the hill, hiding for a moment on one side of the road, and then the other. He was hoping to get Mildred alone.

Why, Brian?

I don't know! Why do you have to keep asking?

He refused to ask himself any more of his silly questions as he kept after Mildred and her charge. He tried to stifle the sounds of his progress, but, nevertheless, he had made himself known. Mildred and the girl had sensed that he was here. Once before they seemed to have noticed him when they had stopped to re-fasten the child's bonnet. And now, a package had just fallen out of the girl's basket. The child bent to retrieve the bundle, and she must have seen him, for she quickly stuffed the bundle down into her basket, and fled up the hill. Leaving Mildred on the road alone.

The girls, was Mildred's first thought as she hurried up the hill, chased by the disturbing boy. *The girls.* Bea, Jean, and Evelyn. How could she possibly protect them from the likes of this child? When she saw him standing down the road, she realized that this was not the first time she had seen him. He had been following her for several days. She had seen him in Winifred's telegraph office — she had thought he was a work-worn runner awaiting another message for his employer; and before that, he had been at Shulman's. He had been the boy loitering in the aisle looking at the suppositories and then the pomade, while she and Bea searched out the price of arnica for Mrs. Stevens. And, of course, there was yesterday's daydream. She wondered now if it had been a daydream at all, or if she, in fact, had actually gone into the Nortons' apartment. It was odd for her not to remember such a thing. Was her mind starting to go? Finally? After all this time? Must be; she could not make sense of any of this.

She had always dreaded coming across someone like him, and she had wondered over the years what she would do, or how she could protect herself and the girls. Her imaginings always led her to expect the worst: his actions, nefarious; her defences against him, inept. And now here it was, being played out just as she had thought. Her older, terrified legs against his nimble, confident strides. Her fear against his compulsion. She knew there was no getting away from him.

As if mocking her fright, he easily closed the gap between them. She would never be able to outrun him. She struggled to hoist the hem of her skirt, but it kept slipping from her grasp as she forced her arms to help propel her short body up the hill. "Samuel," she gasped, invoking her late husband's name. "Samuel!" she called again, choking on the word, barely able to get out the syllables, and again, as always, her husband was not there to answer. If he came at all, it would be too late: mere feet now separated her from the dark child.

Brian could outrun anyone except his brother. His brother had always been far faster. They often raced home from their cave, and Brian would always lose. But, against anyone else, he would always win any race. And so he easily caught up to Mildred — there's no possible way she could beat him, why was she even trying? — when the thoughts of his brother unlocked his secret stash of questions: Why are you here? Why don't you go home? Why don't you listen? Disturbing images tripped over one another as they rushed his brain. He tried to dispel them, but it was no good; they kept coming. He didn't know the answers to these questions. He didn't want the answers. Why didn't he just leave himself alone? But his mind wouldn't listen, and just as Brian reached for Mildred's arm, his brain shouted out one more question: What *do* you want with Mildred?

His fingers landed on her arm and she swung to face him. The fear on her face reminded him of Morna and Natty. And George, even. They all looked like this from time to time. He now knew what he wanted with Mildred. "Someone was killed," he said calmly. There was no need to hurry now. There was nowhere to go on this long, lonely road.

His hand remained on her forearm and he waited for her to reply. She had better hurry. Time has a way of running out. Perhaps she hadn't heard him. "Someone was *killed!*" he repeated urgently, loudly.

"I know," she answered quickly, her words tripping over his own. Then her face suddenly softened, as if surrendering its fear. She stopped struggling against his pull on her arm, and said, "Yes, I know, Brian."

"You do?" he asked cautiously, resisting his own question.

"Yes," she replied, and at that he released her arm and began to turn away. But, then, he stopped himself, and looking up into her kind face he was about to ask another question. You don't need to ask her, he stopped himself. You don't need to know what happened when you were twelve. At that surprising and curious scrap of information from himself — twelve? — the question shot out of his mouth.

"Do you know who was killed, Mildred?"

"Yes," she said gently. "You."

Why else knickers on this frigid autumn day? And a short-sleeved shirt? No vest to warm his small chest, no sweater for his bare arms. Shoes scuffed with mud; knees cut and bruised; the right knee sock torn along its cuff. Another rip on the right shoulder of his shirt. His hair, a dirty red. Scratches that would never heal on his cheeks, chin, and forehead. Mildred just didn't understand why it had taken her until these last several minutes to realize who he was.

"You were only twelve years old, weren't you?" she asked. He didn't speak this time, but she knew she was right about his age — the same age her daughter Sarah was when Samuel passed away. Brian replied by frowning at her as if wondering why she was asking such a silly question, and then he turned and started downhill.

It was useless to call him back. She wouldn't find out any more from him tonight. He would only grapple with the answers, if he knew them at all. At least, he appeared a fraction less troubled. Perhaps he had been waiting forever for someone like her to find out who he was. And now she, and the girls if they were willing, needed to do their best to discover who in God's name had killed Brian.

...---...

Brian closed his eyes to the sound and prayed himself gone — empty, wet rock, black dust. He wished the cave would swallow him whole. Instead, its safe dark turned against him, making him invisible, but not untouchable. The cold wall pressed against his back and into the palm of his left hand. In his right, he held his father's old knife, the one with the stag handle. He kept his head turned, his cheek plastered against the damp, staring hard at the black passageway for the sound of the footsteps.

He stilled his breath and tried unsuccessfully to quiet his heart, which had started pounding when he first heard someone entering the cave. How long ago was that? It felt like hours, or days, but must have been no more than a minute or two. At first he hadn't even heard the footsteps; he hadn't been listening. *Pay attention,* his father was always telling him, but Brian never could. There was always something else to do, or to think about. Like just then, before the footsteps arrived, when he had been reading his father's mail. The words from the stolen letter flew like shrapnel into Brian's brain, because he now understood why he and his brother weren't allowed to come to the cave anymore. He now understood, too late, why the footsteps.

They were hard and heavy, like a man's, and when he realized what he had been hearing, he had reached his hand far into his alcove, past the correspondence and other hidden treasures like his collection of odd-shaped pebbles, to the very back, where he grabbed onto the hilt of his father's knife. Now, the knife comforted his right hand, the wall secured his back, but still he faced danger in the dark passage. There was nowhere to hide. He was already hidden, or so he had thought. This cave was their secret. He and his brother had found it; no one knew about it — they had thought. But recently, they found out their father knew about their cave. And this wasn't his brother sneaking in through the entrance to the cave, down into the passage where Brian desperately wished himself gone.

"Fortunate that Aunt Evelyn doesn't know the truth, isn't it, Jean?" Bea asked, leaning against the open doorway of the woodshed and holding out her lantern light so that it could join Jean's atop the woodpile. "That this isn't much of a punishment."

"You won't say anything?" asked Jean. She was perched on a wide unsplit log, knees up to her chest, pulling spider webs from her fingers.

"Of course not. But she might be getting suspicious, you've been out here for hours."

"One hour. And a half, maybe."

"Alright. I think she's still trying to think up a better punishment, though. You shouldn't have done it, you know."

"I know."

"No, really, Jean. That Irish lace is extremely expensive."

"I know."

"What were you thinking putting the fish in the same basket as the lace? And the onions? When Aunt Evelyn had asked you to sort the baskets specifically so that wouldn't happen?"

"I don't know."

"You do, I think. I don't think you did it because you were upset about me not saying anything about the ghost ship." At this, Jean looked up quickly at Bea and then went back to her weaving. Bea couldn't see Jean's eyes very well because most of her face was in shadow but she knew that she was right. "It's because it's Billy McLeod's fish, is that right?" Jean didn't answer, but started spinning the web faster around her fingers, as if she herself was the spider. "It's not going to stop, you know. She likes him. You can't do anything about that. Well, I guess if you were really nasty and evil, you could."

"It's not that — that she likes him," said Jean.

"What, then?"

"It's that she's kissing him."

"So?"

"What do you mean, 'so?' She's *kissing* him, Bea."

Bea recognized the firm moral authority that she herself had felt at the age of ten. "Is it that she's kissing him or that she's not telling us she's kissing him? That they're courting?"

"That she's kissing him, of course."

"She shouldn't be?"

"People are going to find out. What will everyone think? It's not right. She's a married woman."

"No, she's not. She's a widow. Your dad's been dead six years. Is she never supposed to be courted by another man?" Jean didn't answer, but Bea realized that this conversation wasn't going to go anywhere. "You'd better get going with bringing in the wood, she's beginning to wonder what's taking you so long. That's why she sent me out here. She doesn't know your fascination with spiders like I do."

Jean nodded but didn't put the spider web down nor make any movement to get up. "Bea? What if this was where we lived?" she said, changing the subject suddenly, a habit that Bea found disconcerting.

"Where we lived? Here? In the wood shed?" Bea asked, and Jean nodded. Playing along, Bea looked around. Not bad, she thought. Lots of spider webs and spiders. Jean likes that. A perfect home. Jean was always telling Bea not to kill spiders, not to destroy their webs. Just then, Jean picked a spider off a piece of wood in her wood basket. She set it carefully down on the side of the woodpile. Lovingly. Like a mama spider.

Besides a plethora of wood and spiders, one corner of the shed was stacked with tools, most of them rusty. Many of them hadn't been used since Uncle Ian. Another home for the spiders. Food might be a bit scarce, Bea thought, unless we could live on a diet of fir chips and dead spiders. And we'd get cold. "It'd do," Bea said and a little smile played on Jean's lips. "Cozy. The spider webs make a nice addition, don't you think?"

"No. Really, Bea, stop joking. Can you imagine living in something this small? With only one little window that you can't even see out of?" Jean looked up to where the two sides of the roof came together, and Bea followed her gaze. Jean might imagine she saw windows, but they weren't there. The shed didn't have any windows. They left the door open for light.

"No. I can't imagine it, actually," Bea said. Jean picked up another spider that had settled nicely into its web on the wood. She let it go and it scurried under the woodpile. Bea selected a piece of fir from the top of the pile and put it into Jean's basket.

"Not too heavy," she said.

"I know," Bea said. She stopped filling the basket after the next piece. Even four small pieces were too much for Jean.

"Some people do," she said.

"Some people do what?"

"Live in little spaces like this."

"I suppose they do. Somewhere in the world. Even here, long ago, men used to live in little sheds called fish sheds, did you know that? Isn't that disgusting? Fish sheds? Can you imagine?"

"That's not what I meant."

"No, I didn't think it was," Bea said, and handed Jean a small piece of wood to put in the basket she'd brought.

"And what if you couldn't get out? Of here, your little room?"

"Why couldn't you get out?" Bea asked, almost not wanting to.

"Because of the lock."

"The lock?"

"The door's locked from the outside, did you know that?"

"No. No, Jean. I didn't. What are you talking about? What little room? What locked door?"

"I don't know," she said, and then she went on as if Bea hadn't spoken. "But what if, Bea?"

"What if what, Jean?" Bea asked, starting to feel spooked. It was getting harder to see inside the shed, despite their light. She worked faster. They were almost finished but they'd have to come back for a couple more loads. "Help me," she said.

Bea handed Jean a piece of wood and she stood there with it in her arms, like a baby. She stared at Bea with her large brown eyes. "What if you don't have anywhere to go to the toilet? That would be awful, Bea. Wouldn't that be awful?"

"Absolutely," Bea said, and kicked open the door with her foot. "Let's unload and come back for more. Maybe by the time we get back you'll be daydreaming about a palace instead of some dung-infested jail."

DAY FIVE
Saturday, October 18, 1902

At 2,000 fathoms down, Mildred was of no help to Bea. How could she be, when she was dying? As she tasted the salt water in her mouth and felt it fill her lungs, and as she struggled for air, she managed to think: do ghosts stay in the sea after they die? How terrible to end up forever under water with no air to breathe. What an awful thought.

She sat up straight and took a deep breath. She tried to focus, tried once again to look at the picture of the ship that Bea had laid out on the reading room table. She had always had a fear of deep water. "What are we looking for again, Bea?" she asked quietly, glancing at the foursome seated at the other large table in the reading room, their heads bent over their studies. When she got home last night, Mildred had tried to tell her family about her encounter with Brian. But neither Jean, nor Evelyn, nor Bea believed her story about seeing a ghost. Another age-related delusion, is no doubt what they thought. They had only smiled kindly and nodded, but refused to believe her. Mildred had finally given up in frustration. Let them believe what they wanted; she knew what she had seen — and he was with them right now at the library.

Brian had patiently smiled at the pictures in the book that Bea was looking through. "That's not the cable on the wall," he said to Bea when she flipped to a page of a cable ship, its cable wound in a massive coil on its deck. Mildred didn't fully understand why Bea was looking through the cable book. But Brian seemed to be enjoying himself. She knew by now that Brian had a fascination with cables and the cable ships, the very first ones in particular. The way he'd talked about it, you'd think he'd actually been on the ships. He hadn't, of course; he hadn't even been born. He revelled in the cable stories, so much so that he had made them his own. Mildred looked at Bea and wondered if she'd heard Brian's comment about the cable on the wall. Bea must have, because she turned to another page and then another, as she looked for what she had come to find. So often Bea's mind was leaps and bounds ahead of Mildred. She would often figure out an answer, before Mildred even knew there was a question.

Brian had sat across from Mildred, and she wondered if Bea noticed him. How could she not? The child willed you to him, and you went, whether you wanted to or not. A couple of times, Bea looked left, down the table at him, as if she sought something there — the resolution of a quandary, the answer to a feeling — but then she would resume looking through her book.

Brian stayed only a short time, and left. He smiled goodbye to Mildred and Bea, and then lingered in the doorway of the reading room as if he wanted to stay but couldn't. Mildred waved goodbye to him, and he waved back; a small wave, bereft of energy.

"Need to see the size of the cable," Bea answered, finally, in response to Mildred's earlier question. But she had not spoken nearly as quietly as Mildred, and the four young women and men at the adjacent table looked up as one and scowled. Bea didn't notice. She was closely examining the etching, but then she shook her head and turned to the next page. Mildred placed the tip of her forefinger on the open page of the book and tried to concentrate. She had agreed to help, although she was still baffled by the object of the exercise as she stared at the picture showing a disaster at sea: the transatlantic cable falling off the stern of a ship and into the sea. The sight made her sick. Not because of the cable, the loss of over 300 miles of it, Bea had said. "The first attempt to lay the cable," she had tried to explain to Mildred. Frankly, she didn't understand Bea's fascination with the story. For some reason, Bea found the whole transatlantic affair enthralling. No, for Mildred, it was the thought of being that far out at sea that was nauseating. Sometime, when she was much younger, she must have crossed the ocean to get from Scotland to here. How else would she have come? The trip would have taken three or four months, a quarter to a third of an entire year, yet she had no memory of it. She was too small. She remembered, though, always having a fear of water. She had never liked water above the waist. She could wade in that far, and had done so many times, but not for years and years. Not since Samuel. Her husband would trick her into the sea, and tackle her in the very shallow waters. He never scared her, though, and she liked the thought of him now, of his hands firmly gripping her waist as he lifted her out of the water. She glanced nervously at Bea to see if she noticed her blushing, but Bea's head was still bent over the book as she read the fine print below. Bea shook her head, and turned to the next page. The picture on this page showed what looked like a length of iron cord, or rope. Apparently this was what she had been looking for because at the sight of it, she stood straight up and clapped her hands, inviting a loud collective "Sshh," from the foursome.

"I found it. I knew I was right," Bea said and slammed the book shut. She grinned at the foursome and at the librarian, Miss O'Flaherty, then grabbed her coat and ran out the big heavy doors of the building into the bright sunshine and clear blue sky.

...---...

"*Which part of France?*" Eliza read aloud from the kitchen table. She had taken the letter from Bea, but then had left her standing outside in the hallway. She hadn't invited her in. Bea had been surprised, she could see it in her eyes — at first so welcoming and friendly, and then shrouded by something that Eliza could only interpret as hurt. No doubt Bea imagined their camaraderie at Shulman's the other day as the beginning of a new friendship. But Eliza didn't have friendships. She couldn't.

So she had closed the door almost all the way, leaving it open a half-inch, no more. It didn't really matter. Bea had already seen most of the foyer the other day, including Mother's telegraph machine, which sat on a side table inside the door.

"Does that work, Miss?" Bea had asked just now as Eliza was closing the door.

"That old thing?" asked Eliza, following Bea's precocious gaze. "Hasn't worked in years. Why?"

"No reason," said Bea. "I was just wondering."

Eliza had gazed a second longer into Bea's eyes to see if she was lying, then headed down to the kitchen. On her way she stopped and stared at the inert machine for several seconds as if waiting for it to talk — she fully expected it to — then she forced herself to proceed without glancing back. She desperately wanted to throw it out, no matter how badly her father wanted to keep it: it reminded him of Mother, he said. But it frightened Eliza, and she was certain he knew as much and didn't care. She had been trying so hard to keep her father as happy as was possible these days, and so she would continue to try to cope with the machine.

She sat down at the kitchen table and opened the letter, still refusing to look at the telegraph machine. Her mother had owned it for years and had been happiest when she was sending messages. "Who are you speaking to?" Eliza had asked her repeatedly, but she hadn't replied. She would only shake her head, and rapidly tap out phrases with the key. Seconds later, the machine would respond, always too fast for Eliza to know what it said, but her mother would smile to herself and answer. Eliza didn't know at first if she had one friend or ten who received these messages. The thought of her mother having friends at all was inconceivable.

She hadn't thought too much of it when her mother had come home first with the Morse code instruction manual and, soon after, a learner's telegraph machine. She had thought it humorous, and later had even been mildly impressed with her skill. Her only question had been: "Where did you get the money?" Her mother had looked sly, but she so often did, and she hadn't answered; it wasn't until much later that Eliza realized where the money had come from.

She sat at the table and read over the letter, and despite the door being open only a crack, she could *feel* the girl trying to get a look at the other telegraph relic in the hallway, hanging on the wall. Her father had put both relics in the hallway, as if setting up his own private cable and telegraph museum.

Which part of France? Eliza read again, trying to concentrate on the matter at hand: the response from Penelope.

"What'cha got there?" her father's voice surprised her from the kitchen doorway.

"Papa. Don't sneak up on me like that," she said, turning around to see him standing in the doorway, his box of letters clutched in his hands. She laid her forearm over the letter on the table as she spun to face him. "It's nothing," she replied to his question.

"Not nothing, Eliza. I can see it from here. Someone sent you a letter. Who's sending you letters?"

"No one you know," she said, raising her voice even more so that Bea would be sure to hear. She turned back around to face the table. "Papa, let's have tea, would you like that? Would you mind closing the front door while I make it? Tell Bea she can wait. I won't be long."

He huffed, but turned and limped down the hallway. Bea will probably start running for her life right about now, Eliza thought as she put on the kettle, but she didn't hear the sound of retreating footsteps quite yet, only his cane knocking the wooden floor, and then the creak of the door as he opened it and bellowed, "What's wrong? Think you seen a ghost?"

"No, sir," Bea stuttered.

"She says you're to wait," he said, and as he started to close the door, Eliza bent over the letter again, expecting that would be the last of it. But then she heard the most startling thing:

"If you don't mind, sir," she began to say to him. Bea was actually going to start up a conversation with Eliza's father. Nobody ever did that. Nobody would dare.

"What?" Papa said. He was as shocked as Eliza was.

"The cable on your wall. From '57?" Bea asked boldly.

"Yeah," he said after a few seconds, and she imagined that they were both looking at the cable. In its glass case bolted to the wall, it wound itself like a snake the thickness of a man's forefinger in and amongst ten round pegs and several hooks. Then Eliza realized by the sound of his voice that he was smiling. It was a moment she absolutely hated to witness, and if this didn't drive Bea to silence, she didn't know what would. His smile, if that's what it could be called, started in the corner of his mouth and unzipped slowly across his cracked lips, revealing pale gums and three stained teeth left standing.

But Bea held her ground, even as he barked, "How on earth do you know the year?"

This was getting to be even more interesting than the letter before her, and without turning around, Eliza listened intently to the conversation.

"Iron sheathing," Bea began to reply, and even though her voice was shaky, Eliza admired her pluck. Bea went on: "Not steel. Steel came later, after '58." Her father didn't say anything. "And the size of it, of course. Smaller around than the later ones," she added, and this time her voice had more depth and power, and she sounded slightly stronger.

"Yeah. But it could've been the 1858 cable, couldn't it?"

"Yes," Bea said weakly.

Eliza reached behind her to the counter for her pen and called: "Papa? What are you doing? Your tea's almost ready. Leave the poor child alone." She placed the pen and ink on the table, then dipped her pen into the well and poised it over the paper. She still didn't know how to reply to Penelope.

"None of your business what I'm doing, is it?" he called back.

Eliza made a decision, and quickly wrote two words on the letter. She got up from the table and strode over to the doorway. "Here you go, Bea," she said, smiling and handing her the envelope into which she had placed the letter.

"We're talking," said her father.

"She'll be back, Papa," said Eliza, shutting the door on Bea.

. . . ⋅---⋅ . . .

"*The south?*" Mrs. Stevens gasped when she read the reply. "Hold on a minute, Bea." She left Bea sitting in a chair in the hallway with her coat on while she went into the parlour at the front of the house.

. . . ⋅---⋅ . . .

"You worked for the company that constructed the cable?" asked Bea.

"Damn right."

"Father," Eliza admonished from the kitchen. "Please."

"Don't need you telling me what to say, do I?"

Eliza wasn't sure how she should answer Penelope's latest question: *Near the Italian border or the Spanish border?*

"Which company, sir? Glass, Elliot and Company? Or R.S. Newall?" Bea's question was directed toward Eliza's father, and again Eliza could hardly believe how forthright she was being.

"Glass and Elliot," he answered. "Well, com'on in, for heaven's sake, take a look if ya want. Since ya know so much. Might as well take a gander — that glass thing opens up. And close that damn door. Too damn cold."

"No, Papa," said Eliza, swivelling around in her chair.

"Don't get yourself all twisted this way and that, Eliza. I'm just letting her into the hall for crickey's sake."

"Papa."

"Eliza, stop your nonsense. I swear."

"Just don't let her go anywhere else," she mumbled, and she watched while Bea walked through the front door, which her father shut behind her. It's just the front hall, she reminded herself. Nothing was in the front hall except the cable, a small chair, the side table on which sat the silly telegraph machine, and the coat rack. That was it. No bad can really happen in the front hall. She turned back to the letter.

Eliza thought about what to write. She blocked out the sound of the voices chattering about the transatlantic cable, though every now and then she'd hear her father; it was hard to ignore him, especially now that his hearing was bad and he talked so loudly. "Twelve feet of it," he was saying. "Got it after the '57 run, but you already know that. From the last nautical mile. I made it. Was mine. They gave it to me as a going-away present."

"When you retired?"

"Never retired. Didn't quit, neither. It's all Judson Stevens' fault. It's all in here, every word of it," he said, and he tapped at his box that he was still carrying around with him. "I got the truth about what happened. Everything, right in here," he said, banging on the box again. "In my little red box."

"*Agamemnon*, sir?"

"What'zat?"

"*Agamemnon*. The ship inscribed on the box."

"I suppose. Might be *Niagara*. Forget. Can't see it anymore. What's it to you, anyhow? What do you care about my box?"

"I don't, sir."

"Yer lying."

"Honestly, sir."

"They all lied, too. Every one of 'em. My foreman. Judson. Foreman said when they fired me it had nothing to do with '57. 'What're you talking about, Cyrus?' he says to me. 'Us letting you go has nothing to do with the cable breaking. You had nothing to do with that. No, Cyrus, that's not the reason.' What a liar. I told you about the cable breaking, didn't I?"

"I don't believe you did, sir."

"Well, no one believed me when I told them it was Judson, not me; whadda they call you?"

"Pardon?"

"Your name, goddammit."

"It's Bea, Papa," called Eliza.

"Bea, sir. Bea MacDonald," said Bea.

"Bea. What kind of a name is that? Beatrice, is it?"

"No, sir. Never Beatrice. Just Bea."

"Fine. Have it the way you want it. Bea. Do you know what my foreman said when I came back to get that piece of cable?"

"No, sir."

"Told me to leave."

"He did?"

"You bet. All I was doing was coming back to the shop to get my cable. I told him that that bit of cable's what I'd come back for, that that's all I wanted then I would leave, he rolled his eyes and said 'what the hell,' and he chopped off this bit. Tried to throw it at me across the yard, but he wasn't good enough and it landed in one of the rounds of cable that they'd just dragged out of the factory and started to coil. They'd all been standing around staring at me when I had marched in through the back gate. After it landed in the coil, I went to climb over to get my piece, my little souvenir, but one of the men got to it first and tossed it at another fellow. They tossed it around for a bit. Hated me, they did. Never wanted me near cable again. Couldn't get much work after that."

"Why was that, sir?"

"Don't you know? I told you about the cable breaking, didn't I?"

"I don't believe you did, Papa, and she doesn't need to hear about it," called Eliza from the kitchen. The older he got, the more he would tell his cable story to anyone who would listen.

"What'zat? What'd you say?"

"I was saying, Papa . . . "

"Not you, her. What'd you say?"

"I said that you had dropped something, sir. But then I realized I was mistaken. It was nothing."

"You sure?" her father asked, and Eliza looked just in time to see Bea putting her hand into her pocket.

"*Did* he drop something?" she asked.

"No, Miss Norton."

"I thought I saw you put something in your pocket," said Eliza, joining Bea and her father in the hallway.

"No, Miss," Bea said again, and she pulled out the lining of her pocket to show her. It was empty. Eliza nodded as her father said,

"You're seeing things, Eliza. Time you went anyhow — whadda they call you? Gotta have my tea."

"Just a minute, Papa," Eliza said as she walked Bea to the front door. "Wait out here, Bea . . . "

"That's it — Bea — what kinda name is that . . . " he said.

"I won't be long," continued Eliza. This time, she shut the door tight on Bea. "Come, Papa," she whispered, taking her father's elbow and leading him toward the kitchen.

Several minutes later, she opened the door, but didn't hand Bea the letter. "I think I will drop by for a visit to Mrs. Stevens, Bea, so you needn't bother returning the note. But I have more mending for your aunt, if you don't mind taking it." She handed it to Bea and then laid her hand upon her arm. "Are you certain you didn't find something in here, Bea? Something that's not yours?"

"I'm certain, Miss Norton."

"Well, goodbye for now, then. I think this will be all the running back and forth for today."

"It's delightful to be here, I must say, Mrs. Stevens. You have a tranquil home. Much more so than mine," said Eliza.

"Please call me Penelope." She was again struck by Eliza's defenceless nature. Seeing her up close like this, Penelope realized that her skin was almost translucent. It seemed that the woman's vitality had been extracted, and she supposed it had: Cyrus Norton would suck the vigour out of anybody. She couldn't imagine being his nursemaid and housemate, and daughter, no less.

"Penelope," said Eliza, setting her teacup down on the small table beside her. They were seated in Penelope's parlour: Eliza in the armchair, and Penelope in the loveseat by the window. "I thought it best we talk in person rather than sending notes back and forth."

Penelope nodded. "I agree, Eliza. I'm glad you came by. More tea?"

"Thank you," said Eliza, holding out her cup and saucer. Penelope poured the tea and noticed that Eliza's hand was shaking. Eliza didn't remark on it — perhaps she was always this way and had grown used to it — but added, "You have been asking about France."

"Yes."

"You don't need to tell me why you want to know, but you seemed to think that France might have something to do with the blackmail my father is threatening."

"Yes. That is so."

"I can't answer that, I'm afraid. He doesn't confide his plans in me. I'm sure he knows that I would oppose them. I wish I could prevent him from carrying through with such nefarious activity, but he will not listen to me, as you might have noticed."

Penelope nodded as Eliza continued. "I do wish you and I had begun this small correspondence under better circumstances, and that this business of blackmail and murder had nothing at all to do with it, because . . . " she lowered her eyes and then raised them again to meet Penelope's. Penelope saw that she was blushing. "In fact, I was thrilled that you had initiated a conversation with me, Penelope. I have not had many friends, and it's a relief to talk with someone other than my father. That's no one's fault but my own, I know. I am just not one to initiate relationships with people."

"You are not in the easiest of circumstances to do so, Eliza."

"Yes, but one can't continue to blame one's situation on others. Can one?"

"No, I suppose not," said Penelope. "Still . . . "

"In any case," Eliza said, setting down her teacup. "I didn't come to complain to you about my life. I came to tell you about this." She pulled from her pocket pieces of paper that seemed to have been torn from a book. She looked at them and then at Penelope. "Other than what I've already mentioned about France, the only other article in my possession is this entry of my mother's from when they took their trip to France."

"Your parents went there together?"

"Yes. Eight or nine years ago, when they were both well. Mother had received a small inheritance and, for once — possibly the only time that I can remember — she got her way and insisted on a trip abroad.

She had never been, and she wanted to go before she was too old. I'm glad she got her way; she so seldom did, although I don't know that the trip ended up meeting with her satisfaction." She took a sip of her tea and went on. Penelope was dying to know what was written on the pieces of paper. "She kept a diary, and she took it with her on that trip, though I don't know why she bothered. She so seldom wrote in it. I looked for it after Bea had brought by your last note. I wanted to see if there was anything else that I could tell you. Unfortunately, I only found four entries on the entire trip to France. And they are all of Paris, and so they might not have any bearing on what you would like to know. There is nothing in here about the south of France, which was one of your questions. I know they went to the south, since Father later mentioned it, but Mother wrote nothing of it in her diary. Of the four entries on Paris, one was an entire page on the Champs Élysées. And another on the Eiffel Tower. These sketches of Paris are tedious, to say the least, and I wouldn't bore you by reading them to you. I did bring the other two entries, although they are equally dull."

"You tore them from the diary."

"Yes. It doesn't matter to Mother anymore, I'm sure. I'll read the first one to you if you would like, although I'm sure it's of no significance. Still, they're all I could find."

Penelope nodded, and Eliza took a sip of her tea and began:

"'Cyrus and I had coffee on a small street somewhere near our hotel when the most wonderful thing happened. I had just been reflecting on how much I missed England, when who should come along and sit next to us but an Englishwoman. She was trying to give her order for a good cup of tea — they understand nothing of tea here — and I can't tell you how thrilled I was to hear a good English accent. We invited her to share our table, which she did. It was such a relief to meet a fine Englishwoman. It's getting so tiresome being around all these French people. She felt likewise, and we had a delightful conversation and then we went off together to see that very tall building.'"

"I assume she means the Eiffel Tower."

"Yes. The Eiffel Tower is her next entry. Would you like me to read the last entry?"

"Yes. Please."

"'Freda Murphy — that's our new English friend — and Cyrus went to tour graveyards. I have no interest in such things and declined going because I am feeling poorly today. My back. I have stayed in the hotel to rest. What I wouldn't give for a good cup of tea!'"

It took all of Penelope's will to replace her teacup on the table without having her hand tremble, and then to make small talk with the enervated Eliza Norton until she took her leave.

...---...

After Eliza had left, Penelope went to her desk and looked again at the letter that had arrived in the morning post. She had not mentioned it to Eliza; the woman already carried enough of a burden. It had been addressed simply to 'Stevens,' so she had opened it. The handwriting was better than she would have expected for a man Mr. Norton's age:

Stevens,

Done enough thinking? I'm looking forward to my money. I expect to hear from you before the week is out. Nice son you got.

C. N. Norton.

That cryptic sentence was all the proof she needed to know that Cyrus had attacked George. She had been sure that the attack on George had been connected to the blackmailing. A taste of what was to come, she supposed, should they not follow through on Cyrus's demands.

She stared hard at the words for several more minutes, then got up and strode over to the drapes. She gazed out the window at the autumn-red maple in the front yard and the evergreen hedge beyond. The situation was worse than she had thought. She now had no doubt that he knew about the body that she had buried. Not only had Cyrus been in France, he had met Freda Murphy. The woman must have told him Penelope's secret, as had been told to her by Penelope's mother.

She kept glancing over at the desk. Something else about the note bothered her besides its threat. She walked out of the parlour and into the kitchen, put on an apron, dragged a canister across the counter and dumped a pile of flour onto the large wooden board, then spooned on some salt. With a force of will, she kept her store of bad memories from careening into her mind. She heated water in a bowl on the stove until it was room temperature, added the yeast and the sugar, and set it aside. When the yeast had bubbled to the surface, she slowly poured the mixture over the flour and worked the dough with her hands, adding more and more flour until she had a lovely smooth round that she kneaded professionally: wrapping and pushing down, turning, wrapping and pushing down. The bread-making became meditative, and for the first time in several days, she felt her mind open and reorganize events, feelings, and thoughts into a kind of order. Suddenly she had it. She knew what was wrong with the note. Wiping her hands on her apron, and trailing flour dust and bits of dough in her wake, she ran through the kitchen into the parlour, and with white hands, picked up the letter. She stared at it for a moment, then laid it back down on the desk, and took her magnifying glass out of the drawer. A closer look at the words told her what she had suspected. She had never seen Cyrus Norton's handwriting before, but the reason this handwriting bothered her was that it looked so familiar. It could almost have been penned by Henry.

...---...

"Miss MacDonald, we received the blue enamel earlier today. Do you think you might get an opportunity to unpack it before you leave?" asked Mr. Shulman, without looking up from his ledger.

"Certainly, Mr. Shulman," said Bea as she handed old Mr. Mews his groceries, then walked around the counter to open the front door for him. As he was heading out, Natty's father was heading in.

"Come to get me salt water taffy, Bea," Angus Cooke pronounced in a loud voice, before reaching under his jacket and adjusting the waist of his trousers, as if trying to keep them from falling around his feet.

"I didn't think you ever ate it. Natty loves it, but I didn't think you could eat it," said Bea. He didn't answer her. "Your teeth don't bother you, then?"

"Ya want to sell it to me or not?"

"Oh, no, I'll sell it to you, Mr. Cooke. How much would you like?" she asked, going around the counter, and taking the canister of taffy from the shelf.

"A pound, she . . . a pound'll do me fine."

"A pound it is," Bea said, scooping the taffy into a bag, and weighing it. "On your account, sir?" Bea asked, glancing over at Mr. Shulman, who nodded his assent. Mr. Cooke had not settled last year's account, nor this year's.

"Aye," said Mr. Cooke, grabbing his bag of taffy and striding to the front door. When he reached it, little Angie Buckley was about to come in. He made a gentlemanly display of opening the door wide for her, and then, giving her a small bow, he waltzed out the door.

By the light of the lamp on her desk, Bea copied the words from the scrap of paper onto another piece of paper. She'd forgotten all about the note that she'd found at the Nortons' until just now. What had come over her? Why had she taken it? Without thinking, she had just grabbed it off the floor where Mr. Norton had dropped it, and then she had shoved it into her pocket. Luckily, it was the pocket with the hole so that when Miss Norton asked her about it, she had reached in, and poked the paper into the lining of the coat. She carefully pinched together the hole and withdrew the empty pocket lining. Her coat lining was sewn up along the hem, so she knew the paper wouldn't fall out. Tonight she'd worked the piece of paper back up through the lining and in through the hole of the pocket.

"What are you doing?" asked Jean, getting off the bed and walking barefoot to the far side of their attic room, her long nightgown dragging on the wooden floor. Bea shoved the original into her pocket just as Jean bent over her cousin's shoulder and read what Bea had just written:

June 30, 1900

Dear Sir,

Thank you for your condolences.

Sincerely, HFS

"Maybe you'll know," said Bea after a moment, shoving back her chair so Jean could climb onto her lap.

"Know what?"

Bea didn't answer but took the note from her pocket, examined the information running vertically along the left-hand side of the page, and then copied the information onto her paper. In this case, there were no more words to write — only single characters: *b, g, j, k, m, p, q, 't.'*

"What're those?" asked Jean.

"Well, that's just it, it's awfully odd. I don't know, but it's nagging at me. The thank-you note seems straightforward enough, but why all the single letters? Why were these separate characters lined up on the side of the page like this? Do you know, Jeannie? They're all written on the left-hand side of the letter, just like how I've done it here."

Jean shifted her position on Bea's lap and bent over the desk, the ends of her fine black hair brushing the paper. After several minutes of looking at the letter, she said, "I don't know, Bea."

"Neither do I."

"Why is the *t* in those tiny things, Bea?"

"Inverted commas?"

"Yeah."

"That's one of the things that confuses me. I wish I knew. This is making me crazy. I've been trying to figure it out." They heard someone at the door to their bedroom, and turned around.

"It's just me, girls," said Mildred, going over to sit in her rocking chair.

Bea and Jean nodded, then they leaned over the desk again, intent on their task. Finally, Bea said,

"Jean?"

"Yes, Bea?"

"I think I know the answer. At first I wasn't sure. But this is it, I think." Bea smoothed the paper from the Nortons' on the desk. "See where the letter's been ripped along the bottom?"

"Unh-huh. Why does that matter though?"

"I think some of the characters are missing, and they would have been in the part that was ripped off."

"Alright . . . " said Jean with some hesitation.

Underneath the eight letters — *b, g, j, k, m, p, q, 't'* — that Bea had already written, she now wrote four more: *x, z, v, w.* "All twelve characters are the ones missing."

"Pardon me?" asked Mildred and Jean in unison. Mildred had not made it as far as her rocker, but had been distracted by the goings-on at the desk. She leaned between the two girls, and peered at the note.

"The ones not in the thank-you note. The letters here," Bea said, pointing to the single ones on the side of the page, "are all the ones not in here," she added, pointing to the correspondence itself. She read the correspondence aloud:

June 30, 1900.

Dear Sir,

Thank you for your condolences.

Sincerely, HFS

"You see, every other letter of the alphabet is in the thank-you note. But the single ones on the side of the page, as well as the ones I've just written, are the letters of the alphabet that are *not* in the thank-you note. In the correspondence from *HFS,* there are no *b*'s or *j*'s or *k*'s or any of the other letters from the side of the page," continued Bea. "Do you understand what I mean?" Mildred nodded. She finally understood what Bea was getting at, but she didn't know why it mattered.

Jean thought for another moment, and finally replied, "I think so, Bea. But what about the *t?* There's a *t* in the 'Thank you.'"

"I know. That was really confusing me, Jean. But I think — it's there but it's in a capital letter. All the other ones are in small letters."

"Oh, I see," Jean and Mildred said, without conviction.

"But why would someone want to get all the letters of the alphabet? Why would someone care which ones are missing, I wonder?" Bea asked. She was posing the questions more to herself than to the others. "What would someone do with the information? What would Mr. Norton do with the information?" Just as she finished questioning herself, someone knocked loudly at the front door.

"Who would be coming this late at night?" Mildred asked, going to the doorway of the attic. "You two stay here," she whispered over her shoulder as she headed down the stairs.

Evelyn had cracked the door slightly. "Miss Norton," she said, swinging it open wide. From behind her, Mildred could hear Bea gasp. "What on earth brings you up here at this hour?" The girls had run up behind Mildred, and now Bea stepped further back into the shadows at the top of the stairs.

"I'm so sorry, Mrs. MacDonald. Have I disturbed you?"

"Not at all. Please. Come in. Here, let me take your hat and coat."

Miss Norton had been clutching a cloth bag and her pocketbook. She laid both temporarily on the side table just inside the door while she removed her grey hat and coat. After the garments had been hung, Evelyn guided Miss Norton down the hall toward the kitchen. "Come in. A cup of tea?"

"I don't want to put you to any trouble."

"None at all. Here, sit down, excuse the mess, I'll make us a pot."

Mildred and the girls followed behind, and now all three of them stood in the hallway just back from the doorway of the kitchen. Evelyn pulled out a chair for Miss Norton at the big kitchen table. Tonight, a bolt of rich loden velvet lay over much of the surface, and scattered about were pattern pieces for Mrs. Eve's dress, as well as two pairs of scissors and the loden green thread — a hard colour to match; Evelyn had had to send away to Canada for it. Evelyn shoved aside pattern pieces to make some space at the end of the table where Miss Norton sat, pulled up a chair for herself, and returned to the counter to pour water from the steaming pot that was always ready on the stove. As she did so, she threw Mildred and the girls a glance, as if to say, this is none of your business, upstairs with you. They pretended not to notice the look, but stepped further back into the shadows.

Evelyn made up a tray with tea, milk, sugar, and two slices of fresh pound cake and set it on the table. She took the cups and saucers from the cupboard. She only ever brought these out for special people. The china was the best. It wasn't for just anyone.

"Lovely," said Miss Norton, glancing at the tea service. She reached a hand up to her blond hair and folded a strand behind her ear. The action made her appear even more vulnerable. Evelyn seemed suddenly self-conscious of her own looks, and her hand fled of its own accord to her head, but what it found there was the antithesis of Miss Norton's fine coiffure. Mildred noticed that sometime during the evening, while the three of them had been upstairs, Evelyn had attempted to lasso her thick brown mop with a remnant of the loden velvet. It was of no use. She had cut her hair several days before, and now there was not enough of it to make a tail, and what there was would not be fettered. Bold strands shot sideways and upwards from the cord that had long given up the struggle.

Evelyn's work-worn hand dropped to her lap. "Now tell me," she said. "What brings you here?"

"It's nothing, really, but today I had meant to give a second item to your niece to be mended," said Miss Norton, glancing into the hallway at Mildred. And it's mending that can't wait until morning, wondered Mildred. Nevertheless, Mildred smiled back and then shot a look behind at Bea. One would think Miss Norton knows you've been up there reading that letter, Bea. As if hearing Mildred's thoughts, Bea stepped back a few paces. Miss Norton reached into her sack, and said, "It was lovely to have the pleasure of seeing your niece again today, Mrs. MacDonald. Charming young lady."

"Yes she is."

"She came by on errands for Mrs. Stevens, did she tell you?"

"No, she didn't," said Evelyn, going around the side of the table to find the first item that Miss Norton had sent home with Bea.

"She talked to Papa about his cable. It was really quite wonderful for him. He was thrilled. He loves talking about those days. You'd think he'd laid the whole thing himself, the way he goes on. He'd be happy to have her come by again anytime. So would I; it would save me from having to try to make conversation with him all by myself," she finished, and gazed into the hallway right at Bea even though she wasn't visible in the dark.

"Well, yes, my Bea certainly is fascinated with anything to do with telegraphs."

"It certainly seems that way. And by the way, I'm missing a piece of correspondence. I'm wondering if it got mixed up with the other correspondence Bea was delivering for me from Mrs. Stevens. Do you mind if we ask Bea if she saw it?"

"Not at all," said Evelyn, but as she was about to call out for Bea, Mildred swept into the room and said to Evelyn: "The girls are just about asleep, Evelyn. We'll ask Bea about it tomorrow."

Evelyn hesitated, and turning back, said, "It'll have to be tomorrow,

I'm afraid. I believe the girls are sleeping."

"Are they?" she answered, peering into the hallway.

"Yes. Now, show me what else you brought. Did you still want this garment mended as well?" Evelyn said, nodding at the green bed jacket, which she had already laid out on the table since she had green going. She had already taken its measurements and written them down. All the buttons were sewn tight, and the seams were intact, except for a tear that had opened up along the back seam.

"Oh yes, but you can take your time with that old thing."

"It won't take me a minute. I could do it while we're sitting here, in fact. You know, this doesn't even look to be your size," said Evelyn.

"I lost a few stone when I was quite ill several years ago. You wouldn't even know I was the same person. People didn't, you know. I don't even know why I hang on to that bed jacket. I really ought to give it away."

"It is lovely. This silk is exquisite. Would you like me to fix it now?"

Miss Norton shrugged, and then said, "No, please, don't bother. I'll need to go soon — I can't leave Father alone for so long. If you wouldn't mind taking a look at this, however," she said, pulling a bundle of navy blue cotton from her cloth bag. "This blouse is my favourite."

Mildred walked over to the other side of the table from Evelyn, and took a seat beside Miss Norton. "Hello, I'm Mildred," she said as Miss Norton looked at her. "I won't have any tea, Evelyn, thank you." Evelyn smiled and returned her attention to the fabric that Miss Norton held out. She took it from Miss Norton's hands and laid it out before her on the table, shoving more of the loden velvet out of the way.

"I hope it can be repaired," said Miss Norton.

Mildred and Evelyn exchanged glances. If this was a blouse, then it was almost unrecognizable. The garment had been violated. Its bodice was ripped down the front, the fine tie loops shredded. One sleeve was torn almost off the body, its lace cuff still absurdly pretty and untouched. The other sleeve's shoulder seam gaped open, and the lace cuff at the wrist was mangled.

"Who did this?" they asked in unison.

"Not a particularly nice person," Miss Norton said and then looked away, her eyes scanning the kitchen as if she was taking in every detail of it, her mind far away from the damaged garment.

"Would you like to tell us?" asked Evelyn softly.

Miss Norton shook her head.

"But tell me, Miss Norton, you must be in some kind of danger, are you not? I should think so, from the looks of this."

"Are you ever afraid to go home?" Miss Norton asked suddenly, in way of reply to Evelyn's question, and she turned her aqua-blue eyes on Mildred and then on Evelyn.

Evelyn sat back down on her chair and poured them each a cup of tea, giving herself time to answer. "No, can't say I am. I've been afraid many times, but not of my own home, no."

"I am."

"I see."

"Every time I walk in the door. I don't know what's coming."

"Like this," Evelyn said, nodding at the blouse. They each took a sip of tea and set their cups simultaneously on the saucers.

Miss Norton shrugged. "No. Yes. I don't know." She paused and looked around the table and then gazed again into Evelyn's eyes. Her eyes were unnerving. "I'd rather not talk about it. I've learned to cope."

"Never mind," Evelyn said softly after a moment, when she realized that Miss Norton wasn't going to say more. Evelyn touched the tabletop as if reaching for Miss Norton's hand. "You needn't say any more about it. But the blouse is irreparable, Miss Norton."

"She can order it from the catalogue, Evelyn," Mildred interrupted. "It's in the catalogue, I saw it just the other day, in fact. I recognize the lace and the colour."

Evelyn nodded and said: "I think we can find the exact same thing in the catalogue. We can write up an order tonight. Let's take a look." She pushed back her chair and strode over to the bookshelf.

"Second shelf from the bottom," said Mildred from her chair, as Evelyn searched the shelves for the book. She pointed in the direction of the catalogue, but Evelyn didn't see her. Evelyn turned and smiled at Miss Norton.

"Bea just puts her things away any old way. Jean, of course, is much better." She looked toward the hallway, where Bea and Jean were still standing. They had been completely silent, but could hear every word.

"Still can't find it, Evelyn? You need me, obviously," Mildred said, rising from her chair. "Right here," she said when she got over to her. She pointed to the catalogue hidden between a dozen or so of Bea's old scribblers.

"Ah, see it now. If it were a snake, it would have bit me," Evelyn said, grabbing the catalogue from the shelf. The tower of scribblers fell to the floor, but she just left them where they landed and brought the catalogue back to the table, setting it down in front of Miss Norton. She moved the tea tray, with its untouched cake, back to the kitchen counter.

Mildred and Evelyn stood on either side of Miss Norton while Evelyn reached down and started to flip through the pages.

"Is that it?" Evelyn asked when she got to page 1172.

"No, I don't think so," Miss Norton said, staring at the blouses on the page.

"Did you order from this catalogue?"

"To be honest, I can't remember where I got it."

Mildred and Evelyn exchanged glances again. They knew every garment in the house; hand-me-downs for the children, or their own made from ends of fabrics and, rarely, items like these that they ordered from the catalogue. That was always a big event, the catalogue order. How could you forget such a thing? Evelyn turned back a page.

"There it is. Yes," said Miss Norton. "That's it, the exact same one. Oh, thank goodness, it was my favourite piece." It did look identical. "Alright," she said. "I'll order a new one."

"Good, that makes sense," said Evelyn. She leaned over and grabbed one of Jean's charcoals and a piece of paper. "Alright, let's see: your size. Let's start with your bust measurement?"

"Thirty-eight?"

Evelyn's hand hesitated for a few seconds over the paper. Finally, she wrote down the number and said, "Of course. And your waist?"

"Twenty-nine, I believe."

"Yes, I'd say that would be right," Evelyn said. She couldn't find her measuring stick, so with a string she figured a few more of Miss Norton's measurements — arms, back and neck — then stood up and said, "Well, that's that, then. The blouse should arrive in no time."

Miss Norton rose from her seat. "I'd best be off, then. Thank you, Mrs. MacDonald."

"No trouble at all."

"Say hello to Bea for me."

"I will. Thank you for coming," Evelyn said, as she ushered her out the door. "Take good care of yourself, now."

"What's wrong, Mum?" asked Jean as she took a seat at one end of the table and Bea, a seat at the other. Mildred and Evelyn were sitting at opposite sides of the table, fingering the green bed jacket, when the girls came in.

"Should have noticed it right away. It's so obvious," muttered Evelyn.

"Notice what?" asked Mildred.

"I saw it, I just didn't know I saw it," she said glancing up at the girls.

They nodded, but Bea said, "Aunt Evelyn. What are you talking about?"

Evelyn shook her head and turned the garment inside out. "See those seams?" They all looked where she was pointing: at the seam down the middle of the back, and then at the left shoulder seam. "Do you see what I see?" Nobody answered, because they didn't know what she meant. "These seams have been re-stitched, by hand, but not particularly well. They're different from the other ones, see what I mean?" She showed them a few of the other seams, and now they all nodded. The other seams were far neater, and professionally sewn. A different colour of green thread had also been used. "This garment had also been torn, girls. Not as badly as that," she said, nodding at the navy blue mess that still lay on her sewing table. "But badly enough. The entire back had been ripped down the middle, and a sleeve torn off. I think those are new buttons, as well. Yes, they are. Whatever violence is being done to Eliza now, was being done to her then, when she had lost all that weight. No wonder she had lost weight! I'm surprised she could put it back on again. Bea?"

"Yes, Aunt Evelyn."

"Do you think it could be her father who's doing this to her?"

"Oh, it could be, Aunt Evelyn. He's a horrible man. Although, he's so old now, I don't know if he'd be able to do that," she said, indicating the navy blouse.

"It must be him. She needs our help; why else would she have come up here to see us? She knows that blouse is irreparable. How could she not? No, girls, I think she was here hoping we'd help her, without actually coming out and saying it. The Nortons haven't been here all that long, have they? When did they arrive? This year? Last year?"

"Early this year, I think," mumbled Bea.

"I don't know if she has any friends to call on. She seems to like you, Bea. I should find a way to see how we can help. It's not right, it just isn't." Bea looked guilt-stricken as Evelyn finished talking and turned the bed jacket right-side out, then smoothed it out on the table. Well she might; the note that Bea had stolen weighed even more heavily now. Evelyn folded one sleeve over the front, and was about to fold over the other one when she asked, "How much weight did the poor woman say she had lost?"

"A few stone."

"That's a tremendous amount — even for a woman her size. Forty-two pounds. Unless she was just generalizing. But even if she lost thirty pounds, that's still a lot. Well, that would explain the difference in size," she said, holding the two side seams of the bed jacket. "Bea, put on the kettle, please. Another small cup's all I need."

Bea quickly went over to the stove and set the water to boil, while Jean came over to stand beside her mother. "Jean, get me the off-white thread, please," she said as she picked up the navy blouse and laid it flat on the table, front side up. Jean looked through the sewing basket on the table, and picked out a spool of thread. "That's white, love," Evelyn said, barely glancing at it. "I'll take the off-white; I've more of it." Jean looked again and pulled out another spool. Evelyn nodded and took it from her, then picked a needle from the pincushion. She quickly cut off a length of thread, ran the tip through the eye of the needle, and while Bea made a fresh pot of tea, she laid the bed jacket over top of the navy blouse and basted single vertical seams on each side of the blouse, so that the basting lined up with the side seams of the bed jacket. Bea brought the tea fixings to the table and as she poured, Evelyn bent under the table. "Have you seen my measuring stick, Jean?"

"It's right there," said Mildred, pointing to the box containing orders yet to be filled.

"Here," said Jean, crawling under the table and reaching into the box.

"Thanks, love."

She took the stick and placed it across the bed jacket, and then moved the jacket aside and measured the distance between the newly basted off-white seams on the navy blouse. "Hand me that order form of Miss Norton's, Bea. It's ready to be mailed. Over there, on top of that stack of papers."

Bea went over to the table just inside the kitchen door and saw the envelope addressed to Sears Roebuck. "It's already sealed, Aunt Evelyn."

"That's alright. Open it up." Bea tore open the envelope, and handed the order form to Evelyn. Evelyn glanced at it, then looked back down at the bed jacket on the table.

"Thirty-eight bust, just as she said," Evelyn said, sitting down hard in her chair. Bea pushed Evelyn's tea across the table to her. Evelyn took a sip, then wrapped her hands around the cup. "The bed jacket is a thirty-two, at the most. Well, I suppose if she lost that much weight, as hard as it would be to imagine, she could have lost that many inches off her bust." She slid the order form toward herself and looked it over again.

A far greater inconsistency in one of the measurements was dead obvious to Mildred, who could see it perfectly clearly, and she knew that Evelyn would have seen it as well had she not been so tired, had she not worked a fifteen-hour day, and had she not worked that many days straight. As it was, Evelyn rubbed her eyes, then stood and began to gently fold the bed jacket.

Mildred looked over at Bea. Over the light of the lamp, Bea kept her eyes on the bed jacket as Evelyn folded it; she continued to watch it as Evelyn laid it on the corner of the table, took another swig from her cup, and carried the teacups to the sink. And when Jean pulled on Bea's sleeve and urged her to bed, her attention still remained on the bed jacket as she followed her cousin up the stairs.

After they had put Jean to bed and Bea was musing over the note from the Nortons, Mildred stood beside her and said:

"You saw it, didn't you? Dead obvious, wasn't it?"

Bea nodded and sat back on her chair, gnawing on a fingernail.

"Don't know why Evelyn didn't see it. Unbelievable, really, but then the poor woman's exhausted. Don't know why you didn't tell Evelyn what you saw, Bea," continued Mildred. "Losing weight is one thing, but I've never known anyone to lose inches off the ends of their arms, no matter how much weight they lost."

Bea sighed, and reached for her pen and pad of paper, and wrote:

Sleeves too short on blouse. Why?

Mildred watched to see how Bea would make sense of the rest of her day. As usual, Bea started in the morning:

Nortons' hallway. Cable. 1857. Telegraph machine. Miss Norton's odd behaviour. Strange, cryptic thank-you note. Why the vertical characters? The even stranger blouse. Who ripped the blouse?

Bea paused momentarily, then scribbled:

Henry. Penelope. George. Brian. Have I met Brian?

She put down her pen, and rubbed her temples. Mildred leaned over Bea's shoulder and reviewed the list. She was always glad to find on rare occasions like now, that she noticed what Bea had missed. "From earlier in the day, dear. Something's missing, I believe."

Bea picked up the pen, and muttered, "Almost clear forgot."

Salt water taffy. Natty's father doesn't eat salt water taffy!

...---...

Brian worried about Henry, who sat beside him on the bed. Henry had been trying to write all night, but words wouldn't come. He would get up from the bed, sit at his desk, pick up his pen, and begin, always the same way, "Dear Penelope . . . " He would get one or two sentences into each letter, ten of them now, all crumpled and thrown into the rubbish, then he would stop and return to sit on the bed, as he did now.

"You don't need to worry, Henry. You don't need to talk about it. Nobody needs to know," said Brian, trying to be comforting.

Day Six
Sunday, October 19, 1902

"We've come back again, Mr. Cooke," said Bea. Clara stood behind Bea and peered at Natty's father. Clara had been waiting at the corner, just where she said she would be. She had come by the store yesterday, and when Bea told Clara her plans for coming back here in the mid-afternoon, the girl had insisted on joining her.

"Zat so?" Mr. Cooke said now, and they were hit full on with the stench of his boozy breath. "Didn't bring Bobby this time."

"Billy."

"Whatever you say. Come yourself. Isn't that a bit risky?"

"Could be, I suppose," said Bea.

"You never know about men like me," he said, leering at them and leaning out from the door frame toward them. "What'dya want anyhow?"

"Natty's here, isn't she?"

"Ya can't come in, if that's what yer thinkin'."

"I'm sure she's here, Mr. Cooke."

"If she was, I would have said."

"Yes, sir. But you see," Bea said, glancing down at little Clara, and wishing she could replace her with Billy or Callum. "Why were you in the store yesterday buying Natty's favourite taffy? She can't live without it, she has told me enough times. Has it all to herself, she has told me that, too; says you can't eat it because of your teeth."

"Ya don't say."

"Oh, Pa. Let them in like I said," came Natty's voice from inside the hallway.

"Natty?" said Clara, stepping out from behind Bea.

"You sure? Could be up to no good," said Mr. Cooke to the owner of the voice as he looked back over his shoulder. He suddenly seemed sober.

"I'm sure. They're my friends. Let them in, Pa."

Mr. Cooke opened the door and stepped aside, and there was Natty, alive and evidently perfectly safe. She led them silently through to the kitchen. It was tidier than Bea would have expected, but then she was expecting that Mr. Cooke had taken to living here on his own, or with Natty jailed and locked in a room. She was nothing of the kind, and she nodded for them to take a seat at the small kitchen table. As Natty put her arm around her little friend Clara, Bea was taken by the difference between Natty and the younger girl. Natty had always been the vision of health, with a full, ruddy complexion, clear brown eyes, and shiny brown hair that fell to the top of her shoulders in a soft natural curl. Natty, at seventeen, was already a woman, though only a couple of sizes larger than Jean, small and compact, and vital.

Natty sat in a chair at the table and Clara stood facing her. Natty gently gripped her thin shoulders. The girl had been staring down at the floor and now looked up into Natty's eyes, her own welling with tears. Natty gave her a hug and then glanced over at her father, who had come to stand by the kitchen window, several feet away. Bea looked at him curiously, and then realized what was different: He was no longer drunk. He never had been, she realized with a shock; it had all been an act.

Natty followed Bea's gaze and read her thoughts. "Sorry about that," she remarked. "We didn't know what else to do." She smiled, and her father replied with a toothless grin, then he turned to the stove and removed the steaming kettle.

"Tea?" he asked. They all nodded. It was almost a bit much, thought Bea. This man, so recently drunk and nasty, had now turned into a placid tea-servant.

"I was still too scared when you all came by before. Then, after you'd left, I realized how foolish I was being, not letting you in, or Clara when she'd come a couple of days before. Sorry, Clara. So I sent Pa down to the store to buy the taffy. I knew you'd figure it out, Bea. I didn't want to go out myself. Perhaps in a few minutes you'll understand why." Then she turned to Clara: "You know I'd never leave here without saying where and why."

"Yeah," said Clara, reaching over and gently fingering Natty's curls by way of forgiveness. "Not like your mum did to you."

"Yeah," said Natty. She pulled up a box for Clara to sit down on, and moved it closer to the stove. "Turn up the stove, Pa. Have you been dressing warmly like I said, Clara?"

"Not always," answered Clara, nestling into the little nook beside the stove. She seemed suddenly weary.

"No, I can see," Natty said, removing her shawl from around her shoulders and placing it over Clara's. She took a mug of tea from her father, who said, "Well, I'll let you girls carry on with your business. I got my own to do." He poured himself a cup, and a few seconds later they heard the front door open and close.

Natty handed Clara the mug of sweet tea. "Suppose I better tell you why I left and went into hiding," she said, still looking at Clara, who had taken one sip of her tea, and had then fallen right to sleep with the mug still held between her hands on her lap. Natty went over to her and removed the mug. She picked her up and carried her over to the cot at the far end of the room and laid a blanket over her. When she sat back down at the table, Bea had poured their tea. Natty took a sip of hers and asked, "Bea, have you met Brian?"

Bea shook her head in response to Natty's question. "I was thinking just that last night. No. We've not been introduced."

Natty didn't respond at first, but just gazed at Bea and then at Clara. When she spoke, her voice had become muted, and scared. "I don't know why me," she said absently, almost to herself. Then she went on. "It was always peculiar there. Right from the beginning. At first, I thought it peculiar just because of Mr. Stevens and George. The way they leer."

"Yeah. Don't I know," said Bea.

"Creepy," said Natty. "Especially George. He'd follow me down to the cellar. And Mr. Stevens, with his drinking. Mrs. Stevens was odd, too, the way she was always looking at me suspicious-like, as if I was up to something. She watched me all the time, even listened into our conversations, mine and Clara's. Sometimes we could hear her breathing through the vent in the kitchen.

"Until the end, I thought that in a strange way, Brian was the most normal of the lot. He was clearly demented — I was positive he had some kind of mental affliction — but he was the most friendly. He'd sit with me while I worked. Sometimes he'd come downstairs with me to the cellar and watch me, but he didn't give me the shivers like George. He wasn't as creepy. I didn't think."

"You didn't think?"

"I didn't find out until the day I left, you see. That's why I ran away, why I've been hiding here ever since."

"Because of Brian?"

"Yes. But not only Brian."

"What happened? What did Brian do?" Bea wrapped her hands inside the front opening of her coat.

"He didn't *do* anything, not really."

"What then? Did he say something to you?"

"Well, that was just it, you see. That should have given me a clue. Brian never said very much. He would just wander around after me. Or sit and watch me work. Usually, when I would ask him a question, he would just smile and shrug, almost as if he couldn't hear me very well. I got used to his silences. I knew he was more than a bit touched, you see. I'd talked to Mrs. Stevens about him. There wasn't anything anybody could do for him, she had said. But he was so *odd* sometimes, I really should have figured it out. You would have, Bea, I know you would."

"I don't know about that, Natty. What kinds of things would he do?"

"Several times if he caught me looking for something, even if it was just to get an item out of a cupboard, he would ask, 'What are you looking for?' After I'd tell him — the wheat flour, a stocking under the bed, whatever it was — he'd say, 'Oh, I thought you were looking for Morna.' Sometimes he'd ask me if Morna was dead. Do you know who Morna is, Bea?"

Bea shook her head and Natty went on, "Neither do I. I came to prefer his silences more than when he spoke, because when he spoke he always sounded so serious, as if the whole world was crashing in around him. Even when I first met him, in the kitchen the day I started. He was sitting in the little alcove, you know, on the bench?" Bea nodded.

Natty took a sip of her tea and continued, "He always wore the same little outfit, and it was so ratty, I even wondered if he was related to them; everyone else in the family dressed so immaculately. 'What's your name?' I asked, sitting across from him. 'Brian,' he answered. It took him a long time to reply, as if he had to think about it, and his voice was so soft, and just starting to deepen into a man's. 'Brian Stevens. You're Natty,' he said. I hadn't told him my name, but of course I assumed Mrs. Stevens had. 'Yes,' I said. 'Pleased to meet you.'

"That first supper — I swear to God, Bea, I'll never forget that first supper my entire life. I should have left right then and there. Don't know why I stayed. That night I had set four places and when they had all taken their seats, Mrs. Stevens said, "What is that for, Natty?" At first, I thought 'that' meant Brian, who was already seated, but then I realized 'that' meant the place setting. She said it without hardly moving her head, like she does, you know. Like she's royalty or something. She stared straight ahead down the table. Her chin shifted a half an inch to the right. With the lids of her eyes, she indicated the place setting."

Despite Natty's obvious nervousness and their tension, both she and Bea began to giggle. She had done a perfect imitation of Mrs. Stevens.

"'It's for Brian,' I told her.

"'If you ever want a new job, Natty, you should go into the theatre. That was perfect,' Mrs. Stevens said to me.

"It was the oddest thing. Of course, now I understand it, but then — at first there was utter silence, absolute total silence, and then all at once they all reacted, Mr. and Mrs. Stevens and George. Brian just sat there and didn't say or do a thing. Mr. Stevens leapt out of his chair and screamed, 'What the hell?' George started to laugh and couldn't stop. And Mrs. Stevens frowned and breathed heavily like she was about to scream, but then all of a sudden she seemed really calm and in a very loud voice, she spoke over all the goings-on: 'Well, it's about time he had a place at the family table, don't you think, Henry?'

"Mr. Stevens all of a sudden stopped swearing and jumping about, and looked down the table at his wife like he could kill her, but then he said, 'Quite,' and sat down. George clapped and said, 'Brilliant, Natty. I love it. Who would have thought? And on your first day. How brash of you.' I had no idea what he was talking about. What any of them were talking about. I looked at Brian and shrugged, and he looked at me and shrugged, and I served the meal. When it was done — they didn't say another word the entire meal, I swear, not one word — I took the plates away. Brian hadn't touched his, of course, and George noticed, of course, and said, 'Perhaps he doesn't like stew, Natty. Better luck next time.'

"My last evening there was the strangest of all. It had been a strange day, what with the Nortons being over and the Stevens being in such a state afterward — though they pretended hard not to be — and then the incident with George at supper." Natty started to describe what she had overheard of the conversation between Mr. Norton and Mr. Stevens in the study.

"Did you listen to the whole thing?" asked Bea.

"Not nearly," she said. "Something about cable ships and a cable breaking, and Mr. Stevens' father being to blame."

"Anything about blackmail?" asked Bea.

"Nothing like that. Mrs. Stevens was on to me; I couldn't listen in for long."

Then she told Bea the story that George had relayed of how he got the gash on his forehead and of waking up in an alley covered in blood. "It was horrible, Bea, the way he described it. I don't know why he wasn't more frightened. I would've been. Of all of them, the one who seemed the most scared was Mr. Stevens, if you can believe it. He just sat there the whole time while George spoke, massaging his own forehead, as if he was the one who was injured.

"Later, after supper, I was putting away the new underwear set I'd just got that day, when Brian came up behind me and spoke. He scared me; I didn't hear him approaching. 'He's watching you,' he said. I turned around and dropped the underwear on the floor. He didn't come in; he just stayed in the doorway.

"'Brian, you scared me. Don't creep up on people like that,' I said.

"'Sorry,' he said.

"'What did you say, Brian? Someone's watching me? Who?'

"'Him,' he said, and he looked down at the corset cover that had fallen on the ground.

"'Oh, you mean my secret admirer?'

"'He's not your friend. You shouldn't have opened it.'

"'What? The gift?' I said. 'Why not?'

"'It's not a gift, Natty.'

"'Sure it is, Brian.'

"'No.'

"'What then?'

"'A message. From him.'

"'Brian, what do you mean? It's not a gift, it's a message? What on earth are you talking about? You wouldn't know anything about secret admirers, Brian. You're too young.'

"'I know about letters and messages, Natty. I know about not opening what you shouldn't. I know about what can happen when you're not listening.'

"'Did you, Brian? Open what you shouldn't have?'

"He looked behind his shoulder into the dark of the cellar. 'I don't know. Perhaps. I can't remember.'

"'Alright. If it's a message or a letter or something, then what does it say?'

"'Didn't you read it?' he asked, and he started pushing at the air around his head with the palms of his hands. 'Can't you see?' He stopped thrashing about with his arms and extended his right toward the garment. He pointed his forefinger at the fabric. I followed where he was pointing. I really expected to see something there. And, of course, there was nothing but the garment itself. No writing. No strange letters. I bent down to pick up the corset cover, and when I stood up, Brian was gone. Disappeared as if he had never been. I wanted to run home right then and there. He was more bizarre than usual. The whole incident completely unnerved me. And then the night got even more peculiar, and leave I did. That's when I came home here to hide. Grabbed my new underwear and a few other things. Everything else I left behind."

Bea hugged her arms around her chest as Natty poured more tea for the both of them. Natty handed Bea a plate of biscuits, but she shook her head. She didn't think her stomach could handle anything.

Natty went on: "Later, I wasn't about able to sleep, and I went upstairs to get a glass of water. Mrs. Stevens was there, cleaning a knife in the sink. She asked me whom I had been talking to downstairs earlier in the evening. I said, 'Brian,' thinking nothing of it. We'd had several conversations about Brian and I'd often heard her chatting to Brian too. Of course, I realized later that that was just her way of talking to herself. Anyhow, when I said, 'Brian,' she went berserk. She started yelling, 'Natty, for God's sake, it's enough. What are you trying to do, for heaven's sake? It's not funny anymore. Mind you, I urged you on, I realize. George and I both did. At first, I thought it would be a relief from the everyday; sometimes meals can get to be so tedious. This fantasy of yours seemed to be an entertainment of sorts. I had no idea what had brought it on or what you thought you were up to, but in a way I admired your spunk. Brash, as George called you. And it did lend some humour to our lives. But it's really gone too far, Natty. Tonight, I am just not in the mood for this. I cannot abide this a moment longer. I forbid you to talk about it again.'

"'You don't want me to talk to Brian anymore, ma'am? Why not? I don't understand,' I asked her.

"'For God's sake girl, stop it. Brian's not here. He never has been. Brian's dead.'

"That's what she said, just like that. Standing there in the kitchen. 'Brian's dead.'

"'No, he's not, Mrs. Stevens,' I said, 'I was just talking to him. Downstairs.'

"'I don't know what you're up to, but here. I was just joking when I spoke of him, but clearly you are up to something. Come. Now,' she said. She grabbed my arm and pulled me into the hallway. Bea? You know the portrait of the two boys?"

"George and Brian," said Bea.

"No," said Natty, sounding confused. "Is that what you thought?"

"Yes, but it's also what George told me."

"They're not, not according to Mrs. Stevens."

"Who did she say they were?"

"Henry and his twin."

"No, Natty. No, they're not. The portrait is of George and his twin."

"Oh, no, it can't be, Bea."

"Why not? How do you know that Mrs. Stevens isn't lying?"

"Well, for one thing, Bea, George is much older."

"Than Brian? No he's not."

"At least four years, Bea. Brian is only twelve. And, also, Brian and Henry both have identical scars on their hands. The artist who did the portraits captured them perfectly; didn't you notice, Bea?"

"Scars on the hands? No, I didn't. Are you sure the scars are on the hands? Left or right?"

"Right hands, I'm almost sure. Yes. Right. Why?"

"Nothing," Bea said, but of course it wasn't nothing. Her dream came to mind again. The boy looking in the mirror, raising his right arm up, the cut on the palm.

"I hadn't noticed the scars in the portrait either before my last night there," Natty continued. "But I'd always noticed Brian's. He often scratched behind his right ear. The palm of his right hand looked like someone had taken a cleaver to it."

"George scratches behind his ear as well, have you noticed?"

"No."

"Well, he does. Like an identical twin might do. The same kind of behaviour. Natty, if Brian exists at all, he really must be George's twin."

"George doesn't have a scar on his hand, Bea. He's not one of the boys in the portrait."

"It's healed, then."

"No. These are old scars. Deep and wide."

Like the scar on Mr. Stevens' forehead, Bea thought. "Well, carry on. What else did Mrs. Stevens say?"

"She had told me it was 'Mr. Stevens and his twin' when I had first asked about the portrait, my very first day there. I thought no more of it at the time. But then that last day, she pulled me out into the hall, and said: 'That one's Brian, the one on the left. And the other one, Natty, the one on the right, is Henry. Brian is Henry's brother. And Brian is dead.'

"I must have stared at the portrait for two minutes without speaking. The Brian in the portrait was healthier and happier than the Brian I had met. They didn't even really look like the same person. 'Did he die soon after this, Mrs. Stevens?' I asked.

"Now it was her turn to stare at me. 'How would you know that?' she asked. I shrugged and I didn't tell her that on the day we met, he told me he thought he was twelve. Of course, he never said he died. I don't think he knows. He just said, when I asked, that that's how old he thought he was. I remember thinking it was odd he wasn't sure."

Her hand shook as she reached out to take another sip of her tea. Bea waited. She knew there was more. Natty spoke softly: "'Mrs. Stevens?' I asked. 'How did Brian die?'

"'Well, if you must know, Natty,' she said, in that snooty way of hers — as if we were talking about what vegetables to serve for supper.

'He was murdered. Awful really, but there you have it. Brian was murdered.'"

Neither Bea nor Natty spoke for several seconds, and then Natty continued: '"Who killed him, Mrs. Stevens?' I finally asked her. She kept gazing up at the pictures, from one to the other, and to the cuts on their hands. 'You'll have to ask Henry that, Natty, won't you? I'm sure Henry could tell you.'"

Softly as a ghost, Mildred touched her husband's forehead and waited for him to die. "Stay behind, my love," she whispered. She glanced to her right past his bed; she knew what waited for her beyond the light, where the room went black. "Stay with me, Samuel," she said, and she hoped that death was listening.

Samuel had always liked it when her fingertips rested here on his forehead. She calmed him through everything, after a bender, or a failed job, or both; he often brought these home together. Past the dark eyes of their daughter, he would weave like a pair of drunken sailors into the kitchen to collapse laughing on a chair. Later, he would sober and sit weeping on the stool in front of their stone hearth, his black hair falling straight and oily onto his hands. "Mildred," he would cry to the sounds of little Sarah asleep on the cot in the corner. He couldn't even look at Sarah at times like these. He didn't know how he would feed her for the next month, or the next day. "I'll quit drinking," he always promised Mildred afterward, and she knew he believed it and she would lay her hand on his brow, his skin sweaty beneath her fingers.

Now no more, she knew, feeling the skin of his forehead, cool and dry from dying, and suddenly she knew with a sickening certainty that death had not listened. It was not going to leave his ghost behind.

"Come back," she yelled at his going, but when little Sarah looked up from his body, her eyes puffy, her face glistening from too much crying, Mildred stopped calling and just whispered: "Come back for me, Samuel. Come back, my lovely," using the phrase he had cried at the ship that had abandoned him here in Newfoundland so many years before; words that they had since used between the two of them while joking in bed, making supper, teaching Sarah her letters — Mildred, at least; Samuel had never learned to read.

Death shouldn't be like this, she thought, watching his last breath come, and then go. It should at least fight for what it wants, but with him, now, it didn't. Instead, his last breath evaporated out of him far too easily, and he was gone. He had entirely left her. It surprised her; she thought they would be together forever. Her wishes — for more of his promises, for the way he called her name, for his gentle smile — all died with him. This confirmed what she already knew: death loves loneliness, the kind that comes at night when the world has gone to bed.

After Bea left Natty, she joined Mildred on Signal Hill. They came here when they wanted to think, and now together they stood on the bluff and looked out over the Narrows. But Mildred knew that Bea's view would be different from her own. For Mildred, the world across the water abruptly ended as if it had never been, as if the person who painted the view from here had forgotten the landscape beyond. The black grew bigger the more Mildred watched it and its loneliness yawned, inviting her to join it. Perhaps Samuel would still be there, waiting, all these many years later. A strong gust came in off the Atlantic and swirled around them, bringing with it the hill's surfeit of twigs, dried leaves and tiny pebbles. Bea's scarf almost blew out to sea, and overhead, the stormy sky slouched its heavy worry.

"Let's go home," Mildred said, turning away from the water. "We won't find the answer to Brian here."

Bea made as if to join her, but then strayed toward the three graves that she had built up here — such as they were; they weren't graves in the real sense, just rocks on more rocks. With no bones to put inside, she had put other things: mementoes, a bead from a bracelet, memories. She prayed over them for several seconds, and then set off toward the tower on another part of the hill. On a large rock, she sat down, her back to Cabot Tower, and then moved over so Mildred could join her.

"How do I find out what happened to Brian?" Bea asked.

"I'm sure there's a way, love, we just have to find what it is. And you'll find it well before I do, Bea. You always do."

Bea picked a lonely piece of grass that had found its way up through the rocky ground, and toyed with it between her fingers as they talked. Mildred heard a sound from behind. She glanced back once, then closed her eyes and listened with the back of her head to the tower and the ruins next to it. Only wind walking on rocks, tunnelling through crevices in stone. That's all. Why hadn't she heard that before? Silly. There were no ghosts up here, and she hoped it stayed that way. She hoped Brian wasn't a harbinger of things to come.

"But — what if Natty is right?" Bea interrupted Mildred's thoughts, as she was prone to do.

"About Brian?"

"What if he really is dead?"

"Oh, that's without question, love. But if you don't believe me, or Natty for that matter, there are ways of finding these things out for yourself, love, aren't there?"

"What if he really had been murdered?"

Mildred didn't answer at first. Finally she said, "He'd want us to know, wouldn't he, Bea? He'd want us to discover the truth."

"Did Henry do it? Is that why the Stevens' are being blackmailed?" asked Bea. They waited for the wind to die, and then she added: "I don't know where to begin."

"I know, love, but let's start somewhere," said Mildred, standing up and brushing the dirt from her skirt. The wind took it, and it swirled around Bea. Bea got up and brushed herself off, and they started down the hill. As they passed Cabot Tower, Mildred wondered if there were ghosts in its turrets. The single sandstone tower appeared more ancient today than ever, as if it were a relic from the fifteenth century, instead of what it really was: a freshly built effigy just over two years old. The city fathers should have thought of ghosts before giving approval for its recent construction. It serves them right if ghosts have taken up residence, she thought. Commemorating the dead is only an invitation for the homeless in their midst.

...---...

"Excuse me, lass," said Mrs. Whelan, as she tried to get by Bea. It was a tight squeeze: the stacks of dried fish, Bea, and the horse on one side; the edge of the wharf on the other.

"Sorry, Mrs. Whelan. Can you get past now?" said Bea, cozying up to the thick brown tail of the mare.

"I can, my love. Thank you," said the beshawled woman as she made her way by Bea, her arms laden with bags of provisions. Several feet away, her son, Matty, took them from his mother and helped her into their rowboat. Bea wondered that the thing didn't tip over from the weight of all the goods aboard. They were probably not going to be coming back from their outport before winter set in.

She looked around and realized she had no idea why she had even come down here. She turned and headed back along the wharf. She negotiated past a young girl who was helping her grandfather lay an old grey net over a gallows to dry; the child sat on the wooden wharf, and the old man on a wooden crate on the other side of the gallows. Bea passed them, but then stopped and turned to ask: "Excuse me, but are you Mr. McNeil?"

"Hello?" he said, looking up.

"Is Bea MacDonald, Grandad," said the child, as Bea walked back toward them.

"Bea MacDonald," he said with a smile. "Don't see so well any more. Need the lass for that. How are you there, Bea? How's your aunt?" He held out his hand and she shook it.

"Fine, sir. We're all doing well, sir."

"No 'sir' for me, thank you, Bea. Plain old McNeil's what they call me, but 'sir' gets me old too quick. Don't need any more of that around here, do we, Rosie?"

"No, Grandad," said the little red-haired, freckle-faced girl, smiling up at Bea. She then bent again over the net, un-creasing the folds and pulling it neatly into place around the boards on her end.

"Mr. McNeil, you worked on the cable ships, didn't you?" asked Bea.

"Did. *Great Eastern*, '65 and '66. Both voyages," he said, taking his pipe and tobacco from his pocket, settling in for a conversation.

"That must have been exciting — '66?"

"Like you wouldn't believe, Bea. We all wondered if the cable would ever get laid, and here we were a part of it. I was a lucky man to have sailed on her."

"Did you ever sail on the *Agamemnon* or the *Niagara*?"

"Hard work, though," he said, and Bea smiled at his granddaughter, who tried to stifle a giggle. His ears were going the way of his eyes, it seemed. "But then, what isn't?"

"What did you do on board, sir? Did you work on paying out the cable?"

"Nothing like that. Didn't know a thing about it. Tended sheep, mostly. And pigs and turkeys and what have you. Butchered them too, when their time was up."

"Animals? On board the *Great Eastern*?"

"People gotta eat, don't they? Lucky to have got the job. What with all those Brits and Americans. Who would've thought a little farm boy from Avalon Peninsula would end up working on the ship that finally laid the cable. Got my taste for the sea after her. Would've probably gone back to the farm, if it wasn't for her."

"Did you ever sail on the *Agamemnon* or the *Niagara*?" Bea asked, trying her question again.

He spent some time lighting the pipe before he answered. "Nope. Before my time."

"Do you know anyone around here who did?"

He took a long drag on the pipe, and nodded. "Clement. Know him? Lives north of here aways."

"Do you know how I can get in touch with him?"

"Don't need to go far to do that. He's coming down for a visit next day or two. Comes once a month when the weather's still nice. Long as it doesn't snow — doesn't much feel like it, does it — he'll be here for supper. If you'd like to meet him, why don't you come by have supper with us? We'd like the company, wouldn't we, Rosie?"

"Yeah," she said, smiling.

"Tomorrow?" asked Bea.

"Possibly. Come by — if he hasn't arrived, you can eat with us anyhow."

"You waiting for me, Bea MacDonald?" asked the familiar voice. He had spoken rapidly, as if nervous. But he always was, jittery eyes and fingers, a rapidly tapping foot whenever he was sitting down, which was never for long. But she liked the sound of his voice as much as ever, especially on nights like tonight.

"Now why would I be doing that, Callum McNee?" she asked, not turning to look at him but staring ahead.

He came up behind her, and sat down beside her on the wide flat rock. They sat, side by side, and gazed out into the starry night. The sea would be visible in the day, but now, they could only smell its salt and hear its waves. Callum broke off a twig from a scraggly bit of bush growing next to the rock. He chewed on the twig, and after several minutes, Bea broke the silence:

"Remember how scared you were of ghosts, Callum? Always asking me if my house was haunted?"

"Don't know that I was ever scared," he said, talking to the night, same as her. She didn't challenge him. Of course he'd been scared. He knew it. She knew it.

"Did you ever see any?" she asked.

"Ghosts? Now what's got into you, Bea MacDonald?" he asked, glancing at her, but when she kept staring ahead and didn't answer, he looked out over the bluff. He kept waiting for her to speak, and when she still didn't, he said, "Couldn't sleep tonight?"

"Didn't try."

"Sounds like me, not you," he said. "Darn ghost keeping you up, I guess." He chortled to himself, but when Bea didn't join in his laughter, he said, "No, never saw any ghosts." Again, silence fell between them, and then he added, "Not like you did."

"What're you talking about?" she asked, swinging around to look at him.

"You saw ghosts, Bea, when you were little," he said, gazing at her with his large brown eyes. "Or one ghost, at least. Don't you remember?"

"I never saw any ghosts."

"Sure you did, when you were a little girl. From the time you came here to Newfoundland and moved in with your aunt and uncle, until — I don't know when it stopped, I can't remember. You honestly don't remember?"

"Don't be daft."

"You did. Honest. You talked to her all the time. Seems like she came with us everywhere we went."

"So it was a girl ghost?"

"Aah, c'mon, Bea, you must remember. I can't believe you don't remember."

"Don't remember talking to ghosts, that's for sure. Remember going everywhere with you when we were little. You and Mildred."

"That's it. That was her name; I couldn't remember."

"The ghost? You thought Mildred was a ghost?"

"What did you think she was?"

"She was just Mildred, Callum. Our nursemaid, or maiden aunt; a relative of some kind. I'm not too sure, actually. She lived with us when I was little. She must have been very old. Aunt Evelyn said she'd also been around when she and Aunt Isabella were children."

"And then what — she left?"

"I suppose. I guess. I don't remember. Don't be daft, Callum," Bea said, laughing and looking out over the water. "Of course I remember Mildred. She wasn't a ghost, though, silly."

"Well, if she wasn't a ghost or a spirit or whatever — what was she then, Bea?" he asked, his eyes still focusing on the side of her head.

"I told you — our maiden aunt, or whatever — she helped Aunt Evelyn with me, mostly, then Jean for a bit, until she left."

"Yeah, so you said."

"Whatever led you to believe that she was a ghost for heaven's sake, Callum?"

"Well, for starters, young Bea," he said slowly. "Besides the fact that we all know that you and your kin are all a bit touched — there's this . . . " He paused, and gazed again out over the night. The twig was well chewed by now, but it was odd for him to sound so calm while Bea felt so nervous. She wished he would just get on with it and say what he had to say. He finally looked her in the eye. "Nobody could see Mildred, Bea. Nobody but you. And Jean, of course. But then, our Jean sees more than most."

"My daughter Sarah was only eight years old when I died," Mildred said. "That's why I didn't entirely leave, I imagine. She was far too little and I loved them far too much. And I'm glad I stayed with her. Samuel died four years later, when the child was only twelve. I don't know what Sarah would have done without me, all on her own, such a little bit of a thing." Mildred had been listening in on Bea and Callum's conversation, of course, and felt that an explanation was in order. Normally, she didn't intrude on the private conversations of her wards, but she suspected they would get around to talking about her tonight. And so they had.

But Mildred had been talking out to sea, and when she looked back, she realized she had been talking to herself. Callum had left, and Bea was already a ways ahead, hurrying down the path home. "Wait up, Bea," Mildred called, and Bea slowed, but didn't turn around.

"It was a couple of hundred years ago, Bea. I think. It could be more. I've lost track," Mildred continued, as she got within hearing distance. "In any case, I've been with the family all this time." Bea stopped in the path for a moment and looked back. "It's alright. It's just me," Mildred reassured her. Still, Bea's anxiety forced Mildred to glance behind them toward the outcropping from which they'd just come. Callum was probably already home by now; Bea, as was her wont, had refused his offer to walk her home. Mildred wished she had accepted. She quickened her pace and came up beside Bea.

"Sarah grew into a fine young woman, I must say. Then, she had a daughter of her own. Her daughter had a daughter, and so on, down through the generations. There was the odd son here and there, mind you, and — honestly, Bea, I've lost track of how many generations of girls and boys I've looked after. And, well, Bea, it just never seemed the right time to leave. There was always someone to look out for. You all mattered so much."

"I don't believe in ghosts or spirits . . . " Bea muttered, interrupting Mildred's tale.

"No, of course not. Who would? It might surprise you to know that I hadn't really believed in ghosts, either — until Brian just the other day — never having met one before — though I don't know why not. I'd wished for one, of course. You wish for more than one; you never know what you're going to get. Like up at Cabot Tower, Bea. It's spooky up there, isn't it? I wouldn't doubt if there were ghosts up there, though I can't say I've ever seen them."

"And I certainly don't believe in guardian angels," said Bea, as she stopped and looked directly at Mildred with a questioning look on her face.

Mildred shrugged and answered, "Guardian angel seems a bit farfetched, Bea. All I've been able to figure out is that I'm an ancestor. Although, mind you, I've never been able to understand why I'm here and other ancestors are not. Sometimes I think I simply got stuck between the worlds. But I'm with Sarah's descendents; I'm with the people I love — what can be better than that? I don't really suppose it much matters what you call me, Bea — guardian angel, ancestor, archangel has a nice touch, though I think that's a bit of a stretch — but, really, Bea, I don't prefer ghost. Apparition. Poltergeist. Those words have a fearsome ring to them. I don't like it when people refer to me that way. And they do, don't they? 'Those MacDonald women up on the south shore. Got the sixth sense, don't they? Swear I've seen a ghost up there when I go to visit.' You've heard the rumours, Bea. They've been talking about us for centuries, ever since I've been around, I suppose."

Again Bea interrupted: "If you're here, then why don't I see you?"

"I can't explain it, love. It's the way it always is. You saw me as a child. When you were a little girl, we had the most wonderful conversations — do you remember? The children in this family have always seen me. And some other children, too. But adults seldom do. When people start to become adults they stop seeing me, with the odd exception. It saddens me to say it, Bea, but even our Jean seems to have stopped seeing me. I really thought she'd see me forever."

DAY SEVEN
Monday, October 20, 1902

"Five cents, Bea, isn't that what ya said?"

"Pardon, Mrs. Campbell?"

"Five cents, m'love, not fifty. Ya've written fifty in your book."

"Oh my! Apologies, Mrs. Campbell. Don't know what's come over me."

"Young man, is it?" whispered Mrs. Campbell, leaning her dark, round face across the counter as Bea changed the figure in the ledger. She peered at Bea with eyes almost black, and then winked down at Jean again hiding below the counter. Jean winked back. "She's got Indian blood," Aunt Evelyn would grimace whenever they passed her on the street.

"Pardon, ma'am?" asked Bea, wrapping up the imitation tortoise-shell hairpin, putting it in Mrs. Campbell's cloth bag along with the rest of her purchases, and feeling a blush rise to her cheeks. She had no control over it, and it always made her feel more embarrassed than she already was. What was Mrs. Campbell talking about? What young man?

"Now, m'love, that's alright, dear. It shows on yer face, ya know. I can always tell when the young are in love. But, Bea, this talk of romance's got me baffled. Here I am ready to leave and I forgot what I come for." She turned and walked away from the counter.

Bea was baffled, too — romance was the farthest thing from her mind — and she tried to focus on the ledger in front of her. Get your mind on your job, girl, she scolded herself, but when she tried to add up a column of the day's sales, none of the numbers made any sense whatsoever. Her mind kept shifting between yesterday's talk with Natty and last night's talk with Callum. She hadn't been able to get to sleep for hours after that. Mildred — a ghost? He was having her on. Surely. Though that wasn't like Callum. Bea had rushed home and into the kitchen, but Aunt Evelyn had gone to bed. What a night for her to choose to go to bed early, but when Bea had looked at the clock she realized it wasn't early at all: it was after one. She now forgot about her ledger and started thinking of the questions she wanted to put to Aunt Evelyn whenever she next had a chance, when a dreadful voice interrupted from the other side of the counter.

"The new razors behind you, Bea. How much are they? Hello, Jean."

He rarely shopped for himself; his wife or Natty usually did his bidding. So why was he here? To apologize? Surely not. Bea stepped back from the counter and was about to grab Jean's hand and leave him standing there. Mr. Shulman could deal with him. But then she realized she had heard something in his voice. He was trying to act nonchalant, but underneath his arrogance Bea detected apprehension, as if *he* was leery of *her*. "Hello, Jean," Mr. Stevens said again in his condescending manner, peering at Jean who had tried to crawl further under the counter as soon as she heard his voice, but there was no more room down there and now she sat with her head bowed, pretending she wasn't there.

"Leave her alone," said Bea.

"Pardon me?" asked Mr. Stevens.

"My cousin's not one for talking. What is it I can help you with, Mr. Stevens?" She was trying to keep her voice from betraying her loathing, but she wasn't being particularly successful.

"Razors, Bea. How much are they?" he asked, looking down at the top of Jean's head. The way he kept staring at Jean made Bea want to take the pen that she still held in her hand and ram the nib into his eye.

"Oh, yes, the razors," Bea said, looking over her shoulder at the shelves in between the windows. She grabbed a few for him to look at. She could barely keep her hand steady as she lay the razors down on the counter in front of him. She should have got Mr. Shulman; she didn't know if she could go through with this transaction. To add to her discomfort, she had again seen his smile, and the scar on his forehead: they were without a doubt the images in her dream. So where was the knife, she wondered, gazing at his hands as if expecting the blade to appear out of nowhere. But then again — why was he in here buying razors, of all things? That question absorbed her entirely, and when she again looked over at him, he was shaking his head as if trying to rid himself of a fly. Another case of red ants, if that's what had attacked him in the laundry room? Let's hope, she thought as she reached under the counter for the ledger containing the razor prices. But as she bent to pick it up, she dropped it on the floor. Jean handed it up to her and Bea put it on the counter and flipped through the pages, feeling Jean's gaze concentrated on her. The child had felt the tension, and now would not take her eyes off Bea. "There's quite a difference in price, as I remember," said Bea quickly. She found the page with the razors, and then the column under today's date. "Here we are. German or English, Mr. Stevens? The German's more than double the price."

He glared at her as he scratched his head. He ran his fingers underneath his high, tight collar. He was suddenly looking distinctly uncomfortable and far less smug. Had he got a sudden case of nits? She tried not to show the satisfaction on her face as he continued scratching. He was eventually able to concentrate enough to reply: "Blade's the important thing. Need a good, swift cut."

"The German Bismarck three quarter–inch blade is one dollar and thirty-four cents."

"I'll take one," he said quickly, and clumsily removed his glove, tan kid leather, engraved along the cuff with his initials. He scratched under his collar again; his arrogant demeanour had entirely evaporated. He reached into the breast pocket of his coat for his money.

Bea's gaze travelled back and forth between the cuff of his glove and his bare hand, between his bare hand and the cuff of his glove. Jean's eyes had darkened — Bea knew without even looking that this was so — as she burrowed her focus into the side of Bea's face, trying to determine the cause of Bea's sudden increase in agitation. But Jean couldn't see the glove and the hand; and even if she could, the child wouldn't be able to make sense of it — she hadn't been with Bea at Natty's the day before.

Mr. Stevens handed Bea two eighty-cent notes, grabbed the razor, didn't wait for the change, and as he left the counter to rush out the door, he hissed, "I heard the rumours about you and your family. Didn't think anything of them. But they're true aren't they, you bloody witch?"

Witch? Now wouldn't that be lovely? She wished she were.

When Mildred finished adjusting Mr. Stevens' collar, she was left feeling restless. This so often happened; one of the many reasons she so rarely interfered. There were plenty of other reasons, but she preferred not to dwell on them: she was often left feeling far worse than this.

She needed to do something to rid herself of the last of him, so she wandered the aisles for a few minutes, looking at all the wonderfully modern products. She had always loved shopping for new things and she often suggested items for Evelyn to buy. She hardly ever did. She was so careful with her money. Too frugal, really. Now and again a little treat wouldn't hurt. Mildred particularly liked the tools — they had changed so much since her time — but they were far too pricey, and even though she'd love to see them at work, she couldn't very well ask Evelyn to purchase such a thing. But this Garland Floating Soap, now that wasn't much at all. Twelve bars for forty-two cents. What did they mean by floating soap, she wondered. She really would have to ask Evelyn to buy it so they could try it out.

"Am I interrupting something down there in the bowels?" she heard someone saying from the front of the store. How long had she been wandering about? She'd entirely lost track of time. She hurried over to the front counter, where Mr. Whelan was now standing. He had been leaning over to talk to the girls on the other side.

"Sorry, Mr. Whelan," said Bea, standing up. She had been crouching down, reassuring Jean, no doubt, after that awful encounter with Henry Stevens. "I should have helped you with that."

"As if I'd take aid from a little lass like you? Sorry, Bea, I might be lame, my love, but I'm stronger than any of them," he said, cocking his head toward the harbour, his lined face breaking into a toothless smile. He meant his fellow fishermen, of course. He was correct about his own strength, Mildred thought, admiring the muscles in his arms as he foisted the sack onto the counter. Bea tallied up his order, which included the potatoes, a sack of flour that he went back to get, and a tin of pipe tobacco. As soon as he had finished, and had loaded the sacks out onto his cart parked outside, Mrs Campbell returned to the counter. She had nothing in her hands.

"Couldn't find what else you came in for, Mrs. Campbell?" asked Mildred.

"Got away from me. It must be halfway home by now. Sure enough it'll beat me there and I'll remember when I catch up to it."

Bea smiled as she added up the total of her previous items: "I'm sure you'll remember before that. One dollar ten, Mrs. Campbell. All of it on your account?"

"Aye, Bea. Well, we'll be seeing you, m'love. Good-bye, little Jean."

"Good-bye, Mrs. Campbell," Jean said as Bea handed the woman her parcel.

Mrs. Campbell had reached the front door when Callum came in and held it open for her.

"Good day to you, Mrs. Campbell."

She looked up at him and then back at Bea. "Callum," she said with a smile and a wink at Bea before walking out the door. Callum tipped his cap to her as she left, and strode over to the counter.

"What's she about?" he said, cocking his head at the door. They looked out onto the street as Mrs. Campbell walked by his horse-cart, full to the top with culled fish.

"She thinks we're getting married," said Bea, and Jean started to giggle.

Callum smiled but then went silent. Mildred certainly knew why and she was again surprised that Bea didn't, as again was perfectly obvious from her next statement:

"Gawd," Bea said. "Gawd," she repeated a second later. "I love ya, Callum McNee, but honest to God, it'd be like marrying my own brother. I'd rather die." They'd been friends since Bea first arrived in Newfoundland. One year her senior, he'd been the first person her own age, and the last, ever to have been allowed into her special tent that she'd had as a child. Uncle Ian had built it for her on her seventh birthday. After Uncle Ian died, she'd ripped it down and convinced Callum to get his father to dump it off his boat, and sink it with a rock to the bottom of the deep.

Mildred watched the hurt cross his face — Bea seemed oblivious — and she reached up and gently touched his cheek. He had always been one of her favourite people. A good, solid friend to Bea — to the whole family, in fact. She couldn't stand it when Bea talked to him like this. He lay his fingers over Mildred's, and rallied. "Seen any more ghosts overnight, Bea?" he asked. Bea shook her head and looked down at Jean. Callum nodded and peered over the side of the counter. "Is that you down there, my Jean?" he whispered.

"Aye," Jean whispered back.

"Good to see you, then, isn't it?"

"Aye. You too," said Jean, giggling.

"Any more ghost-ships, love?"

"No," Jean said after a few moments.

"Gawd, Callum, don't be an idiot — will you bloody well leave it alone?" Bea said sharply. He just looked at her, but didn't reply. "Don't need you bringing up that ghost-ship business all over again, do we?" she added.

"If you say so, Bea," he answered after several seconds had elapsed.

He didn't speak for half a minute. Finally he said, "Just come to get my dad his smokes, and I'll be off."

"Would you be heading up our way?" Bea asked as she handed him the tobacco and rolling papers.

"Am. Do you need a ride?"

"I don't, but little Jean here does, if you've got the room."

"Think I can manage such an enormous package," he said to Jean's giggle.

"I've got somewhere to go when I close," said Bea. "It'd be hours before I'd get her home."

... --- ...

"*Great Eastern* was never built as a cable ship, did you know that, Bea?" Clement asked.

Bea nodded and smiled. She was thoroughly enjoying the conversation and waited for them to continue. "Biggest ship ever built," added McNeil.

"Kingdom Brunel built it, didn't he?" asked Bea.

Clement nodded. "Sad, that was. He died before she laid the cable. Never saw her come to good use. Bloody shame."

The three of them nodded. They had been sitting around the small pot-bellied stove in McNeil's galley, beer mugs in hand, pipes for the men. Rosie and McNeil had cleared away the dishes from the stew, and then Rosie had curled up on the bench next to her grandfather. She had tried to keep her eyes open so she could listen to the tales of the *Great Eastern*, but she soon drifted off, lulled to sleep by the voices of the old men and the gentle lapping of the tide against the hull of the boat. The pipe tobacco, the heat from the fire, the gentle rocking of the boat, and the soporific effects of the beer were almost enough to put Bea to sleep as well.

"Aye," said Clement. "There'd never been anything like her."

"But you didn't come to talk about our *Great Eastern* stories, did you, Bea?" asked McNeil.

"No, but I love to hear them nevertheless," she said.

"Still," said McNeil. "It's the *Niagara* you were wondering about. Or was it the *Agamemnon?*"

"Both," she said. "But especially the *Niagara*. Specifically a couple of the people on board."

"Ask away," said Clement. "Sailed on all of them, one time or other. *Niagara* in '57. *Agamemnon* in '58. *Great Eastern* after that. I'll tell you what I can remember."

"Well, '57 is what I'm interested in, Clement. Did you know a man named Judson Stevens?"

"Yup."

"How about Cyrus Norton?"

"Yup. Couldn't help but know 'em."

"Why's that?"

"Everybody knew everybody. Gotta work with them. Sleep with them. Eat with them."

"He's moved here, you know."

"Norton?"

"Yeah."

"Hmm," he said nursing his pipe. "Why'd he want to do that? He's English."

They contemplated that for a bit, and then Bea asked, "Do you know what happened to the cable in '57, Clement?"

"Broke."

"We know that, Clement," said his friend, drawing on his pipe. "What our Miss MacDonald wants to know is *how*."

"Just did, is all. Weren't right, then. It wouldn't have lasted. Look at '58. Got laid, but didn't last, did it? Never worked well until *Great Eastern* laid it in '66 . . . '58, McNeil, how long'd it take for the Queen to send that first message to the President? Twelve hours?"

"Twenty-four, wasn't it?" suggested McNeil.

"Twelve. Twenty-four. What's it matter? Long time, in any case. Who wants to sit around for a whole day waiting for a couple of sentences from somebody?"

"But in '57, Clement . . ."

"Stop drifting, Clement, and try to pay attention to what Bea is asking you," said his friend. "Think you're right, though. Might've been twelve hours. No, maybe it was twenty-four."

Bea smiled, and asked, "Did you ever hear about somebody being held responsible for breaking the cable on the '57 run?"

"Don't think so."

"So nobody ever got blamed?"

"Not so far as I know."

"Not Judson Stevens or Cyrus Norton?"

He shook his head. "If so, I never heard of it, and you'd think I would've. I was around and about as much as the next guy." He pulled his pipe from his mouth and added, "Now what'd I hear about Stevens?"

"Something to do with the cable?" asked Bea.

"Nothing to do with that, I don't think. Something else. Years later. While I was still living over there. Something other." He sat back against the wall behind the bench, so that his head rested on the ledge of the galley window. He smoked on his pipe. "Murder."

"Is that the truth, Clement?" said McNeil.

"That's the truth."

"That so?"

"Yeah."

"Who was murdered?" asked Bea.

"Well, ya see, not sure's I remember. Might have it wrong. Was a long time ago." He pondered this for a time and then put down his mug and went up on deck. After a few minutes, he returned to the galley, holding onto his pipe while he finished doing up his fly. He sat down, took a swig of his beer, and said, "His lad. Had two. Twins. One o' them was killed. Awful thing. He'd lost his wife years before, when the tykes were small. I saw him some time after the boy's murder. But I never made the funeral. Felt bad about that."

"Do you remember the boy's name?"

"Nope. Wouldn't know it if it hit me."

"Did Judson have any idea who might have done it?" asked Bea over the hiss of the fire and the lap of the water against the dock.

"Don't know if he did. But I asked him that same thing when I ran into him some time later, not too long before I came back here to Newfoundland. Remember now."

"What did he say, Clement?" asked Bea, taking a sip of her beer.

"Said, 'I can't say,' which made me think he knew who did it but wasn't telling. Then he said, 'Lost one boy; I'm not going to lose the other.'" After several seconds, Clement continued, "Another thing."

"What's that, Clement?" McNeil asked.

"The other lad, the twin. He was with his father that day I ran into them down on the wharf in Greenwich. Strange boy. Mind you, I might've been if it was my brother who'd just been killed. Still, he struck me as a shifty little thing. Didn't take to him. He was standing right there beside his father when Judson answered my question. When his dad finished speaking, he looked up at him, and then at me. It was the oddest thing, the sense I got from him."

"He must have been upset. Or angry?" asked Bea.

"No, not at all. That was just it. He didn't seem to care. Didn't seem sad about his brother's death at all. Seemed to think our conversation was funny. I could swear he was even going to laugh."

... --- ...

Bea closed her eyes, and floated her hand like a blind person across the muslin, then the satin. She felt the fabric the way Aunt Isabella had taught her. "Listen. Let your skin tell you, love," Aunt Evelyn's sister had advised Bea years ago, before she'd left Newfoundland, first to go to Canada, then to Italy. They hadn't seen her since. But feeling the fabric didn't take her mind off the night. If anything, thoughts of Aunt Isabella only reminded Bea of a world beyond the material and the tactile. Isabella had never seemed afraid of it. God only knew why. Finally, after too long a time trying to make sense of everything, she left Aunt Evelyn's sewing table and went up to bed.

... --- ...

Mildred wasn't surprised that tonight was the night that Bea woke sweating, sitting straight up in bed, staring at the dark as she tried to make it gone. She was only surprised that there had not been more of these nights over the last week. Bea didn't rouse entirely, but lay back down again after a minute or so, and within seconds, she was sleeping again. But the sleep was fitful, and Mildred sat right next to the bed and kept watch while one disturbance after another rolled across her soft face and beneath Bea's fine eyelids. She was glad she was here to tend to Bea's nights. Her daytimes had plenty of company; it was by night that she needed Mildred most.

Day Eight
Tuesday, October 21, 1902

July 1872
Police search for child murderer.
On Sunday afternoon, Mr. Judson Stevens of Greenwich discovered the dead body of one of his twin sons, Brian Stevens. The child's throat had been cut. No weapon has been found. Authorities are investigating but as yet there are no leads. Brian leaves behind his twin brother, Henry.

August 1872
Search for child murderer suspended.
In over a month, no new evidence has been found to implicate anyone in the murder of Master Brian Stevens. Police are refusing to say if they have any suspects. "We've not enough evidence," said Inspector Rand of the Greenwich Constabulary.

The police have decided to call off the investigation. When questioned by the Times, *Mr. Judson Stevens said that, unfortunately, calling off the investigation is the best decision. "It is really the only decision that can be made at this time," he told the* Times. *Mr. Stevens, who is a widower and has been the sole parent to the boys for the past six years, said that he has come to believe that Brian's death must have been a case of mistaken identity. Someone must have killed him by mistake, he said. He said that he sees no reason why anyone would have wanted to hurt his son.*

"There it is, if you can believe it," Bea said when she finished reading the two small newspaper articles, then she leaned over the binder of old newspapers and put her forehead on her hands. "Don't suppose there could be another Brian Stevens, could there?"

"Doubt it, dear," said Mildred.

It had taken Bea more than an hour to find anything on the death.

... --- ...

"I wonder if you could help me with something, Miss O'Flaherty: Do you happen to have English obituaries from the mid-1800s?" Bea had asked.

"Unfortunately yes, Bea," answered the diminutive, elderly woman, shoving back her chair with fervour and marching away from her massive oak desk. Bea followed her past row after high row of books and papers and magazines. "The English take up more space than they should in my little library. Here's their dead; some of them, in any case, not enough if you ask me." They arrived at the end of a long row and she pointed to a set of tall binders with leather covers. "*The Illustrated London News*. Five years at time. What year, Bea?"

"I'm not sure. Let's try 1858 through to '65."

"Then start with these two," she said, hauling a heavy binder off the shelf. "This one's '55 to '59," she said, dumping it unceremoniously on the small table in the aisle; dust billowed around them as she did so. "And that one, Bea, '60 to '64." She indicated the one she meant, which Bea extracted and put on the table. "If you don't get anywhere with these, '65 starts the next one. There are other newspapers when you're done with those. Are ya all right, then?"

"Yes, thank you, Miss O'Flaherty." After Miss O'Flaherty had left her on her own, Bea sat down at the table. "Where to start?" she mused aloud. "Mr. Stevens must be fifty at least, which would mean he would have been born in 1852. So, he would have been twelve in 1864. If he and Brian were twins — gawd, this is too silly for words; I can't believe I'm even doing this — and Brian died when he was twelve, then I'm going to need more of those books. I don't think Mr. Stevens can be older than fifty, but he's probably not younger than forty." Bea opened the binder, and turned to the newspapers starting at 1864.

...---...

"Natty?" asked Bea, standing on her porch.

"Bea!" said Natty, holding the door open wide. "Want to come in? I really could use the company."

"Can't. I'm already late for Shulman's. You know how you told me about the cuts on the twins' hands? Do you know any more about that? How they happened?"

"Yeah, I do, as a matter of fact," Natty said. "One day, Brian was sitting in the kitchen while I worked. I was chopping pork for supper, and I nicked my finger. It was just a little cut, but you know how they bleed. I ran over to the sink and poured water over it and that's when Brian, who had been silent the entire time I'd been working, started talking. 'My hand bled more than that,' he said. 'Did you cut your hand, Brian?' I asked him. 'He cut it,' Brian said. 'Who?' I asked. 'My brother,' Brian said, and then he went on: 'He laughed while the blood fell from my hand and onto his.'"

...---...

Bea had seen it when he removed his glove at the store: Mr. Stevens did have a scar on his hand just as Natty had said, and on the cuffs of his gloves were the initials *HFS*. She decided she had reason enough, and so here she was in his bedroom.

She had rushed over here after her shift at Shulman's, and had poorly pressed three of Mr. Stevens' shirts that were hanging in the laundry room, so that she would have reason to be in the bedroom should Mrs. Stevens find her.

Mr. Stevens' room was remarkably clean and tidy, despite a grimy tinge to the air. It could use a good airing. She certainly wouldn't be the one to do it, she thought, screwing up her nose and glancing to her right at a small bedside table and the single bed with its tight, plaid cover, more like a boy's than a man's. The head of the bed faced the window at the other end of the room, and under the window sat a worn, brown armchair positioned so that the viewer could look over the street. He could see everything from here, she realized. He could see them all coming and going and no one would be the wiser. On the left side of the room and below a smaller window, but separated from the armchair by a partial wall, was a desk. A fireplace directly to her left, an old rug and rocking chair, and a large closet leading into the water closet made up the rest of the room.

With his freshly pressed shirts draped over her left arm, Bea went immediately to the desk and opened the top drawer. She hadn't really expected to find anything; she didn't know what she was looking for, so she was surprised by the first piece of paper she stumbled across.

> *Dear Penelope: I have tried to tell you about the murder, but I have spent so long pretending it never happened . . .*

That was the only sentence. Bea looked around. To the left of the desk, on the floor, sat a copper rubbish bin, and inside it, a number of crumpled pieces of paper. She bent down and picked one of them out of the basket.

Similar to the first, this was also a single sentence long.

> *Dear Penelope: I remember laughing about it. It was the strangest thing.*

Letters to his wife. Why? And why only partially written? She reached down to get another one, but just then the front door slammed.

"Penelope, I'm home!" boomed Henry's arrogant voice.

By the time he had removed his coat and hat and hung them on the coat rack, Bea was on her way down the stairs. His shirts had been hung in his closet, and when she reached the downstairs foyer, she acted like he didn't exist as she strode past him into the kitchen.

. . . --- . . .

When she slowed, they slowed too. When she quickened, so did the footsteps keeping in time with hers. Bea had gone only a few blocks in the dense fog, but nevertheless she was sure of it. There could be an innocent explanation for the person's presence, but she didn't think so.

She was being followed. She was sure of it.

She turned right at the next street, where the light from the streetlamp barely penetrated the fog. The person behind her made the same turn. Bea walked faster and felt along on her right until her hand finally touched up against a large tree. She found her way around to the other side of the tree, feeling her way, hoping its trunk would hide her. The fog should have been doing that well enough, but it hadn't. The person — male or female, she couldn't tell — had had no trouble staying on her tail.

The person walked by while Bea tried to take shallow, silent breaths. The footsteps had gone beyond the tree when they stopped, turned, and listened. Through the fog, Bea couldn't see the person, or even an outline, only a darkening that interrupted the streetlight. Suddenly, the band of fog lifted, opening the night, and immediately the footsteps started up again. Perhaps he was concerned about being discovered; whatever his reason, he started quickly off down the street and away from Bea and her hiding spot. But she had seen all she needed to identify him: the hat on his head and the umbrella in his hand. She had sold him both. The black silk umbrella with its steel rod looked as ominous now as it had then; it had always reminded her of a weapon. Even before tonight. The hat was the new Pure Beaver Black Stiff Hat. They wouldn't be ordering any more of those. They sold poorly. In fact, they had sold only one, and that had been to Mr. Stevens, the day after the shipment had arrived in the spring.

Penelope waited at the top of the stairs for George to leave, then ran softly down to the foyer and took Henry's extra coat and hat off the coat rack. Henry had left again, ages ago, soon after Bea had gone home — he had an important errand to do, he'd said. She hesitated for a moment, listening to make sure that George had left through the gate.

She quickly slipped into Henry's coat, and tucked her strands of hair under the hat. She faced the long hall mirror. She had always been muscular; still, she probably wouldn't pass for a man during the day . . . but on a night like tonight?

… --- …

Like a babe born into an unfriendly world, Brian beat at the cloying mass with his fists. But this new, reeking environment was amorphous. He couldn't push it off. He inhaled its fishy smell and opened his eyes onto its thick, white shroud. His impulse to suck and breathe was strong, but each frigid breath seared his throat, his lungs, his eyes and then, suddenly, he was drowning. Someone was pushing him down by the back of his neck, submerging his whole head in water. Stop! Let me breathe! Stop, he screamed in his head as he thrashed and struggled under water against the powerful pressure on the back of his head.

Just as suddenly, he was up for air. He had been released, and he gasped and choked, and tried to think and act. His cheek on the hard wet floor, he tried to see his attacker. He couldn't see anybody. He might as well be blind. It was so dark in here. Who was trying to kill him? And why? He tried to look around for his alcove, for the safe corners of his cave, his escape route. He couldn't make them out. He couldn't feel them either as he felt forward with his hands. Just sharp shale and pebbles on the damp cave floor.

Pain shot through his head and his neck. His attacker had grabbed him again by his hair, yanking him up off the floor, wrenching his head backward. Brian was propelled forward, and down toward water — he knew now — to drown. He struggled to break free. He scratched and kicked backward, but he was overpowered, and the top of his head hit water. But he didn't go under. Instead, his attacker pulled Brian's dripping head backward, and with vile breath its vanguard, the frightening voice yelled words he had heard before: "Got the message now? Don't ignore me!"

In a flash, Brian was under. Fathoms down, or so it seemed. With nothing to breathe, and no one to save him.

He could breathe here though, funnily enough, as he again smelled overwhelming fish in the dank air. This wasn't his cave, he realized, and there was no one out to get him. Not now, anyhow. He still couldn't see, though. But it was a different kind of not-seeing than the darkness of his cave. This atmospheric shroud that encased him was thick and white and permeable, but it had no substance. What mysterious matter was this? Where was he? Then it occurred to him — he didn't know why he hadn't thought of this before: This was death. And heaven.

Heaven smells like fish and looks like this? For a moment he was utterly disappointed. But then he answered himself:

This isn't death, Silly. It can't be.

Yes. Must be. Look at it.

I can't see a thing.

You see. I told you. It must be death. Maybe it's hell, not heaven.

He waited several seconds without talking to himself while he thought about this. Then, happily, he had a better idea.

Death doesn't smell like fish and salt water and seaweed. If you were dead, Brian, you wouldn't be able to smell, for pity's sake.

Can you smell when you're dead?

Who knows, Silly. Don't worry about it. You're still alive.

So this is life.

Yes.

Not death.

That's right.

If only I could see.

He could walk, though. His bare feet hit ground, slick and hard, and he slipped and almost fell. The ground was familiar — a cobblestone road? And that sound, a horn to warn the ships. More of the familiar. He breathed a little more easily now. So, this then was life and Earth and he was not on some alien planet, or dead and in some strange hell or an even stranger heaven.

He groped the damp elusive blanket around him, blind, but not deaf: he could hear a voice wafting through the din toward him. Go away, he thought automatically. Go home, he said to the voice, get away from here. It's dangerous out here, he realized, and once again he reached for his alcove and once again remembered that it wasn't here. He wanted the voice to leave, but then again, he didn't. Not really. He wanted the company. He walked forward slowly, like a sleepwalker, his arms outstretched. His fingers met a hard and cold object. He jumped backward, almost slipping again. Reaching out, he touched it again: A metal of some kind. He gingerly roamed his hand over the tall, cylindrical object, then, gaining courage, reached up and around it, feeling its height, its cold, and the bumps made by its uniform vertical ridges. He felt strangely comforted. Whatever it was, it existed. Just like him. It was only himself, the voice and the object here together in this wet, smelly world. And there was the voice again; and he clung to it in his mind, trying to figure out how far away it was, or how close. He leaned against the metal object and listened. The words distorted, cleared, distorted, and suddenly George broke through the blanket of white right in front of him.

"Bloody fog," he said.

"Fog?" asked Brian, looking around. Yes, fog, you idiot.

George reached down between them and Brian recognized the sound that followed; it was the creaking of the gate leading out of the front yard onto the street. Brian had been standing on the street side, apparently, and the metal object that he had clung to just now was the lamp post outside the house. You shouldn't worry so much. I shouldn't worry, he thought, and smiled to himself.

No?

He frowned and reached out to touch George on the shoulder, but he was no longer there. He had charged ahead down the street. Don't leave me again, George. I can't see.

"George?" he cried, and he began to run, only to bump right into him. George had gone just a couple of yards before stopping.

"Hell with it," said George, looking around.

"What? What is it?" asked Brian. But he knew what. He could smell something else; something was out to get George. On this street somewhere.

Where?

I don't know.

Get him to turn back.

I'll try. "George!"

"I'm not going to be afraid. That's just silly," George announced, and strode several steps ahead before Brian caught up again.

"No, not silly," said Brian, running out of breath. Not silly at all.

"I'm not going to stay home just because of some stupid . . ."

"Stupid what?" asked Brian.

"Stupid game. Stupid idiot playing a stupid game," answered George.

"Not a game, George. Believe me. Remember? Remember what the message on your stomach said?" What *had* the message said, Brian thought, stopping in his tracks. Now that he had mentioned it, Brian himself was having trouble remembering. "George, wait up," he called.

"It was one of my friends," said George, slowing down until Brian caught up. "If I ever find out which one, he's dead." He stopped and kicked at the road, unearthing broken cobblestone and pebbles.

"I don't know who it was but I'm pretty sure it wasn't one of your friends, George. It didn't seem like a very friendly thing to do."

At that, George stopped again. Brian stopped with him and stretched his senses out into the fog. "You're not being silly, George," he said. "Just turn back. Being courageous won't help you when bad things come out of nowhere and you're trapped before you know it." Trapped how, he wondered as George kept on walking without answering. "If I had known what was going to happen, I never would have left home. Believe me," Brian added, but George wouldn't believe him; George wasn't listening.

"To hell with it," George muttered, striding on ahead.

This time, Brian knew right away that they weren't in George's room. They weren't in an alley, either. This was the road they had just been on. The last he remembered, he had been walking along with George trying to convince him to go home, and now here was George on the ground again, just like last time in the alley, except now he was more awake and grabbing on to a lamppost and pulling himself to his feet.

"You've fallen again, George," he said, but as soon as he'd said the words, he knew they weren't true. Of course he hasn't fallen. He's been hit again.

Look, will you?

Brian looked even though he didn't want to, and there was blood falling from a cut high on George's head this time, and dripping onto his shirt. The shirt would have to go. It was a shame because, this time, George had not wet his pants. George was pulling up his shirt.

"What? This again?" George cried.

"Yes," said Brian, stepping back from George. He couldn't stand this. He wished it would all just go away. Footsteps echoed through the fog toward them and George dropped his shirt and tucked it into his pants. An approaching light penetrated the fog.

"Who's there?" George called.

"Miss Norton. Eliza Norton." Her voice sounded thick and far away. At the sound of her name, Brian stepped further back into the dense curtain of fog behind George. He didn't want her to know he was here.

"Oh. Sorry, Miss Norton. It's George Stevens," George said, glancing behind him and shrugging. He had been about to introduce him, Brian knew, but perhaps because of the direction of the lamp's light, the fog seemed to be acting as a one-way screen so that somehow Brian was still able to see them, but they couldn't see him. "I can't see you," George said to Miss Norton.

"Nor I you. Where are you?" she asked, as the light yellowed the fog in front of George.

"Right here," he said, and she appeared right next to him, lantern in hand.

"Oh. Yes. I could never forget that handsome red hair."

"I got your note."

"What note?" she asked, surprised, and looking at him curiously.

"The one you sent me. Asking me to meet you here, at the end of the block, at 9 P.M."

"Really? Let me see."

As George began to reach into his pant pocket, she glanced down at his coat-less chest and suddenly noticed the blood. "George, what on earth happened to you? You've been hurt, George. Are you alright?"

"I don't know, Miss Norton."

"Eliza."

"Eliza," he said tentatively. "Someone's out to kill me, I think."

She suddenly stepped back, so that fine mists layered her face like a veil. "How horrible. Ghastly. What on earth makes you think so?"

"This is the second time this has happened. Someone knocking me on the head in the dead of night."

"Really?"

"Yes. And he left something else behind."

"What?"

"Markings on my chest and stomach."

"How horrible," she said, shutting her mouth with her hand. And then, stepping toward him, she said, "May I see, George?" Her blue eyes looked brighter. Brian had seen that look on her face before, but now he couldn't tell what made them so.

"Oh, I don't know, Miss . . . Eliza. It's nothing a lady should see."

"Please don't worry, George. I promise I won't faint."

"Oh, alright," said George, and he untucked his shirt and lifted it to show her his bare chest and stomach.

"Oh my," she muttered as he turned his chest toward the light so they could look at the smudges together. She bent forward to get a closer look, but a moment later she stood up straight and glared at him. "Is this some kind of a joke, George?" she cried.

"Sorry?"

"Those words."

"What does it say?"

"You don't know?"

"No, I can't read it."

"Are you certain?"

"Yes. I've never learned Morse. It's Morse, isn't it? Do you know what it says?"

"No. It's illegible. And you're right," she said softly. "Of course. You're right. Perhaps I shouldn't have looked. I'm sorry. This is just too hideous. You poor thing." She laid her gloved hand over his arm, but he stiffened at her touch. "I am sorry, George. Please forgive me. I don't know what made me react like that. I guess you were right about showing it to a lady." She stepped over to a lamppost and leaned up against it.

"I shouldn't have. I'm sorry. It's not your fault. Come," said George, tucking his shirt in again. "I'll walk you home." He reached his arm out toward her.

"Lovely," she said, taking his arm, hooking her hand gently into his elbow. "What a gentleman. Thank you, George. We just won't talk about it on the way, alright?"

"Fine with me. This way?"

Eliza smiled at him and nodded and they started down the road, her lamp lighting the inches in front of them. "Now let me see that note that I supposedly sent you."

He handed it to her, took the lantern from her hand, and held it beside the paper so that she could read. "It is exactly as you said, but George, I'm afraid someone is joking with *you*, although if these injuries are any indication it is certainly not much of a joke. This is not my writing, George, not at all. I never sent you this. I say, George, does the writing seem familiar to you?"

George went silent while he frowned at the note. Finally, he nodded. She put her hand through the crook in his elbow once again and they walked down the street. After they had gone several blocks, George said: "What were you doing out on a night like this?"

"I came out looking for my father. I wondered if he had come this way. He's probably home by now."

Brian remembered what the words on George's belly said. When Eliza had read the words just now, Brian hadn't joined her. He didn't need to look at the message; he knew what he would find. Henry would know, too. This wasn't the first time those words had been written in blood on the belly of a boy.

... --- ...

"We'll just throw them in the fireplace. I'll get you clean clothes, Henry," Brian had whispered as he helped him up the stairs. But Henry's urine-soaked trousers weren't the worst part, and they both knew it. The worst part was the gash on Henry's forehead that still bled profusely. Brian had found him unconscious on the rocky trail leading from their cave. They had been at their cave, and when they left, Henry ran on ahead. Brian had not bothered to try to catch up; Henry was so much faster. Brian found Henry lying on the path, bloody and bruised. All Henry could remember was being hit from behind before falling down the steep embankment.

The twins had sneaked in through the back door and were almost to the top of the stairs when their father called from the study: "Supper's in half an hour."

"Yes, Father," Brian called back, and then to Henry, he said, "We'll have to tell him."

Henry nodded and adjusted the piece of Brian's shirt that he held to his head. "He'll find out anyhow," he muttered.

"Look at me!" Henry gasped as they entered their bedroom.

Henry's face that stared back at them from the dresser mirror was scary and unfamiliar: red ugly scratches along his cheekbone, a swollen lip, and the bloody rag held to his forehead — all of it evidence of his encounter with the hard object that hit him from behind and then the rocky path on which he had fallen.

Brian got a clean cloth for Henry's head and then waited while Henry went to the water closet to wash and change. A few minutes later he emerged, having put on a clean pair of trousers, but not a clean shirt. His blood-splattered shirt hung open.

"Look," said Henry, as Brian came up to him. Henry pulled apart the panels of his shirt to show blood on his chest.

"It's just some more blood, Henry."

"It's not, Brian. Come, look at it over my shoulder."

Brian went to stand beside him and gazed over his brother's shoulder. Something had been written on Henry's chest.

"Can you make it out, Henry?"

"Yes. Can you?"

"Yes."

"We don't need to tell him about what happened to me, Brian. He already knows," whispered Henry.

"Don't ignore me!" their father had yelled at them that morning as they were leaving the house. "I forbid you to go up to your cave. Do as I say, boys, or there will be trouble for you." He had been giving them another lecture about not going up to the cave — and just as they had ignored all the other lectures, they were about to ignore this one. For months, their father had been a changed man: troubled, irritable, but never physically violent, and it had never been directed at them. But that had changed, they both knew, as they peered down again at the words written on Henry's chest. *Don't Ignore Me.*

Penelope started her climb to the Nortons' apartment and tried to calm herself, but it was fruitless. She had gone out to follow George. She knew he would never ask for her help. Today, a messenger had delivered a letter to George, and all afternoon and into the evening he had been acting strange, and oddly excited. She had kept an eye on him, and when he left the house just before 9 P.M., she waited in her room until she heard the gate shut. Through her bedroom window she heard him say, "Bloody fog," and she started down the stairs. But by the time she made it onto the street, she had lost him in the fog. She finally heard him say, "What? This again?" and was about to run up to him, startled by the tone of his voice. He had never been a child to show fear, and when he did, she knew something was terribly wrong. But she had stopped at the sound of footsteps coming from the opposite direction. George had called, "Who's there?" and when she heard Eliza's voice, she had quietly moved away so that she was still within earshot.

Afterwards, she had waited in the fog outside the house until George had returned home. She knew he wouldn't want to see her; he would probably stay in his room for the night. He would be too ashamed to come out. She had slipped back into the house, removed Henry's coat and hat, and tiptoed into the parlour. From the bottom drawer she removed an envelope, and from the envelope took a handful of pound notes. Her mother's money, which Penelope would have posted tomorrow. She hated to take it; she knew how much her mother depended on it. She hoped she would understand.

...---...

Eliza answered the door seconds after the knock. She wasn't surprised to see who it was. What did surprise her, however, was how distraught Penelope looked.

Without preamble, Penelope said: "Is your father still up?"

"No, I'm afraid he's retired for the night."

"Really. On the other hand, why would he be awake? He'd have had someone else do it, wouldn't he?" she said, and without waiting for an answer, she thrust a handful of money into Eliza's palm. "Tell him if he leaves George alone, there will be more." She paused and took a deep breath. Her voice had begun to break, but she composed herself and went on. "Your father is trying to hurt my son."

Eliza averted her gaze and when she next met Penelope's, her eyes had begun to tear over. "Yes, I believe you're correct, Penelope," she whispered, and then in a panic, she hissed, "Oh, Penelope, please don't tell him I just said that. You won't, will you?"

"Eliza, you really should build up a bit of backbone. It would do you some good."

"Please. I beg you, Penelope."

"Fine."

"Thank you, Penelope. You honestly don't know what he can be like. He would kill me."

"Before he kills my son? I doubt it," Penelope said coldly, and pulled her arm away when Eliza reached for it. "He needs you to look after him, doesn't he?"

Eliza nodded.

"You see. You have nothing to worry about. A little cruelty, perhaps. I'm sure you can cope. But my son . . . tell your father . . . tell him — not another attack. My son is all I have."

Eliza nodded to the woman's back as she strode away down the hall and marched down the stairs. When Penelope had reached the second floor, Eliza closed the front door and went down the hall to her bedroom. Her room smelled as it always did, of magnolias. Earlier tonight, lilacs had been in the air.

When she came out of her bedroom a short while later and went to the kitchen, the counters and tabletop were polished to a shine. No smears of any kind anywhere. Nothing to be afraid of here. Everything tidy; everything in its place. And there, where it should be, where she had left it, the single table setting — the scarlet placemat, a knife, two forks, two spoons, the napkin. A water glass. Full, still. But then, it always was, she thought, and giggled aloud at what she had become.

. . . ---. . .

Without taking off her coat, Penelope ran up to George's room as soon as she got home. She listened outside his doorway for movement or sound. "George?" she whispered. He didn't answer, and after several minutes of waiting, Penelope gave up and went downstairs. Henry had returned home, she realized, as she hung her coat on the coat rack. But the weight of her coat had made the thing unbalanced and out of order. She rearranged the coats so that the hooks all the way around had an even amount of weight. She had lifted George's coat to one of the highest hooks when her hand felt something in his pocket. She reached in and took it out. She wouldn't normally read her son's private correspondence; she found that kind of behaviour appalling. But lately, life had gone awry, and she was not being herself, whatever that self might be, recreated as it was from one moment to the next. She opened the paper, and when she did, she was glad she had. So like the other one from Cyrus Norton the other day. This note, requesting a meeting with George at nine that night, had been signed Eliza Norton, but the handwriting did not appear to be hers, or her father's. Penelope wondered if she should talk to Henry about this now. She shoved the paper in her pocket. No, she decided: she would wait for a better time.

Day Nine
Wednesday, October 22, 1902

"Jean, do you remember the Morse code you deciphered for me?" Bea asked as they were getting dressed in the morning, the frigid air nipping at their skin. For the last two days, Bea had been wanting to ask Jean what she knew about Mildred. But the time had never seemed right, and it still wasn't. The Mildred question would have to wait; right now, Bea had to find out what she could about Brian.

"Of course, Bea, but I don't want to talk about it anymore. I told you that," answered Jean, throwing on another petticoat and then her grey wool dress over top.

"I know, but I was thinking," Bea said, pulling her own dress over her head. "What if someone *was* murdered, Jeannie."

"It was someone playing a trick on you. Mum and Billy said so, right?" asked Jean, sitting down on the floor and pulling on her shoes over her leggings.

"Right. But I'd like to be sure."

"Why?"

"I just would. What if it's not a trick, Jeannie? What if someone was really murdered, Jean?"

"I don't care, Bea. Why should I? Anyways, why are you talking to me about this, Bea?" she asked as she stood and turned around so Bea could start to button the back of her dress.

"Why do they put buttons in the back of dresses, it's so silly," Bea muttered, fumbling with the tiny cloth-covered buttons. Jean shrugged as Bea added, "I'm no good at Morse."

"No."

"Please, Jean."

"I said *no*, Bea!" Jean spun around and yelled into Bea's face. "I'm not going to help you with any more Morse code. Learn it yourself. You should've learned it by now, anyhow."

With that she stomped out of the room and down the stairs, her dress open almost all the way down the back.

...---...

"Pardon, dear?" Henry asked, shifting his attention off Bea as she left the room and focusing on his wife at the end of the table. He shovelled an entire banger into his mouth. She hadn't touched hers. A single banger and a small mound of mash sat in the middle of her large plate.

"I didn't say anything."

"Really. I could have sworn you called my name."

"No. I haven't spoken our entire meal."

"Really," he said. He waited a couple more minutes and then lowered his voice and said: "The Nortons. They will be coming for tea tomorrow."

"Is that so? I don't think that's entirely necessary, do you?"

"Of course it is. We can't go on pretending, Penelope. Did you see George this morning? Something happened again last night. It's got to do with Cyrus Norton, I'm sure."

"Are you?"

"I've invited him over for two o'clock. His daughter as well, of course."

"Of course."

"You'll be here?"

"I wouldn't miss it, Henry, but you needn't bother, you know."

"I must make some kind of arrangement."

"What kind of arrangement would that be, dear?"

"Money, no doubt. It's the only thing he'll listen to."

"Would that be wise? One might think we're guilty of something."

"We? Well, one might, I suppose."

"In any case, dear, you needn't bother having them over. I don't believe there will be any more problems with George."

"And why is that?"

"Because I had a little chat last night with Miss Norton. Just between us women, you know. I'm sure there will be no more trouble."

"Really?" he said, standing up and wiping off his mouth. "Then why did I get a note from Mr. Norton this morning, requesting a visit, saying that I'd had more than enough time to 'think it over, Stevens'?"

"Alright. Let's ask, 'Did Henry do it?' Can you do that?" Bea asked Jean, who quickly tapped out the sentence using a block of wood and a piece of kindling. Bea had worked on Jean — berating, cajoling, and finally bribing her with a pound of the taffy that Aunt Evelyn forbade Jean to eat — until she finally consented to help Bea with the Morse code. Bea had brought Jean with her this morning. They finished the breakfast dishes, and then waited until they were alone before descending to the cellar.

They listened intently for a reply to the question. Finally, softly, barely loud enough, they heard an answer.

-- --- .-. -. .- / -.- -. --- .-- ...

"Do you know what it says?" whispered Bea. Jean nodded.

"Morna Knows," said Jean. "Who's Morna, Bea?"

Bea shook her head. "I have no idea," she said. "Ask: 'Where's Morna?'"

Jean stared at Bea for a few seconds, and then turned to her instruments and swiftly tapped out the question. They waited several minutes for an answer, and then Jean tried again.

Brian heard them. He heard them just fine, but what could he say? They knew where Morna was. He'd already told them. She certainly wasn't here, he thought, looking down at his feet against the wooden flooring, before gazing up the steep dark staircase.

DAY NINE

"Jean," said Bea, handing her the tub of lard. "It really must have been someone playing tricks. Aunt Evelyn and Billy are right, I think."

"Who, though, Bea? 'Morna Knows.' What do you suppose that means, Bea? Where is she, Bea? Who's playing tricks on us, Bea? Who's sending the messages?" Jean asked her flurry of questions as she set the lard down next to the flour that Bea had already poured into the bowl, along with a bit of salt.

Bea hadn't really expected to get a Morse code reply down in the cellar, and now she deeply regretted having convinced Jean to help her. "I have no idea. Start cutting it in, alright?" she said, trying to sound unconcerned, honestly glad that Jean had consented to stay with her. "We're running late." She removed an onion, two carrots, the butter and cream from the pantry and placed them on the working table.

Jean reached into the tub and grabbed a handful of lard. She dumped it on top of the flour and started working it in with her hands. "Who would it be?" she asked, her eyes shifting to the cellar door as she started to work. "Mr. Stevens is out. Mrs. Stevens said so, remember? And she's gone out, too."

"What about George? It could have been him."

"No. He went out earlier. When we were talking to Mrs. Stevens in the kitchen. I saw him leave by the front door," said Jean, quickly working the flour and lard with her fingers. Making pastry was one of her favourite chores, and she was good at it. "Who's the other boy, Bea? I just saw him heading upstairs a few minutes ago. He turned and waved. Didn't you see him?"

"No. You sure it wasn't George?"

"No. Although he looks like him, like the boys in the portraits."

"It must have been George, Jean, although I never thought George looked particularly like those boys in the portrait," said Bea, bending down to look further into the pantry shelf. "They're far too sweet."

"You don't think I'm sweet?" said a voice from the doorway. Jean screeched and her flour and lard-covered hands flew to her face. Bea stood up, hitting her head on the shelf above. "Sorry," said George, standing in the doorway with his coat on. "Didn't mean to scare you."

"Don't, then," said Bea, rubbing the top of her head and turning back around to grab the sack of potatoes.

"I think I'm easily as lovable as the boys in the portraits," George said, staring at Jean, who had immediately gone back to working the dough and staring intently into the bowl.

"Leave her alone," said Bea, reaching for a knife and an onion. She changed her mind — she didn't want to risk having the onion make her cry in front of George. She filled a bowl with cold water and began to peel a potato.

"But Bea, she was talking about me. I should know what she was saying."

"She was just saying that she saw you go upstairs just now."

"I didn't. I've just arrived."

"Really," said Bea, finishing that potato, plopping it into the water bowl and starting another. She didn't believe him for a second. "How did you get in? The cellar door?"

"That hasn't been used in years. It's bolted shut from the inside, but I don't even think it needs the lock. It's always been impossible to open."

"So you say."

"I do. Try it yourself. Besides, why would I use the cellar door, pray tell?"

Bea wasn't going to give him the luxury of knowing how scared they had been when they had been downstairs sending Morse code. She changed the subject.

"George?"

"Yeah," he said. Bea looked up from her peeling and noticed that he still hadn't taken his eyes off Jean, who hadn't stopped working the dough; it had reached the pebbly stage ages ago. It seemed the men in this family were intent on scaring the little girl.

"Back to the portrait in the hallway. You and your brother, you said?"

"Of course."

"Brian?"

"Yeah."

Liar. He's not your twin. He's your father's. No one else lives here besides you and your parents, Natty told me, Bea wanted to say, as illogical as it was, but she didn't because she had yet to tell Jean about Natty's experience with Brian, and about her own suspicions about Henry. She didn't want to scare her any more. She finished peeling the last potato and started cutting it.

"He's not around a lot, Brian," said George. "Kind of a funny guy.

He's a bit odd, really. I'm the normal twin." He came into the kitchen and sat at the window bench, picking up a fork on the table and stabbing it into the leftover pie that Bea had put there. "Wanna meet him?" he said with his mouth full.

Bea stopped cutting the potatoes and looked at him. "Really, George."

"I'm certain he would like to meet you."

"Really."

"Yes. He likes the company. Doesn't get out much. People don't talk to him a lot." Bea glanced over at him. "His choice, Bea. Don't get all upset. He's like that. Odd, like I said. A little more than odd, really. You really should meet him to find out for yourself. Natty always liked Brian."

"Did your father do something to him, George?" She couldn't help herself; she had to ask the question.

"Brian? Well, hard to say, really."

"George, you know what I mean," Bea said, shooting a look at Jean that she hoped George would see. She wished Jean wasn't here; she would be able to be far more direct with George.

But George didn't seem to notice what Bea was trying to say. "Did your father have anything to do with it, George?"

"With Brian being addled? Oh, I suppose so. Who knows, really? No one ever talks about it. It's the big family secret, that one. Unless you count the other one."

"What other one?"

"Well, my mother's a bit odd, or haven't you noticed? Shifty, I'd say. You should ask her about it. I never have. I'd be curious to know, though. Strange place to grow up, this house."

He had that right, Bea thought, glancing over at Jean, who had not changed position or stopped working the dough. Bea began to peel a carrot.

"This is all very exciting, girls," he said, putting the fork down on the empty pie plate. In a few minutes, he had eaten the remaining half of the pie. "But I have schoolwork to do, and now I really do have to go out; get some research done down at the reading room. But you wouldn't know about that, would you?" he said, smiling at Bea. She stared right back. Condescending like his father, George seized every opportunity to mention the superiority of his schooling above Bea's.

"It closes early today. Noon," she said, and noticed the look of surprise on his face. What could she possibly know about the hours of the reading room, after all, he must be thinking.

He pulled his watch from his pocket and glanced at it. "Just after eleven now. Still time, I suppose."

"Add the water," Bea said softly as they heard the front door close behind him. She handed Jean a small pitcher of cold water that she had set aside.

Jean poured a few tablespoons into the well of the dough and formed the dough into a ball. Only then did she speak: "It wasn't him."

"Who?"

"The boy I saw on the staircase a little while ago. It wasn't George."

"Really?" said Bea, her knife halting over the carrot she had been slicing. She glanced across to the kitchen doorway.

"No. It was George that I saw leaving the house earlier, but not George who I saw on the staircase." They worked quietly for several seconds, and then Jean asked, "Bea, who's Brian?"

"George's twin, just as he said. They're the boys in the portrait," Bea said. She wished she could tell Jean what Natty had told her about Brian. But she couldn't very tell her now; the child was anxious enough.

"Do you mean the boy I saw on the stairs is George's twin?"

"Must be."

"No, Bea. They don't look anything alike. Not at all. They can't be twins, Bea."

"Really," Bea said, finishing off the carrot and starting another.

"It's not just their faces, or their hair. It's not that," said Jean, busily spreading fresh flour over the worktop, then emptying the dough over it.

"What, then?" Bea said, barely able to speak. She wielded the knife, beheading and then peeling the onion.

Pressing gently at first with the stone rolling pin, and then harder to make a perfect circle, Jean seemed as if she hadn't heard. Bea was about to repeat her question when Jean said: "They're not the same age, Bea. George is older by far. George and Brian are sort of like you and me. And even if we looked alike, people wouldn't take us for twins, would they?" said Jean, looking up at her big cousin.

"No," said Bea, looking down at Jean. "They most certainly wouldn't."

"George is lying about them being twins. He must be the older brother. Where do you suppose the other twin is? The one in the portrait?"

"I don't know, Jean," Bea answered creating criss-cross patterns through the onion, cutting first one way and then the other, then slicing it widthwise so that tiny cubes tumbled onto the counter. She threw all the vegetables in a steaming pot of water to cook. Neither of them spoke while the vegetables were cooking. When the vegetables were tender, but still firm, she drained them.

"Bea?" Jean asked.

"Yes, Jean?" asked Bea as she stacked the vegetables into a deep pie plate, while Jean finished rolling the pastry into a big, thin round. Jean didn't answer her as she wrapped one side of the round over the rolling pin, so Bea continued to work. She shook salt and pepper liberally on the vegetables, coated them in flour, drizzled them with cream, and then she took the rolling pin from Jean's hand. She unwound the pastry over the mound, then with Jean working one side and Bea the other, they folded the sides of the pastry onto itself and then thumb-sealed it onto the edge of the pie plate. With the sharp knife she had used for the vegetables, Bea slashed the top of the pastry three times, brushed it with oil, and put the pie into the oven.

"Forty minutes?" asked Bea, pulling out her watch.

"Yeah," replied Jean. They quickly started to clean up: Jean took the countertop, and Bea took the tea and apple pie mess on the kitchen table.

While Jean finished wiping the last of the flour off the counter surface, Bea swept the floor under the table and around the counter.

"Bea?" Jean asked again as Bea put the broom back in its thin closet to the left of the pantry.

"Yes?" asked Bea, turning around. Jean had walked over to the doorway and was looking out into the hallway toward the stairs.

"Do you know how to get up to the attic?"

Of the two, Mildred decided that the boy on the left was Brian, and the other, Henry. The artist had captured a particular look in Brian's eyes: Wistful. Wistful. She sat down at the foot of the wide staircase to wait for Bea and Jean to finish when she heard a sound from above. She turned and looked up the winding staircase and there was Brian, standing at the top, on the second-floor landing. With a slight movement of his head he motioned for her to follow him, then he ran to his left, down the hallway and out of sight.

When she reached the top of the stairs and glanced in the direction he had gone, he was no longer there. She walked slowly down the corridor until she got to the end. A narrow ladder stood in front of her. She looked up to where it went. Above her head was the trapdoor for an attic and on the dirty wooden handle, a set of child-sized fingerprints.

She was about to reach up to push the door open when she heard a sound like a whisper, and she turned. He was back at the top of the stairs again, and now he was waiting for the girls to follow.

...---...

"Here it is." At the far end of the hall, a narrow ladder stretched upward toward the ceiling. "I'll go up. You stay here," Bea said, glancing back at Jean, who was looking nervously behind her down the hallway.

"You shouldn't, Bea. What if he's up there?"

"Brian? In the attic?"

"Yes."

"I don't think so, Jean. I'll go up. You just stay here, alright? I'll be fine."

"Alright," she said, but as soon as Bea had taken two steps, she said, "Bea?"

"Yes?" Bea asked, gripping the sides of the wooden ladder, and turning to face her.

"I know I said we should go up here. It's alright now though, you don't have to."

"Still. I'm curious. Aren't you? You said this is where Brian went."

"Yes, but it doesn't matter. Let's go."

"I'll just go up quickly before Mrs. Stevens comes home." Bea turned and climbed the eight or so steps to the ceiling. She could hear

Jean coming up behind her. "You don't have to come up, Jean. Just stay down there."

"I don't want to stay here all by myself."

"Alright, but if you come up, I don't want you getting even more frightened."

"I won't."

Above Bea the attic was closed off by a square trapdoor. She pushed on the wooden handle, but the door didn't move. "It doesn't feel like this has been opened in ages," she whispered to Jean, and she tried again. The door lifted off its frame, but as it did, a billow of dust fell over them. She glanced quickly at Jean.

"He couldn't be up here, Bea. He just couldn't."

"I'm sure you're right, Jean, but let's see." She pushed the door open all the way until it crashed over backwards. She popped her head through the opening and called quietly: "Brian? Brian?" Of course he didn't answer; no one answered. She scrambled up to the attic floor, reached down, and helped Jean up. They dusted themselves off, then looked around. They were standing at one end of a long narrow attic that ran the length of the house. A hazy light drifted from a small window built low into the wall on the far side of the attic. Next to the window were two crates, which looked like someone's chairs. Other than these, the place was almost empty, except for the furniture and boxes piled at the other end of the attic, mostly covered with white sheets.

"No one's here," Jean whispered.

"No, absolutely not," said Bea. Dust covered the entire attic. If anyone had been in here, they would have made a mark.

"What's that?" Jean asked, pointing at a small container on the floor near the window.

"I don't know. It doesn't matter. Let's leave it. Come, Jean," Bea said, glancing around at the unwelcoming attic. It was her turn to be scared. It did feel like someone occupied this space. She turned and looked at the white-wrapped furniture as if she expected to see people sitting in it. She turned at the sound of Jean's voice and realized her cousin was no longer standing by the trapdoor. She had gone over to the container and was squatting down beside it. She had reached out a finger toward it, but wasn't touching it.

"Leave it alone, Jean. Let's go," said Bea, as she bent down beside her cousin and realized that what she was seeing was a small box. Bea started to stand up, but then she noticed that a small dust-free circle surrounded the box. "Someone's dusted before they put it here," she said, and flicked her forefinger across the floor near the box. When she looked at the tip of her finger, it was absent of dust. "And not long ago. Today, or yesterday." She stood up and glanced around again. The box with the clean floor beneath it only made her more nervous. She couldn't figure this out. The whole attic was one big dust heap, and yet here, six feet from the window and ten feet from the trapdoor, was a dust-free circle, on top of which sat the little box. Someone had been up here, and placed the box after first cleaning the circle — but how? There were no footsteps in the carpet of thick dust, discounting the ones that she and Jean had just created. She looked over at the window. Had they thrown it inside? Somehow scaled the outside wall of the three-story house, lifted the window, and tossed the box inside? But, even if that was possible, which it wasn't, what of the circle? How could they have cleaned the circle? Then she had a thought: perhaps when the box fell on the floor, the energy of its fall had blown the dust aside. She visualized the impossibility of a square box creating a round circle while she tiptoed along the floor and looked at the window. It was sealed shut. She would swear it had never been opened, or cleaned. Dust covered the panes, the lead trim, and the wooden sash. And the heavy metal latch. No, whoever it was must somehow have come up from inside the house and through the trapdoor. Besides, she thought, who could have gotten through that window? It's far too small for most people. Perhaps a child, but even for Jean, as small as she is, it would be a tight squeeze, never mind the climb up the sheer wall of the house. She peered out onto the street. The gate and the corner of the front yard were visible from here, as was a maple tree in the yard, and part of the shrubbery and the road beyond.

"Look, Bea," said Jean. Bea turned around to see that Jean was wiping a corner of the top of the box with her sleeve. She walked over and stood behind Jean as she wiped some more. The solid tan gave way under her sleeve, revealing a dark red.

"I see," Bea said, glancing back at the window, and then down at Jean. "Keep going." Jean's sleeve had taken on the colour of the dust, but she kept wiping, removing one layer of dust and then the next. As the dust came away, Bea could see that the box was almost identical to Mr. Norton's: red with faded gold lettering. The difference between the two was the ship sketched onto the lid. "The *Niagara*," she said, and as Jean cleaned the last of the dirt, Bea's dream surfaced to the forefront of her mind.

"Shall we open it, Bea?" asked Jean.

"Let's," said Bea, feeling now more excited than afraid, and she let Jean lift the lid off the box. Inside were two compartments. In the compartment on the right, a single piece of paper, folded in quarters. But it was the compartment on the left that commanded her attention. There it was: the small knife from her dream, snuggled on a small pillow of white satin, its blade encrusted with what looked like dirt and rust. Or was it blood? Bea couldn't help but reach out for it when they heard the front gate open and shut.

"Someone's home, Jean!" Bea hissed.

They replaced the box and quickly climbed down the ladder, and Bea yanked the door shut behind them. "Look at us!" Bea cried when they reached the second-floor landing. They were covered in dust, and Jean's sleeve was black. They hurriedly swept themselves off. Bea rolled up Jean's sleeve to hide the dirt, and then they somehow managed to get down the stairs and into the kitchen before the front door opened.

"You're still here, girls?" Mrs. Stevens called from the hallway. "How splendid."

"Let's go back," Jean whispered when they heard the click of the door three flights above. She held tight to the banister with one hand and with the other she clung to Bea's hand.

"You can stay downstairs if you like. Just like I suggested. I have something to find out. I won't be able to sleep another night without knowing," said Bea, continuing her climb to the Nortons'.

"Don't want to stay down here by myself," said Jean.

"Fine then. I just have a few questions to ask. We won't be long."

When they reached the Nortons' apartment, Bea rapped on the door and then they both stared, terrified, at the doorknob. They heard the distinct sound of approaching footsteps, a rustling of skirts, and the door flew open. Even though they had heard her coming, they still gasped and automatically stepped backward. Framing the doorway was Miss Norton — blond, tall. Stunning. Once again Bea was taken aback by how beautiful she was. And then there, coming around the corner at the far end of the hallway, was her antithesis, Old Man Norton.

"Miss MacDonald? How nice to see you so soon. And who's this? Your little cousin?" Miss Norton asked.

"Yes, Miss. Jean's her name."

"Hello, Jean."

Jean didn't speak but just stared at the floor, nodding and clinging to Bea's coat.

"Is everything alright with my order?" asked Miss Norton.

"Everything's fine. Sorry to bother you," Bea said.

"That's no problem, Bea. We haven't had supper. But I thought for a moment you might have found the note that I misplaced, the one I thought you had found."

Bea fussed about in her satchel, and didn't answer or look up at Eliza. She knew if she did, the guilt would have been clearly inscribed on her face. She was saved from answering by Mr. Norton, who called out, "What're you all talking about out here?" while he limped down the hall toward them.

"Nothing, Papa," said Eliza tenderly.

"Don't sweet-talk me, Liza, I know damn well when there's goings-on behind my back. Ah, I see," he said getting up to the door, the foul odour from his mouth hitting them as he spoke. In one hand he held his cane, in the other his old box, clutched between his fingers like claws. Bea had never noticed his fingers before now; so much like the fingers around the box in her dream. "Women. Always got secrets, don't you? I've had enough of that, haven't I? Hey, I recognize you: you're the one wanting to know about my cable. Whadda they call you?"

"Bea MacDonald, sir."

"That's right. Bea. What kind of a name is that for a girl? And who you got there?"

"My cousin, sir."

"Whaddya want here anyhow?"

"I don't know, Papa, she hasn't said."

Bea could tell that Jean was ready to bolt, and she reached down and gripped her hand. Bea had planned what she would say. She had decided on an excuse she would use, but now that she was standing here in front of the Nortons', the words wouldn't come.

"Bea?" asked Eliza. "What is it we can help you with, dear?"

"Research," Bea blurted. "I'm helping down at the *Evening Telegram*."

"I didn't know you worked there as well."

"Only now and again."

"Yes? Research? Go on."

Bea didn't speak for a few seconds, then she released Jean's hand and fumbled in her satchel, withdrawing a pencil and paper. "We're doing a piece on recent immigrants."

"Wouldn't call us that, would you, Liza?" said Mr. Norton. "Don't remember immigrating anywhere."

"That's right, Bea. We're not sure if we're staying. We'll have to see how we like it."

"Yes, of course. But the article will be about the newly-arrived; I think that might be the headline, in fact: 'Newfoundland's Newly Arrived,'" she said, warming to her lie.

"What would you like to know?" asked Eliza.

Bea launched into a number of questions: when did they arrive; where did they come from; how long had they lived in Greenwich; did they have any relatives in Newfoundland? Finally, Bea slipped in the questions that led her to the reason they were here in the first place: how many people are or were in your family?

"Two now. Three before," answered Eliza.

"Before when?"

"Before mother died."

"I'm sorry. And I'm sorry to ask, but how long ago was that?"

"A year, Papa, was it?"

"If you say so," he muttered. "Something like that."

"For the record," asked Bea. "May I get your full names?"

...---...

"Time for a quick cup?" Bea asked.

"Absolutely. Am I glad to see you!" Natty cried. "Hullo, Jean."

"'Lo," said Jean, tightening her grip on Bea's hand. She hadn't wanted to come to old Angus Cooke's house again, especially after having just encountered Mr. Norton, but Bea had no choice but to bring her.

"Pa's driving me batty, he is," said Natty. "Never leaves the house, now I'm around. Don't know if he thinks he's protecting me or what."

"He's home now?" Bea said, as she took a seat at the table and Jean climbed onto her lap.

"No, thank the Lord," Natty said, putting on the kettle. Jean breathed a sigh of relief and climbed off Bea and onto her own chair. "Gone to meet up with some of his mates — is 'bout time. I can't hide here forever. So what if Mrs. Stevens sees me and reams me out? So what if I run into Brian? Better than hanging around here with Pa. Gotta get out of here."

"Well, I might have something for you to do tomorrow, and it'll involve leaving this house."

"What is it, Bea?"

"Keeping an eye on this girl for me. Her mum'll be busy, and I've got an errand to do," she said, patting her cousin on the head.

"Doesn't sound so bad, does it? Hey Jean?" said Natty. "We can find something to do, can't we?"

Jean nodded and smiled.

"When are we talking?" asked Natty.

"Around two, little earlier."

"There's more, isn't there? I can see it in your face," Natty said, pouring the water into the teapot and bringing it over on a tray with mugs and milk and sugar. She sat down, but before Bea could answer, she got up again: "What am I thinking? Been away from people too long, is what it is. Can't have bare-legged tea, can we?" She pulled several buns out of a canister on the counter and took them to the table along with plates, knives, and jam. "Help yourself."

"Thanks," said Bea, prodding Jean with her foot under the table.

"Thanks," said Jean.

Before Natty needed to ask again, Bea said, "I'll need you to come with me to where I'm doing the errand."

"Where's that?"

"The Nortons'."

"The Nortons'? Gawd, Bea. What're you doing there?"

"I'll tell you later," she said to Natty, slipping a sideways glance at Jean, who was munching down on a bun and jam.

"Right," said Natty, catching the look.

"Something else."

"What?"

"You said that Brian talked about Morna."

"That's right."

"What kinds of things did he say?"

"Not a whole lot. Mostly he asked if she was dead, or he asked if I knew her."

"Anything else?"

"Well, yeah, now that you ask. Once or twice he said, *Morna knows.* 'Knows what?' I'd ask him."

"What did he say?"

"He never did. It seemed to confuse him. Once, I remember, he looked at me like it was a really silly question, and then he just turned and walked away. I didn't see him for days after that; I thought I'd said something to bother him."

"Did he say something about it when you saw him again?"

"No. Not at first, but then in the hallway outside the study — he'd like to sit there, waiting for Henry, now I understand why — he looked up at me as I was going in there to dust and said: 'You should ask her.' It had been so long, I didn't know what he was talking about: 'Ask who?' I said. 'Morna,' he answered, and then he got up and walked away and up the stairs."

They each took a sip of their tea. The water on the stove hissed. A gust of wind shook a loose shingle on the roof; water from the day's earlier rain still dripped steadily onto a piece of metal on the porch.

"Natty?" asked Bea.

"Yeah."

"Do you know the name of old Norton's dead wife?"

"No, Bea. I don't. But I have a feeling I know what you're going to say."

"Morna, Natty. Her name was Morna Norton."

After they'd had supper and her father had returned to his work, Eliza sat down at the chair to the right of the third setting and folded her hands on top of the table. She kept glancing over at the setting and then decided that no, she was not crazy. But then, neither was her mother. Her mother had been sane, perfectly sane, but Eliza hadn't realized that until it was far too late. She should have seen it, but she hadn't. Her first inkling should have come two and a half years ago, when she'd decided that her mother was up to something. But even after she did find out, she still thought her mother was crazy. Eliza wished she knew then what she knew now. She would have asked her many more questions. Back then, she had one thing on her mind: to discover the truth behind her mother's activities.

She had decided to follow her mother and had given her a full block's lead, and had waited on the stoop trying desperately to bear no relation to the beetle-like woman disappearing around the end of the block, her shoulders bowed, her hands clawed in front of her chest, grasping her pocketbook. Anyone else would have thought that the worn brown coat, unmatching green hat, and torn leggings were charity donations, for goodness' sake. Clothes can be changed, as can posture, with some work. But a face? What do you do about deep lines and sagging skin that makes you look far, far older than your years? "Pray to God," Eliza had muttered to herself, as she closed her eyes momentarily and vowed that she would never end up resembling her mother.

She closed the door of their row house and went down the few steps onto the street, then stopped to adjust her fashionable straw hat with its wide band of pink satin, and swept her hand down her tan-coloured coat with the matching pink satin cuffs. She started out after her mother, making sure to stay a block or more behind all the way. It didn't matter if she lost sight of her; she knew this much — it was Tuesday, and every Tuesday, her mother sneaked out of the house and scurried through town to the post office. For many years Eliza had ignored this behaviour, as she had the others in her mother's repertoire, some more bizarre than others: the way she talked to herself, her obsession with Greek mythology, but mostly, her relationship to the colour of food.

However, when she reached the post office and watched through the side window as her mother withdrew the mail from her box and then re-locked it, she thought: these are not the actions of a crazy person. Has it all been an act? All those colour-banned years, all those chats with herself, all her conversations over the actions of Greek gods — Clytemnestra and Agamemnon, in particular.

When her mother had finished emptying and re-locking her post office box, Eliza stepped to the side of the window and waited for her to come out the front door. When she didn't emerge after a minute or two, Eliza peeked back in through the window to see that she was still busy at one of the tall counters in the large, high-ceilinged room, and she was addressing an envelope. She licked it and sealed it and walked over to one of the tellers, who smiled at her, stamped the envelope, and took her money. What was in the letter? Eliza was dying to know. She didn't think that her mother had any friends, and all her relations were dead.

After her mother had left the post office and returned home, Eliza waited about twenty minutes before coming down the road. She bought new gloves on the way, so that her mother would think she had been out shopping. Pink, to match her outfit. She was hoping that her mother wouldn't mutter under her breath, as she was prone to do: 'And where does the money come from for things like that?' Eliza had quit her job in the office of Glass and Elliot the month before.

Eliza fingered the scarlet placemat. She should have thought of the red setting years ago. It certainly seemed to help. She glanced at her clean, dry countertops. Nothing wet to write on. Nothing red to write with. If it weren't for the words in red on George's belly last night, she might have thought they were through that episode in their lives. But apparently not. Apparently, it was going to go on forever.

Not long before Eliza's eighteenth birthday, she had come home to find the whole kitchen blazing with colour. For most of her life, her mother had refused to cook red anything. Meat. Tomatoes. Berries. It didn't matter. If it was red, she wouldn't. Orange was next, and then anything in bright yellows. Eliza had been raised on blands and beiges, though for some reason greens were allowed, but even so, her mother would cook them well for a couple of hours until the boiling water had sucked every bit of forest or pine or moss and they all turned the same sickly flesh tone. The day she came home to a blazing kitchen, she smelled it first before she saw it, but when she set eyes on it, she almost vomited from the intensity of colour and chaos. Cubes of carrot and sweet potato and beets and tomatoes filled a massive glass bowl on the counter. On the round kitchen table sat a bowl of beef, thinly sliced and soaking in a burgundy wine. Next to that, a platter of berries of all kinds, and another small dish of dried apricots. Brightly filled bowls and plates covered almost the entire surface of the counter and the table, and worst of all the surfaces left bare were smeared with the juices from this entirely unexpected opulence. Amidst it all stood her mother, the conductor.

"Shouldn't you clean it up, Mother?" asked Eliza, more worried by the unclean surfaces than the food itself. Bad things happen in spills of red or orange or yellow, Eliza had been told often enough, and nothing could convince her mother otherwise, not her husband's anger, not her own daughter telling her, "You have clearly gone quite insane, Mother."

But that day, as her mother looked up from cutting an orange, she was unrecognizable, and not because of the speckles of colour all over her cheeks, chin, even eyelids. No, standing before Eliza was a happy woman. For the very first time ever, Eliza thought — so this is where my beauty comes from.

"We don't need to worry anymore, Eliza. I've figured it out," she said, sounding more lucid and self-assured than Eliza had ever heard.

"Figured out what, Mother?" Eliza asked as tenderly as she could, though she was feeling irritable. She had hated the insecure and insane mother all her life, but had grown accustomed to her and to the relationship they had created. She did not know what to do with the confident and rational woman standing before her, and she didn't like her very much. Her mother must have detected the tone in her voice, because she averted her eyes to the floor, the way she always did when Eliza felt out of sorts. She said softly, almost pleadingly: "This," and with the knife in her right hand, she swept her arm in a wide arc over the food festival. Then with what seemed like a surge of strength, she looked Eliza in the eye. "And, Eliza, I've also figured out the noise I'm always hearing. You hear it too, don't you dear?"

Eliza didn't know what to say. She didn't know that her mother knew she heard it. She could only nod, because she felt like crying.

"It will stop now. Don't you worry. I've been practising, you see, Liza . . ."

"Mother. Please don't call me Liza. Practising what?"

"Sorry, Eliza. Practising how to talk to him." She lowered her voice to a whisper in the way she was prone to do even though it was just the two of them in the house. "I bought a book the other day, a manual, it tells me how." With damp, brightly-stained fingers like rainbow gloves, she picked a book up off the table, where it had been hidden beneath a mountain of vegetable and fruit peelings, and waved it at Eliza. The cover was muddied with colour, and Eliza couldn't see the title. "I can't believe it only took me an hour, Eliza, once I sat down to read it. After all these years, it only took me an hour. All these years worrying about that sound and I can't believe I never thought of it before. It was right there on page ten. Dead. The word 'dead.'"

"Oh, for heaven's sake, Mother."

"No, really, Eliza, you should learn, too. We won't have to worry anymore. Do you want to? We could learn Morse code together."

"No!"

"Alright, dear," she said, tossing the book back down on top of the peelings and going back to cutting the orange. Without looking up she muttered, "If you say so."

Eliza watched her for another minute, not sure what to say or how to say it. "Let's clean up this mess, Mother."

"Alright, dear, but it's just another way of talking to him, that's all. He just wants to talk, Eliza. That's all. He just wants to talk to me."

Eliza had not bothered to ask who "he" was. She had been hearing about "him" all her life, and had long ago decided that he was a figment of a very disturbed imagination. That was then. Now she knew differently. If only her mother hadn't had her accident, her mother could "talk to him," and Eliza wouldn't have to worry anymore about messages written in red, such as the kind she'd found on George's belly the night before.

DAY TEN
Thursday, October 23, 1902

Fear had tiptoed into the building with her, and now stood quietly behind her while she tried to open the locked door with the stolen key. So when Jean harshly whispered, "Bea," terror was ready and waiting and it flung itself at Bea, wrapping itself tightly to her neck.

She spun around and managed to hiss: "Jean! What are you doing here? You're supposed to be waiting outside with Natty."

"She insisted on coming up," whispered Natty breathlessly, running up beside Jean. "I couldn't stop her."

"Go downstairs, Jean. Now," Bea whispered, the key that she had known she would find under the doormat feeling hot in her hand.

"No."

"Do as I say. Don't argue."

"I'm not going. I'm staying right here, with you. What are you doing, anyhow?"

"Nothing you need to worry about," said Bea, pulling her watch from her pocket. "Miss Norton asked me to, see? She gave me the key and asked me to get something for her."

"Then why are you being so secretive? I don't believe you, Bea. I think you're breaking into their place."

"I'm not. And if you don't believe me, that's fine, but you're not staying with me, Jean. Go back outside."

"No."

"Oh, gawd. Alright. But stay here. Do not come into the apartment, whatever you do."

"Alright."

"Promise?"

"Promise."

Bea stared hard at her for a few seconds, then glanced at Natty, who shrugged her shoulders. When Jean was wilful like this, there was nothing anyone could do.

"I'll be back in a minute."

She turned the key and opened the door, and was about to step into the apartment and shut the door behind her when Jean hissed, "Did you hear that?"

"What?" asked Bea, turning and glaring at her. Jean had stepped closer to the doorway.

"Morse code."

"Oh, Jean. Stop it. You're imagining things now."

"No, I'm not. It's coming from there," Jean said, pointing at the ancient telegraph machine just inside the doorway.

"Jean. That's been broken for years, love. Now, wait here. I'll be back in a minute."

Bea went into the apartment and closed the door behind her. She wondered for a moment why on earth she had come. In her pocket she still had the crumpled letter that Mr. Stevens had started to his wife, and she suspected that the knife in the box in the Stevens' attic had been the one used to kill Brian. Neither, of course, gave her cause to now be breaking into the Nortons'. But she did have two other reasons. First, the matching box, Mr. Norton's — so much like the one in the Stevens' attic, both resembling the one in the dream. She couldn't take her mind off it, and she had even wondered if Mr. Norton was the old man in her dream. Especially that smile of his. Gawd. She had thought she was going to be sick when he had smiled at her. But in the end, the box had compelled her more than the smile. She needed to see the inside of it. However, she wouldn't have broken in for that reason alone. The second reason had swayed her: *"Morna Knows,"* the Morse code message from yesterday. Morna Norton had been part of this family. If "Morna knew" something about Brian's death, Bea hoped to find it here.

She looked at her watch: just gone two. The Nortons had gone over to the Stevens' at two — Bea had overheard the Stevens' discussing the matter at breakfast — to talk about the terms of the blackmail, no doubt. It had been a hard choice: stay at the Stevens' and snoop in on the conversation right now taking place between the two families, or use the opportunity of the Nortons' absence to see what she could find out about Brian's death.

She had already decided where she wanted to begin: in Mr. Norton's room. She went quickly down the front hall, turned left at the kitchen — with its table curiously set for three — and into the bedroom hallway. At the end of the hall was the water closet. The door was ajar. The one door on the left side of the hallway and the two on the right were shut tight. Quietly, even though she knew she was alone, she tried the door on her left. It was locked. She moved to the door on her right, closest to the water closet. She knew by the smell when she opened the door that she had found Mr. Norton's room.

The light coming through the dirty window made his room even uglier, exaggerating the thin bedspread crumpled at the end of his narrow bed, the scratched and dented wood of his cheap desk, the worn rag rug crunched on the floor beside his bed. And there, on his dusty desktop, was where she had wanted to begin: the red scratched box that he always carried around with him. Exactly like the box at the Stevens'. She walked up to it, but didn't touch it. She ran her fingers along the outline of the word on the lid of the box. This one spelled *Agamemnon*.

A shiny new lock sealed the lid of the box. Without thinking, Bea started opening the drawers of the desk. In the second one down, she found it: the little key for the lock, not very well hidden under an old ledger. She slipped in the key and opened the lid.

Just like the inside of the Niagara box, this was also divided into two sections. Correspondence, mostly, on both sides. But no knife.

She fingered the stack of papers on the right. She removed a bundle containing several pieces of correspondence, which had been tied together with a thin piece of twine. Without removing the twine, she thumbed through the envelopes. There were seven pieces, each addressed to Mr. Judson Stevens: two pieces of mail from the gas works, bills she supposed; another from the cable company, AAE; two from Mr. Norton; a letter from the Gutta Percha Company; and another from the *London Daily News*. None of the seven pieces had ever been opened.

She put the correspondence on the floor next to the box, in exactly the same order she had found it, and took out a piece of paper that had been underneath the seven pieces. She read the surprising words:

Dear Cyrus,

Another month. Another ten pounds. You know what for. As per usual, I will expect the money within the week.

Forever yours,
Judson Stevens

She put it away and took two other pieces of paper from the box. At first it seemed as if the paper was peach, as in her dream, but then she realized that it wasn't at all. The letters were written in a strong masculine script:

September 20, 1900

Dear Mr. Henry Stevens,

I am looking forward to making your acquaintance once again, and thank you for replying to my letter of condolence regarding the death of your father. I assume my second letter didn't find its way to you, so I thought I would try again. As I had mentioned in my second piece of correspondence to you, please let me know what would be a convenient time to meet. I live within an easy distance from London.

Of course you won't remember the first time we met. You were a youngster and had come by the factory with your father. Did you find the whole operation awe-inspiring? I imagine you would have. For a boy, it must have been quite an experience. Besides the huge lengths of cable and the clanking of it as it settled onto its round, and the smell of metal and copper and sweat, there were the characters your father worked with. Especially Jeremiah, the gutta-percha man — he must have been a sight. I remember that I was shocked the first time I saw him at work, so you must have been doubly so. Shirtless and sweating profusely and huge, he must have weighed almost twenty stone, but he was as tender as a pussycat when it came to cable.

Do you remember? We were permitted to watch from the cabin that perched like an eagle's nest high above the core room. Only two individuals worked the sensitive jointing operation taking place below us: Jeremiah, and his assistant, Cyrus Norton. Do you remember him? While Jeremiah resembled a whale, Cyrus looked like an eel, thin and tall. What a pair they made. Jeremiah waiting patiently for his turn to wrap the gutta-percha while Cyrus did the soldering. But I'm certain you must remember this, I need not refresh your memory.

In any case, Mr. Stevens, that was our first and last introduction to one another, so many years ago. I look forward to seeing you again.

Sincerely yours,
Mr. Jake Adams

Bea re-folded the letter and placed it beside her. She unfolded the next letter and in a few seconds, she read the short note:

September 25, 1900

Dear Sir,

I felt prompted to make certain inquiries since your last letter and my sources have told me that the real Jake Adams is dead. Thus the question arises: who are you and why are you using his name? Please offer me an explanation for your correspondence or I will be forced to go to the authorities with this matter.

Yours,
HFS

She was reaching for more correspondence, when, unbelievably, she heard Jean at the front door.

"Bea!"

She ran to Mr. Norton's bedroom door and hissed, "Jean!" and hoped the whole building didn't hear her. "Close the door, Jean! Get out of here."

"Bea!" This time it was Natty. "It's the Nortons. They're coming!"

Bea ran back to the desk, put all the papers away as she had found them, locked the box, and started out into the bedroom hallway. As she did so, she heard three sounds in quick succession coming from the stairwell. The first was metal on wood, as if a set of keys had fallen to the floor; the second, the clank of a cane on a stair far below; and the third, Miss Norton's voice saying, "Wait here, Father. I'll take these up and then I'll come back down to get you. Sit on the stair."

Later, Bea would hardly remember the next several seconds. Fear threw its cocoon over her, stretching itself downward, tautly anchoring her to the hallway, leaving her immobile. After what seemed like a lifetime, she broke free and her hushed but panicked exit was overlaid with more sounds from the stairwell.

"Out. Quick," she whispered to Natty and Jean when she made it to the front door of the apartment. But out where? Where could they possibly hide? There was nowhere. Then Bea saw it. "There!" she whispered, and pointed to an open closet door at the end of the corridor, the opposite end from the staircase. They were about to run for the closet when they heard another voice from one flight down:

"Can I help you with those, Miss Norton?"

"Gladly, Maxwell. Thank you so much."

"Maxwell" then bounded down the stairs. The threesome glanced at one another — Miss Norton was still two flights down. They started for the closet when Bea stopped. She looked down at her open hand: in her damp and sweaty palm sat the tiny key for Mr. Norton's box.

"You go," she whispered, and motioned to them that she was going to go back inside the Nortons' apartment.

"What are you doing?" Jean whispered, gesturing for Bea with her hands.

Bea wondered that herself, but she just whispered urgently, "Don't worry. Go," and she waited while Natty grabbed Jean's hand and they reluctantly fled to the closet without her.

Bea stepped back into the Nortons' and locked the door behind her. Seconds later, she was back inside Mr. Norton's bedroom. She ran to the desk when she heard: "Thank you, Maxwell. That's fine. I can manage from here." Miss Norton was right outside the front door of the apartment. How had she timed it so wrong? Perhaps they'd only been one flight down, not two. It was now all too perfectly clear that she would not have had time to go back, return the key, and run to the closet where Natty and Jean were hiding.

Miss Norton's key unlocked the front door. Bea thanked heaven that she had thought to lock the door after her. She didn't know what made her think of it, but she was glad she had. As she heard the door open, she looked madly around for a place to hide and, finding nothing other than the closet or under the bed, she tiptoed across the room to the closet and crouched down in its dingy interior.

"Mother. We're home," Miss Norton called as she strode toward the kitchen. She banged something down on the table or the counter and then walked back to the front door, closed it, and returned to the kitchen, where she set down another heavy item. Bea could hear the thunk; it sounded as if she had brought home bags of rocks or wood. "Mother," she called again. "You'd like them. They're white, all white; I found them down by the docks in a couple of bins. I can't imagine why people would leave things like this behind, but there they were for the taking. Perhaps they'd fallen off a ship. Papa and I were taking a stroll down by the wharf like you and I used to do in England, remember, Mother? I didn't want to go to the Stevens' today like Henry had suggested. I kept insisting we not go, so we didn't, and we went down to the ocean instead. Do you remember how I'd play in the ocean and you would come running in after me? You must have thought I was going to drown or something. You'd get all wet. You always seemed so worried about me. You shouldn't have been, Mother. Really. I was fine. I can take care of myself, you know that." She stopped talking. She wasn't speaking in a normal tone of voice but rather in a shout as if she wanted Bea herself to hear. Bea heard more rumbling and thunking as she opened and closed cupboard doors. Bea supposed she was putting away the white things. Whatever on earth they were, Bea had no idea. "Two kinds of white," Miss Norton continued to call out happily, as if she had discovered gold. "Well, if you ignore the outside parts I guess. But just guess, Mother. Just guess what they are. Two kinds. He won't care about these. He couldn't possibly. They're not red." When she said this last sentence, she suddenly lowered her voice to a harsh whisper. Then she started to hum and continued to clatter about in the kitchen.

Bea didn't know what to make of any of this. Miss Norton's mother was dead. Miss Norton was talking to herself. This was behaviour that Bea easily understood; they did the same in her family all the time. But Miss Norton's way of doing it was so unusual — something was extremely odd about the way she spoke. In Bea's experience, people who talked to themselves always did so on the sly — even when they thought they were entirely alone — in a whisper, or a low voice at least. This shouting was most bizarre. Still, perhaps it's what she did to make herself feel not so lonely with just her father for company. She could fill up the whole apartment with a soothing, imaginary conversation with her mother and she could do it only when her father wasn't around. Perhaps that was why she had left him sitting down at the bottom of the stairs for so long. Bea was so wrapped up in trying to figure out Miss Norton's behaviour that at first she didn't hear the shift in sound. And when she did, she instinctively held her breath; Miss Norton had left the kitchen and was heading down the hallway toward Mr. Norton's bedroom.

Bea glanced at his door — she had closed it, thankfully; it was just as it should be, though she didn't remember having shut it — but she realized with horror that she had chosen an idiotic place to hide. As soon as Miss Norton opened his door, the shaft of light from the hallway would shine directly into the closet. The closet had no door. She had been banking on the shadows and Mr. Norton's pants and coats to act as a sufficient screen. She was about to lunge out of the closet toward the space beneath his bed — that was such a disgusting thought that she immediately pushed it away. Besides piles of dirt and dust, no doubt, God knows what all else would be under there — old apple cores she supposed, his dried spit, his filthy underwear. But she instinctively stopped herself from heading for the bed, and, instead, tried to squeeze an extra inch out of the back of the closet. Miss Norton was knocking on the locked door across the hall. "Mother?" Miss Norton whispered. Bea didn't hear an answer, but instead, another sound: a key turning in a lock. Miss Norton had unlocked the locked door. Its hinges creaked as she swung it open.

"Mother, what a mess you've made of yourself again."

Bea had to know who or what was in there. She crept out of the cupboard as she heard Miss Norton stride into the room across the hall. She tiptoed past Mr. Norton's desk to his door and slowly turned the knob. She began to open it, praying that its hinges wouldn't creak. They didn't, thank heavens, but through the small crack she could see nothing but the hallway. She realized that the crack at the hinged end might give her the correct angle to see into the other room, but it would mean she had to open the door further, to give herself more space to see out. Trying not to think what would happen if Miss Norton suddenly decided to depart the room to discover her father's door ajar, she opened it a few more inches and squinted through the crack between the door and the frame.

Miss Norton was still talking loudly, which was good; at least Bea knew where she was and it covered up her own noise. "Mother, you know I really wish you would speak to me when I talk to you. It's most upsetting to be talking to oneself all the time. In any case, Mother, I want you to guess. Quickly now, before I go get Father. I'm sure he's wondering where I could have got to."

Bea could see into the now unlocked room. On the far side was a bed topped with crumpled blankets, much like Mr. Norton's. She couldn't see an actual person on the bed, but she could see lumps, as if someone was underneath the covers. Who was it? And then she saw something else that made her heart stop. A hand. Bea had seen a hand like this before. On the ship on the way over from Scotland; she would never forget it. She remembered thinking that lizards were softer, remembered starting to pull her own hand away as the cold, bony fingers wrapped her young flesh. Skeleton fingers. Just like these that now hung visible up to the second knuckle below the covers on the side of the bed. She blinked away the tears forming over her eyes, and for a terrifying moment when she did so, she thought she saw the tips of the skeletal fingers move rapidly against the wooden frame of the bed. That was impossible and she wiped her eyes, and when she looked again they had stopped, of course. They were dead still. They had never moved in the first place. This hand was a dead hand. This hand belonged to dead Mrs. Norton. It must — who else could it possibly be? Miss Norton wasn't talking to herself. She was talking to a skeleton. They must have brought Mrs. Norton's skeleton with them all the way from England. She couldn't understand it. She had thought of Miss Norton as beautiful and fragile, but despite being saddled with her aggravating father, she also had seen that she was possessed of an inner strength. But now, Bea was overcome by confusion and pity. The poor woman — does she even realize what she's doing? Does she know how insane this is? Bea continued to listen to Miss Norton's mad babble from the other room, and then, for some reason, she remembered the little green bed jacket.

She had found herself thinking about the bed jacket all yesterday afternoon, all throughout their day at the Stevens', in the cellar, in the attic, in the kitchen. She had not known where to begin with her questioning of the Nortons last night — so she had begun with her fib of writing an article, and before long, she still wasn't sure who belonged to the bed jacket, but she had found out who Morna was. Now, she thought, if the bed jacket had in fact belonged to Morna Norton, and if it had been torn from her as the navy blouse had been torn from Eliza Norton, then the common denominator between the two, and the only person likely to have access to both women, was, as Aunt Evelyn had suggested, Cyrus Norton. The thought then occurred to her, and she didn't understand why it had not occurred to her before: had Mr. Norton killed his wife? Was that the reason that Miss Norton kept her mother's skeleton here? As a sort of haunting, a retribution. It truly would be, Bea thought with a shudder.

Bea had seen enough. She quietly closed the door, and just in time, because the next second, Miss Norton said suddenly, "Good-bye, Mother," and walked quickly to the door, locking it behind her. Why on earth would she care if the door was locked, thought Bea, with only a skeleton inside? She stood stock still next to Mr. Norton's door and pondered this madness, then heard Miss Norton return to the front hall, open the front door, and leave. Bea was about to collapse onto the floor when Miss Norton called — she obviously hadn't left after all — "Potatoes and turnips, Mother. Two of your favourites." With that, she closed the door, but it did not sound as if she had locked it behind her.

What did she mean by *potatoes and turnips,* wondered Bea. What further insanity was this? And then she remembered: the two whites. Turnips and potatoes, once you took off the outside.

Feeling disoriented and upset, she was about to run out the door to find Natty and Jean when she glanced down at her own hands. She had forgotten about the key. She would have forgotten once again to return it. She was desperate to leave this apartment, but when she went to put the key back in the drawer, she was overwhelmed by a powerful need to know what else was in this *Agamemnon* box. She had a few seconds to find out. It would take Miss Norton at least that long to get her father all the way up the stairs. She quickly squatted, set the box on the floor, and opened the lid again.

She fingered through the pile to the last letter that she had read, the one signed by Henry Stevens — HFS — and turned it over. On the other side, the characters *j, x, z, v* had been written, and alongside the characters was the phrase: *Simply avoid those letters.*

She put that piece of paper back in the pile and listened for sounds from the stairwell. When she heard none, she thought she had time for one more. She picked out an envelope, soil stained and addressed to Cyrus Norton from Judson Stevens. She started to scan the letter . . .

May 29, 1870

Dear Cyrus,

Please excuse my belated response. I was shocked when I read your letter, I must say. I know that you have always blamed me for breaking Niagara's *cable. And that you think everybody on the ship and off blamed you. I don't really think they did. Why would they?*

. . . but a voice in her head kept insisting she hurry. "It's alright," Bea replied in a whisper, folding the letter carefully and slipping it inside its envelope. "I still have time." She believed she did. She could hear Miss Norton. She had made it to the bottom of the staircase, but getting her father back up again would be another task entirely. Bea set the envelope on the floor beside the bundle. She took another letter out of the box. This one was addressed to Judson Stevens. She started to open the letter when the voice became more insistent. She didn't argue. She returned the letters to the box in the order that she'd found them, and then she placed the bundle of correspondence neatly on top. She had set the box on the desk when she heard the distinct sound of the cane on the stairs. How far down were they? It was hard to tell. She was almost out the door of Mr. Norton's bedroom, when the voice in her head said: "The key, Bea."

She had absently shoved the little key back in her pocket. She seemed determined to keep it. Hurriedly, she ran back, opened the drawer, lifted the ledger, replaced the key, and closed the drawer.

She left Mr. Norton's room, closed his door and ran all the way to the front door. She stopped by the front door for a second and gathered her breath and listened. Finally, she heard it, one flight down, the cane, and she thanked a god she didn't necessarily believe in but hoped fervently for at times like these. She opened and closed the door, not locking it this time, and ran on tiptoes down the hall to the closet. When she reached it, and crouched down between Natty and Jean, Jean flung her arms around her and wept silently. A flood of tears ran down Bea's neck and under her collar as Jean hung on to her and they listened above the muffled sobbing as the Nortons climbed the last flight of stairs and entered their apartment.

For several minutes the only thing the three could hear was their own breathing, and Jean's diminished crying. Eventually, they all glanced at one another and agreed. They slipped out the door of the closet. To Bea's ear the sound of their footsteps was overly loud as they tiptoed as fast as they could past the Nortons' apartment and down the stairs. They didn't stop running until they had reached the water.

Mildred waited for them by the water, skimming rocks into the ocean. She stood on a small band of beach beside the dock, trapped by the tide up to her ankles. She wondered if any of her skimmies ever came back again; the good ones she would like to keep forever, but what's the sense of having an excellent skimmy if you're going to keep it? She had just skipped one of these, a beautiful fiver, when the girls ran down the dock to the very end. They didn't notice her standing there.

She joined them at the dock's end and commented: "Not what you expected, was it, Bea?" Bea wasn't concentrating on what she was saying. Jean's distress had turned to anger.

"Don't ever do that again to me, Bea. Don't ever," she cried, pounding her fists on Bea's arms. Bea took her hands by the wrists, and looked her in the eye.

"I'm sorry, Jean. I'm so sorry. I won't ever again. I promise."

"What nonsense," Mildred said, rolling her eyes and shaking her head. She didn't dispute Bea's absolute belief in her promise. The problem was that it was unnecessary, and, more than that — wrong. Where would they be now if Bea had *not* gone back into the apartment? They now knew a lot more about the whole sordid mess. If Bea had not taken the risk of re-entering the apartment, they would still be no closer to finding out what happened to Brian. They would still be wasting time, and following false leads. Mildred had got her out in time. Jean would have coped fine without the promise.

After Jean and Bea and Natty had had a good cry, they sat down at the end of the dock, and wrapped themselves snugly in their coats, dangling their toes above the high cold sea so only the spray hit them. Three sets of shoes and tights lay behind them on the worn wood. Mildred didn't understand how they could bear the frigid wet on their feet; it wasn't summer, after all.

"Come sit next to me, Jean, dear. You can hear better," Mildred said to the girl. Jean got up and sat next to Mildred, with Bea on Jean's other side, and then Natty next to Bea.

Without any prompting from Mildred, Bea decided to tell Natty and Jean all of what she had found out about Brian. Bea had been leery of telling young Jean about Brian, and she kept glancing over at Jean as she told her story, but the tale didn't frighten the child. In fact, Jean seemed entranced by it and kept nodding, her dark eyes focused on the water in front of her, as if she had suspected the truth all along. Emboldened by her response, Bea decided she would tell both the girls what happened inside the Nortons' apartment. She had originally thought she would save the story to tell Natty when they were alone, but, as Mildred knew she would be, she was strangely reassured in knowing that Jean was privy to the tale. So she told them about the box, the letters and notes, the skeleton, even the white vegetables. That got a smile out of the girls. What an absolutely strange thing to talk to your dead mother about, they all wondered, giggling. Except for Mildred. She had begun to suspect the rationale behind the white vegetables. And she wanted Bea to think a little harder about the body on the bed.

"Was there still flesh on the hand, Bea? Thin, perhaps, but there nevertheless?" Mildred asked her.

Jean glanced over at Mildred and then at Bea, and she asked: "Was it all bone, Bea? Or was there still flesh and skin on the hand?"

Bea looked down at her cousin and Mildred knew that she now regretted having spoken about the skeleton in front of the ten-year-old and that she was wondering if she should answer her. But, once again, Jean surprised her by expressing fascination rather than fear, so Bea said,

"Not flesh really, Jean. There was no fullness at all. Skin though, now that I think about it. Skin on top of the bone."

"If it were a skeleton, it wouldn't have skin, would it Bea?" Mildred suggested.

This time she was surprised that it was Natty, not Jean, who continued this line of thought. "Do skeletons come with skin, Bea?"

"They do if they just died," Bea said.

They all nodded, including Mildred, as their three sets of toes and one pair of boots hovered above the water. None of the girls had ever seen a skeleton before, but all of them had seen someone who had died, and over the next few minutes, they debated the various stages of decomposition. They discussed skeletons with skin and without, and if it still had skin, then was it really a skeleton? "Not really," said Jean.

"Then what is it?" asked Bea, but no one seemed to know, including Mildred.

One thing they eventually agreed on: a skeleton that was years dead would no longer have skin. It would have to be a fairly new skeleton to have skin; but whether that was days new or weeks new or months new, none of them knew.

"If the body just died, and it still has skin, then it can't be Morna. Or can it?" asked Natty.

"What if she only recently died?" asked Bea.

"The smell, Bea," said Jean. "Dead bodies smell, don't they? They smell really awful."

As so often happened between Mildred and the girls, they got to the truth before she did. "Jean's quite right, Bea. You're forgetting about the smell," said Mildred.

"That's right, Jean," Bea said. "There would be a smell if someone had just died. So, it's not recently dead. I've been by the apartment many times in the last ten days, and never once did I smell a dead body."

"Do you know what one smells like?" asked Natty.

"Well, no," said Bea.

"Then how do you know?"

"I've read lots about it," she lied. Lying was coming easier and easier for Bea these days, and Mildred supposed she should be more troubled by it than she was. Bea had never read about dead bodies as far as Mildred knew, but anybody would know that a dead body smells worse than anything you could possibly imagine. Far worse. "It's far, far worse," continued Bea, "than all the other horrible things I smelled in there — strange food, urine, the old man's body odour. You've smelled dead mice and rats?"

The other three nodded.

"It'd be like that but a thousand, no, a million times worse. Never mind," said Bea, standing up and brushing herself off. "Come on, Jean, time to get you home. Enough of skeletons and whatnot. You're not going to have nightmares, are you?" Jean looked at her and shook her head. "I know who to ask about skeletons, in any case," Bea said after they'd put on their stockings and shoes and walked down the wharf. "Mr. Shulman. He'll know."

...---...

Knowledge tried to battle its way to the surface of Bea's mind. Mildred could see it written all over her face as she once again kept vigil over Bea's night. Outside, another storm shook their little house, so Bea's violent dreams had plenty to keep them company. Mildred was amazed that Bea slept right through whatever the dreams were forcing upon her. In the morning, Bea looked calmer than she had in days. Some glimmer of truth had obviously been snatched from the wrestling she had done with her night. Before the day was through, Mildred was sure that Bea would remember what she had found in her sleep.

Day Eleven
Friday, October 24, 1902

Mr. Shulman arrived in the early morning, just after Bea, so she had plenty of time to talk to him without customers around. Still, she wasn't sure how to broach the subject. Finally, she just said: "Can you tell me about body decomposition?" as she added more potatoes to the bin. She had tried to act indifferent and had faced away from him after she asked the question, but now she could feel his eyes burrowed into her back.

"Miss MacDonald?" he said after several seconds. She turned to see him standing staring at her, a box of wart remover in each hand. "You are up to something, yes?"

She hesitated a moment, and then said, "No." He was scrupulously honest, and had always been extremely fair with her. Lying to him made her feel a thousand times worse than being a criminal. As for being a criminal these last few days — burglary, trespassing, lying — she had been waiting for guilt or shame to envelop her, but they hadn't. She had felt those feelings only in meagre quantities, and they were never enough to stop her.

"No? But decomposing bodies on a lovely morning such as this, Miss MacDonald? What makes you think to ask such a thing?" he asked, placing the wart remover on its shelf, then joining Bea by the vegetable bins. "Ah!" he said as she started to speak. "Before you answer with another small fib, let me just say that I've noticed that you are, how do you say it, jittery, of late, am I right?"

"Yes."

"And this decomposing body has something to do with your jittery nature, am I correct?"

"Yes."

"And where have you seen this decomposing body, Miss MacDonald?"

She didn't know how to answer. If she said "at the Nortons'," then surely he would wonder how she ended up there, and if she lied and said she was invited, then he could easily let something slip next time Miss Norton was in the store. She had cornered herself. She should never have asked.

"I'm sorry, Mr. Shulman. As you said, I've been jittery. I shouldn't have brought it up."

He had opened a sack of onions and was emptying it into the onion bin. He stopped and looked over at her, and she could feel his wise eyes on her head as she bent again over the potato bin. "If you will not say where you found this decomposing body, then it is because you can't. I won't force it from you, Bea. You are not deceitful by nature. I will answer your questions. Please, ask."

She stopped and looked up at him, and felt like she was going to cry. She was so lucky to have found work with him.

"How long does it take for a body to become a skeleton, Mr. Shulman?"

"One doesn't really know. It would depend on many factors."

"Such as?"

"Heat, cold, the health of the person before death, their size — very large or very small — predators. But usually, I would say within six weeks, unless the climate is extremely cold, like the Arctic, for instance. Yes, usually by six weeks you would have your skeleton."

"Can the skin stay on?"

"Once it is a skeleton?"

"Yes."

"No."

"Never?"

"Well, nothing's absolute, but, Miss MacDonald, what kind of skin do you mean? Bits of it scattered about, or a complete layer, like this?" and he lay down an onion and held out his right hand, smoothing the fingers of his left over the top and then over the palm. When he met her eye, she could have sworn that he knew it was a hand she was talking about.

"Not like that exactly, but not bits, either."

"What colour is this skin that you speak of?"

"Hmm. Sort of purple."

"Not brown or black?"

"Possibly." She had not been able to tell the colour because of the shadows in the room.

"Are there fingernails?"

"How do you know I'm talking about a hand?" she asked, suddenly feeling alarmed.

"Deduction, Miss MacDonald," he said calmly. "You keep staring at your own as you speak. Your eyes are either on your hands or they're on mine."

"Oh."

"Yes. Fingernails?"

"I don't know."

"You didn't see any?"

"It was too far away."

"So," he said, beginning on the bin of carrots. "What was the temperature of this place where the body was? Hot? Cold?"

"Neither. Just warm."

"Room temperature."

"Yes."

"So it could be a brown or black or purple hand that looks like a skeleton's except that the skin is still on, and it is room temperature. Is that correct?"

"Yes."

"I see." He didn't speak until he had undone the sack of carrots and added a few dozen to the bin. "Did it look as if all of the water had been sucked out from under the skin? Did it look dry?"

"Yes. Yes, in fact it did."

"I don't think your skeleton's a skeleton, Miss MacDonald. It is either not decomposing at all, or it is a mummy."

"A mummy?"

"Yes. You've heard of them of course."

"Of course."

"Mummification is another way for bodies to decompose, Miss MacDonald. The most usual means of decomposition is skeletonization, but under certain circumstances, with dry, non-humid conditions, bodies can mummify. Still, it is hard to believe that you would find a mummy in

Newfoundland, Miss MacDonald. It is not the right climate; far, far too wet. Where I come from, now that is another matter."

"You have seen mummies before?"

"Oh, yes, Miss MacDonald. Not many. Two, I believe. As a young physician ... "

Mr. Shulman had not been allowed to practice as a doctor in Newfoundland. Now, Bea waited eagerly for him to tell her another story from his days as a physician in his native country — this time about mummies. But before he could begin, they were interrupted by the chime of the bell over the front door of the store. Mr. Tattlebaum had arrived for work.

"Ah, Mr. Tattlebaum, top of the morning to you," said Mr. Shulman. He always tried various British phrases on Mr. Tattlebaum. He wanted the old man to speak English whenever Bea was around. But Mr. Tattlebaum usually replied in Hebrew, and then Mr. Shulman would translate. This morning he didn't need to. Mr. Tattlebaum had been practising his new language:

"Top morning, Mr. Shulman, Miss MacDonald," he said, and smiled.

Bea grinned. "And to you."

As they finished setting up the store, Bea pondered the information she had gotten from Mr. Shulman, and she couldn't get a question out of her mind: how on earth could Miss Norton have mummified her mother's body, brought it over on the ship here to wet, chilly Newfoundland, and then have kept it preserved all this time in that room in their apartment?

...---...

"Who is this?" asked Bea to Mrs. Stevens, who was on her way out of the house. "The portrait of this old man?" The portrait hung on the wall near Mr. Stevens' study door.

"Lovely, isn't it? So pleasant to be around, but Henry insists we keep it. I'll never understand," said Mrs. Stevens, pausing in the doorway and adjusting her hat. "That's Henry's father, Judson Stevens. He never saw the sense of getting dressed properly for events, not near the end. That was painted not long before he died, two years ago. He had it done and sent it to Henry. God only knows why. I won't be long, Bea. I'll be back well before two. The Nortons are coming over, or so they say."

Bea was too distracted by the portrait to comment, so she just nodded as Mrs. Stevens closed the door behind her. Why had she not noticed it until today? She must have walked by it half a dozen times. So much was the same: the smile, gums and all; the way the clothes hung from his body; the lax, unshaven jowls; and, most especially, the eyes. The painter was talented. Hatred, Bea thought, must be a difficult feeling to capture.

"Excuse us for not making it by yesterday, Mr. Stevens, Mrs. Stevens," Eliza started to say when her father interrupted:

"I see you took my note seriously."

"I don't know how seriously I'm taking anything you have to say, Mr. Norton," said Henry. "We simply thought it time to deal with this once and for all. Let me introduce my wife, Penelope."

It took every bit of Penelope's strength not to run from the room. She stayed seated on the settee, and with an enormous force of will, she managed to keep her right hand from shaking as she held it out for Cyrus, who shook it before he plunked down into the chair furthest from the fire. He didn't look like a man who could do much damage. If she were a different type of person she might have thought of doing him in, but then, she'd never had an appetite for murder. As she nodded politely at Eliza and caught the look in her eye, Penelope knew that she had succeeded in showing only a calm exterior. She wasn't going to show Cyrus any weakness, not yet, not until he showed her what exactly he knew.

When everyone was settled, Cyrus looked directly at her and spouted: "I know your family's secret, Stevens," and she thought she would collapse. Here it was then, her suspicions again confirmed. But why would he be here when she'd already given him money? She glanced again at Eliza. She's ashamed of her father, Penelope thought. She can't look me in the eye.

"Henry," she said. It's time she just told him everything, so that he wouldn't hear it from Cyrus. She should have told him before now. But he ignored her and said to Cyrus:

"That so?"

"That's right. And because of that, you'll pay up. But first, let me ask you two things."

"What might they be?" interrupted Penelope. "I don't know if there's more about France that I can tell you that you don't already know."

The Nortons and Henry all stared at her. The men seemed baffled, but just as Henry said, "What on earth are you talking about, Penelope?" she caught a look in Eliza's eyes. She had been demurely staring down at her lap, but at the sound of Penelope's voice, her eyes had flickered up onto her face and then down again. *She's petrified that I'm going to let on what she's told me, and that I'll make things worse for her than they already are,* thought Penelope.

"Nothing, Henry," said Penelope, keeping her gaze on Eliza. Immediately, Eliza seemed relieved.

"Fine, then," he said slowly, shifting his gaze from Penelope back to Cyrus. "What were you going to ask me?"

"Whaddya suppose happened to the knife?"

...---...

"Sshh," said Brian, putting his finger to his lip. "You can stand here beside me."

Bea looked down at him. She had chosen Natty's spot to spy — the best place in the house, really — you could see as well as hear: the crack between the double doors that separated the dining room from the study.

...---...

The knife fell into the pit after the body. Penelope had reached out to grab it, as if by some freak of nature, invisible tentacles grew from her fingers. She couldn't catch it, and it landed handle side up, looking every bit like a single birthday candle on a macabre cake: the pink of the dress, the beige of the lye, and the soil — dark brown like chocolate. She had just thrown another shovelful of dirt over the body when the knife had fallen out of her coat pocket and tumbled the six long feet into the pit. She had only used the knife to cut open the bag of lye, and in the absurd wave of thinking that followed, she had thought of climbing down into the hole to retrieve it: someone might think she had used it to kill. But then she had left it, of course, and shovelled more dirt over top until soon the knife was buried, too.

...---...

"I have absolutely no idea what happened to the knife," answered Penelope, and again Henry looked flummoxed, but he didn't say anything. "And your second question?"

"Did you by any chance get a little bundle of money every month in the post?" Cyrus asked Henry as he looked over at Penelope, and then back at Henry. Henry was again taken aback, and didn't reply. "You did, didn't you? Did you ever wonder where the money was coming from? I mean, who would be sending a young man cash every single month?"

"Father, you don't need to be so gruff. Lower your voice," interjected Eliza quietly.

"I can be as loud as I want, Liza. None of your damn business, is it?"

Penelope stared at Cyrus, shocked that he would speak like this in public to his own daughter. But Eliza obviously was used to it. She didn't reply, and returned to staring at her lap. Henry didn't seem to notice the little interruption. Penelope concentrated, trying to comprehend where Cyrus was taking the conversation. What money in the post? She didn't know anything about that.

"I don't know how you know about that," Henry said. "Of course I wondered. I wondered all the time."

"Bet it was called 'Brian's money' or some such thing, am I right?" From the look on Henry's face, it was clear that Cyrus had hit the mark once again. "That's what it said, didn't it?" Henry nodded slowly, and Cyrus continued, "Another funny thing about this money, is that it went on from the time you were, what, twenty or so? Until, hmm, let's say — two years ago. Now that was just about the time your father died? Right again, aren't I?"

At first Henry just stared dumbfounded at him, then he seemed to gather his wits: "Why is it you know so much about this, Norton? You've been spying on us, I take it."

"Nah," said Cyrus. "I don't need to spy, Stevens. Was my money, you see."

"Yours?"

"Yup."

"Why would you be sending me money every month?"

"Well, you see — that's it, isn't it? I wasn't sending it to you, now was I?"

"Who, then? Out with it."

"Your pa, Stevens. For twenty years, I been sending money to your pa every month. We'll call it 'Brian's money,' he said. And it's for Henry, he said."

Henry looked doubly shocked. "Why?" he asked simply.

"Blackmail. You see. It all comes around. For all those years, he was blackmailing me."

"What on earth for?"

"Murder, Stevens. Brian's murder."

Henry turned away and stared into the fire. Cyrus glared at him:

"You see — you know. I was right, wasn't I, Eliza?" She glanced at him, looking exceedingly uncomfortable and nodded. "But you know I didn't do it, though, don't you? You know I didn't kill him."

"Do I?" asked Henry, turning around, but there wasn't a lot of power behind his words. "If you didn't do it, then why did you pay all those years?"

"He had some things of mine that tied me to the murder, or so he said. A letter of mine that I'd written, threatening the two of you. Now why I would have done that I don't know, but anyhow, he said he had it. And a pin that I always wore, with my initials: CNN. Anybody would've known it was mine. Judson said he found it in the cave where Brian was murdered. He said Brian had it in his hand. That's a complete lie, of course. I don't know how he got it, but I had lost the darn thing right around that time. And then he turns up with it. He also had my sweater with my name embroidered into the inside of the collar. That's even more mysterious. Where on earth he would have got that, I have no idea. I searched my brain for years, could never figure it out. In any case, those things were missing. And I got scared. I knew how wily Judson was. He was capable of anything. He'd betrayed me about the cable. He was capable of anything, I figured. So I started to pay. 'Course, once I paid the first time, he had me. I kept paying. Stupid, maybe, but I did. Was never very much every month. That's what baffled me. Why on earth did he never ask for more? Perhaps he knew I couldn't pay more. I don't know."

"But you paid."

"I did. I paid money for a crime I never did to the one who did it. And now I want it all back. Ten times the total of what I paid out over the years. Figure it out yourself."

Penelope couldn't believe what she was hearing. Cyrus wasn't talking about the body that she had buried back in France. Not yet, at least. This was about Brian, Henry's brother. She had always known he had been murdered, but it had never occurred to her that the blackmailing had anything to do with him. Perhaps if she hadn't been so guilt-ridden, she might have figured this out. She glanced over at Eliza and caught her eye. Eliza looked as baffled as Henry and Cyrus had been earlier. She obviously had no idea what her father was up to. But now, Penelope wanted to know something. She looked at Henry, who had fallen silent once again. For the first time in minutes, she spoke: "What do you mean, 'the one who did it'?"

"Well that's obvious, isn't it, Mrs. Stevens," said Cyrus. "Ever feel that your silence was being bought, Henry, heh? Ever think that? Or that it was guilt money? Ever think your father knew that you knew and was trying to keep you quiet? Judson killed Brian, didn't he, Henry? Your own father killed your twin brother."

Penelope looked over at Henry, who was staring into the fireplace. She could tell that Henry knew that Cyrus was telling the truth. He had known all along that his father had killed Brian. That's why he was so afraid of the blackmail Cyrus was holding over his head.

"This is pure nonsense, Norton," said Henry, turning to stare at him. "My father killed my brother? You have gone entirely insane. And what proof do you have that this blackmailing actually took place?"

"The money you got every month, for one."

"You must have something more than that."

"I do, in fact. I have this," Cyrus said, and from his left breast pocket he extracted two letters and handed them over to Henry. "Two of the notes from my blackmailer. He'd send them every month. I burned most of them, then decided I should start to keep them. Just in case, you know." But while he was talking, Henry had glanced down at the letters. Then he looked over at Cyrus with a wide smile on his face.

"When did you say these were written?"

"They're some of the later ones. Sometime in the last ten years. I got the dates written down at home."

"Well, then, Cyrus Newton Norton. I have some shocking news for you. These weren't written by my father."

"What do you mean, not written by your father?" said Cyrus, and for the first time since he arrived, he looked unsettled. As did Eliza. Penelope caught an expression on her face, as she quickly glanced up at Henry. It could only be interpreted as fear.

"It's not his handwriting."

"Don't be a fool. Sure it is. That's the first thing I checked when they very first started to arrive. I checked them against other correspondence that Judson had sent me. I was familiar with his hand. They were an exact match."

"Well, you see, that's just it, isn't it?" Henry said, still smiling and turning back to the fire. "It is similar, extremely similar, maybe even exactly like my father's writing when he was younger. But the thing is, you see, after Brian died, my father's writing got progressively worse. He developed a twitch in his writing hand, his right hand. Before that he'd had a beautiful script. But afterward, his writing was always shaky. Toward the end, he had myself or someone else do the writing for him, it had become so bad."

"I don't believe it," spewed Cyrus.

Instead of answering, Henry strode over to the desk by the bay windows, opened a drawer, and took out several sheets of paper. He strode back and dumped them in Cyrus's lap. "You know, I never knew why I kept these things. Didn't have much affection for my father, as you can imagine. Now I know why I kept them. You can tell by the dates. One of them was written soon after Brian died, six months, possibly. A description of cable-making, funnily enough. I think I needed it for a class project. You can see how his writing is already shaky." Cyrus rifled through the half dozen sheets of paper until he found the one dated almost thirty years before.

"Means nothing," he said, throwing it to the floor. Henry left it there, and continued talking as if Cyrus hadn't commented.

"The rest are letters. Starting when I went away to boarding school, then university, and afterwards. The first one came when I was fourteen or fifteen, the others throughout the years, until I was about thirty. Read them if you like. There's nothing in them that's all that personal. But, as you can see, the script gets progressively worse. I have many more of these, right up until he died. Same time as your blackmailing stopped, you said. Well, that was a smart move on someone's part. How can a dead man be a blackmailer, after all?"

"But I was being blackmailed!" Cyrus screamed, almost whining.

"That may be so, Mr. Norton. But not by my father."

Cyrus bent his head and stared at the letters in his lap. Then he looked up at Henry with an expression of complete calm. "Still, you know I'm correct about your father, Stevens. You know I'm correct about him killing your brother. And you never said a word, did you? Not when you were a boy, not later as a man. An accessory to murder, I think they'd call it."

"Is that so?" asked Henry, trying to sound more confident than he looked.

"Yes, that is so."

"Well, I ask you, sir, what proof do you have that my father killed my brother?"

"The knife, sir. I have your father's knife, the one with the stag handle. You remember it, don't you? You remember watching your father wash off Brian's blood and then hide the knife. I dug it up later. As proof. Kept it all these years."

"Then I assume you have it with you, this knife, as you say. Proof that my father killed Brian?" said Henry, talking to the fireplace.

"No. I didn't bring it."

"And yet you expect me to believe you."

"He will bring it by tomorrow," said Eliza, getting up off her chair. Penelope looked over at her, surprised that she would interrupt these proceedings. Evidently, she had some iota of her own will. Eliza rose from her chair and turned toward Henry and Penelope, who had gone to stand beside her husband at the fireplace. She stepped over to them and lowered her voice so that her father couldn't hear her. Her voice was trembling and her blue eyes were wet from the tears she was holding back. Penelope could see that her fear had turned to real terror. And, not for the first time, Penelope was afraid for her. She wished now that she had done something to help extricate Eliza from her situation. She knew, as women know these things, that Eliza had been begging for her help. She had been too consumed with her own problems of blackmail and the attacks on George to pay her much attention, but now something must have taken place in the course of the conversation to turn Eliza's normal state of anxiety into this palpable fear. Penelope glanced at Cyrus, still sitting glumly in his chair, as Eliza continued: "My father has had enough for one day. I realize that you might find it hard to think that I have affection for him, given his character, but I do. I have to get him home." She reached out to touch Penelope on the hand while she was talking, and her hand was damp with sweat.

"What're you whispering about, you conniving woman?"

Eliza quickly glanced back and said politely, "Nothing, Father," then she turned again to the Stevens'. "I am sorry about all of this. I've tried to stop him from going through with it all. But it's been no use."

"It's not your fault," said Henry.

"But still," she said.

"Please don't apologize," said Penelope. "We can see what's going on, can't we Henry?" Henry nodded, and Penelope added in a lower whisper: "Is there anything we can do? Would you like to stay the night here? Perhaps you don't want to go home tonight."

"Thank you, Mrs. Stevens. How kind. But I can't stay. I hope you understand," she said. She had been looking at the floor as she spoke, and now she looked up at them. "I'm so sorry again. I'll get him home. He'll want to return tomorrow, however, with this knife, as he said, and then you can ask him whatever else you wish." Eliza went over to help her father out of his chair. Despite his horrible behaviour toward her, she continued to be gentle with him. Penelope could never have been so generous. It wasn't in her to be like that. When Eliza had helped her father to standing, she said to Penelope. "I wondered if you might come by tomorrow, Mrs. Stevens?"

"Yes, certainly, I would be happy to."

"That would be lovely. Thank you. Perhaps after Father's visit."

"That would be fine."

"Thank you, Mrs. Stevens. You're most kind. I will need your help with something, and I don't think I can do it on my own."

Bea stood, hands in the pockets of her skirt, staring up at the portrait of the two boys and then glancing now and again down the hall toward the portrait of Judson Stevens. She couldn't see for looking, though; the answer didn't seem to be coming. They didn't have much time: the Stevens' would be home soon. They'd just stepped out for some fresh air, they told Bea. "You've not been able to find out what Morna knows, have you, Bea?" Mildred asked, interrupting Bea's concentration. Without waiting for a reply, she started up the staircase, but when Bea didn't follow, she stopped and turned around. Bea had remained in the hallway, continuing to look at the portrait of Brian and his brother. "You'll not find it there, Bea."

"I don't know where the skeleton fits in, if it does at all. That's the last bit," said Bea.

"It's not the last bit by any means, Bea. But it does fit, Bea. You'll see."

"How could Judson have killed his own son? I just don't believe it. I still think it's Henry."

"Because of the hand?"

"There's the cut on the hand and the scar on the forehead," Bea said, nodding at the portrait. "And there's Clement thinking he was laughing about Brian's death. There's the notes he was writing to his wife. Confessions really, don't you think? He's a horrible man; he was probably an evil child. The rotten twin. It's the only thing that makes sense. Henry must have killed his own brother. Mr. Norton has it wrong. I'm sure of it."

"You're forgetting something, Bea," said Mildred, and Bea looked up the staircase at her, and then glanced past her to the top floor landing. Mildred followed her gaze. Bea had felt Brian standing there; how could she not? His grief was so quiet, she could not help but hear it.

It seemed a lifetime went by while Mildred and Brian waited for Bea to think. It seemed they saw a change in weather. It seemed they felt a shift in seasons. Finally, at some point in the far distant future, Bea finally remembered what she had found in her sleep.

Bea put her lantern on one of the crates by the window in the Stevens' attic, and she sat down on the other crate; then she reached for the *Niagara* box and took out its contents, a single piece of correspondence. "Why *Niagara?* Why not *Agamemnon?*" Bea asked, the letter on her lap. Mildred nodded. Last night, Bea had dreamt again of the box, but this time she was able to read the inscription. Covered with dust, the inscription had eventually come clear: *Niagara*.

Bea didn't touch the knife inside the box, although until she finished reading the letter, she was certain the knife was the one that Henry had used to kill Brian. As Bea returned the letter to the box and closed the lid, Mildred couldn't help but lecture both herself and Bea: "When you hate someone as much as we loathe Henry, it's so easy to have your dreams make all sorts of sense, isn't it, Bea?"

...---...

Someone had been in her bedroom. Penelope saw it as soon as she entered: an old red box sitting on top of her vanity. She walked over, picked up the box, then opened her vanity drawer and withdrew two small sheets of paper. She strode back down the hall to Henry's room.

"Did you deposit this wretched thing in my room, Henry?" she asked as she entered without knocking. He was sitting in the armchair staring out the window.

"Scotch?" he asked, turning to face her.

"Please," she said.

She stood just inside the doorway, ill at ease as always in her husband's room. He poured her a drink, picked up the rocking chair and brought both back to the window with him. He offered her the rocking chair, but she preferred the armchair.

Once they were seated, he answered her question.

"No," he said, looking at the box that she had placed on the windowsill. "Where did you find it?"

"In my bedroom, Henry. Someone put it there. I certainly didn't."

"Well, I didn't either. What is it?"

"It's your father's. Don't you remember? When he came to visit, he brought it with him. He gave it to you and you put it upstairs in the attic. It's been there ever since."

"Throw it out."

"Are you sure?"

"Yes. What on earth was that malarkey about France today, Penelope? What were you getting at?"

"Nothing," she said. "A matter of miscommunication." She didn't think he believed her, but he was looking too despondent about his father and Brian to venture asking anything else. He took a large swig of his scotch, and she sipped hers. Heat filled the back of her throat and her chest as she swallowed. It even went up into her ears; it was a nice feeling, better than she remembered. She usually enjoyed something milder, a sherry, perhaps, or even beer, but this was a pleasant change. "Do you really think he did it? Do you think your father killed Brian?"

"Always have," he said, staring at his scotch, and then out the window.

Penelope decided to ask him no more about it tonight. "I want to see what you think of these," she said, putting her glass on the windowsill. She pulled from her pocket the two pieces of paper and gave them to Henry.

He glanced at the first, and then looked over at her: "A note to George from Eliza Norton requesting a meeting a 9 P.M. Where did you get this, Penelope?"

"From George's coat pocket. Don't look at me like that. These are not normal times, Henry. I'm not one for filching. Take a look at the writing. Do you recognize it?"

He looked back at the note and frowned. Then he picked up the other one. "The note from Cyrus."

"Yes," she said. "That's not what's important. Again, look at the handwriting."

He did, and after a few minutes he said, "Ah. I see what you're getting at. Here, hold these." He handed the notes back to her and walked over to his desk. When he came back, he had several sheets of paper in his hand.

"My writing," he said, handing them all to her. "Compare it to those." He pointed at the notes she had brought. "I think you'll see that there is a similarity, but they are not an exact match. Not even close, actually. Whoever was trying to forge my writing was never able to replicate my *m*'s and my *n*'s, as well as a surfeit of other characters. Did you really think it was I, Penelope? Did you honestly think I wrote these?"

"No, Henry, I didn't. I simply wanted to be sure, that's all."

...---...

When Penelope got back to her bedroom, she returned the notes to her drawer and took out a letter that she had planned on giving to Henry: her departure letter, now no longer necessary. However, she still wasn't sure if she was safe. What of the Nortons' encounter in France with Freda Murphy? Had Freda told Cyrus all she knew about Penelope?

She poured herself a large sherry from the canister on her dresser, curled up in the loveseat by her window, and read over the letter.

> *Dear Henry,*
>
> *If I leave, he will have no reason to blackmail you. Or to harm George. I am sorry that it has come to this. Often, I have wanted to tell you. But then, if I had, would you have married me? All I can say in my defence, Henry, is that I did not push her down the stairs. Nor did I taunt her or scare her or argue with her or do anything that would have precipitated the fall. It really was an accident. I am not a murderer.*
>
> *And, in fact, even while I carried out the series of events that led me to this juncture, I cried. You will be surprised to know that, no doubt, given my propensity for a dry eye, but I had actually grown to like her. I really had, Henry, and was truly sorry that she was dead. Her death, however, gave me new life. A life I never could have imagined, although sometimes I'm not sure it was worth it. It's been torturous being a pretender. You never have anyone to trust.*
>
> *It's true, as no doubt you will find out today when Mr. Norton tells you all — as I have no doubt he will — that I buried her body in the root cellar, and then assumed her identity. It all happened so quickly when I saw her dead body down at the bottom of the stairs. I didn't even think, and once I did, it was already done. Assuming her identity was far easier than one*

could imagine. It had been just the two of us by ourselves at the villa in France. The gardener and the cook had a week off to attend their granddaughter's wedding in the country. They were an elderly married couple, and I abhorred lying to them and leaving them without employment. I left them some of her money as small compensation, along with a letter that told them that we had been called back to England on short notice. I have often wondered if they were able to smell the body in the cellar after their return. I think not. I buried it deep and covered it heavily with lye. If anything, François (his wife was Françoise, isn't that funny?) might have noticed that a sack of lye was missing. He might have put it down to absent-mindedness. I still remember that couple with affection.

When I saw Penelope's body at the bottom of the stairs (that was her name you see, Henry. Mine was, and still is really, Gertie, Gertrude), the idea to become her came to me as if it had always been planned this way since we first met. I still remember that day when, at my mother's urging to get a position in the city, I was hired on as a lady's maid for Penelope. We were both startled when we met one another. We were of the same age, she older by only a few months, the same height, the same build. Her grandfather, her only relative, said it was remarkable how much we were alike: "You two could be identical twins." I suppose that's when I first started to fantasize about being Penelope, so, perhaps, when she fell down the stairs and died, I already was.

She finished reading the rest of the letter, then sat by the window for a few more minutes. Finally she went over to her blazing fire, opened the grate and threw in the letter. Henry might never need to know this now.

...---...

Brian walked to the window where Henry was nursing his third scotch, and pointed to the box on the windowsill.

"Yours was the *Agamemnon*, Brian. Remember?" said Henry, looking at him. "Mine was the *Niagara*. Father made them, and even etched the ships himself. He seemed to have loved us then, didn't he? What happened? Where did you keep your box, Brian? I never saw it after you died. Our cave, I think, in that little alcove of yours. Do you remember that day we cut our hands?"

Brian nodded, though he didn't remember it all that well. He wanted Henry to tell him.

Henry looked thoughtful and sipped on his scotch, and Brian didn't think he was going to continue. Finally, he said: "We were just being silly. Do you remember us asking ourselves: are we insane? I've often wondered since — where had we come up with the idea? I can't remember who first thought of it, you or me, Brian."

"Me."

"Probably was you. You were always the one to get us into trouble. But there we were: to be *real* brothers, we must be blood brothers, and so you took one knife and I the other. How could such a tiny cut hurt so much? It hurts, we hollered — do you remember?"

"No."

". . . as soon as the knives went in. We were like that, weren't we, always saying the same things at the same time, finishing each other's sentences. And then you laughed, and so did I, and we giggled like girls and held our wet red palms together, fingers connected. We raised our two-arms-in-one to the sky. Your blood with mine, flowing down our arms. It stained our white short-sleeved shirts. 'What will Father say?' I said to you. 'What will we do with the shirts?' I asked."

"Burn them."

"Yes, burn them, you said, and then we cried it in unison as loud as we could, but no one could hear us, we were always alone up there on our hill by our cave. We giggled like crazy. I don't remember what we did with the shirts, Brian. Did we burn them? I don't remember whether Father ever knew or asked what had happened to our hands. Did he even care? Had he already stopped loving us? To us, the cuts were so obvious, it's hard to believe he didn't see them right away and scream, 'Where'd you get those cuts on your palms?'"

Brian waited for Henry to finish thinking and to take another sip of his drink. He put his hand on Henry's knee, and then he removed his hand and gently touched the lid of the *Niagara* box. After several moments, Henry reached toward the windowsill.

Day Twelve
Saturday, October 25, 1902

Brian closed his eyes to the sound and prayed himself gone. Face down, he lay still as if dead, his bleeding cheek plastered against the damp, sharp cave floor. And he listened, for the sound of the footsteps.

He could hear the shoes' heels scratching against the shale some short distance away; the noise seemed to be coming from the mouth of the cave. Brian had not been lying on the cave floor for very long this time — a minute, perhaps more. But, already, Cyrus was returning. Where had he gone after he'd stopped trying to drown Brian, after he'd once again released him and dropped him onto the cave floor? Had he gone outside the mouth of the cave? To do what? Was there someone else out there?

Brian tried to stand, but the best he could do was roll, from his stomach onto his back. And there — as if a gift from God — his father's knife.

... --- ...

"It's absolute nonsense," Cyrus barked, glaring at the letter that Henry had handed him. "So you're saying *I* killed Brian?"

"I'm not saying it. My father said it," Henry said. "It's all in this letter. And, I'll have you know, I believe him. I wish I had known before. I hated him for killing Brian. I was sure he had done it. I saw him wash and then bury the knife after all, didn't I? I ignored this letter all these years. He gave it to me years ago, and I never read it. I just left it up there in that box in the attic. I will report your activities to the local constabulary, sir."

They had taken their same seats as on the previous day. The women stayed completely silent as the men's voices rose.

"Will you now? And you have proof, do you?" said Cyrus.

"This letter from my father."

"His word against mine."

"And a good word it is."

"Is it now? You know that, do you? You're forgetting the lies he spread about the cable breaking? Blaming me. Nobody wanted to talk to me or hire me after that. He was deceitful, your father was."

"I looked into what you said, sir, about *Niagara's* cable. Couldn't just take your word for it, could I? I contacted friends and colleagues back in England. Associates of my father, some of them. Others who still work for Glass and Elliot. No one knew anything about you having broken the cable, sir. These lies and rumours that so destroyed you — well, it appears they're all in your mind. No one seemed to think that you had broken the cable. Nor my father, by the way. There is no record that either of you was responsible."

"Nonsense! That's complete horseshit, Stevens, and you know it. It's just what your father tried to tell me. 'Don't know what you're going on about, Cyrus. Nobody blames you.' Horseshit, Stevens! Horseshit!"

"Father," said Eliza, putting her finger to his leg. He swatted away her hand.

"Well, horseshit or not — excuse my language, ladies — that's the response that I received," said Henry.

"They saying Judson wasn't on that cable? Because if they are, they're lying. Or were they saying I was on it?"

"They didn't say either, Mr. Norton. There was some indication that my father had the brakes at the time."

"See! Just as I said!"

"A few remember it that way. Others remember differently."

"Those that are blaming me, no doubt."

"No, in fact, they're not. They didn't mention you. Even when asked, they didn't remember you being on the cable. Whether my father was on the brake or not, nobody appeared to blame him either. It seems that you have exaggerated your role in this event out of all proportion. I suspect, sir, that the real reason nobody would talk to you or hire you after the voyage had nothing to do with the cable breaking."

"You suspect that, do you? What reason would there be instead, pray tell?"

"Your personality, sir. It's somewhat lacking."

"Aah. Twisting this whole thing to blame it on me, aren't you? Just like your father."

"Is that why you killed Brian?"

"Whaddya mean?"

"You resented my father so much, you felt so betrayed by him that you just had to get back at him, had to take from him something he cherished. And you won, didn't you? He ended up losing both of us — Brian through death, me through rancour."

"You're talking gibberish. I'm not going to discuss this any more," Cyrus said, trying to get out of his chair. Eliza stood up to help him. "You want to charge me with Brian's murder, you go ahead and try to prove it. I'm leaving."

"One more thing," Henry said, as Penelope put a hand on Eliza's arm. She sat back down and Cyrus remained in his chair, unable to stand on his own. "George."

"Your son? Only met him once, Stevens. What about him?"

"You bloody well better leave him alone now."

"More gibberish. I have no idea what you're talking about, Stevens."

"You've been attacking George, just like you attacked me that once. I had always thought it was my father who hurt me. So had Brian," said Henry, and he pointed up to the scar on his forehead. "Remember this? Before Brian died, you tried to kill *me*, didn't you?"

"Never tried to *kill* you, Stevens."

"*Don't Ignore Me*. That was the message you sent," said Henry.

As if on cue, a sound at the doorway made them all turn toward it. Against the door frame, barely able to keep himself erect, leaned George, one hand holding his head, the other over the front of his shirt, which was covered with blood.

"George!" cried Penelope, rushing over to him.

"You did this!" cried Henry, running over and reaching out to hold him up. Eliza ran up behind them, and the three of them guided George over to the settee. Penelope ran out into the hallway and grabbed a handful of towels and the box of plasters from the linen closet. When she returned, Cyrus had turned in his chair to stare at the scene with a bemused expression.

"Now, how could I have done that? How would that be possible, heh? I've been here the whole time."

"You hired someone, didn't he, Eliza?" asked Penelope, laying several towels behind George's head. She went over to the sideboard for the pitcher of water, and as she returned and wet one of the towels, she noticed that Eliza was quite white; Penelope was worried that she would faint. She obviously did not have the stomach for violence of any kind, and she seemed incapable of helping under duress. She stood at the end of the settee and did no more to help with George.

Eliza now gazed at Penelope as if stunned, and then glanced back at her father and down at George. She answered softly, her voice quivering: "I don't know if he hired anyone, Mrs. Stevens. Someone's been by, a large man; I didn't know what they were discussing."

"What're you whispering about over there?" called Cyrus.

"Did you see who did it, George?" asked Henry.

"No, Father. I came to at the end of the street."

"Do you think you fell?"

"He didn't fall, Henry. For God's sake. Look at him."

"I didn't fall, Father. Somebody did this. Again. Look." And he held up his shirt. "What is it? What does it say? It's Morse code, isn't it? It says something, doesn't it, Father?"

"No!" exclaimed Eliza, staring at the writing.

Penelope quickly looked at her, and Henry said, "You'd better have a seat, Miss Norton. I believe this is all too much."

Henry started to lead her back to her chair, but she said, "I'll be quite fine, Mr. Stevens. Thank you for your concern. I'd like to help if I could," and they both returned to George and looked down at his exposed stomach.

"George, can you stand up, son?" asked Henry. "My Morse is rusty enough as it is. I can't read in this light."

"Henry . . ."

"He'll be fine, Penelope. I'll try not to take too long."

George nodded, and Henry and Penelope helped him off the settee. While Eliza and Penelope supported George on one side and Penelope held a cloth to his head, Henry took the bulk of George's weight from the other side, and the three of them slowly led George over to the brightest lamp in the room, in front of the double doorway leading to the dining room. "I don't even need to read what it says on my son's stomach, Norton. I know. It's exactly what you wrote on me: *'Don't Ignore Me.'* Correct, aren't I?"

"Bloody nonsense! You can't pin this on me."

"I can pin the other on you, though, can't I? We had always thought it was Father. Can't believe that now."

"What on earth are you talking about, Henry?" said Penelope, as they stopped walking so that she could dab the top of George's forehead with a damp towel.

"Before Brian died, someone attacked me on the path coming back from our cave. Father was furious that we had been sneaking off to our cave — of course, I know now that that was because of Cyrus here; Father knew something we didn't — and when we had left that morning he had yelled, 'Don't ignore me!'"

"Now isn't that a coincidence," said Cyrus.

Henry glared at him and continued: "We could read Morse. We were good at it back then. And guess where a message in Morse had been written."

"On your stomach? Like this?" asked Eliza, massaging a temple with her fingers.

"That's right. In blood; just like this. And it said, *'Don't Ignore Me.'* Why did you write that, Norton?"

"Bloody obvious, isn't it? I'd been sending Judson letters for months. You know, first all I wanted was for him to admit what he'd done . . . "

"You mean about the cable . . . "

"Yes, goddammit. What else? Admit it. Be a bloody man. Apologize. I wanted a goddamn apology! I think I would have been alright if I got that. I think I might have forgiven him even."

"Unlikely, but I take it he didn't apologize."

"Didn't apologize, didn't ever admit it. Kept insisting he didn't do it. In fact he said, if you can believe it, that I did it. I'll never forget that goddamn letter. We'd been writing back and forth and finally he owns up to what he really thinks: 'I don't blame you, of course,' he said, then he went on to tell me all the things wrong with the expedition, lording it over me like he always did, as if I didn't already know all the problems with the expedition: 'The size of the cable, for one. It was too small, wasn't it, Cyrus?' he says to me like I'm a child. 'The paying-out gear, for another. Do you remember the way it would slip off its trough?' Of course I bloody remember! What did he think I was, an idiot? And then at the end of that letter, he says: 'However, if you are asking me if I think you put too much pressure on the brakes and that caused them to break, then the answer would have to be yes, my friend. I'm sorry. I know you've always seen it another way.'"

"Your word against his, once again. Even if he did write that to you, even if he did believe you were responsible, he certainly did not spread malicious rumours about you. It appeared he kept his thoughts to himself. No one I communicated with in England remembers you as the one who broke the cable."

"They did; they just weren't saying. I know they did. I know what he did. I've always known."

"Fine. But this still doesn't really explain why you would attack me, and then kill Brian."

"You're not going to get me to admit to killing Brian."

"Fine. In time. What led you to attack me?"

"After that letter where Judson denied what he'd done and told me that I was to blame, I was furious. I wrote him back. He never replied. I wrote him again. Again he never replied. First he was blaming me for what he'd done, then he told the world about it, then he ignored me. Just like that. Ignored *me!* Finally I wrote, and I said, 'Don't ignore me, you idiot! I can do you more harm than you would believe.' I still didn't hear back from him, if you can believe it. He'd betrayed me, set the world against me, and now he was treating me like I didn't exist. Mr. Judson Stevens was always so much better than little Cyrus Norton, you know? In the next letter, I said to him, if you know what's good for you, you'd protect your sons. Still I didn't hear anything. Then I wrote, 'I'll harm them unless you start paying, Judson, let's say ten pounds a month to start, and I'll forget about all your lies.' I thought that was a good compromise. Don't you? If he was going to be so bull-headed, least I could do was get some money out of him. But he didn't answer, of course. Too bloody good for me, he was. Finally, I thought I'd give him a warning he could not ignore: the top of your head, or was it your forehead?" Cyrus pointed to the scar on Henry's forehead.

"Both. You hit me from behind, or don't you remember? I got this scar on my forehead when I fell and hit a rock. But why did you want money when what you had really wanted was an apology?"

"Oh, I wanted more than an apology. Right from the beginning. He had ruined my life, had a hard time getting work after *Niagara*. Nobody wanted me. And money mattered to him. He always cared about money more than anything. You're fooling yourself if you think otherwise. Didn't seem like he cared about you two at all. Why the hell didn't he respond to my letters if he cared so goddamn much? Why the hell not, heh?"

"Because, Mr. Norton, he never got the goddamn letters, as you put it."

"Whaddya mean? I sent them, didn't I? To the correct address, too. Believe me, I checked that time and again, didn't I?"

"Brian stole them."

"Pardon?"

"Father's correspondence. Father had started to tell us not to go up to our cave   perhaps he'd become suspicious of you from the first set of your letters that he did get. Brian got angry. We both were. But Brian started to steal Father's correspondence. Trying to get back at him, you know. Didn't take everything. Father would have certainly figured that out. But he took enough. Some of them were bills. Others must have been most of your letters. Father must have received at least one of your later letters, though. Otherwise, why would he have become increasingly agitated about us going to our cave, why wouldn't he permit us to go anywhere on our own, why would he follow us home from school?"

"That's why," George muttered. "Why you've been following me."

"Yes it is, George," said Henry. "Sorry."

Cyrus didn't reply, and after a few seconds of glaring at the old man, Henry asked George, "Are you able to hold up your shirt, son?" George weakly grasped his shirt around his upper chest. Before leaning over to look at the marks, Henry glanced at the message and remarked to Penelope: "What I don't understand is why the entire thing is not totally smudged. The message appears to be intact. Remarkable."

"Henry, for God's sake. Could you please just read it?"

"Sorry, Penelope," he said, and bent forward to read the Morse code on his son's belly.

After some hesitation, while muttering, "Now why would *that* be there . . . ?" Haltingly, Henry started to sound the letters aloud: "That first letter is most definitely a *w* . . . "

"Bloody hell, Stevens. Can't you read any faster than that? This is going to take forever. Eliza, you translate it. You're almost as fast as your mother."

Eliza was already leaning down on the other side of George. "Speaking of Mother — there's mention here of a Morna, but it's not Mother, I dare say." She spoke lightly, with a smile. "Morna was my mother's name," she informed Henry and Penelope. Then, standing and looking at George, she asked: "Do you know a Morna, George?"

"Morna?" George muttered, sounding entirely befuddled.

"George," said Eliza, lightheartedly. "I'm afraid your perpetrator is a jealous associate — a school chum, possibly?"

"What do you mean?" asked George.

"What does it say?" asked Penelope, while Henry continued to gaze at the code on George's stomach.

"Other than the delete line at the top of the message — and I can't understand why that would be there — it says: *'Why have you kissed my Morna?'*"

"I never kissed anyone named Morna! That's a lie!"

"Are you sure that's what it says, Miss Norton?" asked Henry, not taking his eyes off the code.

"Are you certain you never kissed someone named Morna, George?" asked Penelope.

"Bloody certain. Sorry, Mother."

"Even if you had too much to drink?" asked Henry.

"Someone obviously is besotted with a young woman named Morna," said Penelope. "And clearly this admirer has confused you with an adversary. Well, we'll certainly have to figure out who is doing this, George . . ." She had started to lead George back to the settee when Henry put out his hand to stop her.

"Are you sure you read it correctly, Miss Norton?"

"Oh, absolutely," Eliza answered.

"The 'my' in the code, that couldn't be a 'me,' could it?"

"Absolutely not," Eliza answered patiently. "If you recall, Mr. Stevens, the *e* is the most common letter in the alphabet, and so is the easiest of all the letters in Morse code. The letter *e* is only one dit, Mr. Stevens — or 'dot,' as it is commonly known. *Y*, on the other hand, is a far longer letter: dah, dit, dah, dah. No, Mr. Stevens, they are quite unalike. One would never get those two letters confused."

But one could get other letters confused. And numbers. And punctuation. And Bea, spying from the dining room on the other side of the double doors, could clearly see at least one major error in Miss Norton's translation. Bea had a clear view of the Morse code on George's stomach. She had spent far too long pondering the significance of the eight dots at the top of the message, which, of course, meant "delete the last word." However, there was no last word. George's skin above the eight dots was clear of blood or other markings. What had the sender been trying to say? Was the delete code a mistake? She had finally gone on to the remainder of the message. The first three words were easy enough.

.-- .... -.-- / -.. .. -.. / ..-

One word was written in the commonly-used shorthand, making her job all that much easier. And when she went on to the rest of the sentence, despite her limited Morse-deciphering ability, Bea gleaned one major error. She was still deliberating about another major error, when George let his shirt drop over his belly.

"What a load of rubbish this is. Eliza! Let's leave," Cyrus barked, and Eliza rushed over to help him off his chair.

"I have to get him home," Eliza said to the Stevens'. "Please excuse us."

"Of course," Penelope and Henry said together.

Without another word, the old man and his daughter exited the study. Penelope accompanied them to the front door, and as they were leaving, Eliza gripped her arm and whispered: "You wouldn't believe what I have to live with. I simply cannot abide living with my father any longer. I know that now. Will you still come by to visit me this afternoon, Mrs. Stevens?" She gazed intently into Penelope's eyes. "I need your help even more now than ever."

"The error, Bea? Was it the same as before? Was it the same as the Morse code you had heard in the Stevens' basement? The same confusion over the dots and dashes? The word 'kiss' instead of the word 'kill'?" asked Mildred, running along beside Bea as they approached the wharf. But Bea didn't reply. She was already calling out for Billy as she ran up to his boat.

"Are my aunt and Jean here, Billy?"

"Just missed them, I'm afraid, Bea. What's wrong? Are you alright?" Out of breath, Bea just nodded. "Here, I'll give you a ride. I offered one to your aunt, but she insisted they needed the walk. She's daft. She'll have wished she'd taken me up on it by now, I don't doubt. We'll find them on the way, I'm sure."

And they did. Evelyn seemed immensely relieved when Mildred and Bea arrived in Billy's cart. Mildred wasn't at all surprised when Evelyn didn't express any curiosity as to why they had caught up to her and Jean. Evelyn willingly took Billy's hand and let him help her into the cart. Nor did she express any curiosity about Jean and Bea's whispered Morse code discussion in the back as Billy started driving to their house. Mildred also paid little heed to the girls' discussion. She was much more interested in Evelyn's day. She had spent it fitting a confirmation dress for the eldest McTavish daughter. "They're a bit of an odd bunch, don't you think, Billy? Especially Mrs. McTavish herself. She seems entirely removed from reality. No wonder, really, what with all those tykes," Evelyn was saying.

Those seven tykes were only the half of it, Mildred began to muse before she overheard Bea saying, "'Kissed' and 'killed,' Jean. That was only one error. I think there was another."

Mildred didn't pay any attention to the end of their conversation, however. She was deathly tired, and she started to drift off, rousing now and again to the soothing voices of Evelyn and Billy as they continued their conversation — the McTavishes; the prospects for next year's fishing season; the state of Billy's boat. It wasn't until Bea called, "Billy! Would you mind stopping a moment?" that Mildred perked up. Billy halted the wagon, and Bea jumped out.

"Bea, for the love of God . . . "

"It's alright, Aunt Evelyn. I've just got to hop back into the city for a moment. I won't be long. I'll fix supper when I get back, Aunt Evelyn. Leave it for me."

"Bea, honestly . . . " started Evelyn. "Well, alright, then, but don't be long. We've another gale coming."

"If you wait until I take your family home, I'll run you down and back, Bea," said Billy.

"Ah, thanks for the offer, Billy, but I'd best just deal with this while it's on my mind." Bea was about to leave when Jean reached out for her. "What is it, Jean?"

"One more thing," said Jean, whispering into Bea's ear.

"Really?" asked Bea. "Are you sure that's what you heard?"

"Yes, Bea. I am," Jean said.

Bea nodded, smiled at Jean, waved them all goodbye and ran down the hill. After Billy had urged his horse along, and the wagon had once again started up the hill, Evelyn broke the silence that had come over them by saying: "Jean, what were you two whispering about in the back?"

"Morse code, Mum."

"I know that, love. I could overhear that much. What of it? What would make Bea charge back into the city this late in the day?"

"Punctuation, Mum. She wanted to know the Morse for certain kinds of punctuation."

"Oh, I see," said Evelyn, though Mildred knew that she didn't see at all, but Evelyn wasn't about to ask Jean to elaborate. Nor would Jean offer. Despite patience on Jean's part, it would only end up being a frustrating conversation for everyone. Even after many attempts by Jean to teach her elders the simplest words in Morse code, they seemed incapable of learning. So, in response to Jean's statement, the three in the front of the wagon simply nodded, and went back to wondering what Bea was up to.

Mildred wondered if she should be worried about where Bea was heading. She should have gone with her. She knew she should be more concerned about Bea's punctuation inquiry. She suspected the punctuation conundrum was somehow pertinent to the whole affair, but Mildred didn't have the energy to try to figure it out. She felt suddenly quite weary. For a moment she struggled against the fatigue, but she knew she wouldn't win. She started to fade, but more questions and concerns kept coming into her mind keeping her awake: Firstly, young Brian — where had he gone after the Stevens'? She had seen him there, listening, as they had been, to the conversations in the study. But then he had left and she hadn't followed. Where was he at this moment? She had no sense of him at all. Was it that she was simply too tired, or had he finally departed? Would she see him again? Was he satisfied with finding out that Cyrus was the murderer? She still had questions about this last point, but she was too tired to give it any serious consideration. Surely Cyrus had murdered Brian. It was the only thing that made sense, really. However, several questions regarding Brian's murder still lingered. One question, though apparently unrelated, kept nagging: What did Morna know? Brian had posed this question often enough, apparently. And the answer, certainly, could only be Cyrus. No doubt, as Cyrus's wife, Morna knew that Cyrus had murdered young Brian. And yet, for some godforsaken reason, the question regarding Morna's knowledge wouldn't settle. It kept niggling at Mildred's mind, as if it was not happy with the answer she had given it. And, of course, this all led to another question she had been avoiding. What of the locked room at the Nortons'? And the supposed skeleton? Of course, she knew the correct answer to this, but it made her sick to think of it. There was a far worse thing than a skeleton in that awful room.

Oh, for some rest. Some real sleep. She really was getting far, far too old for this type of excitement; she got weary so easily these days. Not feeling content, but not unduly concerned about Brian or Bea, she could no longer fight the weariness, and she finally closed her eyes. She would just put her head down for a moment. But with Evelyn's shoulder as a firm, yet friendly pillow, Mildred immediately fell fast asleep.

Henry was on to his fourth scotch when it came to him. He stumbled out of his bedroom, and down the hall to George's room. "D'you still have it, George?" he asked, shoving open the door.

"Have what, Father?" asked George, sitting up in bed. "You're drunk."

"You would be too, George, b'lieve me. The Morse code, do you still have it on your stomach?"

"God no, Father. I washed it off long ago. You think I'd go to bed with that muck on me?"

DAY TWELVE

"Damn!"

"I'm going back to sleep, Father," said George, flopping onto his bed and pulling the covers over his eyes.

Henry shut the door and went back to his own room. Once there, he poured another scotch, and sat in his armchair by the window. A mess of papers lay scattered on the windowsill beside him. He picked one paper off the top. The four-by six-inch white paper showed eight dots separated by a space in the middle. Underneath the two lines of four dots, Henry had written "HH." "It worked, ya know, Brian. They'd never know it was you. But on my own son's stomach? Old boy, what the *devil* are you trying to tell me?" Henry asked the paper as he tilted the writing toward the lamp.

Henry couldn't remember how old they were when they first came up with their secret signal — eight years old? Ten? They had decided that they needed a secret call sign, something that only they would know. A signal to let the other twin know that his brother was calling. No one else would know. It had taken him and Brian a number of tries to come up with just the right thing. It was Brian in the end — he was so much better at Morse — who discovered it. "Eight dots, Henry. That's the . . . "

"Delete code."

"Yes. And everyone else will think it's the delete code. But we'll know — when it's at the very top of the message, Henry, otherwise it really will be a delete, won't it? We'll know it's actually two groups of four dots. The signal . . . "

"For *H!* Brilliant, Brian. Absolutely brilliant."

"Thanks. I was playing around with both our initials at first, but yours work best, don't you think?"

"Absolutely."

... --- ...

The tip of Brian's forefinger moved over the soft wet surface like a ship over water. This was as it should be, Brian thought, because when you draw ships, you should feel them first — how they are in the water, the wind, the waves. Here, the water was still. Like satin, he thought, his finger turning easily toward the west. And as if he was riding a wave, his finger would rise up off the surface then fall gently, rise then fall. He still could not see the design that he had drawn in the lightless room, the shape he had made of the sailing ship, but he knew that he had drawn a battleship, and she was on her way to Newfoundland to set the cable right. He couldn't wait for the light to shine so he could take in his accomplishment: the entire ship, her graceful sails and powerful guns, her elegant bow.

So he was extremely surprised when the haze cleared and he saw that the image before him was not a ship at all. Instead, he had drawn characters: a line across the top, for Henry. And then the code of five words and two pieces of punctuation. The words themselves weren't yet making sense, but he recognized the code — tight and tidy, it was his own, how strange, how different from his brother's; in this one instance they were not identical at all. The writing wasn't the worst part. The worst, by far, was George's blood, which had quickly dried to the tip of his finger.

It was smelly, too. A smell he remembered from somewhere. A red cave angry kind of smell.

... --- ...

With the blood where he had left it, drying to the tip of his finger, Brian had followed George home. He had witnessed the ensuing drama unfold in Henry's study, and when the Nortons left, he left with them. He tailed Cyrus and Eliza down the city streets, and in through the door of the Nortons' apartment building. He followed them as they slowly made their way up the stairs and into their apartment. Cyrus finally got settled in the room across the hall from his bedroom. He sat on his wooden stool in front of the model ship — Brian's favourite, the 1857 *Agamemnon* — and, when the time was right, Brian came up behind him.

"Penelope!" Miss Norton cried as she opened the door, and Bea was so glad that she had decided to come to the Nortons'. She hadn't come for

Miss Norton, but the woman clearly needed help. Bea was even more glad that Mrs. Stevens had said she would drop by later. It was a good thing, because Miss Norton could use someone to befriend her: her father had attacked her once again. The left sleeve of her white blouse hung from its shoulder seam, and the lace of the cuff was in shreds. The left side of the high collar had been ripped as well. Her fine blond hair had been torn from its bun, and now fell in soft, messy curls around her face and shoulders.

"Miss Norton? Are you alright?" Bea could barely get the words out: she could hardly hear her own words, drowned out as they were by the clatter from inside the apartment. At first Bea didn't know where it was coming from, and then she traced its source. It was as Jean had said just now, on the road home. The child had been right: from just inside the Norton's front door, the small telegraph machine sounded a signal. But the strange thing was, its key wasn't moving; it lay perfectly still.

"I'm absolutely fine, Bea. What can I do for you?" Miss Norton said, appearing equally distracted.

"What is it saying?" asked Bea. "Do you know?"

"What are you talking about?" Miss Norton asked, following Bea's gaze to the telegraph machine.

"The telegraph machine. It's sending a signal. Surely you can hear it."

"No, in fact I can't. I don't know what you're talking about. Look, it's perfectly still — how on earth can it be sending a signal when it's perfectly still? Why did you come here, Bea?"

But Bea didn't answer. The telegraph machine overrode all of her ability to think or speak. Finally, after several seconds, she managed to say,

"SOS, Miss Norton. It's sending an SOS. Even I know that. Three dots, three dashes, three . . . "

"I *know* the code for SOS, Bea. Are you saying that this useless old machine is sending out an SOS?"

"That's what I'm hearing, Miss."

"And who do you surmise is sending that SOS, Bea?"

Without thinking how illogical it was to say it, Bea blurted: "Morna."

In her earnest fashion, Jean had said just that when she'd grabbed Bea's arm before she departed the wagon. "SOS, Bea. And *Morna*. Over and over again. That's what I heard it say when we were up at the Nortons' apartment that day, Bea."

"Morna?" asked Miss Norton, stepping back slightly from the door.

"Yes," said Bea, feeling extremely foolish now. The signal had begun to fade, leaving Bea feeling as if she had entirely imagined the whole thing.

"That's just cruel, Bea. My mother is Morna. And my mother is dead, Bea. Are you telling me she is calling us from the grave?"

"No, Miss. I don't know, Miss."

"I'm sure you don't. I've never heard anything more idiotic."

That was true, thought Bea. She didn't know what she could possibly say in her defence. She had been so stupid. The signal had stopped as if it had never been. She had imagined the whole thing. She started to back away.

"I'm awfully sorry, Miss Norton. Really I am . . . " Bea said, starting to leave, but just as she did, the clattering started up again, louder and more persistent than before. She took a step toward the machine, unable to take her eyes off it. She remembered why else she had come. The "SOS. Morna" had just been an afterthought that Jean had thrown her way. Trying to disregard the clatter, she said, "Brian's murder, Miss."

"Brian. I've heard enough of him for one day. What of it?"

"Well . . . "

"Yes? Please, Bea, in case you haven't noticed, I really do need to bathe. It's been a most upsetting day."

"Well, Miss. I was going to say . . . "

"Yes, Bea?"

"Your father — he didn't kill Brian, did he?"

Miss Norton stepped even further away from the door. "Now, Bea, you say that with such authority. I only hope you're correct. But why on earth would you think that?"

"Well, the Morse code, Miss. I happened to be at the Stevens', and I happened to overhear . . . "

"Oh, my, Bea. I can see you're going to have to explain this to us. Come in. We'll discuss this with my father. He'll be most interested in your theory, I'm sure."

"Oh Miss, no, that's alright. I'll just leave. I don't want to talk to your father."

"I insist. Let's settle this question, shall we? Oh, don't worry about

Father. He's had enough for one day," she said, smiling down at her tattered clothes. "He likes you, Bea, and that's a rare thing, let me tell you. Oh, please, don't fret. He'll not harm you, I promise."

Eliza led Bea down to the bedroom hallway, and opened the door on the left — it was unlocked and partly ajar. "After you, Bea," she said, stepping aside to let her enter. "He'll be delighted to see you, I'm sure."

But as soon as Bea stepped into the bedroom, she realized what a fool she had been.

... --- ...

Jean concentrated her gaze not on the storm outside the window, but to her left, past Bea's desk and Mildred's rocking chair — as if she could see right through the far west wall of their attic bedroom. Her woollen frock, leggings, and thick cardigan did little to fend off the damp cold, and she wrapped her arms more tightly about her chest. She sought the answer to her worry in the distance: down the hills of rocks and trees, along the path that followed the harbour, onto the streets of the city. The ocean gale slammed its salty rain against the house, shaking the pane, sending loose shingles flying. Jean ignored it all. Wherever Bea was, that's where the worrying lay.

"Something's happened to our Bea," Jean whispered, turning to her right to face Mildred, who had just joined her at the window. Mildred had continued to sleep after they had returned home. She had just now awoken, as if out of a nightmare, and she came to stand next to the child. But she didn't speak; she was working to quell her own fear made all the more terrible by the look on Jean's face. She touched the girl's cheek, gently brushed away a strand of hair, and finally spoke. "I suspect it's as you think, child. We must hurry. We have little time to spare, and I fear your cousin has even less." But her urgent words went unheeded. Too frightened to listen, let alone act, Jean had turned away again as if still seeking, in the distance, the answer to her worry.

... --- ...

She had been a large model ship; her aft mast, still attached, leaned precariously at a tight angle over her crushed bow. Hanging tattered from the mast, the sail's tip licked at blood that ran like shallow waters under the sinking ship. Embedded in the splintered hull, a valiant anchor — T-side up — stood vigil over the wreckage. Wood, sail, and fine roping lay scattered around the destroyed vessel.

The red waters spilled from a blood-soaked head at the perimetre of the debris. Bea immediately closed her eyes before she could take in the rest of the body. Seconds later, she reopened them, drawn this time to the bed beside her, upon which lay the first of the dead.

Five brittle sets of bones made up the hand. Skin like fine blotting paper — wrinkled, dry, and splotched a faded purple and brown — wrapped each individual finger. Bea couldn't see the wrist; the skeletal hand dangled below the edge of the sheet that drooped over the side of the bed.

At Bea's feet, between her chair and the bed, a moth-eaten, brown woollen blanket lay discarded. Having just now awoken, she began to reach for it — on impulse, to warm the cold bones — but, of course, she couldn't move her arms. Or her legs. She was bound to the chair, a strong rope cutting into her legs, stomach, and chest. Her hands were tied behind her back and a stinking rag was wrapped tightly around her mouth. A movement in the open doorway made her look up. The tiny anchor had also reacted — it waved slowly, from side to side to side, surrendering the ship to the enemy, who had just returned.

... --- ...

When Cyrus had released Brian and the boy had fallen to the cave floor, there, as if a gift from God, was his father's knife. Now, the blade's flat cold steel pressed its comfort into Brian's bare thigh. In a second, Brian's hand had found the hilt. A second was long enough, and when Cyrus returned, Brian was ready. When Cyrus bent down to reach for him, Brian lunged. But Cyrus's scream wasn't the only foreign sound he heard. From the entrance to his cave, Brian heard a second set of footsteps.

Brian never knew whether it was a memory or a dream, whether it belonged to him or someone else, or whether he had made it up altogether;

but he breathed deeply now as it receded. He was no longer in the cave. He was no longer holding the knife. He was in Morna's room, holding on to *Agamemnon's* lines. He had been building a model of the *Agamemnon* ship when the images had interrupted.

He continued tying the lines of the model ship until the knots were peaceful like the prayer; just him, the ropes, and the sound of Morna's breathing from behind. I'm safe, Brian tried to tell himself. It's just me and Morna, the ropes and *Agamemnon*. No footsteps, no one coming to get me. That may be so, but then, what is that next to you, he tried to ask himself.

He ignored himself and tried to concentrate on the knots, tried to remember which line went where. "Not too tight or too loose, give it some slack," his father's voice repeated in his mind. He held fast to his father's words, tying them tighter and tighter into the ropes along the starboard side of the ship. He would make them firm and strong. He could stand anything if he had his father's voice.

He turned around to look at Morna. She was still in bed at the far end of the room, her unchanged sheets stuck to her soiled nightgown as if her body had sucked the wet fabric right into its bone. Nothing about her was different except her breathing — it had become frantic. As if she knew he was there, she tried to lift her right arm and knocked her blanket off, her trembling fingers grabbing for him as though he were the empty air beside her. Silly Morna. Your blanket's fallen onto the floor, Morna. Now you'll be even colder, Morna.

She was trying to tell him something again. She was always trying to tell him something. But he didn't want to know about it; he was tired of listening. So he turned away from her, back to his ropes and *Agamemnon*. He would concentrate and dispose of the bad memory by holding it under until it stopped breathing, until it sank to the bottom of the sea, borne downward by its own weight.

You should stop worrying, he told himself, you're being silly, there are no footsteps. There's no one coming. There's no one here besides Morna.

That might be so, he countered, but then why is there a dead body beside you? Did you kill it, Brian?

I don't know, he told himself as he blinked away the tears that immediately welled in his eyes. Someone had died, that much he remembered. He dropped the ropes and reached up to scratch behind his right ear. His nervous scratch. He didn't want to look at the body. It wasn't real, he knew. He had had his father's knife, that much he remembered. But did he kill Cyrus? Was any of it real? It was just a memory, or a dream, he insisted, but still it wouldn't let him not look. So he braced himself and, shifting his cross-legged position on the floor, he looked quickly — as if to scare it away.

A body lay on the floor beside him. Blood spilled from the head. Brian couldn't see the face. The pool of blood got larger and larger, until it almost touched his knees and *Agamemnon*.

Look, Brian. Look at your hands, Brian.

He couldn't make himself do that, and for several seconds, he looked everywhere but at his hands. He looked at the walls and the high, silly window shut tight against any fresh air. He looked back at Morna, still and stiff again, as if dead. Are you dead, Morna, he wanted to ask her again; he was always asking her that, but now he had other things on his mind. His hands.

He looked. With one hand, he gripped the cords of the *Agamemnon*, and with the other, still sticky with blood, he held tight to his father's knife.

Get the ropes in the right order, Brian. What order was that, he wanted to know. He couldn't remember anymore, and the ropes began to get tangled into one another while, with the knifeless hand, he tried to sort them out. He tried to make the ropes matter more than the dead body at his side and more than the bloody knife in his hand, but it didn't work. He couldn't make the bad go away. He closed his eyes and wished himself gone, and once again his wishes came true because when he opened his eyes and quickly looked down at his hands, the knife was gone, as if it had never been. His hands were clean of blood. They were shaking, but they were clean.

Any rope will do, his father's memory interrupted. Of course it wouldn't, Brian wanted to scream in response. He knew that only the correct rope would do and Father knew that too, but even so he grabbed a cord from the port side and kept threading it and tying it, the ropes all the wrong way now, maybe if I pray, he thought. Now I lay me down to sleep, pray the Lord my soul to keep, but it didn't help. The peace from the childhood prayer had nothing to do with the prayer itself. He knew that, of course he knew that. The peace had only to do with him, his father and his brother, his father in his smoking jacket and slacks, he and his brother in their night shirts, bare knees, bare feet on the cold floor, small elbows leaning down low on the edge of the bed, Father's big elbows on top. Three sets of hands in prayer. Three of them, unbroken, together. He had never been able to remember why it hadn't lasted.

The shoelace came out of nowhere, out of the cold, black damp, out of the wet walls, out of the open doorway. Its hard tip slapped his cheek as the boot flashed by and into *Agamemnon*.

"*Agamemnon,*" said Miss Norton, retracing her steps to the open doorway. She had entered, walked toward the wreckage of the ship, swung back her foot, and kicked. More bits of wood and sail went flying, and she had stood for a moment and watched it. Now at the doorway, pointing a well-manicured finger at the ship wreckage in the corner, she said, "The cable ship. But, of course, you know all about those, don't you, Bea?" Miss Norton looked as beautiful and elegant as ever, despite the torn blouse, but now Bea felt like she was seeing her for the first time. Her distinct air of vulnerability had transformed into malevolence. "Father's work. He's built dozens of model ships. I don't know why he bothers. I always get them in the end." Miss Norton followed Bea's gaze to the black boot on the edge of the circle of destruction. Attached to the boot was the leg of Mr. Norton. He lay inert on the floor, folded in on himself like a baby. Blood pooled from a gash on his head, and spread toward *Agamemnon*.

"He deserved it, don't you think, Bea?" said Miss Norton. "Mother thinks so, don't you, Mother?" Bea's gaze reluctantly shifted to the head of the bed. But there, instead of death, was a very old woman. Bea need not have been afraid of the eyes that stared back at her: they were pale blue and cloudy, and very much alive with concern for Bea herself. Emaciated, balding, toothless, but not dead, not yet. Mr. Shulman had been correct. "If the body is not decomposing, if it is not a mummy or a skeleton, then it could well be that your body is not dead, Miss MacDonald," he had told her. "It could be that your body is still alive."

"I should give him one more kick, don't you think, Mother?" Miss

Norton continued. "Papa always was such a rotten fellow. He really did get to be such a bore." She strode into the room, grabbing on her way a hard-backed chair from beside the doorway. At first, Bea thought she was going to set the chair down on top of him, but instead she placed the chair right next to her father's head so that one of its front legs came down in the pool of blood. She sat gracefully, crossing one leg over the other, and with the tips of her fingers, she adjusted her black skirt and what was left of the high lace collar of her white blouse.

"Oh, yes, the blouse," she said, fingering the tear in the collar. "Pity, that. Mother is such a tyrant. She really is. That little right arm of hers. She can hardly move the thing, just those fingers that rattle away, but when she gets the energy, my, does she have a grip. She's ruined more than two of my blouses that way, hanging on, not letting go, no matter how hard I try to pull her off. Remarkable strength. But I don't really know why she bothers. She's not hurting me, though she'd like to, I know; it's only my clothes. And I always get her back, don't I, Mother?" She smiled over at the woman lying immobile on the bed. "Oh, pardon me, excuse my manners! You two have not been properly introduced, have you? Mother, meet Bea MacDonald, our nosy little miss. And Bea, this is my mother, Mrs. Morna Norton. I'd have you two shake hands, but, well, another day perhaps."

Bea stared at Miss Norton and then at Mrs. Norton. Bea realized that the collar of Mrs. Norton's nightgown was torn from its seam, and that numerous small tears rippled through the off-white fabric of the sleeve. She also had small, bleeding scratches on her neck where Miss Norton's fingernails had got her. Bea glanced up at Miss Norton.

"Oh, Bea. Don't look at me like that. It's not as if she cares. She hardly even knows, does she? I mean, she can't feel anymore, can she? The only problem, really, is that we're running out of clothes, and it is getting to be expensive." Miss Norton smiled over at Bea, and then at her mother, and continued,

"I've always liked you, Bea. You have spirit. I've always liked that in a woman. Too many of us are frightened little things, don't you think? You're more like me. You have courage. Breaking in here whenever you like. I like that. Oh, you didn't think I knew, did you? Leave the doors how you found them next time.

"Too bad you showed up when you did just now. We could have been friends at some point in the future, but not now. I have to depart, you see. In, say, about an hour," she said, looking behind her at a small trunk and two floral canvas bags. "Speaking of friends, we are expecting another guest. She should be here soon." She pulled her watch fob from her skirt pocket, and checked the time. "It didn't quite work out here in Newfoundland as I thought. Still, all is not lost, even though Papa didn't exactly hold up his end. Blackmail's a difficult business, Bea. Isn't that right, Mother? Have you ever tried it, Bea? Well, believe it or not, this pile of bones lying on the bed beside you here is a professional. You wouldn't know it, would you? I learned everything I know from her."

...---...

After several frustrating trips to the post office, where Eliza had no more success in finding out what her mother was up to than she had the first time, she decided that a different tack was required. The next time her mother left the house, Eliza let her go down the block a ways, and then she left the house and rushed down the street.

"What are you up to, Mother?" she said, coming up beside her and snatching her basket from her hand.

"No! Don't," her mother had squeaked, and reached for the basket to try to grab it back.

"You know, Mother. I've had it with your sneaking around. And I've had no luck whatsoever trying to figure out what you've been up to. Aah. I see you've had no idea that I've been following you," said Eliza, smiling down at her mother's shocked face. Her mother blinked rapidly, something she always did when she was nervous. "Almost every Tuesday for two months. How tedious. Out of the house, to the post office, watching while you go through the same ritual every time, opening letters, mailing other letters. Every single time. Then home again. Haven't you noticed that I would come home not long after you on those days?"

Her mother's head started to tremble and she didn't respond. She stared at the ground while they stood at the side of the road. Passers-by pretended not to notice them, and streetcars and buggies drove past, splashing muddy water onto Eliza's new coat.

"Haven't you?" repeated Eliza, grabbing the side of the coat and stepping further away from the road. She grabbed her mother's coat sleeve and yanked her toward her. "I'm asking you a question."

"No, dear, I didn't."

"God, you're stupid. Well, what're you up to, eh?"

"Nothing, dear."

"I'll bet it's nothing. Could be, but I doubt it. If it was nothing, why have you looked so guilty, Mother?"

"I don't know, dear," she said, and then she looked up at Eliza as if she was going to try to be strong. "I have correspondence to attend to every week, dear. That's all. It's nothing special."

"No? Well, let's see." Eliza shoved her hand in her mother's basket and to her mother's "don't, dear," "oh please, dear," she threw the things that didn't matter on the muddy ground: a scarf, a hat (why would she need another when she had one on her head?), an old pair of stockings (why on earth would she be carrying these disgusting things around with her?). At the bottom of the basket sat a fresh new envelope. "Hmm. Let's see what this is, shall we? "

She pulled it out and looked at the address on the front: *Cyrus Newton Norton*. "My, my. A letter to my father. Your own husband. No return address. Not your handwriting, though. Making deliveries for someone, are you?"

"No, certainly not, dear. Look. Your father would be most unhappy to know that you're looking at his correspondence."

"Well, that's too bad, isn't it?" she said as she ripped open the envelope and took out the letter inside.

Dear Cyrus,

Another month. Another ten pounds. Money for murder.
I will expect the money within the week.

Forever yours,
Judson Stevens.

For a moment, Eliza didn't have any words. She didn't know what to say; she was truly shocked. "Is this what I think it is, Mother?"

"What's that, dear?"

"Oh, Mother, please. Don't blather."

Her mother didn't respond and just stared at the ground. The woman was always surprising her. Like now. "And what's this about murder?" Eliza asked, shaking the paper at her mother.

"I don't know, dear, really."

"Really? Well. I have dozens more questions. Such as, what are you doing with the letter in the first place? A fresh, new, unmailed letter, for that matter. Are you working for this . . . Judson Stevens?" asked Eliza, glancing again at the signature on the page.

"Don't be silly."

"Oh. I'm not being silly, Mother. But not to worry. We won't worry about all those questions, now will we? We have one more stop before we can unravel the mystery."

"Is that right, dear? And where is that?"

Really. She could be the most infuriating woman. "The post office. Or have you forgotten?" Before her mother could answer, Eliza tucked her arm through hers and started down the street. They had gone a block when the Gladstones came around the corner.

"Oh, Eliza. Mrs. Norton. How nice to see you," said Mrs. Gladstone while Mr. Gladstone tipped his hat.

"And you." Eliza nodded and smiled, but didn't stop. She didn't want to get into a conversation with them right now.

"Frightening woman," Mrs. Gladstone whispered to her husband as they passed them by and Eliza knew, of course, that they meant her mother.

With Eliza gripping tightly to her mother's arm, they passed several more people that they knew on the way to the post office. Eliza smiled and nodded, but her mother didn't. This habit she had of ignoring people was most infuriating. And embarrassing.

Eliza thrust open the large wooden doors of the post office and they walked into the spacious and airy room. She marched her mother over to the post office box on the wall, their feet clicking echoes on the stone floor. Finally, her mother started to cry. "Must we?" she said.

"Just open it," said Eliza, pushing her mother against the wall of boxes with her hips, but in such a way that no one else would notice.

Her mother took the key out of her coat pocket but her hand was shaking as she tried to put it into the lock. "Here, by all means let me," said Eliza as she grabbed the key and opened the box. At the back sat a single envelope. Eliza pulled it out.

"My, my, my. I was expecting it to say Mrs. Cyrus Norton, but it doesn't, does it?"

"No," her mother muttered, hanging her head.

"Look at me when you talk."

"No, it doesn't say that," she said, trying to meet Eliza's eyes, but her gaze kept shifting to the floor.

"This is rather funny, Mother. And I must say, I'm baffled. The addressee is *Mr. Judson Stevens*, the same fellow that that letter is from. Well, let's see what's inside this one, shall we? Let's see what all your sneaky behaviour has been about."

Eliza tore open the envelope and out fell pound notes. "Money. Well, Mother, you do surprise me. How much do we have here?" She counted it quickly. "Ten pounds. Well, fancy that. Isn't that right, Mother? Fancy that. That is exactly the same amount as was asked for in the first letter."

Her mother didn't say anything. She seemed to have given up; her shoulders had slouched even farther and her arms hung at her sides. She continued to stare at the floor.

"But, Mother," Eliza said without expecting an answer. "There's one more thing, isn't there? The third letter." At this, her mother glanced up. "Remember. I know everything. Everything. Well, almost. I think when we leave here we should go for a cup of tea and a scone, perhaps. It's been a long time since we've gone out together, hasn't it. Never, you say? Well, perhaps you're right. In any case, Mother, we have all this money here, don't we, and we can have a nice hot cup of tea and you can tell me the whole thing, won't you, Mother?" She grabbed for her mother's thin wrist. Her strong fingers circled it easily. She could crush the bones if she wanted to. She let go. Her fingers had left imprints that would turn quickly to bruises to join the other ones there. Her mother had never learned not to challenge her.

"But first, Mother, before we relax, I need to know: what is the other letter? Who is it to, and what is in it?"

"I can't, dear."

"No, Mother. You can," said Eliza, touching her wrist with her fingertip.

"It doesn't really matter, does it, dear?"

"I'm sure it doesn't, Mother, but I really would like to know. Here, I'll help you. We'll go through your Tuesday visit to the post office, step by step. First you get the mail out of your box. We've already done that, correct?" Her mother stared downward and nodded. "And then, you open it, of course, and you take out the money." She nodded again. "Then you take the other envelope out of your purse. The blank one. Let's do that, shall we?" Eliza reached into her mother's basket, found the envelope, and placed it on the high counter next to them. "Then . . . oh, I know what you do now, Mother. I've never been able to see this part of what you do in here. You see, I stand at that window over there," she said, pointing, and her mother turned toward it. "But you're too good at this, aren't you? You don't let anybody see, do you? But I know what you do. I just figured it out. You put the money from this envelope into the new envelope. Am I correct?"

Her mother's silence was her confirmation but still she wanted a better response. "Am I correct?" she asked, leaning over and whispering in the older woman's ear. Her mother nodded. "Say it," Eliza whispered and then, seeing a woman looking at them from the other side of the room, she smiled one of her large, warm smiles, shrugged her shoulders, and shook her head. *The old lady isn't quite right in the head*, she tried to indicate with her non-verbal cues. The woman smiled slightly, but Eliza wasn't sure that she bought the lie. However, Eliza didn't need to worry about it because the woman quickly finished posting her letter, and without another look at them, she turned on her heels and went out the door.

Eliza glanced around at the other customers in the building. No one seemed to be paying them any mind. "Am I correct?" she repeated for a third time, and this time she pressed her gloved fingers around her mother's wrist.

"Yes," said her mother, and she started to sniffle.

"So I thought. Alright," said Eliza. "And then what, Mother? Where does it go?" Eliza nudged her mother up to the counter, grabbed the pen out of the well in the centre of the counter, placed the blank envelope in front of her, and handed her the pen. Without another word of resistance, her mother wrote the name of the addressee: *Mr. Henry Stevens.*

"We'll have a large pot and two of your best scones with cream and preserves, please," Eliza said to the waitress, who wrote on her pad and then turned and headed back to the kitchen.

She had taken a seat across from her mother at the booth by the window. She had chosen the restaurant and the seating for its privacy. They sat in silence, waiting for their tea. Her mother slouched across from her with her head bowed and her hands in her lap. Eliza knew that to absolutely everybody, Eliza herself looked the complete opposite. Elegant. Cultured. Well-bred. Beautiful.

"Mother, please," Eliza said with a smile in case anyone was watching. "Please don't look so peculiar. You're embarrassing me."

"That's always it, isn't it, Liza?" asked her mother suddenly, gazing up at her, her eyes red and sore looking. "You. Does anyone else exist, Eliza, besides you? Do you know what it means to love or care about anyone?"

Eliza stared across at her mother, amazed at her sudden brazen behaviour. It must be because they were in public. She would never be like this at home. Perhaps it had been a mistake to come here.

"Love, Mother? What does love have to do with anything?"

"Oh, I don't know, dear. It just seems that perhaps it's something we should talk about sometime. You seem to think it doesn't matter."

"Does it?"

"Of course."

"And now you're going to tell me you love Father, I suppose."

"No. I did once. Long ago. He ruined everything."

"Yes. I can see that. So. Are there others? Oh, Mother? Are you telling me that you have been having an affaire du coeur? Heavens, who would have thought?"

For the first time her mother smiled, a slow sad smile. "No, dear, that's not it."

"Then who, Mother? Who have you loved? You seem to be an expert on the subject."

"Besides you?" her mother said, but Eliza didn't respond. She just looked away and out the window. The rain had started again. She longed to get away from this country, somewhere warm, exotic. "The boys," her mother said.

"Ah. The boys. Who might they be? Judson and Henry? Are those the boys?" Seeing an expression in her mother's eyes that she took for agreement, she said, "So you've been working for them somehow. Working against your own husband, it seems. How does it work, Mother? Judson sends you the letter and you post it and pick up the money that Father has sent, and then you send that to Henry? There must be a reason for this, though I'm stumped as to what it might be. Oh, yes. I'd almost forgotten. There is the murder." Just as she said the word the server arrived from behind her with the tea and scones. She didn't appear to have heard, but servants are always like that, Eliza had found from the few that she had known. Once the woman had poured their tea and gone, Eliza took a sip of her tea and whispered, "Who was murdered, Mother?"

"Brian," said her mother, without missing a beat, and Eliza glanced over at her, startled. Her response was too prompt. Why was she not resisting anymore? Why was she looking as if she had acquiesced? This wasn't normal for her mother, and Eliza found it far more disconcerting than her typically subservient behaviour.

"Who's Brian?" Eliza asked.

"One of the boys."

"And the other?"

"Henry, Brian's twin."

"And Judson?"

"Their father."

"Alright. So Judson is blackmailing Father for killing his son Brian. Is that what Father did, Mother? And for some bizarre reason you are involved and are forwarding the money on to the other son, Brian's twin, Henry?"

"No."

"What, then?" Eliza she saw that she was going to have to come up with the right questions. Despite her mother's new forthcoming nature, she wasn't going to offer the information freely.

Eliza took another sip of her tea, buttered the scone with the cream and a dollop of strawberry jam, and took a bite. Her mother hadn't touched either her tea or her scone. "Drink, Mother. People will wonder."

"Let them," she said in another audacious display of rebellion.

Eliza glanced about the restaurant, which was almost full at this time of day — teatime — but no one seemed to be paying particular attention to them. Eliza sighed and took another bite, which she chewed slowly, like a lady; she had been practising being a lady all her life. She had another sip of her tea. "The tea's good, you know. Refreshing. Did Father kill Brian, Mother?"

"Yes."

"Really? And how do you know?"

"I followed him. To the cave."

"The cave? This all happened in a cave? Where?"

"Not too far from here, in the country."

"Is that so?"

"Yes."

"So Father killed this boy Brian. For what reason?"

"Revenge. Anger. Rage. Frustration."

"What did the boy have to do with anything?"

"Well, he didn't, you see. That's the point. The boy was an innocent. A sweet little innocent," her mother said, her eyes welling up with tears.

"Let's get to the money, Mother," Eliza said, and her mother glanced at her, and shook her head. "Oh. I know. You think I'm heartless. You always think I'm heartless."

"Aren't you?"

"If that means do I weep about every poor little child in the world, no I don't. Why don't you keep the money, Mother?"

"It's not mine. It belongs to Henry."

"Henry? Why should it belong to Henry?"

"Brian was his twin. Henry lost his other half when Brian died. It's the least I . . . least that could be done."

"You were going to say 'the least I could do.'"

"No I wasn't."

"Yes, you were. But I still don't understand; why were you working for Judson Stevens? To get back at Father?"

"Yes and no."

"Oh, Mother, out with it."

"Yes, I wanted to get back at Cyrus for having killed Brian. And no, I wasn't working for Judson."

"Who were you working for, then?"

"Myself," she said, holding Eliza's gaze.

"Yourself?"

"Yes."

Eliza was confused. Then, her mother pulled from her basket a blank piece of paper and a charcoal. She bent over the paper and wrote a number of lines, and while she did it she hid the writing from Eliza's view. When she was finished, she slid it across the table to Eliza. Eliza looked at the writing, then stared at it harder, dumbfounded, unable to believe what she was seeing. She glanced up at her mother, and for the first time ever, she almost admired her. "It's his writing. Judson Stevens," Eliza said. "It's an exact copy of the blackmailing letter we just opened."

"Yes," said her mother, and a slight smile crossed her lips. "It's a replica, Eliza. I'm very good at it really, I must say." She finally reached for her cup of tea, and took a delicate sip, then another.

"Forgery. You forge Judson Stevens' handwriting. But why?"

Her mother just shrugged and said, "I can forge it to the stroke of each character. I know all the characters. I practised for years first. Lowercase and uppercase, printing and spelling. Your father was very familiar with Judson's handwriting. It had to be perfect."

"My goodness," said Eliza softly, staring again at the writing. And then it all fit into place and she suddenly understood everything. She knew exactly what her mother had been doing all these years, and why.

"Judson Stevens isn't blackmailing Father, is he?"

"No, he's not."

"And no one else is either, are they?"

"No, no in fact they're not, dear."

"It's you, isn't it, Mother?"

"Yes, dear, that's correct. I've been blackmailing your father for — let's see now — going on twenty years, I believe."

"And you'll keep doing it, won't you?"

"No, dear."

"Yes, Mother. You will."

"It's no use, Eliza. It's over. He's dead."

"So you said," said Eliza as she took one of her newly acquired pound notes from her purse and put it on the table. She had heard more than she'd ever thought she would from her mother. Her mother had given her details on the blackmailing, on the murder, and on how she had set the blackmailing in motion. One of the questions that Eliza had had was why had it taken her so long to start blackmailing her father.

"Things like this take a long time to plan," her mother said. "You have to be patient. Do you know about patience, Eliza?" She asked it pointedly, and Eliza suspected that her mother now knew what she herself was planning. "It takes a long time to learn to forge someone's writing, Eliza. At least, it did for me."

"That's alright, Mother," said Eliza, not bothering to pretend that she didn't know what her mother was alluding to. "I don't need to know. You're going to do it for me. But, Mother, heavens, ten pounds a week? Why so little? We'll have to demand much more than that."

"I'm not going to do it for you, Eliza."

"Oh, yes, Mother. You are."

"No, Eliza, I'm not."

Eliza had looked up, but ignored the resolve in her mother's eyes. "We'll talk about it when we get home." She laid the money on the table as her mother said,

"You don't understand, dear. He's dead. Judson's dead. Today was going to be my last letter to your father, anyhow. Judson died two days ago; I just read it in this morning's obituaries, you see, and even though I'm sure your father doesn't check the postmark, sometime he might, and then he'd certainly wonder how Judson could be blackmailing him from the grave. I thought I'd sneak in one more letter and get one more donation for Henry, and then that would be it. Everything comes to an end."

Eliza was in such a state of shock that she hardly spoke. Her visions of how easy it was all going to be were squashed by the news of Judson's death. "What am I supposed to do then, Mother? What? Tell me."

"I don't know, dear," she said, staring at the tabletop.

Eliza watched the same spot on the table for several minutes while the waitress took their money and brought their change. Then a smile spread across her face. "Henry, Mother. I'll get Henry to do it."

...---...

Miss Norton swung out her top leg and kicked her father in the back. He didn't move. "Probably," she said, reading Bea's thoughts. Then, addressing her father, she whispered, "Father, are you dead? Bea wants to know."

He didn't reply, and she looked up at Bea and smiled. "We get a lot of that around here. Always have. 'Are you dead?' How would you like to grow up in a household where every time you turn around somebody is writing in red on counter tops or tables: 'Are you dead?' 'Why did you kill?' Mother said all he wants is to talk. Isn't that right, Mother?" She frowned at Bea, and then down at her boot. "Oh, my, look what I've done to my new boots." She reached forward and flicked a speck of something from the tip of her bi-coloured boot. "You're wondering what happened next. Did I get Henry to do the blackmailing, just as Mother had got Judson to do hers? Say something, Bea. Nod your head, something." Bea nodded. "This really is getting most tiresome talking to myself. Bea? If I remove that thing from around your mouth, will you promise not to yell or scream or anything?"

Bea nodded again and Miss Norton stepped over and gently undid the cloth from around her mouth, but before she removed it she said with a smile, "Promise?" Bea nodded again, and Miss Norton removed the rag. Bea did as she was told; she didn't say a thing, and when Miss Norton could tell that she wasn't going to scream, she returned to her chair.

"There, now. What part of the story were we getting to?" Just then, Miss Norton stopped talking to listen. Someone was knocking loudly at the front door. "Perfect. There she is. Right on time."

"Hurry, my love," Mildred said, more gently this time, but no less insistent. Jean ran out of the attic and down the stairs.

"It's Bea, Mum!" Jean cried from the kitchen doorway.

"What, love? What about her?" said Evelyn, dropping a half-peeled potato on the floor. Billy reached over to grab it as it rolled toward him at the kitchen table, and he seemed about to make a joke about it, when he caught the tone in Evelyn's voice and the look on her face.

"We've got to go, Mum. Now!" Jean cried again, making for the front door.

"What? What is it?" asked Evelyn as she tore off her apron and ran out of the kitchen after Jean. They both donned their coats and hats and were pulling on their gloves as Billy grabbed his own and shut the door behind them.

...---...

"Now, where was I?" said Miss Norton, with her hands on her hips. She was staring at the floor, where Mrs. Stevens lay in a heap. When they had entered the room, Mrs. Stevens had hardly had a chance to be surprised at the three people already here — Bea bound to the chair, Mrs. Norton on the bed, and Mr. Norton dead on the floor — before Miss Norton struck her over the head from behind. "My goodness, what a party. Well, I'll have to get more chairs." Miss Norton left, heading down to the kitchen.

Immediately, Bea whispered harshly, "Mrs. Stevens. Wake up. Mrs. Stevens."

But Miss Norton was back in seconds, chair in hand, and said to Bea, "Don't bother, Bea. It won't do any good. We have to give her time, don't we?" Miss Norton hauled Mrs. Stevens up off the floor, and with the rope that she had left in the corner of the room, she bound her just like Bea and tied the rag around her mouth. "There. Now we wait."

Several minutes later, when Mrs. Stevens started to come around, Miss Norton spoke to her as if they had all been in the middle of a conversation. "Now, I'll tell you what I told Bea. If you scream or yell, I'll have to conk you on the head again, and then we won't be able to have a proper conversation." Mrs. Stevens stared wide-eyed at Miss Norton, but nodded, and Miss Norton removed the gag. "Now where was I? It's funny how things work out. You see, I was *just* about to tell Bea your part of the story, Penelope, so it's interesting that you should show up right at this very moment. Amazing, isn't it, how things keep working out for me? Even when something goes wrong, something else comes along to make everything right. It always works out for me. It always has.

"I'd fill you in on the whole business, Penelope, but I don't have time. I have a ship to catch. So you'll just have to follow along as best you can. Suffice to say that in the story I have come back with my mother to the same restaurant in Greenwich, and we are talking about blackmail and murder, and your Henry, of course." She turned to Bea and added, "Well, I had tried, hadn't I? To learn the art of forgery. But I wasn't any good at it, was I, and besides — I don't know why I didn't realize this earlier — why go through all this hard work of learning forgery just to blackmail my own father? Drain the family coffers, as it were. Simply because that had been Mother's bent, it needn't be mine.

"And Mother was no help whatsoever, just as she had said she wouldn't be. She refused to take part. I must say, forgery was more trouble than I had supposed. I thought — how hard can it be to forge someone's handwriting? You just have to get all the characters just right. Ah, Bea, I can see by the expression on your face that you are finally putting it together. The note you took that day. I knew you had stolen it. Well, now you finally know what it means."

"Yes," said Bea. "I believe I do."

"What are you talking about?" Mrs. Stevens finally asked.

"So, you're with us, are you? This does involve you, after all. Time you paid attention. Why don't you tell her, Bea? I'll give my voice a rest."

Bea glanced over at Mrs. Stevens, then at Miss Norton to see if she was serious, and then back at Mrs. Stevens. "Miss Norton had tried to forge your husband's handwriting."

"That's why the correspondence looked so much like Henry's hand," said Mrs. Stevens.

"Did they really?" said Miss Norton. "Well, I hadn't realized that, I must say. I just wanted the notes to come out looking like they'd been written by a man."

"But why were the forged letters in your father's box?" Bea asked.

"You see, I was correct! You did break in here, you naughty little thing. How thrilling — each of us four women in this room is a criminal, in one way or other. Why did my father have those letters, you ask? Because he had taken to pilfering through my things. He didn't trust me, I suppose. He wanted to know what I was up to. He was always so suspicious; I have no idea why. I have this lovely Cashmere Soap Box where I keep all my private things, but he had taken to going in there, and then taking whatever he wanted back to his room."

Mrs. Stevens shook her head, trying to understand what was going on. "Why would you want to forge my husband's writing?"

"Don't bother telling her why, Bea. If she couldn't get here in time to hear the whole story, then she doesn't get to know."

Mrs. Stevens looked entirely confused while Bea continued, "She wrote your husband two pieces of correspondence, I believe, maybe more."

"No. Just two. You're correct," interjected Miss Norton.

"And he responded. She didn't write as herself. She pretended she was someone else — a Jake Adams."

"Jake Adams," said Mrs. Stevens, with an uncertain nod.

"Yes. I suppose she just wanted your husband's replies. You see, in order to forge his handwriting, she needed all of the letters of the alphabet. After the first response from him, she had some of the letters, but not all, so she had to write again."

"Oh, hurry up, Bea, for heaven's sake, we don't have forever. So I wrote to him again. He wrote back, but this time he knew that I wasn't really Jake — don't ask me how — and his letter was very curt, but still I thought I had enough letters to figure out the remaining ones, like z. Whoever uses z anyhow, I mean really. But you know, I tried to write like him, and it just never looked right. So I gave up. Besides, there was only one thing left to do now that I had caught on to the blackmailing idea, an idea I had come to like very much, I must say."

"What was that?" asked Mrs. Stevens.

"I had to decide on someone else to blackmail — oh, say, Henry himself, perhaps. Of course, I would have to get my mother to do it. I decided to take her out to tea again. I wasn't quite sure how I was going to go about it, she can be so stubborn — can't you, Mother? Oh, Penelope. Heavens. You haven't been introduced, either. That's my mother over there on the bed. Morna is alive after all, isn't she? Morna, Penelope. Penelope, Morna. There now. Anyhow. We are in the restaurant and I started out by asking some innocent questions about Henry. I needed to know more about him, after all. You have to have some reason to blackmail someone, don't you? I didn't realize then quite how lucky I was going to be with this line of questioning.

"So I said, 'Tell me, Mother, what do you know about Henry?' I asked her the same question three times. She had been refusing to answer, playing with her palm as she so often did, until finally, she glared at me and blurted: 'What do you mean?'

"'Well, for instance, how long has he lived in . . . where is it now?'

"'Newfoundland,' she said in that stubborn tone in her voice.

"'Yes. Newfoundland. Now, Mother, is that part of the United States? I'm never too sure about my states.'

"And then the most amazing thing happened, Penelope, and it's when things such as this happen that you know you are on the right course, that events are all being created just as they should be. Before Mother could answer, the woman who had just that moment taken off her coat and hung it on the hook between the booths, and was about to sit in the one behind Mother — well, she bends down toward our table and says, 'No, it's not. And Newfoundland's not part of Canada, either. It's its own dominion.' As if anyone would care about that bit of geography. Really. Then she smiled and went on, 'I am sorry for interrupting, but I couldn't help overhearing you mention Newfoundland and someone named Henry, and I thought to myself: Freda, it's your lucky day. Imagine. There can't be that many Henrys in Newfoundland, can there — it's just a small little outport on the other side of nowhere, isn't it? I was just about to ask you about Henry and then I rudely interrupted you, and what I was wondering was: it's not Gertie — I mean Penelope's — Henry, is it, by any chance?'

"Honest to God, Penelope, that's just what she said," said Miss Norton as Mrs. Stevens stared at her, agape. She had gasped twice during the story, once at the mention of Freda and then of her own name.

"So that was a lie," said Mrs. Stevens.

"What lie was that? There have been many. To which are you referring, Penelope?"

"That your mother and father met a woman in France named Freda Murphy."

"Oh my yes. That was a little fib just to keep you worried. My parents never went to France. They'd never been away from England until we moved here. No, the Freda Murphy story is quite different altogether. If you listen, you'll see what I mean.

"So I said to this Freda woman, 'Penelope?'

"'No, I suppose not,' Freda answered me. 'It couldn't be, that would be too much of a coincidence. Just too much,' Freda said. 'So it's not Henry Stevens, is it?'

"'Well, isn't that strange?' I said to her, amazed at our lucky coincidence myself. Because, you see, already I knew that this woman had something I needed to know. I just knew it, don't ask me how, I'm funny like that. Intuition, I suppose. 'In fact, it is Henry Stevens, isn't it, Mother?' I said to Freda. 'And you are . . . ?'

"'Oh, I am sorry,' she said, and she stepped right up against the end of our table and bent her big bosom toward me as she extended her hand — she was an awfully short, dumpy woman with a toothy smile and silver grey hair coming out in wild curls from under her hat; she made quite a sight — and I took her hand warmly in my own. 'Mrs. Freda Murphy. From Yorkshire,' she said. 'Imagine. Here in Greenwich to visit my niece, and who would have thought I'd run into someone who knows our Gertie — I mean, Penelope.'

"'Well, Mrs. Freda Murphy, I am Miss Eliza Norton and this is my mother, Mrs. Morna Norton. This calls for a celebration, don't you think?' I said, and I gave her one of my warmest smiles. I don't know why I asked her to join us; intuition again, I suppose. And I was correct, wasn't I, Penelope? I usually am; I have excellent instincts. 'Mrs. Murphy,' I said to her. 'We were just about to leave but I think we could do with another pot of tea, don't you, Mother? And Mrs. Murphy, we would love it if you could join us. Mother? Why don't you move over?' Mother shuffled over toward the window side of the booth and throughout the rest of the conversation she didn't say a word, which was just fine with me. After Mrs. Murphy was seated and we ordered the tea, I said to her, 'You keep saying, *Gertie — no I mean Penelope*, Mrs Murphy? Is *Gertie* her childhood name?'

"'Well, no, in fact it isn't,' she said, and she lowered her voice to a whisper and leaned forward toward me on the table. I was dying from suspense, I can tell you. She was ignoring Mother as she talked, but Mother wasn't ignoring her. Without moving her head as she stared out the window, I could tell that she wasn't missing a thing. Mother's hearing was as keen as it had always been. 'But I shouldn't say why . . . ' this Freda woman went on.

"'Shouldn't say why what?' I whispered as the waitress returned with another pot of tea and a second plate of scones. She set them quickly down and walked away.

"'No, really, I promised I wouldn't.'

"'Promised who?'

"'Gertie's mum,' she said. 'She said I can never tell anyone, ever. I said I wouldn't, and one can't break a promise.'

"'No, of course, one can't,' I said and asked, 'Milk?' and she nodded and I poured some in her cup. 'Mother?' But Mother shook her head. She seemed burrowed in on herself, it was really quite embarrassing: the collar of her coat — she had not removed it in the restaurant, not like every other normal customer — well, it was up to her ears and she had slouched into the seat, and the cuffs of her sleeves were pulled up over her hands, and she was doing that pawing thing with her palm. Honestly. I poured milk into my own cup and when I was pouring Mrs. Murphy and myself a cup each, Mrs. Murphy said, 'But one can only bear so much. It really is a terrible secret to have to bear.'

"'Is it, now?' I asked, offering her the plate of scones. 'Jam? Cream?' I said.

"'Both, please, how lovely. One can't hold these things in forever, can one? You won't say anything, will you?'

"'Absolutely not. I wouldn't think of it,' I said, and took a sip of my tea. Those few minutes were horrible because the stupid woman took forever to slather her scone with cream and jam and then she took a walloping bite, and then she had to chew forever, must have been a hundred times, and then, finally, she swallowed. I thought she was never going to get around to telling me the terrible secret about Gertie — no, Penelope — and by now, of course, I really had to know and I didn't want to have to resort to other, less civilized means of getting the information.

"Then, at last, she took a sip of tea and spoke, in a whisper. 'Penelope's not the real Penelope, you see. The real Penelope was a rich girl that our Gertie went to work for. I don't quite know how it happened, but it seems that the real Penelope fell down the stairs and died, and Gertie saw that as a chance to change her identity. The two girls looked remarkably alike, apparently. Gertie's mum met the real Penelope and said that it was spooky — they could have been twins. The real Penelope didn't have any family except for an old grandfather who was almost blind, apparently, so it didn't take much to accomplish the switch.'

"Well, I tell you, ladies, I could not believe my luck. So while we had our tea and while Mrs. Murphy ate the entire plate of scones, I got everything I needed to know about you, Penelope, or Gertie, or whatever you like to call yourself, and the body you buried in France. I got everything I needed to blackmail you. And as luck would have it, I didn't even have to write any letters to you, did I, Penelope? Father decided all on his own, really he did, to come to Newfoundland to get revenge on Henry. It was so easy. Of course, Father never held up his end of things, did he? We were so close to success, weren't we? If he had succeeded in blackmailing Henry, then I would have had money from two sources: from Henry, and from you. Father was going to go by the wayside once his job was done, wasn't he?" She tapped his back with her foot. "I had no more use for him, and he always was such a pain." She stopped talking and looked about the room at the little gathering. "Ah, I can see our little Bea over here is surprised by the news about you, aren't you, Bea?" Before Bea could answer, Miss Norton said to Mrs. Stevens, "But there's one thing I want to know, Penelope."

Mrs. Stevens nodded. "It happened near the Spanish border of southern France. Had you answered 'Italian' in your reply to that question of mine, I'd have known you were given erroneous information. I'd always told Mum 'Italian,' just in case something like this ever happened. Just in case Freda Murphy told someone, and she did. I never trusted Freda Murphy. I didn't want her to know everything, and so therefore I didn't tell Mum everything. But you got around the question, didn't you? You came over to my house instead with your little ruse about your parents' trip to Paris."

Before Miss Norton could respond, Bea asked, "What happened to Mrs. Murphy?"

"Well, now, Penelope here was about to wonder the same thing. Or were you? Ah, I can see you already know."

"You killed her. You killed Freda," said Mrs. Stevens.

"Correct. It's not that hard to understand, really, although Mother never seemed to. 'Why did you have to kill that nice woman?' she was always yattering afterward, weren't you, Mother?" Miss Norton said, glancing over at the still figure on the bed. "You should have stopped asking, shouldn't you have, Mother?"

"You killed Mrs. Murphy?" asked Bea.

"Yes, Bea. That's what I just said, isn't it? For heaven's sake."

"Why did you kill her?" asked Bea.

"Because she would talk," said Mrs. Stevens. "She would tell my mum."

"There you have it. Do you see, Bea? Criminal minds think the same, don't they? The woman was a tattler. I couldn't risk it, could I?" Miss Norton paused and then smiled at Bea, and then at Mrs. Stevens. "Do you want to know how I did it?"

Neither of them answered. "Not really," said Mrs. Stevens finally. "We don't need to know."

"Under the train," said Eliza with a smile. "The sides of the tracks are awfully slippery in Greenwich after a rain. Anybody can slip and fall on the tracks just when the train is coming. We had left the restaurant and were going to cross the tracks. She said, 'We'd better wait until the train passes.' I said, 'That's a good idea.' And so we walked parallel to the tracks for a ways as the train approached and just as it did, by gosh, she slipped right in front of it. Mother reached out to grab her arm, if you can believe it, and I can still see Mrs. Murphy's eyes as they settled on Mother and then on me just before the train ran her over. You could tell that she all of a sudden realized that Mother wasn't crazy after all. It was a common misconception, I can tell you. But it was too late for Freda, wasn't it, Mother?"

"Weren't there any witnesses?" asked Bea, and as she said it, Mrs. Stevens glanced over at the old lady on the bed.

"I see Penelope is cognisant again. Just Mother. I'm too smart for other witnesses."

"Is that why?" asked Bea.

"Why what, Bea? Say what's on your mind. I cannot abide people who fail to express themselves clearly."

"Is that why your mother is the way she is now?"

"Oh, you mean mostly paralysed and essentially a vegetable?"

"Yes."

"Yes."

"How?" asked Mrs. Stevens.

"Well, since we're into confessions, I suppose it doesn't matter anyhow, does it? You'll be next in any case, won't you, Bea? I have no use for you. But Penelope here, she gets to get away. Now why is that, I wonder, Penelope?" Miss Norton asked, taking her watch from her pocket and checking the time. "Not much longer until I have to leave for my ship. Can't be late. How would you like to have it all end, Bea? Have you thought about it while you were sitting here? I have. But I'll let you in on that in a bit. First: Mother." She looked over at her mother and smiled. "She wouldn't let up, would she? 'Why'd you have to kill her, Eliza? Why?' On and on. For months. Now that fate had intervened and I had my Penelope story, I didn't really need Mother any more. I knew when I quit Glass and Elliot that there were easier ways to make money, and I knew I would find just what I needed. I did, didn't I? In any case, back to Mother — well, one day she stopped asking, and I absolutely knew she was up to something. And you know what that was, Bea?"

Bea shook her head, but when Miss Norton didn't continue, she said, "What was it?"

"She actually thought she would get away with it. She was going to turn me into the police. Can you believe it? Her own daughter."

"How did you know?" asked Bea.

"She told me. She was heading out. She'd already got on her coat and her hat and had come upstairs to get something out of her room. That was her big mistake. I grabbed her by the arm at the top of the stairs. Well, you can figure out the rest, can't you, Bea? Penelope has guessed it already, I can tell. I threatened to toss her down the stairs if she didn't tell me what she was up to, and finally, after a lot of yelling on my part and a lot of silence on hers, she did. Told me she couldn't *'let this go on.'* And that I was going to get arrested. And that would be that. And I said I can't *let this go on* either, and I dropped her and kicked her and down she went. I expected her to die, you see, but she didn't, and that was my mistake. I didn't kick her hard enough. Not like father, just now. So I ran downstairs and I was just about to finish her off; in fact, I had my foot poised right over her head, when Father came home and saw the whole thing. He could see what I had done and what I was about to do. I thought he'd be happy. He never seemed to like her very much, so imagine my surprise when he got upset, and even started to cry. He's crying away and I'm telling him, alright Father, I'll leave her alone if you want, but we've got to come up with some kind of an explanation for this, don't we? What will the neighbours think if they never see Mother out for her daily stroll? Especially the Gladstones — they are so bloody nosy, those two. I told him all of this, but he wasn't being very helpful. Honestly, you'd think he loved her or something. And so I came up with my own brilliant suggestion: 'Mother is dead, Papa? Is that what happened?' I said to him. I've kept her alive ever since, I'll have you know; I even changed her nightgown and sheets moments before you came, for heaven's sake. He wanted her alive, and I needed him for the time being. Don't need him any more, though, do I?" She smiled down at her father's body.

No one spoke for a minute, and then Penelope said: "George."

"Yes, George," said Miss Norton. "I wondered when we would get around to him."

"So you did attack him."

"Oh, of course I did. Twice, at least. Hired someone the third time."

"I thought your father was responsible."

"Of course you did. Father gets blamed for everything, poor sod, don't you, Father?" Miss Norton said as she nudged him in the back with her toe.

"But why did you attack George again after I paid you money?"

"Insurance, Penelope. How would I know that you would continue to pay? You hadn't made that clear enough, had you? But more than that — I had no idea how the next meeting between Papa and Henry was going to go. It could go badly for me, and it did. George was my insurance, Penelope. You'd do anything to protect your son." Mrs. Stevens nodded, and was about to speak when Miss Norton interjected, "But! I will have you know that I did not write Morse code on his chest."

"Why did you kiss my Morna?" said Mrs. Stevens.

"Pardon?" asked Miss Norton, and then she laughed. "Oh, for a moment I thought you were asking *me* that. But that's not it. No, no, no, Penelope. That's not what it said."

"That's what you told us."

"Oh, I know. But I couldn't very well tell you the truth, could I? I had read it before, you see. I knew what was there. Once before, on the street. Remember that evening, Penelope? That blasted fog? I knew you were lurking about; you should start wearing another perfume, my dear, something a little less cloying. Lilac is nauseating, actually. I don't know how Henry tolerates it. George showed me his chest that night. And Penelope, it certainly did not read anything about kissing anyone."

"What, then?" asked Mrs. Stevens.

"Why did you kill, Morna?" said Bea. "It was never, *Why did you kiss my Morna?* Or, even, *Why did you kill Morna?* It was: *Why did you kill, Morna?*"

Both women looked at her, and then everyone stared at the old lady on the bed.

"Morna killed someone?" asked Mrs. Stevens. "Your mother killed someone?"

"That is correct!" exclaimed Eliza. "Now, Bea, how did you figure all that out, you wily little thing?"

"The *l*'s were obvious," replied Bea.

"I thought so myself. I'm surprised Henry didn't see it. The *l*'s, Penelope! Don't look so daft. Honestly. Pay attention. There were no *s*'s on George's stomach. It never read *kissed*. There were only *l*'s. It read *killed*. I just made up the kiss bit. Thought it was rather fun, rather fitting for a teenage boy, don't you think?"

"My God," said Mrs. Stevens. "You really are mad."

"Now, now, Penelope. Listen up, will you? Honestly. Bea has more to tell us, don't you, Bea? The *l*'s and *s*'s were the easy part. What's the rest, Bea? Oh, Bea, while you're at it, you might want to mention to Penelope here that you were spying on us in the study. That's how you know all this. Where from, Bea?"

"The dining room, on the other side of the double doors," said Mrs. Stevens.

Bea nodded, then looked at Miss Norton and said, "There should have been a comma."

"Comma?" asked Mrs. Stevens.

"Yes, a comma, Penelope. Please don't interrupt. Please explain it to Penelope, Bea. I'm sure she's too stupid to figure it out herself."

"I doubt she's stupid at all, Miss Norton, but, Mrs. Stevens, do you remember when your husband asked whether the Morse code on George's stomach should have read 'me' instead of 'my'?"

"Yes, I recall that."

"Well, he must have detected something wrong with Miss Norton's translation. He was on the right track. But that wasn't it. Miss Norton had deliberately mistranslated the code for a comma into the combined codes of the letters *m* and *y*.

"And so, the real Morse code read: *Why did you kill, Morna?* But kill whom? And why write such a thing on my son's stomach?" Mrs. Stevens asked, glaring at Eliza.

"Oh! Don't blame me for that, Penelope! I altered the translation; I admit it. But I never wrote on your son's stomach."

"Well, if you didn't write the Morse code, Eliza, and your father didn't do it, then who did?"

"I can't answer the last of your questions. I'm as curious as you are to know who the scribe is, believe me."

"But who did Morna kill?"

"Brian," said Bea, and both she and Mrs. Stevens watched the old woman's face collapse as tears flowed from her eyes.

"Yes. Correct again, Bea. You win another prize. What shall it be? A trip down four flights of stairs? Oh, don't look so frightened, Bea."

"So, your father never did kill Brian, then?" asked Mrs. Stevens

"Oh, heavens, no, Penelope. Of course, that's what we were meant to think. Mother even lied to me about that. And Father certainly thinks so — thought so — I do keep forgetting the poor sod is dead, but no, for the longest time, Morna was the only one who knew who really killed Brian. And the entire time, my father thought that he had done it."

"But somewhere along the way, she made the mistake of telling you," said Mrs. Stevens.

"Quite right. It was long after the nasty Freda affair, and just before Mother's accident. I don't know why Mother suddenly told me, but of course when she did, I thought she had gone absolutely berserk. Not that I didn't believe her. Her story seemed true enough. But afterward I saw no reason why I couldn't use the information for my own gain — oh, I don't know, get money out of *her* or something — but nothing ever came of it, of course, and I soon realized why she told me: she didn't care anymore. She was going to turn herself in to the police on the same day she was going to turn me in."

"But why?" Bea wondered. "That's one thing I couldn't figure out. Why would your mother have killed Brian? And how?" asked Bea, glancing again at old Mrs. Norton.

"You'll have to ask her, won't you? I do have my ship to catch. It's wonderful that you speak Morse, Bea. It's all she speaks any more, I'm afraid," said Miss Norton, gazing at the old lady's thin fingers lying inert against the side of the wooden bed frame. "Now I am sorry to cut short our little soirée." She rose gracefully from her chair, then picked the rag up off the floor, walked over to Bea and wrapped it tightly around her mouth. "Time to go, Penelope." Then, catching the look on Penelope's face as she bent down to undo the ropes at her feet, she said, "Don't you worry. I'm not going to kill you."

"You're not?"

"Of course not, dear. I will continue to need you, won't I? Money, remember? Bea, on the other hand, no longer has a purpose, if she ever did."

"No, you can't! What are you going to do with her?" asked Mrs. Stevens, glancing anxiously at Bea.

"Compassion, Penelope? I'm touched. Aren't you, Bea? You ought to be. Penelope, I was thinking fire. What do you think? It'll get rid of them all," she said, nodding at the dead body and the old lady in the room. "And then some. I never have liked most of the people in this building."

"You can't, Eliza!"

"Oh, be quiet. I can, and you know it. Come," Miss Norton said, grabbing Mrs. Stevens by the elbow and yanking her out of the chair.

By the time Mildred, Jean, Evelyn, and Billy had reached the Nortons', they had acquired two more passengers, Callum and Natty, whom they'd come across walking away from the wharf in the rain. Natty had been helping Callum secure the dried fish in his shed to protect it from the rain. She'd found a new job working for the McNees, and she had begun that very day.

Now Natty and Callum sat in the back with Billy's old carriage blanket wrapped over their legs, and everyone remained quiet while Evelyn interrogated Jean. She had had a chance to reflect and hear Jean's story, and her fear for Bea had gradually turned to anger. As if in support of her mood, the sky had grown even darker as the rain pounded the roof. Billy had dropped Jean's side of the canopy, but his had become stuck halfway down and the rain, infused as always by the salty sea, washed through the opening and soaked his seat, and, behind him, Callum's, and now seeped into their thick wool pants. Crowded beside Billy, Evelyn asked Jean: "Why didn't you tell me any of this before, Jean?"

"Bea wouldn't have wanted me to, Mum."

"She wouldn't, would she? But she'll go breaking into people's apartments and rifling through their things. And now you're telling me that she's up there again, and in danger? Well, I doubt the danger part. Caught perhaps, and well she should be. And poor Miss Norton. Since she came to our house with that blouse, do you think I've found the time to check up on the poor woman? My God. I can't believe what Bea's been up to."

"But Mum, there might even be a live person up there, Mum; that's what I think. Morna. And Brian was murdered."

"*Now* who are we talking about? What is this nonsense about someone being murdered and a live person up there, as if kidnapped or some god-forsaken thing. You were wrong about Natty, weren't you? She wasn't dead or kidnapped, was she? No. She was just hiding out in her own house, weren't you, Natty?"

Behind her Natty nodded, then said, "Yes, Mrs. MacDonald, but the thing is . . . "

"Honestly, Jean," said Evelyn. "I've a mind to turn around and go home, don't you think, Billy? Callum?" She swung to face them, but they both just shrugged.

"Best to stay out of it," suggested Mildred, nodding. They looked in Mildred's direction, as if to beg her assistance. She shook her head in response. They would only lose to Evelyn, no matter what they said.

"Honest to God, Jean," continued Evelyn, glaring again at her. "We should leave Bea here and she can get her just rewards. For heaven's sake."

"No, Mum, you can't," Jean cried, and started to weep again. "You can't. We at least got to know."

"Have to," said Mildred, getting out of the wagon and standing in the rain on Billy's side. "Not 'got to.' Jean, stop crying and use your head." After several seconds, Jean finally asked: "Remember that bed jacket, Mum?"

"What of it?" said Evelyn, roughly adjusting Jean's bonnet against the cold.

"I think it belongs to a person up there in the Nortons'."

"Oh, Jean. You're really reaching for it now, aren't you?"

"She's telling the truth, Mrs. MacDonald," said Natty.

"Is that so?" asked Evelyn, reaching back and adjusting the blanket over Natty's lap.

"The bed jacket wasn't Miss Norton's, Mum. The sleeves were too short, Mum. That's what Bea said."

Evelyn looked confused for a moment, but then it dawned on her what Jean was saying. "Too short for Eliza. Yes, now you mention it. Now, why didn't I see that?"

"You would've noticed if you weren't so tired, Evelyn," Mildred said. "Now for heaven's sake, Evelyn, we don't have time for any more of this." She leaned past Billy and put her hand firmly on Evelyn's knee, and then reached up and brushed her cheek until Evelyn turned toward her. "Bea's up there. And other people as well. It's too late for Cyrus, I'm afraid. And Brian, well, he's departing as we speak, isn't he? Poor tyke — time he had some peace. I'd like to get to him before he's gone. And what if the girls are right, Evelyn? What if there is something to be afraid of up there at the Nortons'? What if Bea is in danger?"

"What if we're right, Mum?" Jean muttered through her tears.

"What if you are, Jean?" said Evelyn. She sat silent for a few seconds, then added, "Well, alright, let's go then, we'll see what nonsense this is all about. But Jean, I swear to God, if we disturb those poor people for no reason, you'll not hear the end of it."

"Evelyn," said Mildred, heading for the door of the apartment building as the party clambered from the wagon. She turned to Evelyn as the group got up to the building. "Leave the poor child alone."

Lamp oil wafted down the staircase from the third floor and as soon as she smelled it, Mildred shouldered her way past everyone, and took the stairs two at a time. "Hurry, Evelyn. Hurry, Jean," she called over her shoulder, and she could hear them pick up their pace. But they were altogether too slow. Bea was not out of danger yet. Mildred ran up to the third floor and along the hallway to the Nortons' apartment. She supposed she should have been surprised to see Penelope — hands bound, a rag over her mouth — tied to the banister of the third floor hallway. But she knew she would be here just as she had known that Eliza would have prepared her bags for travel. There was her luggage now, sitting ready and waiting outside their apartment. Mildred quickly bent down beside Penelope and whispered, "I'd stay and help, Penelope, but I've got to go get our Bea."

She turned to face the open doorway of the apartment just in time to see Eliza step from the apartment and withdraw a match from her skirt pocket. The smell of lamp oil was stronger here, and Mildred realized that Eliza had poured a large amount of it in her apartment and over the rug of the front foyer. "No!" shouted Mildred, rushing at Eliza and confusing her enough so that she whipped around to face the kitchen — had she thought Mildred's voice had come from that direction? — and in so doing, she dropped the unlit match. She bent to pick it up, but as she was about to light it, and just as Mildred was about to rush her once again, the telegraph machine beside her started talking all on its own. Mildred and Eliza both stopped and stared at it.

Mildred couldn't understand the signal, but Eliza obviously could because she was staring at the frenetic chattering of the machine and hissing, "Mildred, Mother? And who in God's green earth is Mildred?" She shoved the unlit match back into the pocket of her skirt, picked up the telegraph machine, ran onto the landing and with a loud holler, threw the machine over the banister. She stayed a second too long to watch the still-chattering telegraph machine crash three floors below. But a second was all that was needed for Billy, Callum, and Natty, with Evelyn and Jean at their heels, to run the rest of the way along the hallway, and the moment Eliza turned away from the banister, they were there to grab her.

Saturated from the downpour, the seven relatives and friends dribbled rainwater onto the scratched wooden floor, and closed tightly into a humid circle around an eighth person. Dead centre in the circle, the eighth — the killer — confessed to the murder. The monologue was difficult to hear at times, seeing as how the words were spoken by a child, and not a verbose or loud child at that. "Who ever would have imagined this to be the murderer?" Mildred muttered to herself, knowing she would not be heard above the rat-tat-tat on the wood frame of the bed and the sound of the child's soft voice. Feeling suddenly claustrophobic, she stepped back from the circle. She longed to go home, plant herself in her rocking chair, and have a think and a cry. She could do neither. She was needed here. A think about the last twelve days would have to wait.

"I never meant to kill him. It was a dreadful, horrific accident," Morna answered Jean. In stark contrast to the child's soft fingers, her hand was ancient, and yet it flew almost as rapidly, tapping out its message. Her fingernails strummed the bed frame, while Jean interpreted the Morse code for the group. Mildred understood none of it. She knew Bea understood some. But none of them could keep up with Morna and Jean's proficiency in the language.

Tears flowed from Morna's eyes as she recounted her story. She was growing increasingly weak, close to death, but she kept tapping, as if driven to finish her story for these complete strangers.

"Cyrus had gone to find Brian. Not to kill him, just to scare him, like he had done to Henry on the road. He wanted Judson to be very frightened, and to stop ignoring him. Cyrus told me later — he always thought he had killed Brian — that there was a pool of water in the cave and he had used it as a weapon. He had plunged the boy's head under water a number of times. As a warning. For Judson.

"I followed Cyrus to the cave. To stop him. I had tried to talk him out of it, but he wouldn't listen. I detested what he was doing to these boys, to this family.

"I should have followed closer behind, because I got lost on the way, and when I finally got there, I was too late. I thought. I had just arrived at the entrance to the cave when I heard Brian's high-pitched scream. I didn't doubt for a second that it was Brian. Who else could it be? Tell me! I didn't doubt for a second that Cyrus had just killed Brian. What else would I have thought?" Morna breathed heavily and laboured to tap out the rest: "Moments later, a blade nicked my calf. In the pitch black, I wrestled the knife from the hand. I didn't stop to think how small the hand — I knew, didn't I, I knew! Without a shred of doubt, I knew that the hand that held the knife belonged to Cyrus, that for some godforsaken reason Cyrus was now trying to kill *me*."

Morna stopped talking and weakly turned her head to look at the opposite corner of the room. The circle of onlookers parted so she could see past them. She focused on the wreckage of the *Agamemnon*. Mildred followed her gaze, as did the others, but there was no one there to see. Brian had departed, finally, as if he could not bear to stay for the end of the story.

Suddenly, just like that, Morna's tears turned to anger, and her fingers shouted on the wood: "Why did you not notice the hair when you held back the head?" Then she stopped, and as her own life began to depart, she turned over her left hand — the palm had been scratched raw. With barely enough energy, she quietly sent her final message: "So soft. Like a child's. Look, he's still there, in the hollow of my hand."

. . . ---- . . .

"Tea?" asked Evelyn, but she didn't wait for an answer from anyone. She quickly poured a round of hot, milky tea, went over to the cupboard where she kept her rum hidden, returned to the table, and added a dollop to her own cup. She set the bottle on the table for anyone who wanted it. Billy poured a shot in his tea, then so did Bea, Natty, and

Callum. Mildred arrived as the bottle was being passed around. She looked longingly at it and, not for the first time, wished she were one of them. The ones who could do so took a good long sip of their tea while everyone waited for someone to speak.

Evelyn was the first: "Who would've thought?" she said, picking an aquamarine glove out of her sewing basket. Bea, sitting next to her, reached down and handed her the matching thread. "Thanks, love. Miss Norton seemed like such a nice woman."

"I never particularly liked her," interjected Mildred, but that wasn't entirely true. She'd fallen for Eliza's charms just like the rest of them.

"Poor old Mrs. Norton. It's amazing she stayed alive as long as she did," Evelyn said.

"Is Mrs. Stevens alright?" Jean interrupted, her little voice hardly audible from under the blanket Evelyn had wrapped around her.

"She's back home. Police sent her there after they came to take Miss Norton away," said Bea.

"They're going to want to ask you some questions, Bea," said Billy.

"I'm sure they will. Don't know what I can tell them. Don't know what they'll believe."

Evelyn nodded and, without being asked, Bea started on the story of the last couple of weeks. Natty helped, and Jean added the last bit. They left gaps in the story, things that Evelyn just didn't need to know, things that Bea, for one, would never tell her. After they had finished, and after a few more rounds of tea and rum had been passed around, and questions had been asked and answered, Callum said, "I suppose we've got to get going. Billy? You heading back?"

"Aye," he said easily, setting his cup on the table and standing.

"Oh, Bea," Evelyn said. "I forgot. In all the goings-on, I clear forgot." She went over to the kitchen counter and pulled an envelope out of her basket. "Came today. A letter, from your father."

Bea looked at the postmark. Hamilton, Ontario. She hadn't seen one of these in years. So long, in fact, she couldn't remember when. She almost didn't want to open it, but finally, she did. After reading all four lines, she put it on the table for anyone to read if they wanted to. But everyone just stared at her. Finally she answered them, saying, "He's coming. Here. And he's bringing my brother."

Bea and Mildred walked the threesome to the door while Evelyn took Jean up to bed. Bea thanked the men, and Billy went out to dry off the wagon. Callum lingered at the front door as Natty and Bea started up a conversation.

"Your secret admirer, Natty," asked Bea. "Did you ever find out who that was?"

"Still don't know, Bea. But he wants to meet."

"He does?"

"Yeah. Wrote and asked me to."

"Are you going to? Do you think that's wise?"

It wasn't wise in the least, thought Mildred, but Natty wasn't about to listen to common sense. She was smitten. Someone loved her, or so she thought. But Mildred had finally remembered seeing the so-called admirer watching Natty peruse the catalogue in Shulman's. When she had initially seen him, she hadn't known that that's what he was doing — he seemed such an unlikely voyeur — and so the memory had never stuck. He had all of them fooled, especially Mildred, and she was ashamed that she hadn't remembered the incident until recently. Now, as she recalled watching him watching Natty, she remembered that he had been feeling something, but it certainly wasn't love. Wasn't even close. Was worse. She'd best have a chat with Natty, or at the very least, with Bea.

"I don't know if I will," said Natty. "I haven't made up my mind." That was a lie, thought Mildred. The decision was written all over her face. Natty started out the door, then turned and said, "The letter from your father, Bea. Does that mean you're going to leave Newfoundland?"

Mildred was not surprised to hear Bea's honest reply, although she was saddened to see the look that flickered across Callum's face as he shoved his hands further in his pockets and left the house; it was a look that Bea didn't seem to notice: "Soon as I can, Natty. I'm not staying around for that little homecoming, now, am I?"

Epilogue
Late Autumn, 1902

North Wales

"Lovely, isn't it?" asked the maid as she held onto Eliza's arm, leading her around the side of the castle-like building. The grounds were immaculate, just the sort Eliza had always wished for. The massive house sat atop a hill, and all around them were green grass, flowers, and more rolling hills in the distance. It felt like spring, with flowers still in bloom; it was hard to believe it was November.

Down the hill from them the gate to the grounds was closed, and the stone walls on either side almost obliterated the view. She was going to have to tear down that whole structure, and why were there such sharp rocks imbedded on top of the walls? To keep intruders out, she realized suddenly. Well, that made sense with a mansion like this. Who knows what the locals are like? Perhaps she would keep the wall and the gate. You can never be too safe. After all, the view was still exquisite. She could see quite a bit of the countryside. The country road wound away from the gate and around one verdant hill, then another and another, before reappearing far in the distance in the town of Denbigh.

She couldn't remember much of the trip across the Atlantic, or why she had come to Wales in the first place. But here she was, and it was everything she had ever wanted. She smiled as she said to the maid, "Yes. Absolutely lovely."

The maid nodded. "We get out once a day."

What an absurd thing to say, thought Eliza, but she smiled and said, "That'll be nice, but I might go out more than that. I'd like to take a look around the countryside."

"Well, we do go on the odd day trip. Now and again, to one of the castles hither and yon."

Real castles. Imagine. Eliza looked up at the building they were circling. No, she hadn't bought a real castle; it just looked like one. The entire time she had lived in England, she had never been to a real castle. Now that she was in Wales, she would see plenty of them, it seemed.

"When is tea served?" asked Eliza.

"Oh, anytime soon, I imagine."

"Scones?"

"I'm sure of it."

"And cream? Clotted?"

"Not here, dear, I'm afraid."

"Really? Well I must have cream with my scones, and a good preserve. Strawberry or raspberry, preferably."

"We'll see what we can do," said the woman, but she was giggling at something behind them as she said it. Eliza followed her gaze to see two broad-chested, muscular men following them.

"What are they doing here?" she asked, bending over and whispering in the shorter woman's ear.

"It's for your own good, dear."

"My good?" she asked. She didn't remember having hired two such burly fellows. For her own good. Heavens. What on earth was the woman talking about?

They rounded the side of the building. The house stretched upwards on her right, four or five floors high. On her left, green grass gave way to a forest, and Eliza imagined King Arthur and the Knights of the Round Table, and damsels in distress, and everyone galloping on horses with manes of gold through woods like these. Again, another dream from her childhood. What a perfect place to live. It was the home she had always wanted, despite the nonsensical woman who seemed to have become attached to her, and the beefy fellows behind.

It was hers, all hers, and she had earned it. She moved her arms to raise them above her head, but they wouldn't budge. She tried and tried but she couldn't bring her hands above her waist. She looked down at her wrists. Wide silly bracelets encircled her wrists. Copper. Or were they silver? She didn't remember buying these. Or them having been given to her. Then again, her memory did seem a bit off. She didn't remember the trip here from Newfoundland, for instance. The last she

EPILOGUE

remembered, she had been about to kill that silly girl, Bea. She supposed she had, and that she had got the money from Penelope — enough to buy this place. But she couldn't remember purchasing this piece of land, and this huge house, nor hiring these stupid people. She would have to fire them, and find some better help.

They kept strolling, passing the front of the building, with its beautiful ornate stonework, but really, there were too many people. When she looked closer, she realized that many of them were in shackles. Were they slaves? Had she hired slaves? People were everywhere. On the lawn. In chairs on a massive veranda. In wheelchairs. Who had hired all these people? Not she, certainly. None of them seemed to be working very hard; some were shuffling along, staring into space, chattering to themselves. Most of them reminded her of her mother.

"We'll have to get rid of them," she whispered to her maid.

The foolish woman glanced behind her again at the men still on their tail, then turned to Eliza and asked sweetly, "Who?"

Eliza wanted to scream. She hated stupid people. Just hated them.

"Them," she screamed, trying to sweep her right hand around to the side. Again, she couldn't move it.

"I'll need to get new bracelets," she said.

The silly woman smiled as if Eliza was some idiot child and said, "We'll see what we can do."

Eliza had about had it. "You're fired," she screamed, but the woman only smiled, and at the same time a blood-curdling scream surged out of a top-floor window. Eliza glanced up in terror to the fourth floor and noticed that all the windows were barred. Why would that be? And what was going on up there? "Oh. My God," she gasped as reality swept in nauseating waves through every part of her. She stepped away from the building, which she now knew was not a house at all, and stared at the maid, who was not a maid at all.

"It's alright, dear," said the nurse, glancing up at the fourth-floor window. "You're in another ward."

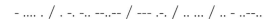